Waiting AT THE Sliprails

Sara Powter

Bible Quotes from King James Version

ISBN: 978-0-6454415-4-3
Paperback

Pacific Wanderland Publications
ABN 99 768 734 831

Kincumber NSW 2251

saragpowter@gmail.com
www.sarapowter.com.au

1st edition 2023 printed by Kindle, an Amazon Company;
available on Kindle Unlimited & KDP

**Cover by
Beckon Creative
beck@beckoncreative.biz**

Cover Painting
By Joseph Lycett
West view of Sydney taken from Grose's farm,
New South Wales, 1819

Girl painting on cover
**by Daniel Ridgway Knight,
Woman in the Flower Garden,
"Ray of Sunshine"**
In Public Domain

Dharug words from:-
https://dharug.dalang.com.au/language/dictionary

Girl Inset
Extract from linograph
By Henry Lawson
See Bibliography

Some story inspirations from
Banjo Patterson and Henry Lawson's Bush stories

Australian Historical Novels

Unlikely Convict Ladies Trilogy
Dancing to her Own Tune
(co-authored by Sheila Hunter & Sara Powter)
Amelia's Tears
A Lady in Irons

Stand Alone Novels
No More, My Love
The Vine Weaver
Waiting at the Sliprails
Scotch at The Rocks *(Sequel to The Vine Weaver)*
Convict Shadows of the Past
In Defence of Her Honour
Gentle Annie Soames
I Can't Stop Tomorrow
Madeline's Boy
Tuppence to Pass
When Upon Life's Billows

Lockleys of Parramatta
Hands Upon the Anvil
Out Where the Brolgas Dance
Diamonds in the Dirt
The Earl's Shadow
Once a Jolly Swagman
Jonty's Journey

Shelia Hunter's Trilogy
Mattie
Ricky *(Ricky, Tad and Will's story)* {*Jonty's Journey is a sequel*}
The Heather to the Hawkesbury

the last three are stand-alone books
and follow the characters met in the other books:-
Matty Paul, Ricky English and Murdoch and Mary Macdonald

#LockleysOfParramatta
#UnlikelyConvictLadies
#AustralianColonialNovels

To the amazing women of the
Australian bush who survived alone.
My mother read "We of the Never-Never" to me as a child,
and I learned that many women were all but alone running farms
while their husbands were out on the runs (properties) for days,
off droving on the 'long-paddock' in drought times or taking stock to market.
We forget that at this time,
many, if not most, of these women were English girls.
I am in awe!

To Stephen, my wonderful husband, who is always so supportive.
Thank you from the bottom of my heart.

And thanks to Roby Aiken,
who patiently corrects all my punctuation errors, thank you too.
To my Beta readers,
Noreen Robertson and Linda Upcroft,
you are all wonderful! Thank you.

Rebekah Robinson for my new cover.

Table of Contents

The grammar and language in this book are
Australian English spelling

Chapter 1   Reminiscing
Mulgoa 1835

$\mathcal{B}$eatrice Dawes knew that her life, as she had known it for the past six years, was drawing to a close. Her term as a convict had only weeks to go until she would attain her Certificate of Freedom. Then what? Her mistress, Mrs Lacey, had already told her she would have to leave. She had arranged other positions for other girls, but not her. No one wanted her. She presumed that if Bea weren't a convict worker, they wouldn't get supplies from Government Stores to cover her food and clothing. She presumed that they had little money to pay staff, and she didn't want another mouth to feed out of their own pocket.

If what the orphanage told her was correct, she was twenty-three. Although where she grew up in may have mixed up the children. One could never tell how accurate their records were as the matron in charge was often drunk, and it was the children who did most of the work in the place. Anyway, she now considered herself as on the shelf.

Bea sat milking her second cow and thought about how she had found herself in this situation. Usually, she would be humming as she milked, but it had all come flooding back to her this day.

Bea had only known life in a London orphanage; when she was just seven, she was pleased to be placed as a laundry maid in a big house in Piccadilly in London. By the time she was twelve, she had been promoted to pantry maid, which meant that she had a tiny room just off the kitchen; it also meant that she had no one to share with. Her delight was that the head cook taught her to make some basic foods.

As she grew, so did the attentions of the owner's son and a young footman. At fourteen, her troubles started. Her tight uniform enhanced her budding breasts.

Miles noticed her, as did Thomas, the footman, whom she had consistently rebuffed, and he was now the night watchman, so he often came to the kitchen after she was asleep.

Miles was the eighteen-year-old son of the household, and she didn't like him at all. He had tried to corner her a few times and kiss her. Thankfully, the cook came in at just the right time and shooed him out of the kitchen.

Bea knew that Mrs Lawrence didn't like her, but Cook knew what Miles's behaviour was like. She liked him much less, so protecting Bea was the lesser of two evils. No girl should have to put up with the master's son having his way with them.

Bea managed to survive unscathed until she was fifteen, as most of that year, Miles was at college.

It was the summer holidays in 1828, and he had brought a friend home with him. Bea knew she had little hope of avoiding both of them. She pleaded with the cook to allow her to move back up into the girls' rooms with the rest of the staff, even just for the holidays, but the cook insisted that she stay put, as someone had to stay in the kitchen if one of the family needed something. Bea's pleading went unnoticed.

Bea finished milking that cow, moved the bucket back, and released the beast. She wiped away tears and said nothing to the two girls in the other stalls.

They also had a bad time on the ship. It was no use complaining, life did nasty things, and you just had to cope as best as you could. No one had ever listened to her; why would she expect that anyone ever would? She was an unwanted orphan.

Bea poured the whole bucket of milk into the vat and knew the next cow would be waiting when she returned to the stall.

She sat down to milk, and her thoughts returned to the past.

That night, of course, the inevitable occurred. Miles caught her, but he was not alone.

Her thoughts ran away back to that horrific late September night. As the memories flooded over her, her tears fell. She had been in bed and had heard someone enter the kitchen. She got up to investigate and see if anyone needed her. It was what she was employed to do. She often had to warm milk for her mistress. She had pulled on her dressing gown and exited her room to find the two young men with their backs to her.

Miles and his friend Cedric knew she would be alone in the kitchen, and as both had been drinking quite heavily, they decided to have some fun with her.

Bea knew there was no lock on her room, and she had no way to keep them out. She had nowhere in the house to go.

Fearing what they would do to her, she ran to the stables. She planned to hide in one of the horses' stalls until they had given up and returned to bed.

It was a good plan, but it backfired severely.

Micky, Miles's tiger, was still grooming his master's horse after his return. He heard her creep into the stables and enter an empty stall. Although Bea had tried to be as quiet as she could, she bumped a bucket as she closed the stall door. It sent her heart into her mouth.

That night her world changed forever.

After Micky had finished grooming the horse, he found her curled up in a corner, weeping silently.

Under the ruse of comforting her, he tore her drawers almost in half, forcing himself on her. When he encountered her virginal resistance, he cursed her violently, "Damn you, girl, why didn't you tell me you'd not been with a man before?" He said, "I would not have taken you if I'd known." However, he didn't stop his abuse.

Bea was horrified and said, "As if that was my fault? You didn't ask; you took! I tried to fight you, and you still forced me." She was still fighting him as he grunted to a finish.

Micky was about to pull himself off her when Miles and Cedric came upon them. Bea's state of undress and compromising position were evidence of their recent activity.

Bea was weeping and obviously distressed.

Despite the fight that Bea put up, they took their fill of her. Cedric went first, then Miles, each egging the other on.

Micky stood and watched, saying nothing, but he smiled. He could have helped her but didn't.

Miles blamed her for not being nice to him and getting him into trouble with the cook. He reeked of alcohol, and vomit covered his vest; he stank. He was so drunk that while Cedric was riding Bea, he vomited on the far side of the stall.

After Cedric finished, Bea hoped they would leave. She lay cowering on the floor. Then Bea saw Miles's boots as he stood over her.

She knew what he would do and lay unresisting. Struggling only made it hurt more.

However, Miles was not content to leave her in distress after he had finished his abuse. He had barely buttoned the flap of his trousers when he laid into her with his shiny hessian boot.

Bea wasn't quick enough to protect herself. Kick after kick rained down upon her. Two kicks hit her face, and more landed around her shoulders. A final blow caught her on the temple and knocked her out.

Bea's world went black.

Only then did the other two men stop Miles from inflicting more injury to the now senseless and bleeding young girl on the floor.

Micky thought she would be all right.

Miles told his groom, "She's only a servant girl, and what do I care? I have the right to use her as I wish, didn't I?

Bea still didn't rouse. She was found an hour later by the night watchman. Her nightgown was still up, and her drawers were bloodied and torn. Her private parts were fully exposed to his gaze. On his rounds, Thomas found her in the seclusion of the stables. If he had looked harder, he would have seen her bleeding face. The bruises should have told him she had been assaulted, but it was dark. He recognised her dressing gown. He knew her to be around somewhere as she was not in her room. He had already tried in there. She roused when she felt she was being violated again, and when she saw who it was and groaned, she pleaded for mercy, knowing what he had tried earlier that night.

Over the past month, he had bailed her up a few times and tried to fondle her breasts. He had exposed them more than once and previously even managed to undo her bodice. Thankfully he had been disturbed by the housekeeper and had fled, throwing a filthy glance at her. What came next made Bea shudder.

At those horrible memories, Bea leaned her head against the cow's warm flank. She was still weeping; she thought about what had happened next. Again, the memories washed over her anew.

He did not immediately call for assistance; Thomas also took his fill of her. Like Miles, Thomas did not like the many times she had rejected his advances. He slapped her for previously refusing his attention. Rather than call for assistance for her, he called in the constabulary and had her arrested.

Realising that she was now unrecognisable from the numerous beatings, Thomas accused her of trespassing and using the stalls in the mews for nefarious purposes. He should know; he'd just used her.

Bea could vaguely remember the Bow Street Runner who had appeared that night. He was aware that she had been assaulted and gently covered her. He had even been kind enough to tie the cord of her dressing gown around her. She remembered that she could hardly see. She knew her face was now severely swollen, but she had no idea how bad it had been.

As she thought back, in hindsight, she excused Thomas with the thought that he may not have recognised her as the pantry maid until his beatings after his act, but then she remembered his words of rejection. No, he had known exactly who she was. She thought he liked her, but not so. He used her while she could not resist. He was just as debased as the rest of them.

It was too late now to do anything about it. Nearly seven years had passed since that fateful September night seven years ago.

Bea was arrested and taken away to Bow Street, then charged. She had stayed in the cells there that night. She had been given a calico gown to wear for her transfer to the gaol the following day. From there, a guard roughly shoved her into the squalid and overcrowded cell in Newgate prison.

The other women just stood back and watched the newcomer's arrival.

Deep in shock, Bea lay on the filthy floor where she had landed, astounded that these four men had used her so badly, and each had blamed her for being a loose woman. The calico gown was reasonably decent, and at least they had let her keep her clothing, even though it was her night clothes. The padded cotton dressing gown was still quite respectable and quite warm. She jumped as the door slammed shut. Moments later, many hands were feeling over her person for valuables. Finding none, they then ignored her.

There was no way to wash, let alone scrub herself. The blood from her drawers had dried, and she knew would eventually stain the fabric. She felt dirty and discarded.

This had been the story of her life to date. She remembered crawling across the filthy prison floor and thinking, what more could go wrong? She knew streetwalkers were normally locked up overnight and had to pay ten shillings to be released. She had no money, but she was not a prostitute.

Again, the memories from the past flooded back over her. She shook her head against the cow's flank. Bea sighed. She finished the milking and prepared for the next cow.

Bea soon found out just how bad things could be. Three weeks after her abuse, Bea realised that she had not had her monthly flow. She had always dreamed of finding a man who would love her, and they would live happily ever after in a cottage with a white picket fence. That would not happen now. To have an illegitimate child under such circumstances is not what she had wanted in life. At fifteen, she was nearly more than a child herself.

When the magistrate heard her case ten weeks later, she was sure she was carrying a child. It was the week before Christmas. She had been so ill that she could barely stand. She had no money to pay for food or clothing, so she lived on the slops and porridge served from prison cauldrons. And her calico night attire was all she still wore. Her appearance in front of the magistrate was almost a technicality. Bea had been arrested on a property that was not hers and found guilty of housebreaking and trespassing. The magistrate told her to be quiet when she opened her mouth to speak. However, she replied, "Innocent," when asked if she was guilty or not, but they didn't believe her. She tried to explain that she was employed at that house, but the magistrate wouldn't listen. She had stolen nothing and done nothing wrong.

His voice boomed, "Quiet girl! Guilty of trespassing as charged. Beatrice Dawes, you will serve seven years and be transported to New South Wales."

Four months in the hulks followed. Now, Bea thought back over those seven years. She spent months sitting in a stinking, leaky hulk in the middle of the Thames River, where food had been scarce and warmth even more precious. Her dressing gown and a prison blanket were her only comfort. She had eventually been allocated a drill prison dress. However, she kept her nightgown on as a petticoat and her dressing gown as an overcoat to assist in her attempt from freezing to death. She hated rats, and there were plenty of those.

Bea thought back to the ship. She had lost the babe she carried at four months along. It was eight weeks after being sentenced. The loss had been a blessing in itself, though she felt sad it had died.

The thin gruel, and cold lumpy porridge were barely enough to keep her body and soul together. It was no wonder the baby had not survived.

She had discarded the tiny four-inch-long bloodied body into the effluent bucket as she had nowhere else to put it. The child was thrown away, just like she had been. The baby was another unwanted life in this evil world of horror. At least she had lost it before being loaded into the *Lucy Davidson* convict transport in July of that same year.

Tears flowed again. That situation is not what Bea dreamed would happen to her.

Bea was concentrating on the cow she was currently milking. Her hands were heated by the warmth of the cow's udder. Bessie was always the last cow to come for milking. The cows, Daisy, Gertrude, and Bessie, were the three that preferred her to the other girls, Mary and Peg. She laughed that they always went in the same order and to the same person and the same stall. None of the three even need to be tied up. They grazed as she milked them. Bessie would stand still and chew her cud while Bea stripped her milk. When Bea finished milking her, Bessie always turned around and licked her. It was like she was saying thank you.

Bea's mind drifted back to those early years in London; Mrs Lawrence, the cook, came to mind as she milked. The woman could have come and spoken up for her in court, but she hadn't. Bea had no one to turn to.

Thankfully, Mrs Lacey was nothing like the old cook. Overall, Bea loved her time on Lacey's farm; her mistress was kind. Bea had been there for five years. She had come here seven months after her arrival in Sydney Cove. Here, she was safe, and no one had abused her. She remembered the soldier who had picked her out from the group of women in the prison. He looked familiar but couldn't remember where she had seen him before. She had hung back from the assignment auction and been scared to present herself to be claimed by one of the disgusting-looking men who normally took the women. The soldier had pointed to her first and then to Kathy, one of the other younger girls.

The two girls the soldier picked had been loaded on a wagon; each was given a parcel of new clothing and a blanket from stores.

As they departed, Bea saw the blond soldier look at them with a smile. He had lifted a hand as a sort of salute.

On arrival at the farm, Mrs Lacey permitted them the rest of the day to settle, bathe, and recuperate. The work on the farm was not arduous. Bea loved learning the way a dairy ran. Kathy had too, but she had gone some years later.

Bea had been there for three years when a governess, Maddie and her boy arrived. The nice Major had brought them, but he was not in uniform. Maddie attempted to teach them how to write their names. Then Maddie left abruptly after eighteen months.

As Bea leaned into Bessie, a few tears fell onto the ground. Maddie had been so nice and had told her God loved her. No one else did, so she doubted that her words were true. Maddie kept telling her it was so.

Bea's thoughts turned back to the ship. The trip out here had been horrible. Bea had taken a back bunk as she was advised by the kind lady, Mrs Fry, who had visited the prison. She was told that she was less likely to be abused if she was out of direct sight. The lady had known she was with child and had given her a baby bundle. It included lots of material and some sewing needles and thread. She loved sewing and was thrilled to find that amongst the fabric was a long length of muslin. Although she lost the baby, she kept the fabric. By the time she arrived in Sydney, that length looked like an extensive length of lace.

Bea's thoughts dwelt on those horrible months. The soldiers on the *Lucy Davidson* were worse than those guarding them on the hulks. Once they left the river, the cells were left unlocked. This was supposedly for their safety, but it allowed easy access to the one hundred female convicts for the crew and soldiers. However, Mrs Fry's suggestion that Bea would be safe at the back was very, very wrong. She was thankful she never conceived again, even though the violations on board were constant. Some of the girls who were closer to the main stairs were regular targets. Unfortunately, the men took whom they wanted and as often as they wished. Even those who had children or were expecting one were not protected from the sexual onslaught of the sailors. Captain Wiseman left the convict supervision to the soldiers, and Doctor Osborne couldn't protect everyone, so the abuse continued.

Bea kept milking. With the bucket half full, she changed teats.

Those months on board were traumatic, but she was thankful they had no significant storms on the trip out as conditions below deck were bad enough, and food was minimal. While on the voyage here, she was thankful they were allowed to wash occasionally in saltwater tubs on the deck. This exercise was also traumatic as they were given no privacy, and some girls were raped when they were stripped off to bathe. Bea learned not to be one of the first girls to wash as the sailors and soldiers had often slaked their lusts by the time it was her turn.

Their arrival in Sydney occurred in stinking hot weather. The women were left locked below stairs for more than two weeks in quarantine before being unloaded, as there was supposedly a danger of whooping cough that had hit them half was out.

During these weeks, they had been inspected and informed of what would occur. They were told they would be taken to Parramatta and put into the new Female Factory before being assigned. They would be expected to work while there, like in a workhouse in England. They would be weaving, spinning, or doing other jobs. They were told not to make any complaints as they had no rights. They all knew that already!

When they finally threw open the hatches, the light was blinding. Cellblock by cell, they were escorted out of their stinking dungeon into the scorching sunlight and melting heat. It had almost been cooler below deck.

Each woman was covering their eyes yet trying to look around them. What met their gaze was nothing like the overbuilt and filthy London riverbanks but an assortment of almost tumbledown buildings in a sparsely populated town.

The women and seventeen children were lined up on deck and told they had to climb down a rope ladder into a small line of crafts waiting to take them ashore. Even coming down the ladder, some sailors enjoyed the last grasp of a leg or feel of a buttock as they handed the girls into the rocking boat. Brushing their wandering hands aside would only bring a jeer or a pinch, so none resisted.

Bea had become resigned to a lack of privacy early in her life, but she still didn't like other people pawing her. When she was little, she remembered being called a 'whore's brat' by the matron at the orphanage. She didn't know what that was. When she turned fourteen, she had asked Mrs Lawrence and been horrified at her graphic description of a man's body and where it would get put. How could any woman let a man do that to them willingly? Bea was determined not to have that happen to her, but it had. Within a year, she had, in essence, become just what her mother had been. She was used and abused, but it was not of her choosing. Saying no had never been an option.

Bea finished milking Bessie and moved the bucket, so her charge could leave the stall. Once she had gone, Bea took the milk and added it to the vat. Mary and Peg had already finished their cows and added their milk. Bea had yet to skim the cream from the milk. This job also gave her time to continue with her reverie. Today she had to make butter and check the cheeses she had made yesterday.

She thought back to her entry into the gates of the Female Factory in the open cart was a memory she would not forget. She remembered seeing the soft creamy orange sandstone edifice and thinking later how it belied the cruelty of what awaited them. On entry, they were given an 'A' grade status. It sounded good, but she later learned that it was because they were new arrivals. If she thought the ship was cramped, it was nothing compared to the Female Factory. She remembered hearing that they would have to share three to a bunk. In this heat, she had preferred to sleep on the stone floor. During the day, they made linen from flax, spun wool, and wove fabric for use in the colony. She didn't mind spinning at home in cold weather, but the heat made the fleeces sticky and hard to both card and spin.

In the dairy, Bea didn't stop working while these thoughts flooded through her. With the milk left to raise the cream, she had cleaned and sloshed out the stalls with clean water, ready for use the following day.

Bea returned to the full vat and started scooping the floating cream from the milk. Once this was done, she had to transfer it into the butter churn and then sit, turning the handle until the mixture thickened. Knowing she had yet to make the butter into pats, she set aside the first jug full in the cool room. She set to work with the milk skimmer again, but her thoughts kept flooding in on her.

For six months, Bea stayed in the overcrowded Female Factory, working hard and staying out of trouble. She learned to keep quiet and try as hard as possible to be overlooked by everyone.

During those months, things began to change for the better. Many female convicts left after being assigned. Even the night-time abuse by the warders stopped. Some of the convict women had broken out and never were found. Some, like her, just tried hard to stay silent. She had not left the dormitory when the riot occurred. She had stayed hidden under a bed.

For the first weeks when she was in the Female Factory, night warders would occasionally have their way with some of the girls. As the place was overcrowded, she was sleeping on the floor; she would slide under a bunk and hide. Thankfully, she had escaped the warder's notice.

Only last month, she heard from Mary, one of the new girls, that some of the women prisoners kidnapped a visiting woman. She had arrived with the Governor, his daughter, and the friendly blonde Major. After the lady was released, all the prisoners were served meat, fruit, and fresh bread. For the first time in six months, they had full stomachs. Mary said the nice Major had removed the leading offending man and the abusive guards. New soldiers from Sydney took over as warders, and the nocturnal abuse had ceased.

From then on, there was decent food, more clothing, and even new blankets. The girls there were now asked if they wished to be assigned to their new places.

Bea remembered her placement and how the kindly Major had chosen her. She smiled at the thought. After meeting Mrs Lacey, Bea was happy to stay on her farm. She didn't regret that, but she had little choice in her placement. She was amazed that now the girls could refuse to go if they didn't like the men to whom they were assigned.

Bea finished skimming the cream and poured it into the butter churn when a shadow darkened the doorway. The other girls should have been at their various chores, so she was surprised that anyone was there. Her job was to do the dairy while they did the chickens, pigs, and vegetable garden.

Bea looked up and saw a black billy and a pair of trouser-clad, long legs. Her eyes travelled up the legs, taking in the tattered jacket; she saw a swag over the man's shoulder and a tattered hat on his head. He stood silhouetted in the sunlight, so she couldn't see his face until he came indoors.

When he was inside, her eyes saw the man's face. His piercing blue eyes met hers, and he smiled. Rather than the filthy teeth of a tobacco-chewing swagman, his teeth were perfectly straight and pearly white. His face was covered in only a short growth of facial hair, which looked reasonably clean. She could not help but notice his body was muscular rather than gaunt, and though he carried a swag, his stance was upright and confident.

His smile made her heart leap. She angrily brushed away the remnants of her tears.

It was as though this man had stepped from her dreams. He was a man's man. If the size of his arms were anything to go by, he was someone who was not afraid to get his obviously capable hands dirty.

She was about to sit and churn the butter, but instead, she turned to the unexpected visitor and asked, "Hello, sir. Is there something I can assist you with?"

The scruffy blue-eyed Adonis smiled again, and in a voice that could have been heard in the best drawing rooms in London, he said, "Ma'am, I would love a glass of milk if you have any spare. For I am parched."

He had obviously been hard at work, as she could see callouses and blisters on the hand that held his mug. Did he want just a glass of milk? She would give him the entire vat of the stuff if he smiled at her like that again.

Bea filled his tin mug with fresh milk and waited for him to finish before offering a refill.

His big moustache was dripping with the snowy drops of refreshing liquid; she wished she could dab them away. She was itching to brush off those drips. She wondered what kissing a man with facial hair would be like. Would it be soft?

His eyes were smiling at her.

Bea didn't even know that eyes could smile, but his did. Her heart sang as he smiled at her again. Few words were spoken, but an entire lifetime of conversation passed in those few glances. Her breath hitched. It was as though he could read her whole history, and he didn't care one bit.

Chapter 2   Meeting Jack

*J*ack Barnes had introduced himself as a drover, and he said he was passing through. Having been on the road for two weeks from his home and had run out of water that morning after leaving Emu Plains. He said he was parched, and Bea could believe that, as it hadn't rained for months. She had heard Mr Lacey talking about a new shepherd, but she had no idea what a drover did; she knew what a shepherd was. She knew they stayed in the fields watching over sheep. She presumed that a drover did the same thing, only making them move. She didn't want to look too keen, but after she had handed him his milk, which he drank quickly, He handed his mug over for more and then refilled his cup for the third time; she abandoned the cream and escorted him to the homestead. Reluctantly she left the exceedingly handsome man with the big moustache with Mrs Lacey and returned to the waiting cream.

Bea sat turning the churn handle until it separated into butter. She could now hear the slosh of the whey and knew the mixture was ready. Opening the churn, she carefully scooped out the creamy yellow butter globs. Scoop by scoop, she sat, turning the creamy butter into even-sized pats. Without even thinking, she decorated the outside of each pat with the stripes from the paddles. All were identical in size, and each was placed on a marble slab to put in the cool room. She had just started the eighth pat when she felt she was being watched. Her heart was beating like a tattoo. Jack had returned. She released a gentle sigh of delight.

Jack gave her a heart-melting smile. "Hello again, miss. Mrs Lacey said I could wait here until the boss returns. Do you mind if I sit and chat while you work?"

Bea's heart did a flip. "I'd be delighted, sir. My mind has been far too preoccupied with my past, not to mention my uncertain future."

Jack made himself comfortable against the wall to watch while she worked. Mrs Lacey had made him a large mug of tea and given him some damper and treacle. He had brought both into the cool dairy to consume. The presence of a lovely young lady certainly didn't hurt either. He asked, "Was it bad? Your past, I mean."

A slight frown passed across her face. "My life wasn't too bad until I turned fifteen. Things happened, and I was sent here. We all say we are innocent, but in my case, it was true. I was charged with trespassing at the place I was paid to work. There's more to my story, but that's all you need to know." Bea started on the next pat, wondering if he would want to stay.

"Miss, many of us had a bad time in the past. How you deal with those things makes a difference to your future. This new job is to be a path for my future. I have a small selection about two weeks' walk from here, and I have come here for work and possibly a wife."

Bea's head jerked up and gazed at him. "A wife? But you can't just get a wife like that. You have to meet her and woo her unless you go to the factory and get a convict one." Her dreams of a romantic relationship didn't include a business-like relationship.

Jack drained the remainder of his tea and sat nibbling, almost delicately, on his damper. "Sadly, I'm not going to have much time for wooing. I need to find someone to marry me quickly and look after the farm if I'm away. I've left the place with my native overseer and his wife, but I want my own wife." He glanced at her. "I'm lonely, miss, I need companionship, and well, I need a wife, a friend, and hopefully children." Amazingly, he blushed.

Bea didn't know what to say. Was that a proposition? Was he asking her? What had Mrs Lacey said to him? She returned her concentration to the butter. She didn't know how to reply.

After watching her make two more pats, Jack said, "Mrs Lacey said you must leave in a couple of weeks. Miss, what plans do you have? Would you consider me as a partner? Would you be interested in being my wife? I promise I don't drink strong drinks. I have never been drunk and never intend to be. I've never hit a woman; I've seen too much of that in my life. I don't chew tobacco or swear, and I already have a house of sorts to live in." His words were hasty and showed his nervousness.

Bea stopped working and turned to him. "Me? Why me, sir?"

Jack gave her another divine smile. "Why, miss? Because you have nowhere to go, and I want to get to know you better. I don't think I'm too objectionable to the eye, and I know you certainly are not. You are downright pretty, miss." Jack blushed again.

Bea gave a huff of frustration. Yes, this man was very handsome, and his manners were exemplary; she had always hated bad manners. Rather than answer his question, she asked, "How long are you here for?"

Jack saw a spark of hope. She had not outright refused him. "Three weeks miss; then I have to go to Sydney to collect the stock for the boss and bring them back here."

Bea was relieved. "Good! I have four weeks until my time expires. But before I decide, can we get to know each other a bit and see what happens? I'll give you my answer before you leave." She had three weeks to get to know the man who may become her husband. Three weeks to spend her precious free time with a very handsome man who wanted to marry her. Not just sleep with her but put a ring on her finger and do things properly. A house with a white fence flashed through her mind. One with roses and a big verandah like Mrs Lacey's. Bea had almost decided, but she wouldn't tell him that yet. She would marry Jack Barnes unless something terrible happened in the following weeks. In reality, she had little choice. When her term was up, she had to go to town and look for work. It was either that or go to Sydney and probably becoming a prostitute. It was far better to marry a man she at least liked a bit rather than have no choice at all who bedded her. She had all but decided to become a drover's wife; she could cope with whatever that meant. A wave of happiness flooded over her.

By the end of the first week, Jack told Bea that Mrs Lacey had said they could walk along the dry creek bed. Jack had sought her out at every opportunity. He would appear each day before their outing and assist her with her chores. He had washed and shaved everything off but his moustache. If she had washing to carry, he would be at her side. He turned the crank handle for the butter churn and helped clean the stalls after the milking. He was at a loose end until he had to leave for town, and he used the time to get to know her. They all ate together in the big kitchen.

Bea was so excited as she had never walked out with a man before, and for Mrs Lacey to actively encourage them gave her confidence. "Yes, dear, I trust you will be safe with Jack. He's a good man and means what he says."

Jack promised they would not go out of sight, but it would just be the two of them.

Bea dressed in her only clean gown and waited for him in the dairy, out of sight of prying eyes. It was her Sunday dress, but they had no church nearby.

Jack greeted her with his devastating smile, then held out his arm for her to hold. They left the dairy and walked down to the creek. In the shade of the trees, he asked, "Bea, I was wondering if I need to ask my question again?" He wondered if she had considered his question.

Bea was nervous but shook her head. "No, Jack, there is no need, for I know my answer. It is yes; I will marry you."

Jack had been so nervous that he had stepped away from her. He swung around, "You mean it? You really will become my wife?" His grin was so broad that she felt like throwing herself into his arms.

Bea had never had anyone so intent on pleasing her. In six short days, she realised she possibly had fallen in love with this handsome man. He was so very nice. Whether she was just bowled over by his good-looking face or seriously in love, she didn't know, as she had no experience in any emotional situations and so nothing to compare her feelings to. But as husbands go, conjugal relations with this man would be tolerable at the very least, but more than likely, they would be very pleasant. That side of marriage would be no shock to her. Her first experiences of that side of things were abusive, but Jack assured her that he would be gentle and considerate, and for some reason, she trusted him. Bea thought she might as well find out what being close to him was like, and a kiss would be an excellent place to start. "Jack, we'll still need to get to know each other properly, but as we're now engaged, maybe a kiss would be a good way to start." Her voice shook as she spoke. She was so forward, but she had to know if she had made a bad mistake or not.

"Are you sure, Bea? I don't want to push you into anything. And it will only be a kiss until we're married. Just so you know, I don't agree with anything else. I'm not the sort of man who does that; I will treat you as a lady. I respect you already and know you had a bad time before coming here. You told me that yourself, so I'm not going to add to it." He turned to her and slid his arms around her tiny waist as he spoke, but he didn't draw her too close.

She was unsure what to do, but her hands automatically went to his chest. She lifted her face and waited.

Jack gently brushed his lips against hers and gave her a gentle kiss. He then lifted his head. He was smiling. He said, "That was nice."

Bea was shocked. "I meant a real kiss, Jack, we're engaged, so, yes, that was nice, but I mean a proper kiss, oh, you know!"

Jack blushed. "I don't actually, Bea. I've never kissed a girl before. I've never had much chance to," he admitted shyly.

"Oh!" She blushed and said, "I have only been kissed against my will, so this will be new for us both." She slid her arms around his neck and took a step closer. "Try again, Jack."

Jack's arms tightened around her back as he pulled her to him. Then he let his emotions take over. His lips seemed to know what they wanted, and she responded in kind.

Bea's fingers somehow found themselves in his clean thick wavy hair, and she liked how she felt inside. He did not threaten her.

Jack's hands didn't stay still. He found himself slowly drawing her closer and rubbing her back. Their kiss deepened. How long they would have stayed like they didn't know, but a tan and white dog came bounding up to them and nipping at Jack's heels. Only then did Jack raise his head.

Bea saw the dog and said, "Down, Bounder!" The young dog obediently sat at her command. "Sorry, Jack. He's young and has taken it upon himself to be my guard dog. I give him some milk most days, and he loves it."

Jack ignored the dog. His emotions were in tumult. "Was that better than just nice?" He had hardly taken his eyes from her face.

Bea was delighted. "Much better, thank you. We could try again if you want."

Jack certainly wanted to; he wanted her much more than he felt he should. "One more; I don't trust myself more than that." His emotions were raging. He looked warily at the dog. "He won't bite properly, will he?" The thing looked like it could bring a pig down easily.

Bea shook her head; she had suddenly become shy. She nodded her assent to another kiss. She more than liked their first kiss too. She drew close again and, this time, pushed her body hard against his as he once more lowered his mouth to her already reddened lips.

This kiss emboldened her to open her mouth slightly to his, and she ran her tongue over his beautiful, even teeth.

Jack's hand slid up to her neck and then into her hair. He was clinging tightly to her. When her tongue met his, he crushed her against him before suddenly pushing her away. "Cor, Bea! Where did you learn that? I won't be able to control myself if you do that. Give a bloke a fair go! I'm only mortal."

He had now released her and was bent over double and breathing deeply. Parts of his body had almost exploded when their tongues touched.

Bea had felt his physical reaction as she was so close to him. She didn't intend for that to occur, but she liked that he found her attractive. "Sorry, Jack! I don't want to make it hard for either of us. I won't do that again. At least not until we're married." She gave him a sly glance. "It was nice though, really nice. Even more than nice," she said with an impish grin.

He discovered she had two small lopsided dimples. "It was good, wasn't it? I didn't know a simple kiss could do that to a bloke."

By now, he had recovered and had taken her hand. "Let's walk; it's safer." They slowly walked along the creek edge. "Bea, I can send away for a marriage licence tomorrow if you're happy. We can have Banns called and get married in Parramatta while I'm there. I know the minister at St John's as I lived in town for a while, so I have friends there. It used to be my regular church. Mrs Lacey said you could leave with me if you're happy to come. She'll even release you early and give me a letter to send in when I send for permission. We can't get married without a lot of extra paperwork until after you are free; otherwise, I would suggest a Special Licence. Then you can come home to my valley with me after I collect the mob of sheep."

Bea's heart was thumping with excitement. "You really mean we could be married in a month? And here was I wondering what I was going to do with my life and how I'd find either a husband, a job, or I didn't even want to contemplate the only other option, and you walk into the dairy."

"I saw you had been crying when I arrived, Bea. I asked Mrs Lacey why, and she told me you soon had to leave." Jack glanced at her. He was wondering if his honesty would upset her.

They talked and talked as they strolled along the creek. The sun was nearly on the horizon, and Bea had chores to do. Reluctantly she said they must return. "Jack, can I have another of your nice kisses?" She was giggling at her words.

"I think I could manage that, but no tongue!" Jack chuckled and added, "Yet!" Jack checked to see if the dog was around. He liked dogs, just not this one. Bounder was beside her, and Jack wondered if he would be permitted to kiss Bea again without being nipped.

The overgrown pup had not left her side; he wasn't sure of Jack but saw that Bea did not mind the man being so close to her. Again, the emotions stirred by their embrace surprised them both.

Bounder decided he had given them enough time and forced his way between the legs but didn't nip Jack this time. Now separated by the overprotective mongrel, the happy couple reluctantly drew apart and wandered back to the homestead hand in hand.

Jack looked down at the girl at his side. Her mob cap was crooked, and her lips still reddened from their recent activity. But he could see she was smiling, as was he. "Bea, will you mind being a drover's wife? Do you know what that means?" Jack presumed that she knew what it meant.

Bea still had not questioned him as to what it entailed. "I know you will look after sheep, which means you won't always be home at night."

Jack nodded. "Yes, sweet Bea, but a drover can be gone for long times too. If there is a drought, it could even be months or longer. That depends on rain."

Bea was stunned. "Months? What, gone all that time? Away from home?"

Jack slid his arm reassuringly along her shoulders. "Yes, but only in the drought times; the rest of the time, I'll be home most nights."

Bea said, "Oh!" But she wasn't sure she would like being alone in the bush. "Can I come too? You know, on the road with you if you have to leave. I'm not sure I would like to be alone all that time." A thought occurred to her. "Jack, what about children? You said you wanted them, but how far is this place of yours out of town? And what's the house like?" Bea realised how little she knew about his life.

Jack thought about the scrub he had spent the last year clearing. The saplings he had trimmed were then used to build a wattle and daub cabin with his soldier friends, Humphrey and Tim. The completion of the small cabin was followed by an extension to the log hut. The house itself was basic, but it was his, and it was solid. He wanted to find some lime wash in town and planned to buy a small cart or wagon and pony so he could carry goods. Finances weren't going to be a problem as he was told his money was coming from home. He could have hired a proper builder and had a team of convicts help, but he wanted to do it by himself. If Bea could learn to drive a cart, she could visit the neighbours if they moved in. So far, there was no one living near them. "Bea, there isn't a town nearby, just a few small farms. But we're the only one that is cleared. I have Netty and Billy, who live on the farm in their *gunya* a few hundred yards away, but there's no one else near." Jack looked down to gauge her reaction. "The other farms are some miles on the other side of my valley."

"Who are they? Convicts?" she asked, puzzled at the names.

"No, they are an Aboriginal couple who are my caretakers. They speak good English, and Netty is a great cook. Billy is my stockman and does much of the fencing. He also keeps his eye on the vegetables and other maintenance. Billy has an old nag I bought for him, and he can ride like the wind, so you won't see much of him. He watches the stock and fences. Netty is in and out of the house as she wishes. They have children, but they are normally out of sight. I rarely see them. I don't even know their names. I'm sure you'll love Netty. She's great fun. She's always singing in an off-key sing-song voice and often giggles."

Jack smiled, and this gave Bea confidence. She had decided that whatever she was going to was better than any other option.

They had walked and talked and had not even noticed they were being observed. Mrs Lacey was standing on the verandah with her hands in her apron pockets. She had watched them since they emerged from the creek area. Bounder was still in Bea's shadow. She smiled as she knew Jack would not be allowed to get too close to Bounder's charge. She knew the dog followed the lass everywhere possible. As the couple drew close to the house, she quietly said, "I'm guessing you have made up your mind, Beatrice? Do I say congratulations?" She didn't move but watched as Jack dropped his arm from around Bea.

Bea smiled at her fiancé. "Yes, Mrs Lacey, I have. I also wish to thank you for allowing me the afternoon off. I needed to ask him many questions about what was before me."

Mrs Lacey smiled. "Did he tell you I'm happy for you to leave with him when he goes next week?" She saw Bea nod. "Good, because on your return trip with the stock, you can hunt around in Parramatta and see if you can find me a replacement for Bea. Ask that nice Major friend of yours, Jack." She turned to Bea and said, "Mr Lacey has known Jack for some time and knows him to be both reliable and responsible. Otherwise, Hugh would not trust him with our flocks. I'm content you will have a happy life with him; otherwise, I would have forbidden him to even speak to you. All of you girls have had a rough start in life, and you all deserve some happiness. If you had refused him, I would have found you a paid job, but it may take some time."

Bea was stunned; she turned to Jack and said, "You never even mentioned that you knew Mr Lacey."

Jack grinned. "We went to Eton together in England. That was another lifetime ago, Bea. Here I'm Jack, the farmer and occasional drover. Hugh asked me if I would bring some stock up from the coast for him. When I arrived, I saw a pretty girl so deep in thought and weeping that she didn't even notice me watching her. Sorry, sweet Bea, but I knew I had met my dream girl even before you spoke. Corny, but there it is!" Jack bent and gave her a swift peck on the lips. He didn't dare admit that he'd first seen her more than a year before when he had come for a visit to his friend.

Bea gave Jack a gentle thump on his chest. "You could have said!" she sounded a little peeved.

Jack smiled and chuckled. "I could have, but it may have tainted your decision. I wanted you to choose me for being just me. Selfish, but that's me giving you free will as I always intend to do."

Bea thought she understood. She knew it had been entirely her decision, and he had applied no pressure. If she had known, she might have been swayed by that knowledge. She gave a slight nod of agreement.

Jack watched her indecision, then contentment of what he had said cross her face, then flee. "Bea, Heather said she had a parcel for you inside. When you leave here, you will not be in convict garb. When we go from the farm, you will be all but free. We'll be doing some shopping in Parramatta while we are there and you can buy what you need in town, including some proper clothes and a box of fabrics. I believe you can sew? I shouldn't presume, but I know most women can." He kicked himself that he had made a presumption.

Bea smiled. "Yes, I can sew, Jack; Mrs Lacey has had me making dresses for her." Bea had no idea how needed those sewing lessons as a child would be. Her skills were used as a laundry maid as she had to learn how to repair the family's clothing. Then she transferred to pantry maid; she learned to cook a few things. Bea spent much time sewing on the voyage out and had learned to do drawn threadwork on muslin and cheesecloth. Bea was stunned that Jack called Mrs Lacey by her Christian name. What more would she find out about this man?

Jack once again assisted her with the late afternoon milking. Being early winter, the cows were already waiting even though the sun was on the horizon. Bea was late, and her three cows were mooing with impatience. The other girls had finished their first cows and were onto the next one. Rather than stand and watch, Jack pulled up a box and milked from the other side. With Jack's assistance, their three cows were finished simultaneously with the other cows.

Jack shooed Mary and Peg away, saying he would help Bea do the cream separation and clean up. Jack told the girls he and Bea were engaged. They hugged and kissed Bea before they left, giggling.

As soon as the two girls had gone, he took Bea in his arms and kissed her deeply, "Just to make sure I have not forgotten how this works." He took his time in showing his feelings.

Bea was content in his arms; she felt safe and secure.

After some time, Jack lifted his head, and as he wanted to make sure she hadn't changed her mind, he asked, "Bea, do you mind that I didn't tell you I knew Hugh?"

Bea was still a little lightheaded from his kisses but said, "No, Jack, I understand why, but it was a shock. I'm a convict; they are not. And if you went to Eton, then you are gentry too. I gather you weren't a convict either?" She'd not asked him that. She had just presumed he was.

"No, not a convict, but I am a second son, Bea. Yes, my family are landed gentry, and my older brother will inherit everything. I have no titles or anything but some money, and they have a big farm in Kent and my father's folly nearby. A few years before I left, Father had planted walnut seedlings at a farm in Yalding. He lost interest as they would take some fifteen years or more to mature. Since I left a few years ago, I've not heard from my family. I don't know what happened to the place or even my brother, but I knew the inheritance would never be mine. Our family is not close, so I left as soon as possible and came here when I came of age." He paused, wondering how she would accept that he had all but rejected everything she had craved all her life. "My home was not a loving place." One day he would be able to explain what growing up to society's expectations meant. He could not remember ever being hugged by either parent. He had been farmed out to staff from birth, not even being fed at his mother's breast. He had wet nurses and nannies, governesses and tutors galore. Few stayed for long, so he had never been permitted to get close to any of them. He was given everything a small boy could want except love. It had been sadly missing in his life. The atmosphere at his friend Hugh's house next door was vastly different; the two boys were permitted to visit them. He had seen his friend hugged by his mother, and she questioned his whereabouts if they had been on an adventurous jaunt. His friend begrudged answering her inquisition until Jack said his parents didn't care where he was or what he was doing. He doubted that they would even notice if he were missing should he run away. His nanny at the time may miss him, and his tutor too, but no one else cared enough about him to worry.

After some minutes of silence, he said, "Bea, I love the freedom of life here. I have no traditions I must follow and no expectations of anyone but myself. There is no pressure or fancy satin knee-breeches or Drawing Rooms to attend or have my mother dangle me in front of some society miss. Here, I can be my own man, a man and not a painted tainted puppet. If I don't work, I don't eat. I'm not prepared to live off the bounty of a comfortable birth; having been born with a silver spoon in my mouth, I'm not prepared to live that sort of life."

As they worked, Bea told Jack about her life in the orphanage. She was a child with a dubious background, one she wasn't sure would be a suitable wife for a gentleman's son. She knew she had to tell Jack before it was too late. Unsure of exactly how to word what she had to say, she blurted it out. "Jack, to my knowledge, my mother was a whore. I have no idea who she was, let alone know my father. I was named 'Dawes' as that was a play on words because I was found abandoned in a doorway at a church. The minister wasn't married, so they couldn't keep me. Apparently, I was a pretty baby, so he named me Beatrice. That means 'one who brings joy.' Apparently, I was giggling and not screeching. There was no note, letter, or trinket left with me. All I know is that it was a Sunday morning. The most affection I have ever known was from Mrs Lacey. I want you to know that if you still want me, I'll be the best wife I can be, but I don't exactly know what that entails. I have had no one to learn from. Also, Jack, I must tell you that I fell with child due to what happened to me but lost it at about four months along."

Jack had just finished scooping the cream from the vat of milk. He gasped when he heard her final comment. She had lost a child? After a few moments of hesitation at what to say, he took her in his arms and said, "Bea, I don't care about your background. It's who you are now that matters to me. I've never been a husband, and my family was certainly dysfunctional, so we'll learn to be a family together. We had servants for everything at home, so living alone has been a sharp learning curve for me too. I had never even dressed without a valet until I left home when I was twenty-one." He bent and gave her a quick peck on her lips. "Let's get this butter churned and get inside to the warmth."

They finished the clean-up in the dairy and set to churning the evening batch of butter. It was to be sent to market tomorrow and had to be set aside in the cool room before wrapping in waxed wrappers. Bea knew it would typically take about fifteen minutes if she didn't take too many breaks.

Jack took over, and she could hear the whey separation in less than ten minutes. Unlike her, he had not taken a break from turning the crank, and his strong arms made the job quick. He had obviously made butter pats too, and soon they had the next dozen pats ready for the cool room.

While they worked, they chatted about his farm and their future. Jack spoke about the size of their new home and tried to explain what it looked like and what he wanted one day.

She had no idea what a wattle and daub cabin was or even a log wall, but he made it sound pretty.

Chapter 3   Leaving the Laceys

$\mathcal{T}$he following day Jack sent in their application to marry, with the driver who came to take the butter to market. Jack addressed his letter to his friend, Major Ned Grace. It was he who had arranged her placement. Bea was surprised that Jack knew Major Grace. She liked him, as the tall blonde Major had been kind to all the female convicts in the prison. She had not seen him since he brought the governess and Chip. She felt she had met him before, in England, but couldn't place where that had been. He showed no sign of recognition of her. Major Grace never caused problems with any of the girls. They felt safe when he was around, and Bea found that the Major had been the one to have the matron's husband removed as a warder. After she left, some of the women reported that the matron's husband was responsible for the nocturnal violations of the convict women. When queried by Bea, Jack just said he knew of him from home. Bea didn't ask more. If Jack wanted her to know, he would tell her. She had discovered that he was open and honest if asked, but she had also learnt to trust him. She already knew from Mrs Lacey that she could trust him, which meant a lot. She realised her future husband was a bit like an onion. He had so many layers; it was as though she was peeling off the crusty outer shell.

Jack had walked from his farm to Lacey's place, but he would need a horse if not a wagon. He intended to buy a multi-purpose vehicle in Parramatta and drive it home.

Bea had never ridden before and was afraid. The stock horse Hugh Lacey had chosen for Jack was Trigger, a large but gentle beast. The saddle was an English saddle that didn't have a stockman pommel but a slight rise at the front. Each day for a week, Jack taught Bea how to ride side-saddle in front of him. He had told her she would probably need to ride astride on their farm. She gasped when he told her that, as it was not ladylike. After finishing her morning dairy work, Jack would saddle Trigger and give her a lesson. He would double her to the creek, then when out of sight of the farmhouse, he would make her walk astride in front of him. They would walk along the dry creek bed for some distance. Once far enough away, they could kiss in private.

Jack liked how she could wrap her knees around the front rise of the saddle and then wrap her arms around his waist. He cradled her in his arms, and they would ride like this for some distance. The wife he had chosen for convenience was becoming far more than that. Far from any lack of emotion, Jack was beginning to feel far more for her than he had ever imagined he could. He wasn't sure it was love, but she had wormed her way into his heart as he didn't know anyone could. He thought it was an appendage he had missed out on owning. It was true that her pretty face had initially attracted him, but he didn't realise he had fallen in love with his fiancé. He knew she liked him, and he had seen her give a hop of happiness a few times when she didn't think he was watching her. Having her snuggled up to him was a pure delight. She had the ability to show her appreciation for any affection offered to her without being clingy. He wished to protect her.

It had been a week since he sent his request to Ned Grace, and while Bea was busy with the morning milking, a note finally arrived back. Jack read his friend's message.

Dear Jack,

I have spoken to the minister, and Banns have already been read once. By the time you come next week, you will only have two more Sundays to wait. I have also arranged for Beatrice's Certificate of Freedom. I will hand-deliver it when you come, but it's finalised already. She is free.

I am glad you have found your life partner. I look forward to standing up with you as your witness for your wedding. Take care, my friend, and congratulations.

Ned

Jack was now able to tell Bea that she was free. He wished to make the news special, and another kiss would hopefully follow. She now had to make her final decision. It was still not too late to pull out of their arrangement. He felt he had to give her that option, even though it would now break his heart. If it came, this next kiss would be between two free people. He was determined to let her know before they dismounted. He wanted to be holding her close when she discovered her new status.

They found a sunny spot out of the chilly wind, and Jack pulled up Trigger. However, he didn't release her. "Bea, I have news. I've waited to tell you, as I want this day to be special. I've had a reply to my note. My friend, Ned, has arranged our wedding at St John's in Parramatta, but sweet Bea, he has already fast-tracked your Certificate of Freedom. As of last Wednesday, you are an emancipist. Free! No longer beholden to anyone; therefore, if you want to withdraw from this agreement, you can." As he hoped, she tensed against him and unwound her arms.

"Don't you want me anymore?" Her beautiful eyes instantly filled with tears, but they remained unshed.

Jack smiled. "Are you kidding? You see, Bea, I have a big problem; I no longer have a heart; I find it has de-camped into the body of a competent young lady." Bea looked puzzled. Jack quickly kissed her. "Bea, what I'm trying to say and failing dismally, is that I have fallen in love with you. Completely and wholeheartedly! Having said that, I will not hold you to your promise as you are now free. You have a choice over your future as you have never had before. As Heather said, she could find you a job."

Bea collapsed against him, weeping. "I thought you didn't want me anymore." She wrapped her arms around him again and lifted her face for the promised kiss. The kiss was the deep and passionate one he desperately needed. He, too, had feared rejection. She drew back from him and said, "I may have your heart in here..." She touched her chest, "...but it is alone, for I gave you mine some time ago. Jack, don't ever leave me. I love you so much that sometimes it's hard to breathe even just thinking about you. I didn't know love could feel like that."

Jack didn't reply. He dismounted and flicked Trigger's long reins around a low branch. He returned and lifted Bea down, and they walked further up the creek embankment. As usual, Bea had been sitting on an oilskin coat to pad her seat. He took the coat with them as they left; Trigger was now hobbled and left to graze. Jack knew being alone with her was unwise as she could stir his emotions with a simple tongue kiss, and he was determined to control himself until after they were married. However, he wished so much to kiss her and hold her close. Now she had declared her feelings for him; he was ecstatic hers were the same. He knew now that their marriage would have a good foundation. Something his parents had never shown to either each other or either of their sons.

Jack stroked her cheek. "Bea, I want to kiss you, just that and nothing more. Not yet, but I need to touch and hold you close, with no dog to come between us." He didn't wait for an answer but spread the oilskin on the ground and then sat. He held his hand for Bea, and she joined him by falling into his outstretched arms. He flipped her around, and she reached up for him while lying on her back. This would be the first long kiss with them declaring their love for each other.

Jack lay leaning over Bea; he gently moved a lock of her hair from her forehead, then lowered his lips to hers.

Her arms locked around his neck, and she drew him down to her. Contrary to her promise, her mouth opened to his involuntarily. It was more to flick his moustache out of the way than intentionally stirring him. He didn't draw back this time, but only moments later, he quickly pulled back and lay on his back, trying to regain control.

Bea watched the pain cross his face. "Are you all right, Jack?"

Jack nodded. He uttered a strangled "Yes," but he was biting his lips. "I want you, and I'm fighting myself. Give me a few minutes. I just wish we were married already."

Bea started, "We could...."

"No, Bea, we couldn't! We aren't going to be together that way until we are married. I love you and respect you too much for that. It's only weeks away now. I was wrong to bring you here, as we are too alone, and you are too great a temptation." After a few minutes, he gathered her to him, and they lay cuddling, but no more kissing. "Bea, I've never felt this way before. I feel like a young lad with a big treat, only much, much better. For you to return my affection is way beyond my expectations."

She rolled onto her stomach, laid a hand on his chest, and kissed him quickly. "I know what you mean, Jack. I keep expecting you to do something hurtful or say something cutting. I find it hard to believe you know everything about me and still want me." Bea wanted to know more about their home. "Tell me about your farm, Jack. What's on it?"

With his breathing now under control, he folded his arms under his head and answered her. "Not much at the moment, Bea, but I have fenced some yards ready for stock." She lay curled to him on the grassy embankment talking about the chickens, the lambs, and calves he wished to buy that would need hand feeding for some months. He yet had to purchase the animals he wanted, but he knew they needed them to make their farm self-sufficient. He also described his dream home to her.

Bea knew how to make cheese and butter, she had also learned to spin and weave in the orphanage, but that was a long time ago. As a pantry maid, Mrs Lawrence taught her the basics of cooking, but again, she had yet to gain much experience doing this alone. "Jack, I'm scared," she rolled over onto her back as she spoke, and they looked at the winter sunshine above them. She admitted, "I don't know how to run a house or do half the things you need me to do. I'm just scared I'll let you down." She rolled over and buried her face in his chest. She expected that he would be frustrated, but he just laughed.

Jack gazed at her and gave her another quick kiss before saying, "Sweetheart, I don't expect you to know how. Do you remember I said we'd learn together? I know some things, and you know some things. Netty is very capable in the kitchen, but they may go 'walkabout' sometimes soon. By the time they leave, we'll cope as best we can. Most of these animals I don't even have yet. I have a paddock of potatoes and two more of grain. I've been busy fencing the rest of the farm boundary with split rail fencing before buying the stock. I have built a pigsty but have no pigs and a chicken coop with no hens. And a round holding yard with a slip rail gate for the horses. Then, six scrub bulls appeared, and none of my neighbours owned them, so I have no idea where they came from. I even placed advertisements in the paper; no one has claimed them. They are unapproachable, so I plan to sell them if I can get them to market."

She didn't know what he had described and asked, "What's a *slip rail* gate, Jack?"

Jack explained. "It's a stock gate but usually made from whole sapling logs about four inches thick. There are normally two or three of them, and they sit on the tops of the split logs and slide aside to make a gate."

They talked for some time about the bush farm and his plans. He moved an arm and drew her close to him. He was content, and the feeling stunned him.

Within the week, Mrs Lacey had arranged for Bea to borrow the stockman coat for a trip to Parramatta. Their trip would be at a walking pace all the way and would take an entire day. From the Mulgoa farm, the journey to town would generally take half a day on horseback, but that included some sections of galloping and long spells of cantering.

Bea had only made the trip once, on the back of a flatbed wagon that had brought her to their farm over five years before. She discovered that Jack had been back and forth often. He knew where to go and, more importantly, where the waterholes were. Bea had never looked at the fancy visitors the Laceys had to stay, so she had never noticed him.

Mrs Lacey had given them a lovely picnic that filled the saddlebags, and they stopped by a large waterhole near Rooty Hill and settled for a leisurely lunch. Someone had chopped the centre out of a log and made it into a water trough for the horses. Considering there was a creek nearby, Bea wondered why they had done this. She said as much to Jack.

Jack smiled. "I asked the same question when I first saw this, then one day, I had to fill the trough. The rope on the bucket had broken, and I had to stand in the water to fill it. Leeches! I've never seen so many of the nasty bloodsucking beasties. I found that out, as I have five attached to me; therefore, the log is there."

Bea immediately lifted her skirts high and checked her feet. "I hate those things."

Jack was hesitant but lifted the back of her dress and checked the back of her legs. One was looping its way up her half-boot and was about to latch on to her calf. "Bea, stay still; I'll just get a stick."

Bea froze but lifted her skirt to well above her knees and yelled, "Get it off me. Jack, quick, get it off now!" She was almost panicking.

Jack took a stick and waited until it 'walked' onto the stick, then attempted to crush it with his boot. "Gosh, they are tough little beggars." He twisted his boot in the gravel, and the thing still wiggled.

Bea quickly packed up their picnic, now keen to continue their trip and leave the bloodsucking grassy area. She folded the oilskin and placed it on the front of the saddle. Not that she would say anything to Jack, but her butt was getting sore. He lifted her onto the horse and saw another small thin leech looping along her boot. He flicked it off and checked his boots before preparing to mount. They only had a few hours of riding ahead of them; the sun was already on the afternoon side of noon. Bea was about to lean forward so Jack could mount when he asked. "Have you ever ridden cantering?" She shook her head. "Ah! Of course, you haven't. No one is around, so do you think you could have a try astride? If you sit in front of me like when we were on the farm. I will hold you tightly, and we can canter for a bit. We can cut quite a bit of time from the trip." Jack smiled at her, "Game?"

Bea nodded, she had seen horses cantering, and they went fast. She wasn't sure how she would like that. If Jack said it was safe, she would do it.

Jack was still holding Trigger. "Good girl! You must hop off unless you can hitch up your skirts and flip around."

She did as he said with little effort and flipped her leg over the horse's other side. "Oh, this is far more comfortable." She wiggled and moved the coat on which she was sitting.

Jack congratulated her. "Okay, lean forward, and I'll hop up behind you." With one swift movement, Jack was up and settled himself. He bent and kissed her neck. "You amaze me, you know. You will try anything I ask of you." He pulled her back to him and wrapped his arm around her. "Ready?"

She nodded. She was holding the low arch of the saddle as hard as she could. With Jack holding her tightly to him, she could feel the strength of his arm. She knew she trusted him.

He set off at a trot, but that was very uncomfortable. He said, "Hold on!" He nodded, then kicked Trigger up to a canter. The movement of the two bodies pressed closely together was smooth and comfortable. Bea was breathless at the speed they were travelling. Jack was holding her tightly, and she felt safe and secure. She started giggling, then threw her head back and laughed with delight. They kept up a canter for about twenty minutes until Jack slowed them to a walk. "Are you okay? How do you feel?"

"Oh, Jack, that was wonderful fun. I've never been so fast before." She leaned back against him and relaxed.

Jack nuzzled her neck giving her lots of kisses; he chuckled. "You, my love, need speed. We'll give Trigger a rest and then have another canter. You must sit the other way when we get closer to town, as your delightful legs show too much."

Bea tried to pull her skirts down but only achieved in giving him a better view of her legs. As they walked along, she wiggled enough to get the oilskin jacket from under her butt. She spread it over her legs and covered herself as best she could while still moving.

Jack had eased his hold on her while she moved. "Hmmm, pity, I was enjoying that view."

She gave a choked laugh. "You'll see enough of them in two weeks, future husband of mine. But if I go into town looking like that, I'll never live it down, nor would you. I'm sure there will be some busybody who'll spread nasty comments around. Most towns have one or two like that." She settled herself back against him and enjoyed the journey.

After some time, Jack asked if she was ready for another canter. He felt her nod, and she braced herself. He tightened his grip on her waist, and they set off.

Trigger's movement was a long, comfortable stride, and Jack pulled him up after only about fifteen minutes.

"What's wrong, Jack?" Bea asked.

"Nothing with him, but having you so close is, let me just say, distracting. We will be within sight of town once we get over that hill. I demand a long and loving kiss before we are that close because we must be on our best behaviour after that. Which means no time alone." He flicked his leg over Trigger and was soon on the ground. He kept the reins in his hand while he lifted Bea off. She slid down his firm body, and her arms snaked around his neck. She didn't care that her skirts were still almost around her waist. His kiss took her breath away.

Again, Jack broke away. "I need to get you to town before I drag you off into the bush and ravish you." He was nuzzling her neck as he spoke. "You drive me wild, Bea; I'm looking forward to being married to you." He groaned with desire. "If I were at home, I would have a wife chosen for me, and I would be lucky if I were allowed near her more than once before the wedding. I doubt there would be any fondness at all. To have someone of my choosing and who returns my affection is wonderful." He dropped a peck on her lips and helped tug down her crushed skirts. "One more kiss, and we'll be on our way."

Their trip was delayed as Bea needed to find a private spot for ablutions before completing the journey. Jack also took the opportunity to relieve himself. On return, Jack lifted her onto the saddle. Once again, she was side-saddle and decently covered. However, she had also put on the oilskin coat as the temperature dropped. Jack dug his jacket out of his swag, and soon they were off again.

Bea wrapped her arms around his waist but under his coat. Her head against his chest, "I would travel with you forever like this, Jack," she said, not expecting him to answer.

Jack kissed the top of her head. "I might get you to come with me on some shorter trips sometimes, sweetheart. We will need to visit Bathurst occasionally. However, I would ride off into the sunset with you cradled to my heart like this. I truly would love it. Sadly, my dear, the sunset is too close, and there's the town." Jack kicked up Trigger and hastened his walking speed from the dawdling pace he had kept up most of the day. As they topped the rise and Bea looked down on the small town, the smoke from the many fires covered the town like a soft fluffy blanket.

Bea shivered as the cold began to permeate through her thin cotton gown. Jack felt her action and encouraged Trigger to keep moving. "Bea, you will be staying with friends of mine who own one of the nicer inns in town. Bill and Molly Miller will look after you. I'll stay with my friend, Ned, at the barracks. Once we're married, I'll come and have a few days with you at the inn before I must leave to collect the flock in Sydney, but we'll do some shopping in the meantime."

Bea nodded. That sounded like he was going to leave her alone for a while. "Can't I come too, Jack?" She wasn't too sure about being left with strangers at an inn. She had heard they were often rough places.

He started with surprise; he forgot that although she was English, she was really a colonial lass now, not a lily-livered society miss. "We'll see," was all he replied.

From the crest of the hill, they turned into the wide street and soon arrived at a building surrounded by a wide verandah. The Rear Admiral Duncan Inn looked clean and had no drunks hanging around it like one of the two-story inns they had passed.

A lady stood waiting on the verandah, and as they drew closer, she waved at Jack. "Hello, Jack; the Major has booked you in for the night. I was looking to see if you were near."

Jack lifted a hand in greeting. "Not for me, Molly, but for my lovely lady here. She will be staying with you until we marry."

They had arrived at the railing in front of the inn. Jack dismounted and flicked the reins over the hitching post. He then returned to assist Bea down. He gave her a quick peck on her lips to boost her confidence. He whispered, "Trust me, Bea, you will love this family."

Molly laughed. "Enough of that, you two; wait until you get inside. We run a nice establishment, so no cavorting in public, please. None in private, for that matter, either until after your ceremony." Her strict words belied the manner in which she delivered them. Molly Miller loved a good romance as much as anyone. Jack had mentioned to her husband, Bill, that he was looking for a wife, and now he had obviously found one. She was here for a couple of weeks until they married.

"Sorry, Molly, I will behave," Jack said, making him sound like a chastised child.

Molly chuckled. "Oh, get away with you, Jack. Bring your lady inside out of the cold, then take your steed to Charles's stables." Molly walked to the door and held it open for Bea. "Down the hall and to the right, dear. There's a fire in the sitting room where you can warm up. The children are asleep, so make the most of the silence, as tomorrow they will be up and probably screaming, as children are wont to do."

Bea followed her instructions and found a comfortable room. She walked to the fire to warm up. She figured that Jack would be about half an hour, so she stretched and, with no one watching, rubbed some feeling back into her aching butt.

Molly returned and chuckled. "Sitting like that isn't very comfortable, is it? As soon as we're out of town, I sit straddled in front of Bill. Not ladylike, but I'm no lady. You make yourself comfortable, dear, and you can have some hearty hot stew when your man returns. That will warm you up. In the meantime, here's a mug of hot tea." Molly handed Bea a steaming mug of sweet black tea. "That should do the trick."

"Thank you, Mrs Miller, I..." Bea was interrupted by Molly.

"I'm Molly dear; yes, true, I'm Missus Miller too, but we're equals, and here we do not stand on ceremony. Just Molly will do nicely," Molly said with another laugh.

Bea nodded; she liked this lady already. "All right, thank you, Molly. Jack didn't introduce us, but as he said, we will be married as soon as Banns have been completed at church. I'm Beatrice Dawes, Bea to nearly everyone, and my term has just finished." Bea wondered how the lovely lady would take the news that she was an emancipist.

Molly pointed to a comfortable seat and said, "We are too, dear, but Jack isn't. We judge no one and welcome all. It is how our good Lord taught us. No one of us is more important than another to Him. He will judge us all at the right time in His own way. There are enough people in this place who look down on the likes of us, but you'll not find that here." Molly saw relief flood over Bea's face.

"Really? You were too?" Bea asked, amazed.

Molly smiled. "Yes, and so were our good friends at the Jolly Sailor Inn. You'll meet them tomorrow. Charles and Sal are wonderful. We try to meet up after church for a bit of a chin wag before we come home and prepare for work on Monday. So, I'll introduce you to them tomorrow morning."

Bea sipped her hot tea, and the heat started warming her. Molly chatted about nothing in particular while she drank. In the distance, they heard a door close. "That will be Jack."

Sure enough, Jack came in carrying Bea's bag. He carefully placed it just inside the door. "Hi, Mol, I'm back. Is Bill in the taproom? I'll stick my head in before he shuts up. I could do with a pint."

"He is, lad, but mind, you only have one. We could lose the licence if he gets done for staying open past closing time again. We're supposed to be an accommodation inn, but Bill wanted to build a small taproom to reach out to some of the lonely well-to-do men." Molly spoke brusquely again, but both listeners knew it was her manner.

Jack grinned an acknowledgement, "Just one, I promise, and then I'll bring him back. I may help him clean up first." Jack bent and kissed Bea on the top of her head. "I promise I won't be long, love."

Jack left, and Molly took Bea to her room. Again, she chatted non-stop, and Bea learnt a lot about many things. "We can sleep seventeen in beds, dear. Most other inns only have hammocks, although our friends have a room or two, which they use if necessary. Their children get moved to the floor as they have no spare beds for paying visitors. They have a storeroom under the house but use it as a refuge room if women need to hide. Most locals don't know it exists. Only women know about it; we don't spread the word in town about that. I don't imagine Jack will ever be the sort of man you must flee from, but know that we have a safe room."

By the time Molly had finished the story, they had reached a room that opened onto the back verandah. Bea didn't realise that the inn was two-story at the back, and she could also hear water. She found out that it overlooked the Parramatta River. She had stayed silent as Molly rattled on. Bea had talked more in the past three weeks than she had done for the rest of her life. In the orphanage, they weren't allowed to make noise; then, as a laundry maid and later in the kitchen, she was only allowed to speak when spoken to, which was not often. She didn't wish to talk much to anyone in prison or on the hulks. On the farm, Mrs Lacey allowed the girls to chat, but she had never gossiped; she usually just listened to Mary and Peg. She hadn't made friends with the other girls as she didn't know how. Her friendship with Maddie was mostly listening to her teaching. Her conversations with Jack were often her asking him things and his lengthy reply. Suddenly she was afraid.

Molly flicked the blue curtains closed and kindled the fire. "I put you in the big room, dear; as Jack said, you will stay here for a while after you are married. So, this will save you from moving rooms. If you put that big log on just before you go to bed, it should burn most of the night."

Bea opened the bag that Jack had brought in for her and was surprised to see that Mrs Lacey had included the new dress that Bea had made for her. It had a note pinned to it. Bea took it and looked at it with a frown on her brow. "Molly, can you read?"

Molly nodded; she thanked Bill for making her learn so many years ago. She took the note and read it to Bea.

My dear Bea,

You have nothing, and I have so much. I know you made this gown for me, but I wanted you to have something nice to be married in. Consider it a wedding gift. I know you will be a good wife for Jack, and he will be a good husband for you. Take care, dear girl, and don't hesitate to let us know if we can assist at any time.

Heather Lacey.

Molly put the note down and picked up the beautiful gown. "You made this?" Molly held up the exquisite creation. It looked like alternating lines of lace, gimp, and insertion spokes. Mrs Lacey also included various spools of narrow ribbon that could change the colour highlights of the gown. "It's beautiful, Bea. You are so clever."

Bea blushed. "Mrs Lacey purchased everything, and I just sewed them together. You're clever as you can read; I was never properly taught. I learned to write my name, but that's all." Bea blushed again. "And it is ages since I have had a chance to practise my writing."

Molly touched Bea's arm. "Dear, many here can't even do that. At least you know your letters. As a surprise for Jack, we might work on that over the next weeks so you can sign the church register. My oldest boy, Timmy, now thirteen, goes to a school in Sydney with Charles and Sal's second son, Eddie, but the rest of our children attend the charity school in town."

Bea looked excited. "Could we do that, Molly? I'd love to have something to do while I'm here. I hate having idle hands, and I doubt you have cows I could milk?" Bea had unpacked her few items; they were all government issues. The nightgown and robe she wore when she was arrested years before had long since worn out.

Molly noticed how little was in the bag, but knowing that Jack had said they were to go shopping, she wasn't too worried. Bea only had one spare pair of calico drawers, a calico nightgown and her Sunday best mob cap, and one clean gown made from blue drill fabric. All were government issue items. Molly gulped, thinking of the lovely gowns hanging in her wardrobe. She was so blessed that Bill was such a good provider. She swallowed back tears, remembering her journey out here. Although her trip out had been safe, some things were better forgotten. She remembered arriving with only the clothing on her back. Although she had not been accosted, the emotional scars were still there. The memories of the horrors on board swept over her.

Bea watched Molly's face display a wave of sadness.

Molly shook her head, took a deep breath and said, "Bea, Gracie will help you. Our eldest girl is eleven and can read and write well." Molly stood to leave but said, "Come and help with our supper, dear. Jack won't mind eating in the kitchen, so I hope you won't either."

A micro frown crossed Bea's brow. "No, Molly, I'd love to. It is where we normally ate on the farm unless they had visitors." Bea laid aside her items and followed Molly. She would hang her dresses later. With so few items, putting things away would only take minutes. She had loved making the gown for Mrs Lacey; now it was hers. She had decided to make the pulled thread overskirt as it looked like lace. It suited her name, Heather Lacey. To be given it for a wedding gown was a delight. Molly led her into the big kitchen and found both men sitting at the table, deep in conversation, and they stood as the women entered.

Jack went to Bea's side. He slipped his hand into hers and said, "Bill, this is Beatrice, my wife-to-be. Bea, this is my friend Bill Miller."

Molly and Bill noticed the softening of Jack's face when Bea entered. The look of adoration on both faces surprised them. This marriage was supposed to be one of convenience, yet it had developed into more. They exchanged pleasantries; the men seated themselves again. Molly told Bea that she had everything in hand, and soon the four of them were enjoying a hearty stew and fresh crusty bread with thick butter.

Soon enough, Jack had to leave. He had to settle into his accommodation at his friend's place. Molly sent them into the sitting room for a private goodnight. As soon as the door closed behind Molly, Jack reached out for Bea. "It feels like hours since I held you in my arms. We'll have to keep busy for the next two weeks, or I'll want to stay here like this. However, I will enjoy any private moments we can grab." There was no talking for some time. Eventually, Jack pushed her slightly away from him. "I really must leave, sweetheart. Ned will wonder where I am as it is. He'll be on dawn duty as the service is at seven, so I have to say goodnight. I'll see you at church in the morning and walk you back here afterwards." He went to leave, then returned and pulled her back into his arms for another passionate kiss. With a slight groan, he stroked her cheek, pushed himself away from her again, and finally left.

Bea watched the door close behind him. The silence of the room made her feel so alone. She sat and wondered what to do. She saw a shelf of old books and wondered what they were.

Molly soon tapped on the door. "Has he gone, love?" she asked as she stuck her head around the door.

Bea nodded. "He said he'd see me at church. I gather that you all go?"

Molly looked surprised. "Yes, dear, we all do. It's a time when we relax, listen, and learn. As I said before, we catch up with friends afterwards. But it's where God fills us up so we can cope with the week's stresses ahead. I like describing it as the more we shovel out goodwill, God shovels it back in faster. I say that because God has a bigger spade." She saw her description had not helped Bea at all. She smiled, then added, "When it's fine weather, like it should be tomorrow, we have a picnic with all the children. All the inns are closed on Sundays, and it's the only time we can spend with friends. The only people who come to us on Sundays are women who, for some reason, have been beaten or abused by their men. Reverend Marsden and Reverend Cowper know all about it, but they also keep our safe room quiet. Anyway, the children romp, play, and run, and we catch up on the week's happenings. Major Ned normally can join us for luncheon as he tries to work the morning duty, and then he goes to Lockley's inn for dinner each Sunday night. With Jack here, Sal might invite you to join them for a meal. I do hope so, as you'll love them."

Bea was surprised that Molly enjoyed church. "I've never been able to get to church service, so I know little about what it's all about." She knew she had much to discover in the new life before her. She supposed she might as well start by finding out about the church. She realised it meant a lot to Jack; therefore, she needed to learn. She knew nothing about church except Maddie loved it too. She knew it had something to do with someone called Jesus but didn't know what. She brightened when she realised she could ask Jack tomorrow. If Maddie, Tim, Molly, and Jack believed in whomever this Jesus was, then He must be good.

Chapter 4   Till Death Us Do Part

*T*he two weeks in Parramatta passed in a flurry of activity.

Jack took her shopping on Monday and bought her two rings. One was an emerald embedded into a filigree band. He slid it on her finger and kissed her in front of the jeweller.

She blushed. "Jack, not here. It's too public."

The jeweller discreetly looked away. Jack laughed. "I'm just claiming you as my own. At least you will be soon." He leaned over and kissed her again while the man still had his back turned.

The other ring was a plain band. The jeweller put it into a box and handed it to Jack. Jack sent her to the other side of the store to look around while he finalised the payment. He chose a necklace for her and added a locket too. He would put a lock of hair from each of them in it. He said, "Done, sweetheart, now for some clothes for you. Oh, before that, we must put a notice in the paper. The Gazette Office is only just up the street." They headed there next.

The bell clanged behind them as they departed from the newspaper office. "Job done; now to find you some clothing and furnishings for our home, my sweet." Jack planned to visit a few stores for some shopping. Since leaving, a new general store had opened on George Street. Mr James Foulcher had advertised in the paper, and Jack had read the notice while in Ned's room last night. Jack knew stock changed regularly, depending on what each ship had as cargo, but he hoped there would be some fabric that Bea liked, if not some finished dresses available. He wasn't that worried about them as Ned had told him of a new place in Sydney.

Jack ushered her in through the open door. "Bea, I want you to see if you might like any fabric here. You will need a good supply of it out at home as no shops are nearby. The house needs a woman's touch, and there are no curtains or anything fancy. It's more of a rough shack than a house. But I'm planning to build us a proper home one day." Jack looked at her apologetically.

Bea didn't really care. It would be a roof over her head, and it would be her home. She would make it the best place she could for her new family. She liked the Lacey's, and Molly's family was lovely. Somehow, they could become a family. Not that she even understood what *being a family* was, as she had never had one. Miles certainly didn't listen to his parents, and Jack had left his family and home.

While Mr Foulcher was digging out some more stock for them to look at, Bea said quietly, "Jack, I don't know what being in a family is. I've never had one, and I am unsure how to make one. I don't mean babies, but setting up a home and making it look comfortable. I don't know much about being a wife, and I'm frightened."

Jack wanted to take her in his arms to comfort her; however, he knew this was not the place. He took her hand and caressed it lovingly. "Bea, we'll work that out later; just choose some fabric you like. Don't select any loud patterns; just something you won't get sick of. If we buy the full bolt, there should be enough for whatever we need. I would suggest something thick, dark, and quite plain. Then we can decorate the place with furnishings. If also we get a bolt of white muslin and even some cheesecloth for the windows, it can be multipurpose."

Bea looked confused. "I like the blue drill, but why do you want cheesecloth on the windows?"

Jack chuckled. "It keeps out the flies but lets in the light. You tack it over the openings. Oh, tacks, I'll need to make a trip to the blacksmith too. The flies get pretty annoying in summer. If you are cooking, they come in plague proportions."

Bowing to his wisdom, they chose three bolts of material. One was royal blue gaberdine for curtains, one of calico, and one of bleached cheesecloth. Bea knew that if they could get some cows, she could use the loose weave cloth to make cheeses. She could also do drawn thread work with it and make it look like lace. Jack ordered five dress lengths of designs he liked and a bolt of blue dungaree. He knew that if Bea could sew, she could make trousers for Billy and him. The drill fabric was also suitable for work aprons.

Jack was poking around in the corner and saw an interesting-looking tin. He flicked it open and gasped. "Bea, look at this; you said you can sew. Would this be of any use?"

The tin was jam-packed with a kaleidoscope of coloured embroidery threads, needles, two thimbles, and some small spools of ribbon.

Bea came to his side and gasped. "Oh, Jack, this is my dream of heaven. Why there must be over a hundred colours in there." She fingered the stranded silks carefully and replaced the one she had picked up.

Mr Foulcher had seen what they were looking at and said, "Miss, there are one hundred and fifty colours with quadruples of white, black and triples of the primary colours."

"We'll have it thank you, sir; add that to the total, along with ten more each of black and white silks and some spools of sewing thread. Two each of black and white. And we'll have a pair of large dressmaking scissors, a box of pins, a ruler, a tape measure and...."

Mr Foulcher interrupted, "Sir, most of those things are included in the kit. The dressmaking scissors could be larger, but there are some small ones."

Jack knew that scissors were always useful, and he had also seen a set of sharp kitchen knives. He only had a few odd bits of cutlery. "Oh, thank you; then we'll add the large scissors, black and white threads, plus a set of those knives and a new canteen of cutlery. Only the small set, as I don't expect we'll get many visitors." Jack walked around the store, adding more to the pile. He knew he needed a new saucepan, a large frying pan, wooden spoons, a ladle, and a few other bits. He had existed with what he could carry on his back. And that was a frying pan, plate, mug, and knife. Jack spun around and said, "Sir, change that cutlery canteen for the large set, please. Who knows who will visit."

Bea watched him. "Jack, how are we going to get all this home?" She looked at the immense pile of things he had sitting on the counter. They had arrived on horseback, and the horse had to be returned on the way back.

Jack looked at Mr Foulcher and took Bea to the other side of the room. "Sweetheart, I have decided that we will purchase two vehicles while we are here. One will be a big wagon, and another will be a small cart or buggy for you. Unless I can work out a way to connect the two, I may have to leave the cart until the next trip, or I might be able to find someone to come with us and then return Hugh's horse. The Lord will work it all out. The wagon I want will fit all this and more. I need one for the farm anyway." He glanced at the storekeeper and saw he was still out of earshot. "Bea, I have decided that next Monday, depending on the tides, I will take you to Sydney for the day, and we'll visit the Bond stores on the waterfront and a few other shops and buy you some ready-made gowns. Ned also told me there is a dress store associated with St James Church in town. The clothes are made by the convicts here. They apparently have some ready-made gowns for sale." He hoped they could purchase completed gowns at the bond store, but Ned's description of the convict-made clothes at the church charity shop sounded good. However, he had to wait until there was a high tide morning and evening so they could travel by ferry. The other option was catching the mail coach. There had been a few accidents on the bad roads, so he wasn't too keen on that. A thought occurred to him. "Sweetheart, would you like to have a few days in Sydney after we are married rather than here? I should have asked you earlier."

Bea looked at Jack with surprise etched on her face. "I don't know, Jack; I've never been to a town for pleasure. Even in London, I wasn't permitted to go out alone or shop and buy anything. My pay went towards a warm coat, and I was never paid for my last month, and I was not permitted to get my clothing once arrested. As a child servant, I only earned £1 a year; my clothing was all hand-me-down or uniforms." She had never expected to have her wishes consulted. She had been ordered around all her life. Now, she was going to have to get used to these considerations from Jack. The more she knew him, the safer she felt.

Jack was grieved. "Oh, Bea, I'm so selfish I never even thought about that. How about we spend a couple of days there, after we get married? There's a nice hotel we can stay in called The King's Arms."

She nodded. Ned had told him that a man had a wagon for sale in town, and he planned to look at it next week. "Wonderful; then we will have a few days in town before returning here."

Mr Foulcher asked where to deliver the goods, and Jack gave Molly's address. He paid for their goods, and they made their farewells. Once outside, Jack said, "What would you like to do now, sweetie? Shopping, teahouse, or sightseeing?"

Bea clung tightly to his arm. "I have no idea, Jack. I told you, I've never had a day of pleasure in any town. I don't even know how to buy anything. This is all so new for me. You tell me this place is smaller than Sydney, but I would not know."

Jack realised she was scared. "Then let's see if there is a tearoom in town." She realised she was almost shaking with fear. "Or would you rather return to Molly's for a while?"

"Yes, please, Jack. Before we go out somewhere, I want to ask you some things. I don't think Molly will mind. You both might even be able to help me." She glanced up at Jack, and this time, he was puzzled. Another couple was walking by, and she waited until they were out of earshot. "Jack, I want to learn how to use a knife and fork properly and how to even drink nicely from a mug, let alone a cup with the dish under it."

Jack now understood what she meant. "They are called saucers, sweetie." Stunned that she had no idea how to use utensils properly, he realised that they had drunk from tin mugs and always had picnics. To eat at a family table with proper cutlery was something she had not done before. She could eat stew, as the convict staff were only ever given spoons. Few convicts were ever permitted to handle any type of knife. "Sweet Bea, I'm so sorry. I should have thought about this. Molly will certainly help, as will I. Because she used to work in a big house in England and knows the way of things, we'll have a few lessons, get her to cook some of her famous feather-like scones, and pretend we are out somewhere special. How about that?"

Bea beamed. "Oh, could we? I'd love that. Jack, I don't wish to embarrass you, but I have so much to learn. Please don't be afraid to correct me. We'll have to make up a sign like a gentle tap under the table or something like that. But I'll watch what you do, just in case."

Jack smiled. "If we make it fun, you will learn more quickly." Jack also wished to kiss her again, so taking her back to Molly's fitted his wishes too. These were things he took for granted but were vastly foreign to her. He realised he'd have to take things easy with her.

Bea asked, learned, rehearsed, and practised for the next week.

Jack made the learning fun, and Molly was a great teacher. These also included assignments with her writing, but Jack didn't know about those. Soon the old lessons from Bea's childhood came back to her. Her writing was big and childlike; if she couldn't spell a word, she sounded it out and wrote like that. Gracie turned out to be a good teacher and helped her read stories to her two smaller siblings. Bill had imparted some of his learning to his older children. He had let slip one evening that his education was a little more than merely basic. Molly admitted to her later that Bill had a university degree from Oxford. They dared not tell her that he was dux in both subjects that he had done while there, hence the books in the sitting room.

The first Sunday after their arrival, the minister had welcomed them at church, and by the following week, Bea knew what to expect. She didn't know the words of the service like the others did, but she would learn. She was determined to learn everything. Jack had arranged for them to be married after the morning service two weeks after their arrival. The Banns would have been completed, so Jack had asked if their wedding service could be after the Sunday morning service. She didn't like crowds and hoped no one would be around. The minister hummed and hawed, then agreed. He didn't like doing weddings on Sundays, but he knew Jack and that he needed to leave town that week. The marriage was arranged for late Sunday morning.

Bea, Molly and Gracie fussed over Bea's dress. It was washed, dried, and ironed, and the gorgeous gown hung in her room.

On the day of the ceremony, Molly refused to allow Jack to see Bea before the wedding service. Bea was not even allowed to sit with Jack for the morning service.

Bill offered to walk her down the aisle, and Bea willingly agreed. When she was taken from the vestry around the outside to the church's front doors, she was stunned to see that the building was nearly full. She expected most of the morning congregation to have gone. She was so excited when she saw Major Tim, Maddie, and Chip, sitting in the row behind Molly.

Bill chuckled. "Everyone loves a wedding, dear, and we all know Jack. He lived in town for a while; we all wanted him to find his special lady. You are a fortunate girl, Beatrice; Jack is a wonderful man and will look after you."

Bea's heart swelled with pride. "He already has Bill; I feel safe with him. Safer than I have ever felt, and Bill, I love him, so all else is just cream." With that, Bea and Bill started their walk down the long aisle.

Jack had turned as she entered the church. He had had a good scrub, and he looked amazing. He was now clean-shaven, had his long hair cut fashionably, and looked jaw-droppingly handsome. He had shaved his moustache off and looked like one of the affluent gentlemen she had seen in London.

Bea's mouth dropped open when she saw him.

Jack thought the same about Bea. He had not seen the gown she had made but knew about it from Heather. Molly had hidden it from him. The work that she had put into it was incredible. The muslin overskirt looked like it was made of pure lace. Bea had told him that it was what she called pulled thread work. It gave the effect of a luxurious fabric when it was just one of the cheapest fabrics available. She looked so beautiful. Jack could not tear his eyes from her smiling face. She looked incredible and almost regal as she floated down the aisle towards him. She could easily pass muster in a royal court, and she would be his forever. What was more, he loved her! He still found it hard to believe that his marriage of convenience had become a love match. His heart sang.

She arrived at his side, and he held his hand to her; she willingly took it, and their fingers interlaced. She relaxed; Jack still wanted her. Little Bea, whom no one loved or wanted, had found a home and heart. And that home would be wherever this man wanted her to live. She would make their family and home the best she could, and she would do it with her whole heart. Her place was by his side and in his arms.

The marriage service started; Bill gave her away to Jack.

Bea thought it was funny, though appropriate, that a stranger gave her away, as she did not know her background. Jack saw her smile as Bill voiced the words. She gave Jack's hand a quick squeeze. She would explain later.

They came to the vows. Bea hadn't heard the words of a marriage service until earlier that week. As they met with the minister for an interview, he walked them through the service, and she followed his instructions until he said the words *till death us do part*. She had shrunk closer to Jack; the words confused her. Jack had explained them to her. They meant they would be together until one of them died.

Bea had teared up and turned to Jack. "I don't want to talk of death and losing you when we aren't even married yet." She had wept into his shoulder at the words. She had cried and had clung tighter to Jack. She didn't want to lose him now or ever; he had become her security. It took a bit of coaxing and much explanation before she was happy to continue. Now, she was happy about repeating the words at the service.

Then for their vows, Jack said, "I take thee, Beatrice Sunshine Dawes, as my lawful wedded wife." The smile he gave her warmed her heart.

Bea gasped, then smiled and relaxed once more. She repeated her vows error-free. She had been worried about messing up the lines she had to repeat. The minister pronounced them husband and wife. John Robert Barnes was now her husband.

Jack had looked forward to the following words for some time.

The minister looked at Jack and smiled. "You may now kiss your wife."

Jack did. He slid his arm around her and drew her to him. "Bea, I have not told you I love you today, but I do; I wholeheartedly do."

Bea was given no chance to reply as Jack's lips claimed hers. It was not a soft, quick kiss as she expected. Bea was crushed into his arms and kissed silly. He used his tongue to full effect.

The minister had to clear his throat three times before Jack released her from his grasp. However, he didn't remove his arm from around her; he kept her close and whispered, "I love you, you know, Bea Barnes!"

Bea just beamed and leaned into his shoulder. She heard Maddie chuckle as she walked up to her.

They signed the register with Maddie and Ned signing as witnesses.

Bea had practised and practised over the past week and made a grand effort as she wrote Beatrice Dawes for the last time ever.

Jack leaned down and murmured, "Well done, sweet Bea."

After they signed the register, Jack escorted her to the Sanctuary steps, and there they stood, waiting in front of the packed church.

The minister motioned for everyone to be upstanding, then said, "I have the great pleasure of introducing you to Mr and Mrs John Barnes." With that, everyone broke into applause.

Bea was stunned at their reaction. Most of these people didn't even know her, but they had opened their hearts to her. She had had nothing but kindness and welcome from everyone she had met. Embarrassed, she stepped closer to Jack. He squeezed her fingers to show his care. They walked down the church aisle to the applause of the congregation and out into the winter sunshine. Maddie caught her eye and blew her a kiss.

They left the church and walked into the sunshine.

Again, Jack took her in his arms for a long kiss. "My wife," he said as he lifted his head. He slowly released her and, holding her close, said, "I love you, Mrs Barnes; just remember that if I forget to say it one day."

They were soon swamped with well-wishers. A shower of flower petals covered them. Jack still held her hand securely.

As Bea had never been to a wedding, she was somewhat overwhelmed with what everyone was doing to her. She didn't like people unknown to her being that close to her. Hugs and kisses from strangers were not something she would ever want. She shrank closer to Jack until her friend Maddie and Tim came and hugged her quickly before others took her place.

On their first Sunday in town, Jack had introduced her to his friend, Ned Grace. She had been surprised to see it was the nice Major from the gaol. Then later that day, Charles and Sal Lockley had invited them for dinner. It was there that Bea realised she needed to learn proper table manners. She had seen that even their children knew how to hold the eating utensils properly. She had just copied Jack and what he did, but her efforts had been awkward. Jack had since taught her the basics of eating politely, and he was thrilled she had asked him for lessons.

Sal Lockley and Molly were now at her side, congratulating her.

Sal then asked them for Sunday dinner again. This time for a roast instead of a stew.

Bea beamed; she now had the confidence to accept the invitation for Sunday night dinner when Sal Lockley asked her. Yes, it was their wedding night, and they would stay at Molly's place for that, as they would not catch the ferry to town until the following day. They had to eat somewhere, so Bea tugged at Jack's hand and repeated Sal's invitation.

He saw Bea subtly nod, so he accepted the invitation gratefully. He was proud of her already, and they hadn't even been married for an hour.

Chapter 5   Honeymoon Shopping

*J*ack had stored the bulk of his clothing with Ned and had brought one big case out of storage. From the wedding day, he was now attired in his London clothes, so Bea felt quite inadequately dressed when in his company.

Jack had hoped that this was how she would feel as it made buying her some gowns somewhat easier. He planned that they would travel to Sydney on the morning ferry; they would spend the few days shopping, sightseeing and, as Jack said, teaching Bea how to relax.

Their wedding night had been a delight to them both. After dinner, they returned from the Lockleys at the Jolly Sailor Inn and dawdled back to The Rear Admiral Duncan.

Jack had felt like picking up Bea and ravishing her as soon as they reached their room. However, the cold evening had meant Bea had become chilled on her return to their warm room. Her teeth were chattering. Jack decided that the first thing he would buy her was a warm coat. By the time they climbed the back steps to their room, her lips were blue with cold even though she was now in his coat.

The inn was in darkness except for the rear lamp and another lantern in their room. Jack was so worried about her being cold that he scooped Bea up in his arms and carried her up the remaining stairs to their room. He placed her down, extinguished the external lamp, and shut their door. He drew the curtains and went to warm his wife.

Bea reached out to Jack. He didn't even realise she had already removed her clothing while he was preparing their room and stoking the fire. He quickly stripped off his garments and joined her under the many blankets. He knew that body heat was the best way to warm someone; however, he discovered that the heat produced when holding a naked nubile new wife in one's arms was very different to having two sheepdogs sitting on your swag when huddled close to a fire.

Bea did not take long to warm through. She then warmed him in a way he had not experienced before. As promised, she reached out and kissed him like the first day by the creek. What followed left them both exhausted but also satisfied and content.

"Bea, I had no idea that marriage was like this," Jack said, grinning broadly.

Bea snuggled into his warm body. She, too, had been surprised by her responses to him. "Jack, I had no idea either. My other experiences were taken, not given, and they were nothing like that!" She murmured drowsily while still enfolded in his arms. "Better than just nice, Jack, way better than nice. I didn't know that I would feel so very… well, nice."

They fell asleep in each other's arms soon afterwards.

Before they caught the ferry the following day, Bea had woken with the knowledge that the act of marriage with this man was a delight. He was no longer a stranger but the love of her life. She gazed at her husband for some time before reaching and gently lifting a lock of hair from his face.

He opened his blue eyes and smiled as she touched him. He reached out for her.

She had discovered that laying curled up next to an unclad virile husband had a different effect than sleeping with cold, smelly, hungry orphans. She was going to enjoy being married to this caring man.

Later that morning, the ferry pulled up to the King's Wharf near the Lockley's Inn. Their trip to Sydney in the little paddle wheel steam ferry was a delight for Bea. They had not ended up taking a trip to Sydney before their marriage as the tides were not suitable for a return journey in one day, and he would not compromise her in the eyes of society.

On the ferry, Jack had his arms around her as they stood at the railings of the ferry. He had done this trip a few times since the ferry began running, so he pointed out some places of interest. He adored holding her so close and having her lean back against him, trusting that he would keep her safe. He was still overwhelmed that his plan for a marriage of convenience had led him to such contentment. Every day he spent with this unsophisticated girl, who had been born with nothing, was sheer delight. When he thought of the females his mother had shoved at him in London, he drew Bea closer. This girl had such a pure and loving spirit.

The ferry arrived in Sydney Cove very slowly, as the small craft had to dodge the many other boats and ships moving around the quay.

Once safely landed, Jack and Bea walked up the hill to the hotel where he had reserved a room for a few days. He arranged for a cab to deliver their bags to the hotel.

The King's Arms Hotel was one of the better establishments in town, where Jack had often stayed on his various visits.

Their arrival at this impressive building made Bea shrink closer to Jack. "We can't go in there, Jack. I'm not dressed properly."

Jack smiled at her hesitation. "We can love, as this is where we're staying. We'll go shopping for some gowns for you as soon as we have checked in. We will first try the Benevolent Society Shop at St James' Church. We'll fit you out like a queen, and then we will find other stores from there."

As they entered and walked into the double doors of the impressive facade, Jack was greeted by name by a uniformed man at the door. "Welcome, Mr Barnes, ma'am; I hope you had a good trip?"

"Good morning, Mr Stewart; we did, thank you. May I introduce my wife?"

Bea was stunned that this well-dressed man knew her husband's name. Instead of just nodding her head in recognition of the introduction, she was about to give a servant's curtsy when she felt Jack's hand hold her up. Realising her error, she stopped in time. The man should bow to her.

They were soon settled into their suite, which overlooked the bay. The elevated hotel room gave them a northward view, overlooking Sydney Cove and the docklands. "Jack, this is incredible. I've never been to a place like this. Even where I worked in London, I was not permitted upstairs. I was either in the laundry or kitchen." She turned in Jack's arms. "Jack, I'm scared! I nearly did a servant's bob to that man. I'm not fit for this sort of life. You told me you were a shepherd. I can cope with that. But I can't live a lah-de-dah life. I don't know how." She dissolved into tears on his shoulder.

This place was merely passable for Jack compared to what he had left behind. His life as a shepherd had been a rude shock to him but one he'd learned to love. So, he knew what she was feeling. "I thought that we could eat in our room tonight. Then you don't have to face the people in the dining room. We can do the same for breakfast, but I have booked a picnic basket for our luncheon, and we'll go out to Mrs Macquarie's Chair for our picnic."

Bea had no idea what that place was, so she just nodded. "Whatever you say, Jack, just don't be surprised if I don't know what to do or say when meeting people. Last month I was a dairymaid, and now I'm supposed to be a lady. I can't do it, Jack."

Jack stood cradling this lovely lady who had come to mean so much to him. "You are more of a lady than many titled ones I know. However, I will not leave you, Bea. If in doubt, look to me." He felt her head nod against his chest. "Now, we will have to get ready to go shopping. Again, don't worry; I'll direct you to what will suit you and what we'll need. I have many other things to buy, and I know what will be suitable. I insist you have some nice gowns for when we are in town." Again, she nodded against his chest.

"Do we have to go straight away?" She gave him a saucy look.

"No," Jack said with a grin. Their shopping trip was delayed about half an hour as Jack willingly accepted her delectable invitation.

Their first stop was the Benevolent Society charity store at St James' church. There they purchased six new gowns and a large selection of lawn undergarments, some of which she put on immediately. They left five gowns for alterations while they shopped for the rest of their goods. The sixth gown was a warm woollen one with a matching cape that fitted perfectly, and Jack insisted that she wear it. The shop would return her clothes to the hotel with her new gowns. Little did she realise just what Jack had in mind for their day. He had worded Mr Stewart up, and other than the gowns for Bea, all their purchases would be stored in a downstairs store room.

They had been to John Solomon's store and purchased various essential items. These included an extensive medical kit, Jack wanted some accounting ledgers, but he found that the man stocked carpentry and coopering repair tools, too. Jack knew that with vehicles on the property, he would need equipment to make repairs. They could easily get all his purchases home as he planned to buy a large wagon.

From Solomon's store, they went to Mrs Horden's new shop, and Jack bought a selection of coats, including the warmest woollen one he could buy for Bea. There were also hats, bedding, and more serviceable work gowns and aprons. He had also bought himself a range of new shirts and two pairs of work dungarees. Bea's current thin coat was relegated to the 'send to the hotel' pile of items, and she was now dressed in the latest fashion of a long woollen coat. It nearly wrapped around her, and it matched the new poke bonnet that Jack had chosen. There was only one item she had asked to have; this was a split habit that Jack had found tucked at the back of a shelf.

Far from being embarrassed, Bea was delighted. He had assured her that funds were no issue. However, she was thrilled that he had bought some things for himself. The next stop was for shoes.

She noticed they passed John Hamilton's bookmakers store on the way to Horden's shop, but Jack turned into a small shopfront. The bell jangled as the door opened. The man looked up as they entered. He looked like a shrivelled monkey, but Bea realised he had a bit of a hunchback. However, the smile he gave them was welcoming. "Hello, Mr Jack; how did those boots go?" The voice asking the question was well-modulated and friendly.

Jack reached out and shook the man's hand. "They are wonderfully comfortable, thanks, Mr Iles. Hence, we are back for more. May I introduce my wife?"

Jack and Bea spent the next hour choosing half-boots, riding boots, and work boots for Bea. She also needed some house slippers, and Jack needed two more pairs of work boots. He also asked for a couple of extra-wide, size eleven boots for Billy. Netty had refused any footwear, but Mr Iles had some fluffy sheepskin Indian-style moccasin slippers, and Jack purchased four pairs of these for them. Bea had never seen such things before, but Jack knew how cold it could get in the cabin. It had not snowed last winter, but Billy told him it often did. From the bootmaker, they returned to the hotel. They arrived back in time to collect a luncheon basket, and Mr Stewart suggested that the hotel carriage drop them off with their picnic and collect them two hours later.

Bea had not had a proper English picnic before, but she was glad there would be only the two of them. Mrs Macquarie's Chair was a colossal sandstone rock made into a long seat. It had been carved for the Governor's wife over twenty years before.

As the sun was out and it was cool in the shade of the overhanging trees, Jack set out a rug on the grass, and they sat in the sunshine enjoying their picnic.

The picnic basket contained an entire crockery set, and the food was packed in straw to stay warm.

After eating their fill of hard-boiled eggs, hot roast pullet chicken, lamb cutlets, pressed tongue, tiny pork pies, pickles, and assorted other treats, they lay back on the picnic rug enjoying the warmth of the afternoon. Jack fed Bea bite-size apple tartlets topped with thick clotted cream. She had never been hand fed before and was initially so embarrassed that she blushed. With their appetites sated, they lay back and enjoyed the view of the ships shuffling around the harbour.

Jack wished they could be more private, but even in the convict town, he could not pull her into his arms and do what he wished. He did lean over and gave her a quick kiss. "Bea, my sweet, as much as I would love to drag you back to the hotel and spend the afternoon in our bed, we have more shopping to do, and I also have to find out when the ship bringing the sheep is due in. Then we will have all tonight to enjoy together. Tomorrow, I must find a man named Richards and see if Laban White's vehicle is suitable for our purposes; if not, I'll see what else they have for sale. We also must stock up on dried foodstuffs, and we then need to buy some furniture and so much more. So, my beloved, we have a lot to do."

Bea grinned wickedly. "And the quicker we get it done, the sooner we can return to our room this afternoon."

Jack gave a shout of laughter and said, "Absolutely, my love, and I can't wait."

By the time the hotel carriage collected them and dropped them off at Mr Richards' coach yards, Jack had made a list of foodstuffs that he thought they would need.

The hotel coachman suggested, "Sir, try the Levice and Younger store in Market Street; they have a fresh stock of dry goods and other bits and bobs." He dropped them off before the shop and returned to the hotel.

The smell of the fresh food assailed their nostrils as they opened the door. Again, a little bell rang as it swung open, and a man appeared from behind a curtain. He had a white cap on his head and a big apron covering his clothing.

Twenty minutes later, they left having placed an order for raisins, tea, salt, sugar, flour, rice, treacle, and a new stoneware demijohn for brewing ginger beer and many other items. Bea wondered how she would ever use them. She had found some butter paddles, a cream skimmer, an earthenware milk vat, some cheese moulds and a butter churn. "Jack, do you have a cow? If not, can we get one? I could use these and make our own food."

Jack knew that now he was married meant the prospect of children; having a dairy cow would be good, but would one be enough? He had never worried before, but he knew that looking after a cow or two would give Bea something familiar to do each day. Any excess cheeses they could sell or trade with passing vehicles. He would build her a small dairy room, and he and Billy would dig out an underground cool room and line it with shelves.

These items were added to the growing pile, along with half a dozen coopered buckets and other dairy paraphernalia. Jack knew he had yet to buy a new bed and some other furniture, but he decided that after the Bond store, they would have done enough shopping for the day.

From the food shop, Jack said, "I need some lime wash, and the Bond store has it. They also have some other stock I need." He wished to visit the main town Bond store down near the quay. They strolled down to the harbour with Bea clinging to his arm.

Bea had never seen an emporium like this before, and her eyes almost popped when she entered. "Jack, I didn't know places like this existed. You can buy anything you want here. Look, they have milk vats too, and what's in those huge barrels?"

Jack smirked. "Those barrels are full of salt pork, sweetie, and that one is salt beef. That ghastly-looking stuff is sauerkraut. It stops scurvy on the ships. We won't be buying any of that as our vegetable garden supplies us with what we need. But I would like to see if we can buy some vegetable seeds and fruit tree plants and take them home." They spent over an hour meandering through nearly everything on the shelves. Jack had told her to choose whatever she liked, so she did. She was like a child in a lolly shop for the first time.

Exhausted after their shopping spree, they still had to walk up the hill to the hotel. They entered the building as the sun was hitting the horizon, as it was mid-winter, and the days finished early. Bea didn't mind. Her head was whirling as she had done so many new things today. However, her new shoes were rubbing a little, and she was sure she was getting a blister. With two hours until dinner, she hoped that Jack would suggest a late afternoon rest.

Mr Stewart had handed Jack a letter on their return. It was from the shipping office to say that a ship had just arrived and mentioned that the expected flock was still some days away on a following vessel. It had yet to finish unloading in Port Phillip Bay. The earliest it would arrive would be Friday morning. This took the pressure off the shopping for the next day. Jack glanced over at his young wife. She was lying invitingly, hoping that his letter wasn't too important. Usually, it would have frustrated him that his schedule was now behind time, but today, with a Bea nearby, he was delighted. "Sweetheart, we have two choices; that letter was to say the ship is delayed, it will not be here until Friday, so we either go back to Parramatta for a couple of days, or we stay here and then have to find a paddock for the sheep on the way home."

Bea didn't care and said saucily, "As long as I'm with you, I don't care if we sleep on the beach or in a feather bed."

Jack laughed. "Then, sweet Bea, I suggest we go on Wednesday, as I must order goods from Mr Tindale. He's the Parramatta blacksmith, and then that takes the pressure off tomorrow's shopping. Hopefully, we'll have our own wagon to travel back in, so we won't have to rely on the ferry. Tomorrow we must buy the cart or wagon and beasts to pull it and then find somewhere to sell us some cows. We also must buy our new bed, which we can do from Mr Riley's store in the James building. Currently, I sleep on a grass-stuffed canvas mattress, which isn't very pleasant. I'm determined to buy a bed where we can be comfortable, amongst other things." By now, he was sitting next to her on the bed. "Any idea what those other things might be?"

They spent the next half hour occupied as honeymooners do. And afterwards, lay discussing what furniture they would need besides a bed. Bea wanted a chest of drawers at some stage. She thought they could double as a baby's bed but didn't wish to mention that.

It was Jack who suggested that she turn her thoughts to a family. After their recent activity, Jack said to the naked lady curled up next to him, "Sweet Bea, you mentioned that you fell with child and lost it. So, you know far more about that sort of thing than I do, but I have no idea what a child would need. I know we have fabric, but what else does a baby need? I realise it's early to think of these things, but we have no shops nearby." Jack didn't want to stir up bad memories for her, but they had to think of their future. She had no idea yet how far out of Parramatta they would live. Jack knew that Bathurst was the closest town, and it wasn't very big. It certainly didn't have the supplies available. The only benefit of his farm is that they had access to the main Bathurst to Parramatta Road.

Bea didn't mind his question. "Jack, I've had little to do with children either. Yes, I fell with child after I was abused, and as I said, I lost it at about four months along. Conditions were not suitable to have brought a healthy child into this world anyway, so, although sad about it, I wasn't that concerned. Although, for some reason, I cried a lot after losing it, even though I was pleased it was gone." She snuggled closer. "You said that Netty has children; if I need her, hopefully, she'll be there. If not, it will be up to you to deliver our babies, Jack. When we go back, can we talk to Molly? She will know what to do. Even if she can give us the basics, that would be a big help."

Bea had no idea what was in front of her. She had seen a stunned look on his face. She knew there was something he wasn't telling her.

The next day when they left the hotel, they were again a bit later getting started than they had hoped. However, neither of them was complaining. They were totally comfortable with each other and became more so as time passed. That day's shopping was far beyond anything Bea had ever done before. As usual, she stayed silent for most of it, absorbing the new things happening around her. By the time they returned to the hotel, Jack had purchased a wagon, a cart, five horses and other assorted stock and a swathe of dismantled furniture that he could re-assemble once they reached home. They would place the feather mattress on top of all their purchases and sleep on it on the return journey. Jack had walked for two weeks, but it could take much longer with him droving Hugh's flock and Bea driving the wagon. But they were in no hurry. They had their lives ahead of them, and it boded to be a good one.

Chapter 6   The Adventure Begins

*T*he return to Parramatta was made by wagon. Jack used this trip to teach Bea how to drive the new vehicle. It was the only lesson she would have before they made the journey home. The four horses were harnessed as a team, and rather than start learning to drive with one beast; she had to learn to drive four of them at once. To complicate matters, these four animals had never worked as a team.

Much to her surprise, when the wagon arrived at the hotel, she found Jack had ordered a covering for the top. Jack had securely tied the small cart to the wagon's rear; they were now a long vehicle. Mr Stewart had his staff assist in loading their purchased items.

Within two hours, Jack and Bea were on the road and heading west. He drove out of town before he handed over the reins.

Bea was more nervous than she'd ever been before. Unable to see through her tears, she wailed, "I can't do this, Jack. It's too big."

"You can, Bea, and you have to, or we can't get all this home." Jack lay back, grinning, his hands behind his head. "Sweet Bea, you can do absolutely anything you put your mind to, you know. You have achieved so much already; what makes you think you can't do this?"

"I'm frightened," she said as she ably flicked the long whip to get only the lead horse to keep moving.

Jack chuckled. "Did you see what you just did? A beginner would have stuffed that and made them all move as a unit. You're a natural, sweetheart."

Her tears eased, and with renewed confidence, she kept going.

By the time they stopped for lunch, Bea had relaxed into her new role. Jack only had to take the reins once, and that was when they were going downhill, and the horses decided to trot. She squealed, and he grabbed the reins and slowed the team down.

They arrived in Parramatta safely, and Jack took the reins as they approached the town and drove the loaded wagon to the holding yard. He knew he could leave the full wagon in the Lockley's barn and hoped to drove Hugh's flock directly there. He had intentionally left the small cart empty, as he had to take it to the blacksmiths the following day and stock up with the hardware they needed. Then the smithy's stock would be repacked into the wagon. The cart would be loaded with pre-purchased breeding stock on the way home. In the meantime, he also intended to show Bea around the town. They would use the cart for transport.

Sal warmly welcomed them. Their eldest son, Charlie, appeared to help with the horses. As they had spent much of the trip only walking, they only needed a cursory rub down; then, the four horses were released into the paddock with Trigger.

Jack and Bea walked up the hill to Molly and Bill's inn. They knew their room awaited them, and the temperature had dropped as the sun had nearly set. Soon they were snug in their room and awaiting a call for dinner. As they were the only occupants, it was kangaroo tail stew again, but Molly's stew and dumplings were delicious.

The next day, their jaunt around town saw them head up to Mr Tindale's blacksmith forge and place a sizeable order for things. Jack could change a horseshoe and farrier the hoofs, but he needed the nails and shoe blanks. He'd had little need before as he only had the two old beasts, both were unshod.

They left the smithy and headed off on a discovery tour around town. Jack knew of places to visit, and the government dairy at the back of the official residence was a favourite spot of his. He knew Governor Bourke from his youth, and he had arrived in town soon after the Governor's wife had died. Since then, he had various debates with him, and the latest one over land ownership saw Jack leave town and take a significant grant of land, which had a tribe of natives living on it. It had not taken long for him to make friends and assure them they could stay. Although Jack agreed with the abolition of transportation and the lessening of the cruel conditions of the convicts, he did not agree with Governor Bourke's new policy of *Terra nullius*.

This was one of the conversations he and Bea had on the trip yesterday. "This means Bea that the natives here have no rights to their land. I have tried to tell the Governor about their culture and community system, but he is just not that interested. Sadly, they can only think about the wealth of the land and what it can bring them. It was why I claimed the valley I did, as I knew this was where the tribe now lived. It was the only way I could keep them safe."

Bea knew nothing about these dark-skinned ghosts of the bush. She'd had little to do with any of them. "Terra, what, Jack? But how can they own the land, Jack? They didn't have to buy it."

"*Terra nullius*, Bea. It is Latin for 'empty land,' or the literal translation is 'nobody's land'. The Governor is very wrong. If what Billy tells me is true, and I have no reason to doubt him, they have been here for hundreds of years, if not thousands. He calls their history their *Dreamtime*, and they have creator stories, too, like the stories in Genesis about God creating our world and the stars. They have as much right to this land as landowners in England. When we whites arrived, we marched roughshod over their rituals and land. We have built on their hunting grounds and destroyed their ancient systems that enabled them to live in harmony with the land and the animals. They only took what they needed and then moved on without leaving any sign they had even been there."

"But they had no houses or towns; how can you say they owned it?" she asked, genuinely interested.

Jack glanced at her. "They didn't need towns as they are nomadic. They move with the seasons and animals. They live in bark *humpies* and *gunyas* and can leave little or no trace that the tribe was even there. They may leave a cleared area or a fireplace when they move on, but little else. It's like us when we camp. We take our things with us. Bea, they know how to manage the land, build fish traps, and take only what food they need. We, on the other hand, plan for the future. We plant, sow, reap, and store our excess goods or trade them for what we don't have. They don't do that. They subsist, living off the land then moving on." Jack thought of what he'd learned from Billy. "You will see that when you get to our place that Billy and Netty have their own *gunya*, but I built my shack where they said I could. Yes, the land is in my name, but I refused to shoo away the tribe that lives there. I ask them permission to do what I have done in exchange for letting them stay. They will always be welcome, knowing they are safe in my place. They don't mind me farming it or clearing the land, but there are areas I can't and won't enter. There's a hill with a seam of silver in the rock that is sacred ground for them. There is also a small gully no man can enter. If word ever got out about the silver being up there, there would be a rush on the stuff. I know there is gold in the creeks as I did some panning for fun, but I'm keeping quiet about my finds. I don't need the money yet, and we would be inundated if word spread. The news will get out one day, but in the meantime, I like living near them and learning about how they survive. In particular, it's their bush medicines that intrigue me."

Bea was surprised. "They have bush medicines? Like what?"

Jack chuckled. "In England, if we have a headache or pain, we take a mix of willow bark, or if you have a heart condition, you use fox gloves. These are English plant medicines that we know work. There is also honey for burns, other herbs, and things we have used for centuries. Nicholas Culpepper wrote about this over a hundred years ago, and his book is still used. These people have different plants to access and know much about what works best. Here they call it bush medicine, and that's just what it is. Things like yellow puff mushrooms that fix pus-filled infections. Squashed witchetty grubs that they spread on burns and all sorts of other revolting things that work brilliantly. I only know about those two, as Netty has used them on me. I nearly vomited when I learned about the grubs, but it worked. Look!" He pulled up the sleeve of his shirt and showed her his arm.

Bea had seen a few small scars but had never asked him about them.

Jack explained, "I tripped over a log and landed on the edge of my campfire. Netty doctored me with their treatments. First, she cleaned me up and smothered the burn with a thick gooey dark honey. The next day, Billy arrived back with a *coolamon* of wiggling dirt. He had gone and collected these particular wiggling creatures, and I had presumed they were to eat. I have tried them cooked before, and they taste like rancid nuts. Netty didn't tell me, but she appeared with a smooth cream, and after she had cleaned off the honey, she put this cream on. It helped greatly, and twice daily; she put on more. I realised what was in the cream when Billy left to get more grubs."

"Eew, yuck!" She exclaimed. "But what's a *coolamon*, Jack?" she asked.

Jack saw Bea's interest. "It's a sort of a wooden bowl, but it's made from part of a tree trunk that they hollow out. They use them to carry things and come in various sizes, from small ones for berries to huge ones for wood and babies. They also use bigger ones as baby cradles. They also have wooden throwing sticks called *woomeras*, musical instruments named *didgeridoos*, but I call them a *didge* and of course spears and other things. The *woomeras* are smoothed holders with a spike used to throw a spear, and the *didgeridoo* is an instrument with an unusually deep, haunting sound that men play at a *corroboree*; that's a tribal dance. Most of their tools are wooden and strong. Their digging sticks are often made of *mulga* wood, and it's almost as strong as iron. About the only other thing they use is the stone axes. They shape these from grey river rocks, and it's why they come down to Emu Plains. They sit at the ford and make them. I asked why they don't use the rocks in our creek, but Billy said, "Not good stone.""

"So, you had an argument with the Governor about these people?" Bea was somewhat concerned that her husband even knew the Governor.

Jack nodded. "My family knew Richard Bourke from home. I stayed there for a while when I first arrived. After my argument, I moved to Bill and Molly's inn. I also had many discussions with him about the separation of church and state. At least, that is one thing we agreed on. Now each of the denominations can worship as they wish. Before, everyone had to be Church of England; he has thankfully freed that up as I've heard he's changed that rule."

Their conversations of late had often led back to his faith. Bea was willing to learn all he taught her. She knew that Jack had a strong belief in God, and he often brought this up when chatting. It had not taken her long to realise it was the centre of his life and that Hugh Lacey was partially responsible.

After spending the day tripping around in the small cart, they returned to the blacksmith and loaded up their order. There were horseshoes, files and clippers, four boxes of assorted nails, double-pointed looped fencing nails, and hinges for the window shutters that Jack wanted to build. He had seen a double-ended saw and added one, then added an assortment of other tools. There were shearing clippers, welding irons and solder, two rolls of plain wire, hoof picks, and vices.

Bea also asked Jack if she could have an iron that you filled with coals. She had seen one sitting on a shelf in the forge shop. They looked around to see what else Mr Tindale had, and there was a box of odds and ends of experimental items. In there, Jack found some strange pliers, a brace and bit frame with some homemade drills, a meat cleaver with no wooden handle, and for some reason, there was also a leather hole punch. Jack added all of these to the large order of goods.

Mr Tindale tallied up the account, and Jack pulled out a wad of notes from his pocket and paid in cash. "I'll collect the wheel frames and rivets when I come through next week; thanks, sir. It's a real pleasure doing business with you." He gave the smith's apprentice, young Charlie Lockley, a wave and went to join Bea.

It was a week before word came through that the ship carrying the stock had finally arrived in Sydney. This delay had given the honeymoon couple a luxuriously lazy time together. They enjoyed the time getting to know each other as well as the town. They saw Jack's friend Ned frequently and ate with the Lockleys a few times. Jack even managed to persuade Bea to dine with the Governor one evening.

She would only accept the invitation once the Governor knew she was an emancipated convict.

Jack had assured her that she would be welcomed. He and Richard Bourke discussed inclusion in a society for emancipated offenders. For Jack to have married one proved his point. That thought brought him up with a jolt; one thing he had not yet done was to write and tell his family he was now married. He wondered how to word his letter. He decided to let Richard Bourke or even Hugh Lacey write and tell his family. Richard could wax lyrical about her, and he would be believed. Ned couldn't write to anyone, as Jack knew his identity was secret, and though his family knew he was in Australia, they didn't know the name he was using. However, Richard knew Jack's father well enough to word the letter appropriately. Thankfully when Richard's daughter, Anne Deas Thompson, met Bea, the two ladies hit it off.

Bea initially had not realised that she was also the first lady, as she had stepped into that role when her mother had died. Bea's gentle and loving nature won over the Governor's daughter soon after meeting that evening. When they had retired after dinner, they had sat discussing the condition of convicts in the Factory.

Bea gave Anne a genuine description of what conditions were like in gaol. Bea had been surprised to find that Anne had visited the prison twice. Bea had been horrified and said, "Ma'am, that is no place for a genteel lady." Bea then discovered that Anne had been the mysterious other lady accompanying the kidnapped lady. She filled Anne in on the rape of the convict women and what the matron's husband was like.

Anne revealed that the poor matron was unaware of what her husband was up to or that he was siphoning funds from the Female Factory allocation. She had taken Bea's hand, patting it comfortingly as they talked.

There was one topic Bea dearly wished to know. She was very hesitant when she voiced her worry. "Ma'am, I am a convict, now married to a wonderful man who even considers my wishes and desires, but I am inadequate to know how to be a wife and mother to any future children. Having been raised in an orphanage, I have never known what a family is, and I have rarely seen how a family should work. Jack expects that we will learn together, but there are some things we will need to learn together that we won't be able to muddle through." Bea looked up to see an amused look on the first lady's face. "Babies, ma'am. We know nothing about children other than how they are made."

Anne smiled. "I presumed as much, my dear. Children are a wonderful gift from God Bea, but they don't come neatly packaged or with an instruction book." Anne saw Bea's confusion. She continued, "Dear, all of us must muddle through as best we can. If you have another lady with you who has children, that will help, but each child is an individual and must be treated as such."

Bea's nervousness made her say, "The only other woman is a native lady. She has children, but I have no idea what she's like."

Anne was still holding Bea's hand. "Bea, babies are the same, black or white, boys or girls, they are all born the same way. This native lady will have as much experience as a white woman, if not more. She will probably even have more knowledge than we do. Never underestimate their knowledge; they have survived here far longer than we have. I agree with Jack, dear, they may not have built towns and solid houses, but they certainly have lived in this rough country. If Jack says you can trust this woman, then do so. Even if it's because you trust Jack." Anne wondered what the reaction would be and was encouraged when Bea smiled and nodded.

Bea gazed at her trustingly. "I've hardly ever seen someone with different coloured skin, Anne. As a matter of fact, I've spoken to very few people from anywhere other than London." Bea's eyes were wide with anxiety.

Anne smiled at her comments. Her father's work had thrown her into the diverse pool of humanity. "We all bleed red, Bea. The colour of our skin is quite literally skin deep. We all have feelings; we laugh in the same way and feel hurt just as deeply. Do you as a convict feel hurts or loves any less than I do as Governor's daughter?"

Bea shook her head.

"They are the same, aren't they?" Anne asked gently.

Bea teared up, "Yes," she said meekly. "Only no one ever asked me for my ideas or wishes before Jack. No one has ever cared before." Bea was overwhelmed with emotion. "No one ever wanted me, ever. Even my mother gave me away."

Anne took a teary Bea in her arms.

Soon, Bea was weeping freely on her new friend's shoulder. The words Bea muttered were difficult to understand, but Anne got the gist of what she meant. "I've never been loved before, and it's all so strange. I've never been consulted about what I want, and to tell the truth, I don't know what I want." Bea sniffed and delicately blew her nose. "I've been told what to do, where to be, and what to wear all my life. I've never dared argue or stand up for what I believe, as I don't know what I believe. Jack leaves so much for me to decide, but I don't know how." Again, the tears flowed.

Anne had had free will all her life; her wishes were rarely denied by either her husband or her father. Her heart went out to this adorable, abandoned girl in her arms. Bea's beauty was far beyond a pretty face. She didn't even know how exquisite she was. Although very pretty, her true loveliness came from deep within. The trust she had for Jack was visible to all who saw them together, and it was evident that Jack adored her.

That fact became patently obvious when Anne's husband, Edward, and Jack entered the room moments later. Jack saw Bea's distress. Disregarding protocol, he knelt before her and gathered her to him. "Darling Bea, what is wrong?"

Bea just shook her head and remained silent. She was too upset to put the words together.

Anne answered for her. "Jack, she's somewhat overwhelmed that you care for her and give her free will; and also that you are concerned about her wishes. She has never had such love, compassion, or freedom, and it's a lot to absorb. Also, she's fearful she'll fail you."

Jack was now seated beside her. "Sweet Bea, you will not be alone in whatever is in front of us. We will face the future together, whether in a fancy house like this one or in a wattle and daub hut in the bush like where we will be living. Darling sweet Bea, together we will make a good life and a home for ourselves and, if God blesses us, a family too. Something that neither of us has experienced."

Bea lifted her head, and she saw him nod. She softly asked, "Sure? I don't want to let you down."

Jack kissed the top of her head. "You haven't, my darling girl, and you won't. Sure, we'll both make mistakes and probably have some fights along the way." He felt her stiffen in his arms.

Anne noticed and quickly added, "Bea, all married couples have disagreements at some time. It's how you work through them that makes a marriage strong. A marriage is a partnership, and it must work both ways. If one person always tells the other what they must do, say, or even think, that is not helpful. Jack knows that, and it's why he asks for your input. Bea, you must learn to give Jack honest answers to his enquiries." She turned to her childhood friend and said, "Jack, you must give her both time and guidance. Bea, I have known Jack for many years; he is truly a wonderful man. You can trust that he will only ever want what's best for you. He could have chosen a wife from all the society ladies he knows, but he chose a girl with an honest heart." Anne met her husband's puzzled stare.

Jack took over, "I chose you because you were the essence of goodness. Unbeknownst to you, we had met before. I have visited the farm a couple of times in different guises. More often as Hugh's friend, but on each visit, I saw that you were not only beautiful but that the world had not tainted you or changed the beauty within. It shines out of you, sweet Bea. You had been hurt and abused, but your beautiful soul shone through. It was that which drew me. I could not get you out of my mind; you haunted me. I told Tim about you soon after he married Maddie. When I came through on the last visit and found you weeping, I wished to take you in my arms and march you to the altar. But I needed to woo you, and also, we needed to get to know each other. I didn't care for your status, for I looked much deeper into who you were. I learned that one's status in life is but a facade. My parents both have status, but they are not nice people. I shunned the society that my older brother adores."

Bea was now curled to his side in quite an unladylike position, but she felt safe. "You loved me even then?" she asked in amazement, gazing up into his face.

Jack gently kissed her. "Bea, I'm not sure if I was full-blown lovesick then as I am now, but I wanted to get married, and your face kept coming to mind for months. I turned to the good Lord and asked him to lead me to the wife He wanted me to have. Again, your face came to mind. Soon I could not get it out of my mind or even my dreams. Then I arrived and found you in the milking shed in tears. Bea, I knew you were the girl for me. Anne can vouch that I had done the rounds of the Drawing Rooms and presentations in London and saw the shallowness of the silly girls I met, present company excepted, Anne."

Bea looked up and saw Anne nodding in agreement.

Anne chuckled. "He trod on my toes more than on the ballroom floor."

"I'm a good dancer, Anne!" Jack said indignantly. "Bea, I left the country very disillusioned and sought solace in a distant nation. I had heard that the Bourke's had come to New South Wales, and knowing Hugh was here somewhere too, followed some months after their arrival. However, I arrived at a melancholy time, with Anne's good mother passing. She was the dear lady whom I called Aunt Betsy. She was more of a mother to me than my own. I stayed and stood as a friend for them through that horrible time. I was welcomed here and settled in. Anne and I are of an age, and although good friends, it was never more than that." Jack looked up and saw Edward glance towards Anne. "No, Edward, nothing more; we were like brother and sister. No more than we are now; I was thrilled when you two were married; otherwise, I would not be sitting here cradling my wife in front of you both. You are more family to me than my own. Anne, you know that."

Anne nodded; she looked at the surprise on her husband's face, "T'is true, Edward. Jack is very much like my younger brother, Dick. We spent many happy days in our childhood playing on the foreshores on the Isle of Wight, for our fathers were friends. The boys spent many hours together getting into trouble, and I spent as many getting them out of it." She gave a joyous chuckle.

Bea frowned. "Should I not be in your arms, Jack?" she asked in all innocence.

Jack chortled. "No, my beloved, but as I just said, they are almost family. It will be permitted here in this intimate setting, but I would not even be allowed to touch your hand elsewhere. It's one of the things I hate about society and another of the things I love about you. You are all that is true and honest." He brushed back a wayward curl and kissed her forehead. "That would also not be allowed if we had visitors," he said while chuckling.

A voice from the doorway said, "And that should not be permitted here even without visitors, my boy. Decorum, Jack; some societal rules should not be allowed to slip." Governor Bourke joined them as the tea tray was brought in. "Sorry I was delayed; pressing business needed to be sorted." He appraised the situation, "Tears, dear? Whatever for?"

Again, Anne filled him in on the previous conversations.

Sir Richard settled into his winged armchair. "Ahh, the blessings of a good wife! I miss my Betsy beyond all reason, for she was a queen amongst women. For my beloved to pass so soon after our arrival here was a bitter blow. I thought the warmer climate here would be good for her. However, she is now at peace and out of pain. She had been unwell for many years, as my Anne will vouch. But, Beatrice, the wonderful years we had together and the children we shared fills my mind with happy memories; they shall never pass. My beloved Betsy lies on the hill in a grave not far from here. Yet I know she is also with our good Lord in Heaven. I visit her grave as often as I can." He saw Jack's glance. "Yes, lad, I know she is not there. Her earthly husk remains and, by now, will have returned to the dust from which we are made, so I should not grieve. Yet, her passing tore my heart in two, and I shall miss her until the day I die, and I shall once again be joined with her. Sadly though, I feel that shall not occur in this country."

Jack felt Bea stiffen in his arms.

She looked up at him and said, "That's what those words in the marriage service mean, isn't it? Till death us do part. I'm beginning to understand the depth of love now. Coming from someone who has never experienced it before, can I say it's nice, Jack. It's nice to have someone to turn to if I'm fearful or unsure of what to do. I've never had that before. I've not known a mother's love or what a family is like. There are so many new things I have experienced with you. I had not even walked in the sea until last week." She turned to Anne, "I'd never had a picnic until I met Jack, nor had I been shopping before. Have you any idea how amazing it is to walk into a store and buy things you could previously only dream about? Many of the items in the stores I did not even know existed."

She had no idea how the words she said affected the four listeners. All had grown up not worrying about their place in a family; or where their food would come from. Even Jack had that security, just not love from his parents. However, Bea knew none of that.

Jack just held her closer, loving her more dearly. All present knew that many convicts were in similar situations, but few were untainted like Bea. They, too, had come from poor and dysfunctional families and homes, if they even had those. Many, like Bea, would have grown up in orphanages or on the streets in London and other cities in Britain. Eking out an existence as best they could. For Bea to not be resentful of what she saw and what they had, amazed them all. She was neither possessive nor bitter. She just wished to be the best wife that she could be for Jack. She would work hard and try to give her future family everything she had missed.

All four sat in awe of this lovely young woman who had taught them more love, compassion, and humility than they had thought possible.

Chapter 7   The Boat Comes In

*F*or two days, Jack and Bea unloaded the wagon and replaced everything again so the mattress could lay flat on top. The canopy would cover the load and give them some privacy from the other drovers.

There were only fifty sheep to collect for Hugh; However, as Jack had added some other beasts to the herd, he employed four other drovers to assist him with the mob.

He was now confident that Bea could drive the wagon for much of the time; having others on hand meant that he would take the reins and guide the wagon up and down the rough or steep road sections over the mountain's complex and uneven roads. That, in turn, would make Bea a lot happier. She was becoming more important to him daily. He thought back to the evening at Government House in Parramatta. He was astounded that a tiny slip-of-a-girl could bring him to his knees with her watery eyes. She had no idea just how vital her happiness had become to him. He didn't care if his family objected to her; she was now his priority. He had no intention of returning home anyway. She had asked for nothing for herself but an iron that you filled with coals and a split riding habit. He had chuckled over them, but he had showered her with more than she could ever dream. Nothing would be too good for her, and he decided to build her a beautiful home one day with a wide verandah all the way around it as she wished. It would have a summer sleepout and every modern convenience he could buy. He wanted to buy her diamonds, but she would rather have his kisses. He offered her a servant, and she had chosen three puppies, all of which were runts. How these Scottish border pups would fit into their farm would be interesting. These three black and white fur-balls were half-grown and chewing everything. Bea had fallen in love with the three scruffy imps on sight. When Jack said they were heading out to look at them with plans to get one for Bea, Molly had refused to allow any dogs indoors. Consequently, they had to stay with the owner for the week until they collected them on the way out of town.

Jack found that saying goodbye to Bea for at least a three-day absence was unpleasant. Both had known that had to occur; however, neither liked the temporary separation. Jack felt he was leaving her alone for months rather than a mere few nights, four at the most. She would be kept safe in the room at Molly's Inn. The night before he left, they had once again lay entwined. Her warm and supple body stirred him more than once.

A reluctant Jack saddled Trigger and set off just after dawn on Thursday morning. He would be in town by lunchtime and see about unloading the flock. The new drovers were to meet him at the docks, and he intended to drive the sheep to the church glebe and corral them there overnight. That, hopefully, would only take a few hours, as it wasn't far from the dockland. Afterwards, he had rounded up his other beasts he purchased, and the five men, mounted on their own steeds, would leave around dawn on Friday morning. They would return on Sunday or Monday if all went well unless he could move the herd along at a good pace. Normally such a mixed mob dawdled. He didn't like working on a Sunday, but the animals had to eat. It would be better to reach Charles's paddock, and they could graze it down. He knew the knee-high grasses were a summer fire hazard, and Charles said he would have to scythe it soon. Putting fifty sheep and assorted other beasts in there for the weekend would fix the problem. Hopefully, there would be a beast that would set a good pace; he had found in the past that there was often one who took charge.

Having left a little late, the herd had settled by the time they were an hour out of town. One of the milking cows had taken over as the lead beast, and the other animals willingly followed her. Jack wondered if she had come from out this way. She confidently led the hotchpotch herd as if she were a queen. She raised her head and occasionally mooed, ensuring everyone knew she was in charge. Behind her came a six-month-old black bull calf that Jack had chosen to be the herd bull. He would reach maturity by the time the cows had calved and were ready to mate again. Droving a bull in mating season would be problematic; the half-grown calf solved this problem. This calf would replace the stray bulls on his farm. Their sale would go to pay off some of his debt to Hugh. Jack smiled at that thought. They were a God-given gift so he could start afresh with Bea. He had hoped his money would be through from home by now.

He had purchased two other horses and six sheep for the beginning of his own flock; one was a young ram for his farm. The bull calf had been hand raised, so he was also approachable, if not affectionate. Near him were three other cows; one had a month-old calf at foot, and the other two were in calf and should drop in a month or so. Hugh's fifty merino ewes were used to being penned together. Hopefully, they would stay that way.

Sitting on the horse while droving, he found his mind had little to occupy itself. He recalled another purchase he had made the day before at the barracks office when visiting Tim Hinds and Humphrey Downes. Jack had also bought four piglets to be collected from the government farm at Rooty Hill. He was surprised to learn that female piglets were not called sows. They called them gilts if they had not had babies; however, all males were called boars. So, they had yet to collect one boar and three gilt piglets from Rooty Hill. He had to find and source a cage for them in Parramatta.

They hoped to arrange to use a roadside yard at the government farm the first night out of Parramatta when collecting the new breeding stock. Depending on how the mixed herd went, they should reach Hugh's farm only a day or so later. If Bea's puppies scattered the sheep, they could be in real trouble, but they were supposed to be sheepdogs, so he hoped they would have some natural instinct for herding animals.

Jack found that his time away from Bea was challenging. His mind was constantly on her in some way or another. Sometimes he thought of how to please her or what she looked like in bed. He smiled and knew it would not be long until he saw her again. With that in mind, he gave Trigger a nudge to hurry him up.

Jack expected to spend two nights on the road between Sydney and Parramatta. To cover the sixteen miles in only two days was unreasonable with such an assortment of beasts. They would be unpredictable. He knew they should cover about six or seven miles daily, but he wondered if they would get more than five miles with such a mixed mob. More would be astounding, and less would be frustrating.

The four drovers were men recommended by Ned. He had used them before for Government jobs, and they were four bedraggled ex-convicts who hired themselves out whenever possible. They were itinerant workers at the government farms but generally based on the main farm in town. Hiring them, though, meant that Bea could not be left alone for a moment once she joined them. He didn't trust them, or anyone else, with his new wife. Thankfully he could sleep in the wagon with her *en route*.

Strawberry, as Jack had named his lead red cow, was powering along. Her long sharp horns were held high, and her nose was in the air. She was headed westward and hardly stopped to graze or drink. She chewed her cud as she powered along, and the herd followed her lead.

They covered seven miles on the first day, which was an extraordinary feat. If Strawberry could keep up this pace, they would reach Parramatta around dusk on Saturday night. It would be better than staying only a mile out of town and sitting up all night with them. The drovers could remain in Lockley's barn in hammocks, knowing the fenced paddocks awaiting the stock. Jack knew he could wallow in the luxury of his comfortable, warm bed with Bea cradled in his arms. The thought of her waiting was enough to stir him to another smile. It wasn't all that stirred; he was now sitting uncomfortably in his saddle; he tried to get his mind back to the work afoot. He had to find somewhere to keep the flock safe overnight.

As the sun neared the horizon, the drovers told him of an area used for holding travelling stock. On arrival, they found it was currently empty, so Jack willingly opened the slip rail and ushered Strawberry into the paddock. He was surprised he had not noticed this yard before but travelling with experienced drovers helped. They told him about a series of these stockyards along the main road to Penrith. Most were out of sight from the road. Beyond that, the only ones were at the convict stockades. They had not been available the only time Jack had done any droving. That had been the year before and was to bring some of Hugh's new breeding stock from across the mountains.

Jack carried rope hobbles for the horses, but they could be in with the herd in the stockyards. There was plenty of grass, and he saw a wooden coopered bucket and discovered a small weir in a nearby creek where they could draw water to fill the trough.

The men took turns watching the beasts, but they were safe as they were fenced in. Every two hours watch changed. As it was mid-winter, they all slept close to the fire.

At this campsite, they could stay near the fire while on watch and at least stay warm. Once on the range on the Bathurst Road, they would have to be two up at a time on two hourly shifts. He wasn't looking forward to that. Two weeks of frigid nights and crossing the range mid-winter was certainly not the best time to travel.

The four men's names were Joe, Tom, Iain, and Fred. All four refused to give their surnames, saying, "Names ain't needed for us in this caper, Mr Jack," muttered Tom, the spokesman. "We's all got our tickets, as Major Grace knows, and the government e'en uses our services." The others spoke only to tell the next man it was time to change shifts at night.

Throughout the evening, Jack heard one or other of them singing. He took the midnight to two o'clock shift as he knew he would have time to get back to sleep after his shift. He hated the two to four o'clock slot as they had to rise at five anyway.

The night passed with five cold, hungry men huddling around a dying fire in the frosty pre-dawn light. They first made tea and added some oats to a second billy of boiling water. Jack was keen to get the herd moving. If they had a good day today, he would be with Bea tonight. The promise of a good feed and a warm place to sleep stirred the drovers to break camp quickly.

Yesterday they had a bit of a late start by the time they had assembled the beasts; it had been seven o'clock and an hour after sun-up before they were on the road. With Strawberry again in the lead, the mob set off at a good pace. They had grazed the yard to nearly ground level. Strawberry trotted along quickly, and the others followed in her wake. They had obviously all grazed during the night on the lush grass in the stockyard. By near sunset, they were on the outskirts of Parramatta.

The hard part was to get Strawberry to where she could lead the mob. In the end, Jack had to tie a rope halter around her horns and led the eclectic herd down Parramatta's main street, then into Phillip Street, and towards the paddock behind the inn in George Street.

Word saying the drovers were approaching had spread to Miller's Inn. As soon as Bea heard, she flew out of the inn and ran to greet the unusual procession. Rather than stand and watch, she didn't stop until she was beside Jack. "Hi, Jack, lift me."

Grinning at her willingness to greet him, he said, "Darling sweet Bea, I missed you so much."

"Me too, Jack; hoist me up, and I'll welcome you as no one else can." Knowing she would be cradled in his arms, he pulled her up.

Now up before him, doubling as they led the cow into Charles's paddock. With Strawberry still on the rope and now trailing behind him, he greeted his wife with a passionate kiss.

Although it was nearly dark, the prying eyes of the town's busybody still saw them. He lifted his head when he heard the bitter words.

Mrs Jenkins' catty voice carried far. "Such rude behaviour. I don't know what the town is coming to with such flagrant disregard for decency and flouting society's rules. I suppose you can't expect more from convicts."

Jack groaned. He should have known better, but he had missed Bea so much. He knew the recently widowed, Mrs Jenkins's cutting tongue would have their activity all over church tomorrow.

Charles had the slip rails down and waited for the stock to arrive. Jack and Bea led Strawberry into the paddock and released her from the rope halter. The cow moved further in, and the rest of the herd followed. Soon the mob was safely enclosed in the large paddock and started to graze even before they had the slip rail up again. Jack turned Trigger loose and carried his saddle and swag back to the barn. He knew he should give him a brush down, but the horse wasn't even sweating. He had been gently walking all day.

Iain saw them and said, "I'll fix him, Mister Jack."

Charles had returned to the inn and left Jack to show the drovers where to sleep. No one would need to keep watch tonight, so once Sal fed the drovers, they could all sleep in the warmth of the enclosed barn. All four had said they would join the family for Sunday services in the morning. All knew church attendance was part of them having a Ticket of Leave.

Jack and Bea put Trigger's saddle on the storage log, along with the drovers' saddles; then, they headed up the hill to their room. Jack had Bea under his arm. The cold was seeping through her woollen gown, and she was getting chilled. The cold had settled, and she had not put on her coat as she ran to meet him. She didn't care; her man was back. She was almost dancing with excitement at his early return. As it was now dark, their walk up the hill took a little longer than expected. Jack stopped several times and enfolded her in his arms for a long, loving kiss. Their warm room awaited them, and he anxiously awaited their time to be alone. He knew he had yet to be sociable to Molly and Bill, and then he would hurry Bea to bed. He had only been gone for a few days, but it felt like months. He wanted Bea, and he wanted her now. They decided to sneak up the back steps and have a proper welcome before he announced he was back. Whether Molly or Bill knew, they didn't care.

When they eventually appeared, neither looked embarrassed, just happy. However, Molly was chuckling when they finally entered the kitchen for dinner, so they figured they had been caught out.

As they ate the hearty and warming stew, Jack filled them in about the drove so far. His description of Strawberry and her leading stance had them all in stitches. The calf he had named Bruce and Jack was sure Bea would choose a suitable name for the other three cows.

"You bought four cows, and some are in calf? Really? Have you any idea how much milk they give Jack? There's only us; what will we do with the rest of it?" Bea was astounded.

Jack looked abashed. "I have no idea, Bea; how much?"

Bea chuckled. "A normal cow will give five to ten gallons a day for about ten months of the year. Of course, you don't have to strip it all, but that is a lot of milk. We'll have to leave the calves with them to use most of the milk."

Molly had her head resting on her arms on the table. Her shoulders were shaking with unbridled mirth.

Bill didn't hold back; he threw his head back and laughed heartily.

Jack had the expression of a naughty schoolboy on his face. "Well, I told you we had to learn together; if that's my biggest problem, it's not too bad. We'll put up a shingle on the road saying fresh milk for sale. I'm hoping you can make some cheeses and other things to sell. We did buy the stuff to make it. Actually, I'd love to have a shop one day. It would be a great idea if we could make it a coach stop, with clean facilities for ladies to use. Tell me about cheese, Bea."

Bea shook her head. She took a deep breath. "Jack, it takes about one and a quarter gallons of milk to make a pound of cheese. I can make the rennet out of thistle or stinging nettle, but I'll need lemon or vinegar to curdle the milk, and even then, that will only make soft cheeses. I need animal rennet for the hard cheeses and a cool room too, but they take time to mature. Mrs Lacey taught me to make proper rennet, so I know how. We have what we need for moulds and stuff, but that's still a lot of cheese."

WAITING AT THE SLIPRAILS

The grin Jack gave her was a delight. "So, we can do it? We can buy what we need on Monday and add it to the wagon. There's no hurry to leave on Tuesday if Charles's paddock survives. I knew about the need for the rennet stuff, but I figured we could get some here. If you can make it, that's wonderful."

Bea said, "I can make it, but you need to use the fourth stomach from a slaughtered calf. Mrs Lacey may let me have some and take it home with us as I don't really want to kill one of the few calves we'll have."

Jack nodded, "Okay, Bea, the deal for the cows was 'take one, take all', and I knew you could milk. I was sort of hoping we could start a proper roadside shop. There are no stores in our area, and we could get other farms to add their produce too. What do you think? Ned knows of places down the Hawkesbury River that make things to sell, baskets, honey, and the like. But that is down the track at a future date."

The three others at the table were astounded.

Bea looked at her husband with delight. "You knew, didn't you? You've thought about it and worked out this idea."

Jack nodded with a smile. "I'm hoping we can start a trend of roadside shops of fresh produce. Oh, and something else we have to collect on the way west are four piglets, a cage of hens, and a rooster. I've already paid for them, but we need cages to transport them from the government farm at Rooty Hill."

Bea's expressive face lit up, "You bought me some chickens? I love chooks! What sort?"

Jack knew what he wanted, but what she would choose was probably different; however, he replied, "I have ordered Buff Orpington's and Dominique's. One is plain black, and the other is black and white speckled." With a chuckle, he added, "They fit the colour scheme of the other animals except for the lead cow. It seems that other than Strawberry, all the rest are either black or white. All the chickens are the same price, so we'll see what they have available when we get there. The pigs, I presume are the black ones; I didn't even ask."

Soon after, the group conversation drew to a close. Bea and Molly did the dishes while Jack had a wash and shave and got ready for bed. Bea had bathed earlier and only had to clean her teeth. The women hurriedly cleaned the kitchen before both retired to their rooms.

Jack had just finished shaving when Bea entered. He had nicked himself and had a trickle of blood on his lip. Bea took her handkerchief and dabbed the ooze away. The gentle action of love took Jack's breath away. She was wrong if she thought the love was directed all her way. Jack, too needed, and craved, the affection she willingly gave him. He, too, had never known the love or caress of a woman. He remembered hugs from his nanny but barely remembered her name. She had been dismissed when he was a small boy. He didn't recall other hugs except on one stormy night when he was little, he had climbed into his brother's bed, and they had hugged each other as the storm raged outside. Their father found them asleep in his brother's bed the morning after the storm and belted them both. Neither understood their punishment; Jack still didn't know his reason, but the boys never repeated the action. For Bea to willingly give everything she had, was new to him.

He woke at six the following day. They had spent a few hours talking before finally falling asleep, still entwined. The soft dawn light partially exposed her warm body; he enjoyed the view. His body responded to the sight before him. His fingers trailing down her cheek woke her. Knowing that they had to ready themselves for church and that Jack had to check the stock before they left, their morning welcome was short and sweet before they rose and got on with the day's activities.

Chapter 8   Delayed Departure

*A*fter the Sunday church service, they spent the day with the Lockley and Miller families, as they had organised another picnic on the river's edge.

Ned joined them after church, and although he had come in uniform, he relaxed, hatless in the sunshine with his friends. The children were often clustered around the tall blonde man. He often had three or four of them in his arms, or he was playing a game with them. His joyous deep laugh rang out across the grassy bank.

Bea was somewhat in awe of this soldier gentleman. He was the man she had met in gaol, where he had stood out even then. It took some adjustment to realise that a red-coated soldier could be an ordinary man; however, as he relaxed and removed his coat this morning, she gazed at him wondering, he looked so familiar, and she had just realised why. It was not because he had brought Maddie, but that also was not where she knew him from.

Jack saw her interest in his friend. He whispered, "Bea, what's wrong?"

She started at his question. "Sorry, Jack, I just find it hard to reconcile the Major at work and the man relaxing. It has also just occurred to me who he reminds me of. One of my master's friends could have been his brother. I heard whispers of some scandal about him, a broken engagement and marrying his brother's fiancé. He was a Marquess named David something or other." As she spoke, she saw Jack blanch. "Jack, have I said something wrong?"

Jack shook his head. His voice lowered so only she could hear; he said, "No, sweetheart, but I can't tell you here. Whatever you do, say nothing about this to anyone until we have spoken privately, promise?"

Bea nodded, but her eyes were now as big as saucers. Was there a connection between Major Ned and Marquess David?

Jack had recovered his equilibrium and murmured so only she could hear, "I'll tell you later, but it's vital for Ned that you say absolutely nothing, understand?" His heart was pounding. He had thought his biggest worry that morning was facing the catty Mrs Jenkins at church. That woman never shut up; she was constantly being catty about someone or other. However, that had been a breeze compared to the conversations this incident would produce. Fancy Bea meeting Ned's brother in London? Now he had to tell Ned that Bea had all but worked out who he was.

Ned roused himself and asked if anyone wished to take an excursion along the river edge. The children were always the first to volunteer for an activity; today was no different.

Jack pulled Bea up from their rug on the grass and said to Ned they would join him. Jack raised an eyebrow at his friend.

Ned took the hint. They followed the scampering children off on a wander. The two older couples stayed to pack up their picnic.

Jack waited until the children had run off and were far enough away from the others for them not to overhear. He suggested to Bea that she check on the small ones while he spoke with his friend. She heard a soft, "Please go, Bea; I'll chat to Ned."

She nodded and followed the children's path.

When she was out of earshot, Jack said, "Ned, Bea met David in London and knows about his marriage to Elouise. Well, she actually said, 'his brother's fiancé' rather than her name. What do I say to her? How much do I tell her?"

Ned started at the information. Jack heard him groan softly. Would that woman never stop haunting him? Ned sighed and said, "Tell her what you wish, Jack; just ask her to keep it private. She's met me often enough before and has not said anything. Not even when I was delivering Maddie and Chip to the farm." He blew his cheeks out in frustration. "If it were not Bea, I'd say, tell her nothing, but from what I have seen of her, she will stay silent." Ned shook his head in sadness. "But Jack, please explain to her that I would not marry that shrew if she were the last woman on earth. She may not know that the woman who was after Chip was Elouise's cousin. I have discovered that the female prisoners in the gaols here had better morals than Elouise, and she was a so-called lady of quality. I soon discovered her behaviour in our very short engagement. I interrupted her intimately cavorting with another man in the garden at a ball. Nothing was left to my imagination as she sat straddled on his lap, and their motion showed their actions. It proved to me that goodness is not something you are born with; I know now that it's a God-given blessing. When I informed my parents of what had occurred, my mother agreed and suggested that I cry off. I did not need to, as she had met David by then. She dropped me faster than a lump of hot coal, then proceeded to rub it in my face that she had already ensnared David. She had done; hence I'm here at David's bidding, not hiding from her."

Jack was stunned. "Cor, Ned, I had no idea. I had heard whispers from your brother, Paul, but such behaviour is often left to the older women. The immorality of society is why I finally left." There was no way that Jack would ever tell Ned that his ex-fiancé had made a move on him. Her young cousin, Geraldine, had also flirted with him. Geraldine and Elouise were two peas in a pod. "Ned, I wished for a wife who would love me for who I am and not what position or wealth I could bring them. For that reason, I chose a convict girl and fell in love with her. Ned, even though my parents disliked each other intensely, Mother stayed faithful to Father. At least, I am pretty sure she did. She would have been too scared of him to have strayed. He had a way with his fists that left no visible bruises." Jack spoke very matter-of-factly.

Ned took a swift glance at Jack. He had no idea of such animosity between his friend's parents. His own adored the very air each other breathed. "Your Bea has that goodness in spades, Jack, and she was both a servant and a convict. But I'd give her a place at a Ducal table any day over the ladies and painted misses of society. I tried to warn David about Elouise wanting a title, but she tricked him. From what I have heard from the occasional whisper and newspapers, she has led him a pretty dance." Ned saw Jack nod and realised he knew more than he'd admitted. A single fair eyebrow raised questioningly.

Jack was dubious about saying anything, but he needed an explanation. "I know Ned; I met Elouise a few times at things in London. You don't need to know."

Ned grimaced. "I try hard not to read the London gossip. However, the old newspapers sometimes mention them; I usually won't read the society pages for that reason. However, they also sometimes mention my parents, whom I miss dearly. I do so hope David doesn't hold it against me. Jack, I am only here because he asked me to leave, not because I ran away. I was only nineteen; what was I supposed to feel? I arrived as a lad with a broken heart."

Jack nodded, not really understanding the desertion of his family but certainly commiserating with his friend.

Ned smiled. "As you know, I love this new life as you do. I hope I never have to return home; David is only a year older than I. But as you well know, we have two younger brothers, and both are married with sons. Here, I have good friends, and my best friend is a convict. I have a great life where I can help the less fortunate; the climate is much better overall." He paused before adding, "And I'm happy, Jack. What more could a man ask?"

Jack thanked Ned; he had permission to tell Bea and knew she would stay silent. Jack had known about Ned's broken engagement but didn't know the details. Elouise was known as a woman of loose morals. However, for Ned to catch her *in flagrante delicto* at a ball was a shock. Ned hurt enough already. Elouise Wickham, aka Marquesses Allingmere, Ned's ex-fiancé and now sister-in-law, was known as 'Alley Cat'. She was also one of the reasons Jack had left London. He had watched her warm the beds of many of the peers of England. When she set her sights on him, he had fled. Her morals were more like a whore, and due to her shrewish behaviour, she was ostracised by many, yet her beautiful face drew men like bees to a honey pot. She wouldn't take 'no' for an answer once she had you in her sights. Jack swallowed nervously. He would protect Ned all he could. "Ned, I'll tell Bea but will swear her to silence about it."

"Thanks, Jack," Ned said with a hint of resignation. "I fear it will never end. I thought I could escape Elouise's evil talons over here. However, her behaviour is so abominable that word travels to even the Antipodes. It's why I have no wish to have my identity revealed." At this, Ned's attitude brightened. "On the plus side, we can talk about home freely when I am alone with you both. I do miss that."

Jack smiled. "You are welcome to come whenever you wish." Trust Ned to find the silver lining in such a situation.

With a hint of resignation and sadness, Ned replied, "Thanks, Jack; I will certainly take you up on that offer when you have a room for me."

Jack put a hand on his old school friend's shoulder. "Then let's change the subject. How's young Eddie going at school?"

Eddie, Charles and Sal's second son, was born on Ned's twenty-second birthday and named after him. The boy had a special place in Ned's heart, and he sponsored him to go to a good Sydney school. Eddie was currently at Cape's Academy in Sydney with thirteen-year-old Timmy Miller. Charlie, Eddie's older brother, had taken his position at the forge when Eddie had left for school. They were now young teenagers and had grown into two wonderful young boys.

Ned said, "Eddie's doing well, Jack, but he has no idea what he wants to do with his life. He now is well-read and speaks and reads Latin, plus he speaks French like a Parisian. Ed runs rings around me when talking about mathematics, geography or even theology. However, his passion is still at the blacksmith's forge. He has plans, big plans for its growth. I don't know if he had discussed this with Thomas Tindale yet, but he also mentioned a foundry to me when I saw him last."

Jack was stunned. "Eddie wants to build a foundry? Seriously?"

Ned chuckled. "Yes, and I have no doubts that he will return here, and that's exactly what he'll do one day, as I doubt he'll remain just the blacksmith's apprentice for long. He's a strapping lad now, and I think Thomas will offer him a partnership soon. Ed has caught up with Tim's height and now dwarfs him."

They chatted about the achievements of his namesake for some time. They had now caught up with Bea and the children. She was once again clinging to Jack's arm as they walked.

Ned asked them when they had to leave and was saddened to find that Jack had plans to head west on Tuesday. Neither knew when they would meet again. Again, they invited Ned to visit whenever he wished. Their farm was about a day's ride east of Bathurst, and they would always make room for him. He smiled at the offer. "I'll come, but not until you have a separate room for me, Jack. I do get out that way occasionally. At least I occasionally must go to Bathurst, so I will take every opportunity to come a bit earlier. I had other friends in Newcastle and Sydney. However, I'm at a bit of a loose end for holidays, as most have returned home to England."

Jack called the children back, and they raced along the riverbank with Charlie and Gracie sedately bringing up the rear. At fifteen and eleven, they took control of their young siblings.

Jack noticed how young Charlie looked longingly at the attractive girl beside him. He treated her as a princess. He smiled at the young man, understanding the feelings stirring in him. He wondered if Charlie would marry her, but that was at least seven years away as he knew Molly and Bill would not let Gracie wed until she was eighteen. Charlie's two sisters, Liza and Anna, each had a small brother in hand. At nine and seven, the two younger boys were often into some mischief and usually returned home filthy. Today was no exception. The two young boys had both slipped in the river mud. Seven-year-old Sam Miller followed them with their sister and Ellen in tow. She was just five and as game as a pebble. Gracie's young brother and sister, amazingly, were still clean. The two little ones were, more often than not, in as much mess as the two Lockley boys. Thankfully, today they had escaped unscathed.

Ellen adored the three big boys, as she called them, and the four were often off on some adventure, and often it involved some indigenous children. Sometimes she even wore some of their clothing.

When the waiting adults saw the state of the two youngest Lockley boys, they knew the picnic was over. These two wet boys needed a bath, and quickly. Luke had also cut his leg, and it required treatment.

They folded the picnic blankets and packed the baskets then the children's parents led the group back up the hill.

The sticky tidal mud stank and clung to the two boys like black custard. As the boys walked, clods of the dark grey gloop were left in their wake.

Ned, Jack, and Bea brought up the rear, ensuring no one was left behind.

Ned chuckled. "Sometimes, I don't envy Charles and Sal. Those two lads lead them on a merry dance; the two older boys did the same when little, but I also love how Charles and Sal allow them to play with the local

Aboriginal children. You never know what any of them will get into next. Molly and Bill's two youngest are normally just as bad."

The group had wandered back to the inn, the two boys bathed in the frigid outside trough, and it was some time before Sal considered them clean enough to race naked into the tiny sitting room and don their night attire. They were rarely permitted to have dinner in nightshirts, but being winter, they were allowed to get warm in front of the fire. As soon as dinner was over, they would be sent to bed.

Bea and Jack would join the Lockleys and Ned for Sunday night dinner. Bea absorbed the joyousness of the loving bond of this family. That bond was what she would strive towards with her future family when the time came. The Lockley children all had good table manners, as did the Millers, and all knew how to behave. Even the youngest Lockley, Luke, could be quieted with a stern look from either his father or Ned.

However, the evening meal was still some hours away, and Bea and Jack had some things to do. Molly said she would light their fire in the room and leave the rear lamp on for them. They could creep in and go directly to bed.

Jack checked on the stock and made sure the four drovers were settled. They assured him that they were fine. They loved the warmth of the brazier in the barn and the comfortable hammocks in the heated upstairs loft. Sal had fed them lashings of stew and potatoes and followed that with treacle dumplings with clotted cream. Charles had home-brew fresh ginger beer on tap, and they had liberally helped themselves.

After dinner, Jack and Bea accompanied Ned out of the inn. It was too cold to stay outside for long, but just out of earshot of the inn, Ned said to Bea, "Jack will fill you in on my story, Bea; I'm fine with you knowing, but please, under no circumstances say anything. My life here would be horrendous if word got out. Even out here, I don't know if anyone can hear. None of my new friends here know anything. Only you two, Hugh and Heather, and Harry Moffatt, the magistrate, knows the truth."

"Of course, sir, I promise." Bea couldn't bring herself to call the tall soldier anything but sir. "While we are alone, sir, I'd like to thank you for hastening my freedom. I've not had a private chance before."

Ned slightly bowed. "It was a pleasure, my dear. Jack is an old friend. He will stand by you, but please know you can call on me whenever necessary."

Jack smiled. "Same goes with you, Ned. If you need an escape at any time, come to us. Give me a few months as I haven't built a spare room for you yet, but I will. I've told Hugh I won't drove his sheep unless there's a drought. I want to get our place fixed up first. I won't go droving for anyone else now that I'm married."

Ned wondered exactly what was awaiting Bea. "Jack, I have a team of convicts I could send up in spring. They are a good crew, and I'm looking for a project for them as they are nearly finished building a big job. Have a think about it and let me know what you decide. Do you have an idea of what you want to build?"

Jack shook his head. "Not really; I'm not even sure I will. I have a dream, but that's not viable."

The two men chattered about what an ideal house would be for a few minutes until Bea shivered under Jack's arm. "Sorry, sweetie, Ned, I'll… no, we will put our thinking caps on and get back to you."

Bea gently tugged his arm. "I would love a big verandah like Mrs Lacey's place, Jack. I used to sit outside, card the fleeces, and spin the yarn. It was so nice. And in the rain, it meant the children had somewhere outdoors to play, and it also gave protection in the heat in summer."

Jack quickly kissed her. "Then, my sweet, a verandah you shall have. Ned, we have a starting point; it must have a full wide verandah and possibly three rooms, one for us, another for our future family and one for visitors." He laughed. "You have given me something to think about. I truly will get on to it as I now have a wife to think of. I had not considered that in my plans. And talking about that, she's cold. I must get her inside. We're not leaving until Tuesday, so I'll see you tomorrow. Goodnight, my friend!" He was about to walk off when he remembered. "Oh, and if you can arrange another girl for Heather, we can take her with us. She'll have to sleep on the front seat for a night, but it's safer than the mail coach for a girl travelling alone, especially a convict girl."

Ned gave a bow and walked to the barracks as Jack escorted Bea to the inn.

Knowing their lovely comfortable, warm bedroom awaited, they didn't dawdle. Bea went in and changed while Jack extinguished the outside lamp, shut their door, drew the curtains and stoked the fire. The room was toasty warm, and she soon had a wash and slipped between the sheets to wait for Jack.

He wasn't long, and soon they lay in the afterglow, cradling his wife. They lay discussing Ned and the connection to David. Bea had not wished to bring up the topic, but she was itching to know the mysterious connection.

Jack had his arm around her, and her hand rested on his chest. His voice was low enough for her to hear, but no one else. "Bea, as our friend said, what I'm about to tell you is private. If word got out, his life here would be intolerable. I won't mention names in case we are overheard, but you know who I'm talking about. Our friend is the younger brother of the person you mentioned earlier. And yes, the rumour you heard was true to some extent. He discovered she had played him for a fool and was, in essence, no better than a whore. Her reputation over there now is disgusting. Even though she is married and has a title, only a few of the nicer families invite her anywhere unless they must. Her husband, on the other hand, is much loved and pitied. He is involved in Parliament. He fights to support injured soldiers and sailors. The couple now lives all but separate lives. I'm unsure Ned knows that, and I'll not tell him. They have no children, so I think you realise what that means."

He felt Bea nod her understanding.

"He is next in the line of succession. His family at home know he is here, but not the name he's using. In the meantime, he has a real life that he is thoroughly enjoying, and what's more, he is useful. His friends here like and love him for himself and not for what he was born to. He will only return to Kent if he must, but he has no wish to do that. Like me, he prefers this life where people are not born with a silver spoon in their mouths. Our friends here are the salt of the earth sort and make something of their lives. You are a perfect example. In England, society would have forbidden us to marry. To them, we are of different classes, and you have proven just how ridiculous that class system is. My love, you could pass as a Duchess in the royal court in London. You have more grace and dignity than many of them." Jack felt her stiffen in his arms.

Bea knew he was correct; however, she was also horrified. "Don't even make a joke about me doing that. Here I can be in your arms and proud to be your chosen wife. Don't ever make me go back there. I am a nothing, a discarded love child or less if Matron was correct. My status is lower than the lowest class. I know how they treated me; it was toffs' sons from high society who caused my ruin." She hid her face in his chest and mumbled, "I'll never say or do anything to hurt him, Jack, because I know how hurtful those same people can be. He picked me from the prison and sent me to Lacey's."

Knowing they had much to do the next day, Jack turned out the lamp, and they slept, still entwined.

~

The screech of a cockatoo in the tree just outside their window woke them. They had slept through the early dawn chorus and well beyond their normal waking time. It was well after seven when they finally moved from their bed. They had been married for over two weeks, and Bea was expecting her monthly flow on this day. Since she lost the baby on the ship, she was very regular. She had to tell Jack about her menstrual flow and that they couldn't be together intimately during her bleeding. After their time together that morning, she explained the situation before they arose.

Jack had no sister, so he had no idea of this occurrence. "You tell me when you're ready for me, Bea."

She smiled and said, "I will, but it should be fine this morning as it won't come until this afternoon. It might make travelling a little awkward, though, as I might need to stop often," Bea said shyly. "The first day or so are often heaviest."

Jack nodded. "We travel very slowly, so that won't be a problem. Today, we only need to prepare the wagon and get everything packed. We must find cages for the piglets and chickens. Oh, all sorts of last-minute things and cripes, and we must get the wheel hoops from Thomas Tindale. So, we'd better get moving."

Molly greeted them with a chuckle. "Afternoon, sleepyheads." She handed them two sizeable steaming bowls of cracked barley porridge. "Get this into you."

Jack greeted her with a kiss on her cheek. "We are officially still on our honeymoon, Mol. We stayed up late talking as Ned had sown the seed of us building a proper homestead, and amongst other things, we were trying to work out what we wanted. Bea has narrowed her choice down to a bedroom, a kitchen, and a wide verandah, but it might have to have a least one guest room." Jack grinned at his wife. Her wishes were simple, but simple is what he had already. It was not what he planned to build for her. One day he would build her his dream home. She would get the best he could construct. After she had gone to sleep last night, he lay thinking of Hugh and Heather's house. He loved their place, but he also wanted something with a possibility of a second story or some more rooms sometime down the track. While Bea was having her morning ablutions, he had sketched what he needed. He would leave the drawing with Ned, along with money for the building supplies, and leave the rest to him. He added a list of rooms he wanted, and which were bedrooms plus a staff bedroom, and they could discuss where Bea wanted them before starting the build. He so looked forward to life with this amazing girl. She surprised him with her ability to show her affection for him. She was just so easy to love. Earlier, he had sat on the bed watching her bathe and praised God for her; he did so again now. She was better than any dream wife he had imagined.

After breakfast, they headed down to Charles's barn. He hoped that today he would get the letter to say his money had arrived.

The drovers had checked the stock and saw that they needed water. Charles was thrilled that the large paddock would no longer need scything. The sheep had eaten what the cattle and horses had left. However, there was still plenty left, and Charles also had a second paddock that had one unfenced side down near the ferry wharf that could be quickly roped off if required.

Jack and Bea arrived at the barn as they heard a shout followed by a thud. Jack was beside Charles in an instant. "Bea, get Sal now, then call a doctor; he's broken his leg."

Bea fled. Shouting at the top of her voice, "Sal, Sally, come quickly, Sally, run."

Sal emerged from the kitchen covered in flour. "Bea, whatever is the matter?"

Breathless, Bea said, "It's Charles; he's fallen from the loft and broken his leg. Jack is with him, but I'll go for the doctor."

Sal was already on her way across the courtyard. "Bea, get Charlie from the smithy once you've done that. And hurry love; please hurry."

Liza had heard the shouting and appeared at the door; Bea saw her and said, "Keep the children inside, Liza, and watch them. Your papa has had a fall."

Bea ran to Molly. She didn't know where the doctor was or would be, but Molly would. Molly told her to leave the doctor for Bill, and she was to go and fetch Charlie.

Soon everyone was scurrying to fetch their quarries. Bea hitched up her skirts and ran as fast as she could. She didn't care who saw her. Sal needed Charlie at home.

Molly locked up her inn, took her three children, and went to look after the Lockley children for Sal.

Bill and the doctor arrived in his gig less than ten minutes later. Bea had seen them coming down the hill as she and Charlie ran towards the inn.

Jack had not moved from Charles's side, but he had managed to turn him on his side and ease the pressure from his buckled leg. Charles was conscious but in agony. Once the doctor came, Jack said he would go and find Ned. Charlie and Sal needed him to be at his side, not him.

Bea returned with Charlie, who went directly to his father's side. He had instructed her to tell the ferryman to get Eddie from school. She waited until she heard that Charles was all right other than his leg. Thankfully he had fallen on some hay, but his leg had snapped. She took off down the grassy hill to the ferry. The ferry was due to leave, but she had to get the message to the captain.

Jack saw her go and worked out where she had gone. He relinquished his position beside Charles to Charlie. He then left to find and tell Ned.

Ned arrived back with three hefty soldiers and a long thin thing. He realised Charles would need to be moved inside, so he brought a military stretcher. When the doctor finished his initial assessment of Charles, he instructed the men to roll him over and gently get him onto the stretcher.

Charles groaned in agony and finally passed out as the doctor moved his leg.

The doctor sighed with relief. "Quickly get him inside before he comes round. I'll be able to set his leg properly while he's out cold, but gently does it, fellows. We don't want any more harm done to him."

Sal held Charles's hands on his chest, and Charlie opened the doors leading to his parent's room. Sal called for him to get the washing off the bed and to pull back the blankets.

In a short time, Charles was in bed, and the doctor had set his bones. Thankfully, neither bone had poked through the skin, but his lower leg had an extra bend. As the soldiers carried their patient, the doctor was madly writing a note. When Charles was in bed, two soldiers were dispatched to the hospital with the doctor's note for a leather splint, bandages, and other needed items.

Molly stood at the bedroom door, waiting to give support if needed. Sal would need assistance and be there to do what she could. Gracie and Liza had the little ones under control; Molly had told them what had occurred.

With his teary eyes wide open and obviously scared, little Luke asked, "Dar's broke?"

Molly gathered the little lad into her arms; Wills watched as Molly explained, "Boys, your Dar fell from the loft and has broken his leg. He should be fine, but he will not be able to walk for a long time. You will have to help your Mama and be good for her. Can you all do that?"

All four children nodded. Anna teared up, and Molly gathered her into her loving arms. "I'm sure he'll be okay, sweetheart; we must help your Mama."

The seven young children waited in the dining room in front of the fire. Molly hovered and was in and out, waiting for news. Gracie was Liza's best friend, and she read them a story to keep them quiet.

It took half an hour before Charles eventually roused. The doctor had set his leg. It was now splinted in a buckled leather sheath and then fully immobilised by a large wire brace with bars up the side. Although still in pain Charles only moaned softly. With the bones now set, the pain had eased a little. His recovery would take a long, long time.

A few patrons arrived and found the taproom shut. Molly sent Bill home to open their small bar and remove the curious customers. Molly packed clothing for the four children and soon followed Bill to their Inn. Each child carried their night attire and clean undergarments, and they would bunk down in her children's rooms as they had many times before. Sal didn't need the worry of caring for the little ones until tomorrow or later.

Jack and Bea had remained close by and were on hand as runners if needed. Bea had managed to tell Sal that she had sent a message to Eddie. Sal asked them to meet the evening ferry and fill him in when he arrived.

The day passed in a blur for everyone but the four drovers. They were being paid to sit and relax, but they took over the milking and care of the inn's animals. Then, being bored, they watered the vegetable garden. For them, it was a change and a welcome one. They were being comfortably fed and housed, so they were content. All realised their departure would be delayed, so they roped off the next field and put in the larger animals to graze it down.

Hours came and went; Jack and Bea rugged up and went to wait for Eddie at the small jetty on the river. Ned met them there and stayed as he wished to prepare his Godson for the news that he would probably now have to leave school. Ed was due home for the holidays anyway. Charlie now had to take over running the inn, and Eddie would need to return to the blacksmith. Ned knew he would not mind that, but it's tough when life makes the major decisions for you. He was a bright lad, and he could have done anything. Ned was sad for him, and he wondered where life would take him.

The small ferry chuffed up the river with the rising tide. Eddie was standing at the railing, waiting impatiently. Ned raised a hand in greeting and received the same in reply.

As the teenager alighted, he held out a hand to greet Ned, only to be pulled into a bear hug by the tall blonde giant. He received a few words from Ned, and Eddie's worried face soon eased.

Ned told Eddie, "Lad, your Dar has rallied and is now wrapped up in bed and smiling. Of course, he is still in pain, but there seem to be no further injuries than his leg. This, however, means that Charlie will have to leave the forge and return to the inn."

Eddie looked at the Major, "Sir, I was in two minds about returning after the holidays anyway. I have passed everything but excelled at nothing. I'm not like Timmy, who's top of most classes. My heart is at the anvil, sir. So, this will not be a hardship for me. I was to leave school for holidays tomorrow anyway."

Ned smiled; it seemed that the Lord had already been at work in Eddie's life.

Jack and Bea had hardly been acknowledged, and giving a nod of farewell to the two fair-haired men, they returned to Molly.

In their absence, Bill had put Jack's long-awaited letter on his bed.

Chapter 9   Westward Ho

*T*he morning after the accident, Jack set about the delayed project of obtaining the required cages for the piglets and chickens. Both pens would need to fit on the small cart. The final items to be collected from the blacksmith were the wheel rims. Ned also had to collect a replacement convict girl for Heather and Hugh. The long-awaited letter last night had brought news that his money from home had arrived. He quickly accessed some funds and transferred the money he owed into Hugh's account. Ned returned to work once he walked Eddie home. His presence at the inn had raised eyebrows, but Charles was his friend, and he wished to make sure he was all right. With Eddie now home, Charlie would have to cope with running the inn himself and all it entailed. As Ned lay in bed that night thinking over the day's trauma, he had forgotten Jack's request for a replacement for Bea. The new milkmaid's selection must be his first duty for the morning. Few knew how many girls he saved from the horrific circle of abuse and a life of struggle. He knew of a few timid girls who needed a safe placement and had recently sent some to Walker's small farm on the Hawkesbury River. To secure a safe assignment for the younger convict girls was wonderful. He sighed and rolled over to sleep. He was thankful to his friends in Sydney, Tim and Humphrey, as they both did similar things.

Sun-up brought the usual flurry of activity in all houses. Ned was the dawn muster duty to send out the convict gangs. As he woke, Ned had thought of two young sisters who ideally would wish to be placed together. He may send them both. As he dressed, he smiled at this idea; Ned would set about arranging the paperwork. Two more were rescued from the mire of what was, in essence, legalised prostitution. He knew that many unskilled younger girls would be kept as all but bed warmers. He did everything possible to rescue as many as he could. He had learned the hard way with his friend Jimmy's sister, Amelia. She had been placed when he was with friends in Newcastle, and she had been abused violently for three months until her keeper was killed. Sadly, during this time, she had conceived a child. Eventually, he was able to get her a transfer and placement at Government House in Sydney as a governess, and from there, things looked up. However, she now had a child at her side. He had thought that life for her would be challenging, but then Ned had discovered that the man who had taken her from gaol had married her in one of Reverend Marsden's quickie marriages. Amelia's child was legitimate, and she was legally a widow. Ned had delighted to tell Amelia that, and then supplied her with a legal marriage certificate. She could return to England as a widow and get her life back on track. However, the memories of her abuse would take longer to heal, but Amelia would be all right with love and support. She had left only a short while ago and was still *en route* home. He had arranged an Absolute Pardon for her. Hopefully, her life as a teacher at Sam Garney's school would be happy. He then visited Jack and asked about possibly taking the two girls to the farm. He also had to confess that he had forgotten his request but had a possibility of a solution. He also arranged that there were poultry cages from Government stores that he could borrow. They could be collected on the next government wagon passing through Bathurst Road.

Over at the Rear Admiral Duncan Inn, Jack woke to Bea sitting in bed and gazing down at him. The strange look on her face puzzled him. "Bea, what's wrong?"

"I'm late; I'm never late. They didn't come," she said.

"What's late, sweetie? What didn't come?" Jack wasn't quite fully awake, but something was concerning her.

Bea lay down and curled up to his side. "Jack, I told you yesterday that my monthly flow was due, and it didn't come. I'm normally spot on every twenty-eight days, and even to the hour, two o'clock on the dot, but it didn't come."

He lay silently for a bit, digesting the information. Then a strange mixture of fear, delight, and amazement washed over him. "Are you with child? Is that what you mean?"

Bea nodded against his chest. "I may be, but it's only one day late, Jack. It could be all the stresses of yesterday, but we have given it a good possibility."

"Cor, Bea! That's amazing, my love. When will you know for sure?" Jack had no idea how to respond to the impending news of fatherhood. It was way beyond his frame of reference. He drew her close to him and wrapped her in his arms. Life would certainly be different if this were the case. It meant that he would undoubtedly tell Ned to send a team to him to build Bea her new house, and he would need it done fast. If she was with child, they only had less than nine months until it was born. "A child, Bea, we're going to be parents." He was stunned.

Bea nuzzled his neck. "Jack, I won't be sure for some weeks. I need to talk to Molly, and I want you with me. I have some questions."

"I'll do anything, Bea. Just tell me what you want me to do. I have some questions too." He didn't know if they could continue their marital relations if she were carrying a child. Hopefully, Bea would ask Molly about that.

Although the day didn't start as planned, he was delighted. They were late, teased again by Molly. When Ned arrived after his morning drill, they sat in the kitchen eating breakfast. Bill was cleaning up the taproom for the opening at ten, so Ned sat down and joined them in the kitchen. "Just to fill you all in, I dropped by Charles on the way up here. He slept a bit through the night, but Molly, we will all have to help where we can, and it will take months for him to get back on his feet. I'll arrange to get an extra convict or two to be assigned to both inns for a while until Sal can sort out what will happen. Thankfully Eddie is back, and he has decided to leave school, which will free up Charlie to take over where he can. Molly, can you do meals for Sal and the needy this week, as she'll have her hands full? I saw the four little Lockleys are here. Can they stay for a couple of days?"

Molly nodded. "We'll do anything that is needed, Major. Of course, the children can stay as long as needed. They all get along well."

Bea was sitting silently, with a glazed stare, as she blindly looked out the kitchen window. Molly watched her, somewhat concerned. Molly caught Jack's eye, and with a tilt of her head and lift of an eyebrow towards Bea, she then frowned.

Jack slid his arm along Bea's shoulder and whispered something to her. She replied with only a subtle smile. Jack turned to Ned so he could watch his face. "We think we shall be parents in just under nine months. Hence, we're a little distracted. We only realised this morning. It's early, but Molly, we must talk to you before we leave tomorrow."

A grin appeared on Ned's face. "Wonderful news for you both. I'm delighted." He remembered Sal was the same. When he first saw Sal, she stood out from the other convict women because she was clean. Ned had been with Charles and Jack Turner. From the moment Charles saw her, neither had eyes for anyone else. Sal had only known him for a week before they started officially courting. They married only weeks later. Being convicts, Ned fast-tracked their application to marry. Charlie was born nine months after their wedding.

Molly reached out and put her hand on Bea's. "I'm here when you need me, dear. Let me get the older children off to school, and then we'll talk while we chop vegetables for the stew."

Bea nodded, relieved. "Thanks, Molly. It's very early, and I may be wrong, but…" She looked at Ned, then shrugged. "I fell with child when I was raped; when on the hulks, I lost it about four months along. I was only fifteen, and conditions were far from good, but I've always been regular. It's only one day late, and we did have a lot of stress yesterday, but I was sure back then, and I'm pretty sure now." If she went down in Ned's estimation, then so be it. None of it was her fault.

Ned met her sad eyes. He had seen such abuse far too often. "You will get no condemnation from me, Bea. I know what you girls get put through and that most of you are more than unwilling participants in such treatment. I do what I can, placing young people like you in safe houses. I'm here to ask if you will take two young girls to Hugh instead of just one. They are sisters, and so far, they have escaped such abuse. I want to keep it that way, and Hugh's farm will be the best place for them. Can you fit them in?"

Jack watched Bea's face relax, then smiled at Ned's last words. She said, "Yes, we'll take them, Major. Mrs Lacey has two spare beds in the girl's room."

Jack added, "We should only have one night on the road, but they will need extra blankets as there will be no room on the wagon for two."

Ned returned her smile. "Actually, I have an idea about that too. Jack, I believe that you are to collect the piglets from Rooty Hill?"

Jack nodded, "Chickens too."

Ned smiled. "Good! They have a stockyard for itinerant use there and a barn of sorts. You can pull your wagon into the barn, and the girls can sleep near the brazier. The drovers can have the loft. No one else is droving that way at the moment, so you should have the building to yourself. You should arrive at Hugh's the next day."

Jack was delighted. "Yes, we'll take them, Ned. And thank you, that will be one less night in the cold for the men. Now on another issue, with the prospect of a child coming sooner than I'd thought, I will kindly accept your offer of the building crew." He dug out a sheet of paper and handed it to Ned. "This is what I'm thinking of building. I don't have proper plans, though. Eventually, a second story or extra rooms would be good, but it depends on the expertise of what your crew can build. Can you get an architect onto it and sort it from this end? I will clear the land and prepare the foundations."

Ned glanced at the drawing of the two-story building on the paper before him and saw that he also held a large bank note. He nodded and tucked the papers into his coat pocket. Jack had told him that morning that he was now flush with funds but didn't realise the house would be a vast mansion-like building. He wondered if Bea knew about it and thought probably not. She would be the owner of a magnificent homestead. "I'll get on to it, Jack. Leave all the details with me. Greenway can do the structural drawings, and when the timber is cut, I'll send it up. I'd go for the single-story for the moment. This team are good, but not that good. There are termites out that way, so I suggest cedar and stone. I recommend stone for the building base with cedar cladding for the main house. There's a glut of the stone blocks as most of Macquarie's buildings are now done. Because of that, many private houses were built using brick as it is quicker, so many stone blocks are sitting unused. Would you mind?"

Again, Jack was delighted. "Not at all, Ned; stone is wonderful. I want a cool room basement and hopefully a cellar and a dairy too. So, add them to the plan. Eventually, we want a store on the road as well." He glanced at Bea. She still was not fully concentrating. She was sitting with her hand on her stomach, and he realised her mind was preoccupied with becoming a mother. This time it would be a much-wanted child. Jack still had to deliver the sheep to Hugh and get his own stock home. The sooner they hit the road, the better. After finishing their tea, he left with Ned to sort out the two cages for the stock. Bea would help Molly get the seven children off to school and then help her make the stew for the two families. They also had to make the bread that Molly had started when she rose that morning. It also was a double batch. Sal's bread from yesterday was still sitting unmixed on her kitchen table as she needed to attend to Charles.

By lunchtime, the wagon was packed. There was one remaining small bag to stow, and the new girls' blankets and dresses from Government stores sat on the top. The convict girls would be brought to Molly's inn at noon when Ned finished his shift. They would sleep in front of the fire in the sitting room for the night. Bea remembered how she had delighted in being warm after so many months of shivering at night in gaol. She didn't care about sleeping on the floor as the wooden beds at the prison were no better.

Ned arrived with two girls clad in gaol drill gowns. They had calico mob caps, a shawl and little else. The girls were greeted by Molly and Bea, who each gave them a big hug. Harriet and Dorothea, called Harry and Reah, were red-haired Scottish lasses caught stealing food in London. Both were stunned to find that taking food was a transportable offence in England, as it was not in Scotland. At only fourteen and fifteen, they were fearful of nearly everything. Either they were holding hands or clinging tightly to each other almost constantly. Ned was right; these two needed to be kept together. On arrival, Bea sat with them and told them of their new placement and that they would be safe. She outlined the travel plans and that if scared, they were to seek her out. They would travel on the wagon with her for the two-day trip. She again assured them of their safety. Bea saw them both relax. With all now set for the departure the next day, Jack sought out Ned to say farewell and chat about the new house. They had checked with Sal how Charles was doing and found that if he stayed still, the pain was tolerable.

Molly said, "Sal, all the children must be permitted to see and talk to their father to assure them he will be fine. They are fretting and don't believe me that he is well other than his leg."

Charles's two youngest sons were greatly relieved when they saw their father sitting up in bed. They had not seen him since the accident, and both were acting up. Charles delivered his rules. "Boys, I need you to step up and help your mother, brothers and sisters. I will be unable to work for some time and need your help. Will you do that for me?"

Two small fair-haired heads nodded willingly. "Yes, Dar, we'll be as good as gold." Both soon settled and treated their stay with Molly and Bill as a holiday. Gracie, Liza, and Anna would return each morning to do their chores before school. They needed little supervision, leaving Molly to look after the two little boys and her youngest two, Sammy and Ellen. The four little ones took the longest to prepare for the day ahead. Once the seven children were gone, peace reigned. Molly was waiting for the children's return from school when Ned once again came to the door.

Behind him was another bedraggled girl. "Hello, Molly; I have some help for you too. This lass needs to get out of the system. She is your new help while you have all the children, but she can stay if you wish. I don't want her to return to the gaol if possible. Can you help out with Esme for me?"

Molly saw the woe-begotten, tear-stained face of a young girl that reminded her of herself. Her heart went out to the poor girl. "Oh, lassie, of course, you can stay, dearie; you'll have to sleep in the sitting room with Harry and Reah tonight, but tomorrow you can have a room to yourself until I can arrange something different." She saw the girl flinch when she mentioned the names. Suddenly realising she thought they were men, she added, "Dear, Harry is actually Harriet, and Reah is her sister Dorothea. You will be safe and warm." Silent tears slid unnoticed down the girl's dirty face. The girl crouched down and sobbed with relief. Molly squatted and took her in her arms. "I know what it's like, dear; I've been there too. Here we are all friends, and you are secure. Major Ned is a good man, and you will now be kept safe. Do you understand?" The tear-streaked face looked up at her Adonis-like saviour; she nodded and smiled. Holding her so close, Molly noticed she badly needed a bath. The other two girls had just finished, and she only needed to add some more hot water. Soon three giggling girls sat drying their hair in front of a roaring fire. They had been in different sections of the gaol and had not met. It was wonderful to have others in the same situation and not expected to do much work on their first night out. Once they were clothed in clean frocks, Molly sent in the seven other children. All ten children ate their stew in the warm room and settled for the evening. The three newcomers were not much older than Gracie, but none could read. Gracie occupied the ten young people by reading them a story from the Bible. She loved the story of Ruth, but the boys always wanted the one about David and Goliath. She compromised by reading both stories. Now relaxed and fed, Harry, Reah, and Esme were asleep before she completed the second story. When Gracie finished reading, they snuck out of the room and left the three new girls in peace.

Jack and Bea had been busy all day preparing for their journey. Bea's flow still had not started, and Jack refused to allow her to carry anything heavy just in case. Molly had taken them aside after Jack had returned from

Government Stores with Ned, and she gave the couple masses of information about babies. She even gave them a crash course on how to deliver one. Bea left to use the outhouse at one stage, and Molly turned to Jack and said, "This is personal, Jack, but something you need to know. Men tend to use soap to cleanse too much in certain areas of their bodies. They use caustic soap and lots of it. If you have ever had the stuff in your eyes, it burns, and let me assure you, it hurts girls. Down there is external for men, but it isn't for girls. It burns as it has lye in it. Use only water." She turned her back to him as soon as she finished so he would not see her cheeks flush with a crimson blush. Molly heard Jack mutter, "Oh golly gosh, I had no idea, Molly. Thanks, I'll remember." He realised that Bea would never have told him. He was indeed guilty as charged. She may not even have realised that he could have been the cause of any discomfort she had. He would not forget that bit of wisdom. They were sitting drinking hot sweet tea when Bea returned. He stood at her entry and suggested they prepare to check the load. Molly had enough to do; they had to pack the final items and prepare the cart for the cages.

Pre-dawn the following day saw the drovers hitching up the four horses and intermittently warming their hands at the brazier. They had not enjoyed leaving their warm swags before dawn or breaking the ice on the water pump to wash. Sal was already up and brought a tray of hot sweet tea and cracked barley porridge and honey for their first breakfast. Sal would cook bacon and eggs later when everyone else was up.

Charles had slept well and was in less pain. The doctor had said not to give him willow bark as it could cause internal bleeding. Instead, Sal cracked the ice from the pump water bucket, wrapped it in a towel, and put it on his leg. She knew that ice coldness helped with the swelling if used immediately after the injury. Thankfully it was mid-winter, and they had access to ice. Her biggest problem now was trying to keep her usually active husband occupied. He had probably six months ahead of him where he had to remain inactive. If he didn't, his leg may not heal and may need an amputation. She would growl, yell, bribe, cajole and inveigle, but he would stay immobilised if she had any say. Ned would back up Charlie and Eddie. Life for the next months would be different. She would even get Charles to teach their youngest boys to read while confined to bed. She had two new girls that the Major had sent her, and they were sleeping in the downstairs storeroom. It was a secret safe room for beaten-up women, but it had six bunks and a brazier. The girls set to work, and Sal appreciated their help. The cows were milked, and the bread was already cooking. Sal was sure the Major had worded them up. Molly still had the four youngest children, but the two eldest always pulled their weight. They would manage; they had to! Sal sighed and shot up a prayer, "Thank you, God, for good friends. You must see us through this because I can't do it alone." Sal had just returned indoors when Jack and Bea arrived with Harry and Reah close behind. The day was just breaking as they left to harness the horses. Their bits and bridles were jangling in the cold dawn morning. Everyone's breath fogged as they breathed. They knew they had to get on the road soon, or they would not reach Rooty Hill before dark. Hopefully, Strawberry would once again set the pace. Harry and Reah discovered they had been given new woollen serge dresses and thick blankets from Stores. Bea suggested they put on her coats and snuggle under their new blankets. Mrs Lacey would buy them whatever else they needed, but Bea's new coats would keep them warm while sitting in the chill air. She had never had more than the bare necessities in life, and now owning three overcoats and four cloaks, she was willing to share her good fortune with the two girls who still had virtually nothing.

As dawn broke, Sal arrived with another tray. This time the tray was piled with bacon, fried eggs, and buttered toast. She also handed Bea a basket for lunch. The farmer with the pups decided to bring them in rather than have them collected, so the three fur balls were placed in the back and promptly went to sleep. Everyone quickly demolished the food, and soon the wagon was being driven out of the yard by Jack. Once in the courtyard, he handed the reins to Bea, who waited for the mob to lead the way. One of the drovers led Strawberry, and the herd followed her. Jack closed the gate and was at the wagon's reins until they left the town. Trigger was saddled but tied behind the extended wagon caravan. Bea waved farewell to Sal as they followed the flock up the roadway. While Jack sat up front, the two girls sat under the canopy on the mattress with the pups; both girls grinning broadly. Bill, Molly, and the children were on the verandah shouting their goodbyes, and the little ones were bouncing with joyous farewells.

The eclectic cavalcade made its way up Phillip Street and turned south onto Church Street, making its way out of town. Although still being led, Strawberry had her horned head held high again and led the herd willingly. Bruce, the bull calf, had nuzzled two cows and stripped off their milk, so he kept close to his surrogate mothers. The other two expectant cows were behind them, and the sheep followed the larger animals. Two of Jack's new horses were tied as pack horses to the drovers. From the rear, Jack could see his six sheep as he had put red blobs of dye on their backs. They were spread evenly through the herd. Half an hour after dawn, the town was well behind them. Strawberry was untied, but following a drover, she still led the herd along the road. The fog sat low on the ground, and the Blue Mountains were invisible under the fluffy blanket of white mist.

Jack pulled up the wagon and handed Bea the reins. "Take her steady, Bea; we're in no hurry. The horses should be content to walk with the mob in front of us. I'll take over if necessary, but you should be fine until we hit the mountains." He gave her a passionate kiss that made the two girls giggle; then he untied Trigger from the back. He told them, "Hop up next to Bea, girls and keep warm under the blankets." Jack quickly mounted and came to

Bea for another quick kiss. "You right now, sweetie?"

Bea nodded, and he wheeled off to join the drovers. She was still not over the shock that she could be expecting a child, but it would mean she didn't have to worry about her flow for the next year or so. That brightened her immensely; she hated that time of the month. She hated both the mess and inconvenience of the monthly bleed. That would certainly be a relief. Even better news was when Molly told her that her flow would probably not return until she fully weaned her child. She always detested that part of womanhood. Mrs Lawrence was the one to explain to her what had occurred when she had her first one. She had thought she was bleeding to death. Now, she beckoned the two girls to join her and to bring both blankets. The three girls sat huddling under the new thick grey blankets in the cold morning light.

Jack was correct. The four horses drawing the extended wagon train were content to walk behind the mob. Twice they had to pull off the road. Once was for the mail coach and again for a doctor in a gig racing to a call out. They had a lot of ground to cover today and planned for no lunch stop. The wagon could pull over if required, as it could easily catch up. The girls took a rest stop, and all three used the time to relieve themselves before re-joining the drovers. Mid-afternoon, Bea got the girls to dig out the packed food, and one by one, the drovers came alongside, were handed a wrapped sandwich, and had their mugs filled with the warm tea from the ceramic ginger beer demijohn. Bea had made this with scaldingly hot water and stored it in a straw box, hoping it would stay warm. Even tepid, it was better than just water in the day's chill. All were appreciative. The mob kept up a good pace. Bruce learned to drink while walking, and Strawberry tried to shoo him away with a hoof kick. Bea learned not to travel too close as the cows and horses often chose to lift their tails while walking. It was bad enough with the carriage horses, but they could see that when they raised their tails, the girls would hide under the blanket until they finished once they were distracted and got splattered. It caused giggles rather than disgust. Bea heard their story as they travelled. They had been taken as maids from Edinburgh to London and then dismissed when the family carriage crashed just before reaching London. The family that employed them had been killed, and the girls had no way of returning home to Scotland, so they had become stranded in London. Hungry and homeless, the girls had picked up some leftover bread from the markets only to be arrested, convicted for theft and transported. Neither could work out what they had done wrong until Major Ned told them that Scotland's rules differed from England's. He had explained that his mother was Scottish. He had spent some holidays up there when he was younger and had found out that being poor in Scotland was not a crime; in England, it was. Their accents may have saved them, as Ned singled them out on arrival and set them apart for 'special allocation', as he called it. She found that Esme had arrived on the next ship and had been put to work in the Female Factory sick bay to keep her out of harm's way. Ned had rescued quite a few younger and more traumatised girls. Mrs Walker on the Hawkesbury had taken more than her fair share, and others had gone to various government buildings and rectories. Hugh Lacey had as many as he could house, and with Bea's time now up, he would take two more.

Bea didn't realise that Ned had told his friend, Hugh, about her. This explained why the Laceys had taken her. He had heard of her traumatic experiences and was determined to find somewhere for her. She was just sixteen when she arrived, cowed and demoralised. Ned had never even made eye contact with Bea. She had been one of his early rescues. He smiled at that; Jack didn't even know what he had done for her.

Unbeknownst to Ned, Molly soon realised the connection between Bea's placement with Hugh Lacey and Jack and Ned's friendship. She knew Ned was sending girls out to Hetty Walker's place on the Hawkesbury River and others sent into other safe houses. There was the Turner's Inn in Emu Plains, plus a minister in Newcastle; even the occasional Governor had girls especially selected by Ned. Other rectories around the area were sent some, and now businessman Henry Gates's home in Windsor was also taking the occasional girl for the shop in town. Bea sat discussing it with Sal, and she put the jigsaw together for Molly. Molly and Bill also had met Ned's brother in London, but they stayed silent about the connection. Neither had mentioned that they knew who Ned was.

Sal had told Bea that Charles had seen her on the day of her assignment. Ned and Charles had arrived on the same ship. Ned and Charles had become friends when Charles reported a planned mutiny. It was Ned's first week in town, and they were on the way to the Female Factory to seek a staff member for a friend. They chose Sal. Both men had noticed her standing a little aside from the rest of the women. Charles had asked Ned to save her, and he did. She had been the first of his rescues. More followed. Although Molly had arrived as a convict, she had been assigned to her mother before being allowed to marry Bill. Sal said, "When the Whites left the colony, we were asked to run the inn here on condition Charles take over the Government Stores too. We willingly agreed. The secret room downstairs for women was Ned's idea too." Over time, Molly and Sal had assisted and kept their work a secret.

While making yesterday's stew, Molly told Bea that Charles and Sal had mentioned what Ned Grace did for the young and frightened girls. He couldn't save them all, but he saved as many as possible. Bea had gasped, and the penny had dropped; she had been one of the Major's rescues, and the Laceys were assigned Bea at Ned's request. She knew Maddie and Chip had also been sent there for safety. All these bits of information had run through her mind as the girls told their stories. She wondered if Jack knew, and if he did, why had he not told her.

Chapter 10 Pups and Piglets

*T*he walk behind the mob was painfully slow; Bea wished to ask Jack about his involvement in the safe houses. The two girls had hopped off to find a bush to hide behind to relieve themselves. Jack saw the girls run into the bush and turned to wave as he occasionally did, and she beckoned him over. Jack dropped back, and Trigger walked alongside the wagon. Bea asked, "Jack did you know of Ned's involvement with the Laceys and others arranging placements for us convict girls?"

Jack looked somewhat embarrassed. "I know he helps lots of them, but I didn't realise it was widely known or quite so organised. It doesn't surprise me, though, Bea, as Ned has always stood up for the underdog. He was like that as a kid. His brother is a bit of a snob and bully; Ned's the opposite. If David was downright rude, Ned would apologise on his behalf. His younger brothers are the same. Hugh and I were some of the boys he befriended, but there were many of us. He was our mentor. He had one himself at school and challenged us to do the same for younger boys. So we did. Ned was a senior boy who taught us to look after the less fortunate and opened our eyes to see how the other half lived. He set a great example. The fact that we have all ended up here shows that we all live what we say." Jack smiled. "It's so typical of Ned that he said nothing to me, you know. He doesn't let his left hand know what his right hand is doing." He had just finished his explanation when three sheep bolted from the mob. Jack was about to kick up Trigger and round them up when at that moment, the three puppies, who they thought had been asleep on the mattress, jumped off with a yelp.

Within seconds, three black and white bullets were scooting around the wayward beasts outside flank, and they had them back in the flock in minutes.

Jack watched them with his mouth open. "Did you see that, Bea? They will be worth every penny of their dinner if they are that good."

Once the sheep were again contained, the three half-grown pups scrambled up on the back of the wagon and settled down again. All were panting as they had not had a drink all day. Bea had forgotten they were even there as they had been quiet all trip.

The fog had burnt off into a sunny winter's day, and Strawberry kept up a pretty good pace; the mob were content to stay behind her. Occasionally she would slow the pace at a grassy spot, and the herd would all grab a bite to eat before kicking along again. Jack returned to his duty.

Hopefully, they would arrive at the yards with enough light to collect the piglets and chickens. If not, they would have to get them in the morning. Tomorrow would be much shorter, and they would have time to sort things out if required.

The cold seeped into the three girls as they huddled under the blankets. Eventually, Bea encouraged the three pups onto their laps. At least the men on the horses wore their leathers and long oilskin coats over the top. As the girls snuggled under the blankets, their breath fogged as they spoke to each other.

The sun was now on the horizon, and thankfully the government piggery at Rooty Hill was in sight. The long day had been worth it.

The mob was safely ensconced in the stockyard by the fading twilight.

Harry and Reah set about preparing something hot to eat for them all. They didn't have time for a stew, but when Bea showed them what food they had, and as they were buying laying chickens, they suggested an omelette with oat cakes.

Soon the delectable smell of cooking onions wafted through the barn. The dogs found that Bea had some meaty dried kangaroo bones for them to gnaw on, and by the time the horses had been unharnessed, brushed, and set to pasture with the mob, the five men that returned were ravenous.

The drovers were each handed a mug of hot sweet tea. They couldn't believe the girls had a proper dinner cooking. The smell of onion was replaced by frying bacon bits. Reah was beating the egg whites to a fluffy mass. Harry worked on the onion and bacon mix, and she had removed them from the fire. They were cooling while Reah worked.

Bea watched, intrigued; she had never seen an omelette made like this. The men didn't care; it smelled delicious.

Harry sat next to Bea as they watched and waited.

Harry watched her sister and saw her nod. She poured in the egg yolk and onion mix and then returned the now-empty pan to the coals on the fire's edge.

Reah delicately incorporated the concoction, then gently poured it into the sizzling pan and covered it with the lid.

The low heat of the coals cooked the egg mix; soon, Reah poked the top to see if it was set. It was, and with the skill of something done often, she flipped the dish onto an enamel plate and slid it back into the pan to cook the other side.

The five men watched her work, salivating with anticipation at the forthcoming tasty hot meal.

Jack could resist no longer. "What are you making, Reah? It smells delicious."

Harry answered, "Mama worked in a big house as a cook, and one day a Lord arrived with his own French chef. He taught Mama to make these. We call them French omelettes. They are light, fluffy, and delicious. Like a soufflé, but they won't sink in the middle. You can add all sorts of things to them, too, like asparagus."

The pups had quickly found a trough of water to quench their thirst; they had devoured the dried kangaroo legs, known as 'roo meat,' and settled near the fire for the night.

Bea found that Molly had added a couple of loaves of bread that she had sliced and wrapped in a clean cloth. She pulled one out and placed it on the bench. Next to that was a pat of butter, a tub of jam, a tin of treacle, and a jar of her best clover honey. Bea had helped Molly make her special Lilli Pilli cordial, and Molly had shown her the benefit of the various flavours of honey. Clover and yellow box were delicate flavours for cooking and sweetening, and leatherwood, mixed gum and tea tree were far more bitter honey's, but better for healing things like sore throats.

Bea set out the various toppings and found a toasting fork on the wall of the barn along with a basin. She filled the basin and suggested that everyone wash their hands before eating as they had been with animals all day. Jack had already done so, but to set an example for the drovers did as requested. The others had just dried their hands when Reah said dinner was ready.

Jack gave thanks to God for their meal before Reah served the food.

The fat, spicy omelette was cut into eight, five large serves and three smaller ones for the girls. Harry served it on the tin plates that each drover carried. Bea had produced four plates for them from under the mattress.

Silence reigned until Tom muttered, "Nice tucker, miss. You're a good cook, miss. We would 'a' had beans 'n' jerky, but I'll eat this again any day."

The giant omelette had hit the spot. It was followed by Molly's bread and creamy butter spread thickly on the fresh slices. As the men had done most of the work with the horses, the girls did the dishes and set the cracked barley porridge to soak overnight to cook in the morning. They settled to sleep soon afterwards. Snores from the loft were quickly accompanied by whimpers from the puppies as they doggie-dreamed.

Jack and Bea had snuggled under the covers in the wagon. Both stayed clothed but lay entwined before falling asleep in each other's arms. The morning would be cold, and another long day of inactivity would be ahead.

The cacophony of the bevy of competing roosters from the farm woke the travellers long before dawn. Jack checked his fob watch in a shaft of moonlight and saw it was four o'clock. Wearily he knew that he had to get up and rouse the others. As everyone else was still asleep, Bea detained him delightfully for fifteen minutes. With a final kiss, he dragged himself out into the icy morning.

The fire embers were still warm, and he soon had the fire going. The pups were quickly at his heels and annoying him for some food. Jack dug out another couple of dried roo legs for them, and they settled down to chew. They would get whatever porridge was left over. Jack then filled the large billy and hung it on the tri-frame over the fire. Hanging on the shed's wall, he found a sizeable cast-iron water boiler, called a water fountain, and soon had that on the fire frame too. Bea's idea of the demijohn filled with hot tea was excellent. Although not hot, it was warm and thirst-quenching. They would need it again today, so he filled the water fountain to the top and put it on a low hook to boil.

Bea was soon at his side. While the others were still dozing, he took the opportunity to give her another good morning kiss. They were disturbed by a giggle from one of the stirring girls. Bea set about making sandwiches for lunch on the road. She didn't have any more pressed tongue or ham, but Molly had added some sliced roasted, pickled pork, and Bea made this up for luncheon. Again, food had to be mobile as they would not be stopping. They had some eggs left, so she put these on to boil.

Breakfast had soon been prepared and consumed. The three pups waited anxiously for any scraps; they devoured the scraping of all eight plates and then cleaned up the remainder of the porridge pot. The girls cleaned up the dishes and campsite. Jack and Tom took the two cages and his receipt to the resident Major to fill their animal order.

The three pups were turning out to be obedient little dogs. Bea had discovered that one would come to her and scratch her when it wanted something. She missed Bounder, and these three runts would be great companions. With the wagon now packed, she spent some time with her pups. She thought about names for them, and there was one that seemed to be more alert than the other two. He was a better sheepdog, so she thought of Shep for him. The other two were more challenging. One liked digging in under the bedding, so he became Digger, and the third one was always cold, and as he had the shortest hair, Bea decided to name him Blue.

The three girls packed up the campsite and made the demijohn of tea. Bea decided to preheat the ceramic bottle before filling it this time. Hopefully, it would stay hot longer. The hot hard-boiled eggs were packed in the straw around the flask; these could be kept warm too. She sliced and buttered the rest of the bread so everyone could eat the eggs in the bread if they wished.

Bea reorganised the back of the wagon and arranged for a bowl of water for the pups. She had unearthed the ropes they had brought to attach the cages, and while they waited for the return of the men and cages, Iain and the girls harnessed up the nine horses so they could head off as soon as possible. The horses stomped in the chill morning air as they waited in the traces.

Jack and Tom arrived first. They carried a large cage of ten chickens and a rooster. Jack returned, requesting two of the other men to join them. Jack excitedly showed Bea his new birds. "Look, Bea, they gave us four hens that had nearly finished laying. They only produce an egg or two a week, but one is a red one. I thought we could breed some, and sweetie wait until you see the piglets. Dare I call them cute? We have six of them. They have thrown in two injured ones that they can't sell and don't want to keep. They were a penny each."

Jack was so excited that Bea giggled. Bea saw the other cage being carried by two drovers and two soldiers. "Oh, Jack, one is pink. What sort are they?" The four men were having a tough time carrying the wiggling animals.

Jack was untangling the tie ropes. "They are all crossbreed ones, as they grow fastest. As they get older, they often have more babies. I'm hoping we'll get six piglets a litter, and that's thirty babies a year at least, but they can breed twice a year. Bea, I'll have to build a smokehouse if we get that many." He rattled on with the various facts he'd just learned. "Did you know that pigs can even be used to prepare a paddock for vegetables as they eat all the roots? This is why I wanted them, but it's why they call this place Rooty Hill. It was the first place that the colony had their pig farms, and they prepared the ground for the rest of the herds. Although it's still used for a government farm, they have diversified to other animals. Oh, Bea, my sweet, I'm so excited." He grabbed her and swung her around.

She was giggling as it was, but his joy was infectious. The four men were still struggling with the weight of their charges. To get the overfilled cage up on the cart, all seven men had to lift it onto the tray. The chickens were to sit on top of the piglets, but so they wouldn't get dirty, a sheet of oilskin off-cut was placed on top. The two cages were then tied down. Once ready, Shep and Digger rounded up the mob and herded them out of the holding yard. Fifteen minutes later, the caravan was once more underway.

"Cor, Bea, those two are brilliant." Jack had heard her yelling at the dogs. "What did you name them?"

"Shep is the black one, and the two-tone pup is Digger. Blue is the lazy one with short hair because he's always cold." At that moment, Blue was crawling up the bedding and snuggling under the blankets.

Jack chuckled. "You realise Digger and Blue are girls, don't you? They call them bitches."

Bea blushed, shaking her head. She was beetroot red with embarrassment. "I've never had much to do with dogs other than Bounder, so I didn't know. They have pointy sticking-out bits at that end, but I didn't look too hard, but I thought it would grow as they did. It never occurred to me they were girl dogs."

Jack grinned. "I used to breed hunting dogs when a lad. It's why I got Shep, as he's from a different litter, so we can breed them too. Blue can stay as a house dog if you like, as she seems to like you a great deal. I'll train the other two as working dogs. Although, I don't think they will need much training. I'm amazed at the instinct that an animal inherits."

The two pups had the mob moving much faster than expected. The frost crackled under the hooves of the stock, and the drovers soon took over and had them moving at a good pace. The exhausted pups returned to the wagon. They both leapt onto the back in an effortless jump.

Jack had looped Trigger on the back of the cart and took the reins until they reached the road. He gave Bea a long kiss. "I'll drive for a bit, love; I'm so glad you like your new pets."

Bea nodded. Content that Jack was beside her for a while, she snuggled close to him.

Harry and Reah giggled again as they watched the passionate embrace. They were snuggled on the mattress and under their blankets. The cold pups sat on their laps.

Once the group reached the road, the two now exhausted pups slept. They were wet and tired. The blanket's warmth soon dried them off, and soon all three were whimpering with doggie dreams.

The caravan progressed further west.

Bruce led out the mob this morning. He was frisky and kicking up his heels. Strawberry gave a moo, and he turned and fell into step beside her. Again, the mountains were shrouded in the morning fog. This boded well for another sunny day.

The progress was a little slower until the low fog lifted. The pups, once warmed, climbed on top of the mattress and watched the proceedings of the herd from their padded perch. Shep took off when he saw a sheep break away, and the men didn't even have to move.

Bea heard Jack yell, "I'm keeping that dog, Bea; he's mine. He's wonderful! Shep, the shepherd, I love it." He then roared with laughter.

Soon the fog had completely burnt off, and the girls could discard the blanket. They donned hats as protection from the sun. The three pups now sat behind them, watching the activities before them. Occasionally one or the other jumped off and headed a straggler back to the mob.

The herd kept plodding along the road.

When the sun reached its zenith, Bea sent the girls back into the wagon for the sandwiches and hard-boiled eggs. The men came alongside one by one, and each was handed food. Once everyone had eaten, she would serve the mugs of tea the same way. If the eggs were anything to go by, the tea would still be hot.

It was, and Bea was delighted.

By the time they reached the river near the foothills of the Blue Mountains, the sun rested on the tree tops. The caravan was turning into the road to Lacey's farm. The group would have finished the most challenging part of the journey in half an hour.

As they were about half a mile away, Jack called to Bea, "I'll ride ahead and open the gates." He was itching for a canter and gently kicked Trigger to up his pace. They took off up the dusty road and soon arrived at the farm's main gate. The side gate stood open, and he rode through and up to the house.

Hugh had seen the dust and stood waiting for them to arrive. "Hi, Jack. Did they travel well?"

Jack dismounted in one swift movement. "Wonderfully well, Hughie." It was over a month since he and Bea had left to get married.

Heather appeared at her husband's side.

Jack said, "Before they arrive, I want to tell you both that Bea may be expecting. It's far too early to confirm, but she's not to do any heavy work, just in case she is. Just so you know."

Heather was delighted, saying, "That's wonderful news, Jack; you've only been married for three weeks, though."

Jack nodded and grinned. "Not quite that, but yes, she said she's missed whatever you women get. She should have had it earlier this week. So, as I say really too early to know, but she's not to do any work at all just in case. I have her driving the wagon behind the mob, and she's done brilliantly."

As he spoke, Strawberry and Bruce trotted through the open gate.

Hugh saw them and said, "Funny sheep, Jack. Yours, I presume?"

Jack laughed and nodded. He now stood beside Hugh on the verandah. "Yes, and you should see what else we have on board. Oh, and there are two new girls for you, too, Harriet and Dorothea, known as Harry and Reah. Timid Scottish sisters, but Ned sent them. And, by the way, Hugh, I want to ask you about something. Did Ned send Bea to you to keep her safe?" He looked at his friend's face, now suffused with a red glow.

Hugh just nodded.

Jack was flabbergasted. "Why didn't you tell me?"

Hugh shrugged. "You didn't need to know, and what difference would it have made? All the girls here are sent at his suggestion. Most are convicts; some are just in hiding. We are a safe house for very young or timid girls. The abused ones go to another farm. I presume it's why these two have come."

Jack gently shook his head. He was amazed at what he had just learned about his friend. "Well, I never! Ned's a dark horse, isn't he?"

Hugh frowned. "No, he's just putting his faith into action. Protecting the little ones as he did with us at school, Jack, only he does it literally for work. Do you remember that first day at school? I was petrified until Ned came and showed us the ropes."

Jack nodded. He had loved the friends he made at school; it was why he was here now.

Hugh continued, "Don't spread it around, Jack; it would only hinder our work. When you are set up on your farm, you can join us if you wish. Bea would be perfect for helping with what we are doing. Even better than even Heather or Hetty Walker. She's one, too, you know. Loganberry Farm has taken more than its fair share over the years."

Jack looked at his friend anew. "You're kidding? Hetty too? How many more?" Her first husband, Joel, had been another of their senior school friends.

"A few, mostly rectories, but I'll tell you later." Hugh walked down to the side paddock and pulled back the slip rail.

Strawberry stopped at the moving opening. She tried to back out. Bruce then stopped, and soon pandemonium ensued. The sheep fled everywhere, and the drovers yelled for Bea to shut the main gate.

Thankfully Reah had already jumped down and done just that. The sleepy pups woke at that moment, and the three of them soon scarpered off the wagon and had the herd in the yard by nipping at their heels. The mob was under control in only a few minutes.

Tom sat on his horse, watching the young pups at work. "Cor, sir, wouldn't it slay ya! Who'd a known such young pups could do that? You won't need us on the trip, Mister Jack, with them doggie pups."

Tom's friends nodded in agreement. Iain said, "We'll be out of a job if word of them working doggies spreads."

Jack left them and went to Bea in the wagon. He slid up beside her and steered the vehicle into the barn. "Sweet Bea, I was wondering if you'd mind if we stayed here for a day or so?"

He saw her face brighten. "Can we, Jack? I would love to thank Mrs Lacey properly, and also, I'd like to help the girls settle in. I know you have things to sort at home, and I admit I'm a little anxious about that, but a day or two here would be lovely."

Harry had jumped off the wagon when the pups had; now they were alone. In the twilight, Jack bent and brushed his lips over Bea's as they drove the wagon into the barn. They had just pulled up when everyone appeared to assist. Hugh didn't have a pigsty, but he did have an old large empty chicken coop. He had just completed a new one for his fowl. The pigs and chickens would all have to go in the old yard. If they were to stay for a few days, the pigs and chickens would need to be released.

The perishables had been unpacked by nightfall, and the piglets and chickens were released into the coop. There had already been a few raucous interchanges between the two. Feathers flew, and the pigs squealed until the rooster and chickens took refuge on a high perch.

The three pups decided to stand guard over the cantankerous inmates. With their guards in situ, Jack escorted Bea towards the homestead.

Bea snuggled under her husband's arm. "It's going to be strange staying inside the house and not getting up at dawn to do the milking. I won't know what to do with myself. We're staying where the governess stayed." She paused briefly before adding, "A couple of years ago, Maddie and Chip were here for a bit over a year; they vanished when a stranger turned up. However, Maddie had married Major Tim by then. Here they could be together. He came out most weeks for a night. I didn't even get to say goodbye to them when they first left. I had seen a strange man around the front gate and told Mrs Lacey. Next thing I know is Maddie and Chip had fled." She reached up and kissed him. "She had been my only friend up until then. She did come back and say farewell later. It's why I wanted her at our wedding."

Jack knew the girl Bea had mentioned and knew Ned had placed her here for the boy's safety. After Ned left school, Hugh mentored Tim and Humphrey. Jack knew who these people were, but Ned had told him not to talk about Maddie or Chip. He knew they had left and briefly went to Hetty's farm along the Hawkesbury River. The reason for hiding was no longer relevant, so they were back in Sydney. One day he would take Bea to see them again. She was not to know that Chip was an Earl and would return to England when he came of age. To divert her attention, he stopped and pulled Bea into his arms, "I can think of a way to keep you busy, my sweet." He crushed her to him. His firm body inferred precisely what he was thinking. Jack whispered, "Has your flow come yet? I told them you are not to do any lifting just in case."

Bea shook her head. "No, but it's still early. I lost the last one at about four months. Jack, I'm only three days late, so anything could happen. Molly warned me about that."

Jack slid his arm along her shoulder as they kept walking. "Then you are not to lift anything heavier than your reticule, love."

She chuckled. "I don't have one of those, Jack."

He had not thought to purchase one of those for her. He added it to the mental list of things for Ned to send, not that she would have anywhere to go with it once on his farm.

Sadly, Hugh called them inside, "Dinner's ready! Where are you two love birds?"

They appeared out of the gloom and walked hand in hand into the house. Rather than walk in through the main door, they entered via the large kitchen to check that the new girls and drovers had settled. The men would bunk down in the shearing shed in hammocks, and the girls would be in

Bea's old room with the other girls.

Bea was still somewhat overwhelmed that she would be in the impressive guest room with Jack. She had cleaned it weekly for over five years, even when Maddie was there.

Tonight, there would even be a fire in their room. Oh, the luxury! The red cedar furniture was lovely, the bed had a thick feather mattress that didn't sag, and there were numerous warm blankets. Bea was now far more confident than the unmarried young girl who had left here only weeks before. She knew her table manners now and was content that she would not embarrass Jack at dinner. She had yet to thank Mrs Lacey for her wedding gown. Bea had spent weeks making it and had never imagined that she would wear it herself. Therefore, she still felt nervous about staying here as a visitor. Her five years here had been happy; they were also healing times.

She had shed few tears over those years; the ones in her eyes when Jack arrived were rare. They had not been of sadness but more of self-pity and despair at leaving this wonderful place of sanctuary. For him to have walked in and seen her wallowing in self-absorbed unhappiness made her feel a little guilty. Now, she knew he loved her as much as she loved him. She would hold her head high and make him proud of her. If she could call Ned, who was a Duke's son, by his Christian name, and she knew he had a title, then she could cope with the evening ahead. She had eaten numerous meals with Ned while in Parramatta.

Jack felt the pressure on his hand and saw her change of stance. There was now a look of determination on her face. She was ready to face Hugh and Heather on a different level. From today they would be friends for them both.

Heather greeted Bea with a big hug on their entry and led her into the front guest room.

Jack followed Hugh and watched the relationship between their wives change as they walked.

Heather stopped as they entered the bedroom and turned Bea around by her shoulders. "Bea dear, I hear you have discovered a little of what we do here. You and the other girls have been kept safe and hopefully have learnt much. I want you to know that you will be my friend from now on. While you are here, we will let you know more of our little project, and you never know; you may even wish to join our string of safe houses." Heather cupped her cheek and leaned in to kiss Bea's forehead. She noticed the glassy eyes of her quiet friend.

"I'd love that, Mrs Lacey," Bea said softly. "Were Maddie and Chip in hiding? I often wondered."

Heather nodded but added nothing more. "Call me Heather, dear; friends call each other by their given names. I shall leave you to get ready for dinner. The children are itching to see you again, so don't be long." She saw the men had hung back, so she asked, "Are you happy, dear girl?"

Bea nodded. "Very much so, Mrs... um... Heather."

Heather was so pleased that Bea was content. She knew Jack to be a good man.

Jack had walked in behind Bea. He carefully put their bag on the blanket box at the foot of their bed. Soon they were alone in the lovely warm room.

Bea turned to him. "Jack, how can I be so happy? I don't deserve it or you." With a teary face, she sought refuge in Jack's arms. Her emotional tenderness was more proof of her condition. It took very little to set her off weeping or laughing. Her emotions were somewhat of a see-saw. He held her, bringing comfort and stability after the tumultuous changes that her life had undergone in the past six weeks. "Sorry, Jack, I'm not usually a fountain. It's another reason I am certain I am carrying a child. I was like this last time. Only in the hold of a convict ship I found no solace." With the fortification of a long kiss, they left their private haven to join their hosts for a meal.

Dinner was a delightful event; the children greeted Bea with open arms and much laughter. However, they didn't stay long, as Jack and Bea retired to bed soon after dinner; they had been up before dawn and were tired. The soft bed welcomed them, and soon both were asleep.

The pre-dawn light brought a rude awakening for everyone. The sound of a dogfight echoed through the stillness. The noise was not coming from the chook pen or the pigs. The ruckus was emanating from the sheep paddock beside their room.

Bea had forgotten to feed the three pups and had left them to roam all night.

Jack flung back the bedding and went to the window. He could see the three black and white bullets chasing a sandy-coloured dingo away from the sheep. "Bea, those three pups of yours will be worth their weight in gold. They have just chased off a dingo. I shall certainly be breeding them. They are amazing."

Bea had not moved from under the warm blankets. "They are good foot warmers too." Seeing he was cold, she said, "Talking of which, darling Jack, stoke the fire and come back to bed; I'll warm you up."

He did, but they did not return to sleep. Bea lay cocooned in his arms. "Jack, Heather said something about us joining their safe house program. If we have just a small house, we could only have one girl, if that. There are so many like me and...."

Jack put his finger to her lips to silence her. "Before you finish that thought, I need to confess something. You heard me instruct Ned about building us a house. Although not a mansion, and not what I had planned, it will be larger than a new verandah and a single room. It will be much bigger than either of us planned. If we are going to do this, then we'll do it well.

Bea, yes, we will live in the shack I built until the new house is erected. Ned has a building team at a loose end in spring, and I've given him the money and the go-ahead to get on with the new homestead. My money has arrived from home; I'm quite flush with funds even after I have paid Hugh back. I left Ned enough to fund the project; the labour is free. I have said that I will have the foundation area cleared by the end of September, so it only gives us a few weeks to settle in before it gets started. If the drovers aren't in a hurry to return, I might employ them for some timber felling with me." He felt Bea stiffen in his arms. "Tim and Humphrey came and helped with the first clearing, and they helped cut the logs for the shack."

"I don't want to live in a huge house, though, Jack; I will be happy in a cottage with you," she admitted somewhat sadly.

Jack replied to her comment with a kiss. "I know, sweetheart, but if we don't build, we can't help others. This will be for them. I'll turn the cottage into a dairy or use it for something else. Maybe even staff quarters; you can help with what else we'll need."

Bea nodded, "If I must, Jack, but if it's just for me, then I don't want the house; I just want you."

Jack's heart soared. "I know, my beautiful Bea, and it's part of the reason I love you. You just love me as me, not for a title or position in society. You don't want diamonds; you only want my kisses; you just want me as I am. Like you, I've never had that acceptance before. Trust me; it takes some getting used to."

Chapter 11 Going Home

*A*fter six days at the Laceys, the much-reduced caravan crossed the Blue Mountains and headed to Bea's new home. The frigid nights on the range were a trial, but they coped. After leaving the Laceys at Orchard Hills, they stayed the first night on the road at Emu Plains at the Turner's Inn. Jack had stayed with this family before. He wanted to ask about their involvement in the safe house project on this visit. He was stunned to discover that Jack Turner had arrived on the same ship as Charles and Ned. They stayed for this visit, knowing they were another of Ned's safe houses.

After one night with the Turners, they set off on the slow crawl over the chilly mountain pass. The small mob of beasts came over the hill and dawdled along the two-wheel track. Strawberry was still in the lead with Bruce beside her, but her pace slowed. She was followed by the other three cows and the six sheep.

Jack was now mounted on one of his new stock horses as Trigger had been returned to Hugh. It was a seal-brown stallion with a shiny brown body, black mane and tail, and an odd-shaped star on his nose. He was a stunning-looking beast and responded to Jack's every wish. He could turn on a sixpence and run like the wind. Bea named him Thunderbolt as the big horse had a pounding gait, and he could easily carry them both. They had been delayed setting out from Hugh's place as Josie, one of the cows, had just given birth. Jack had no idea she was that advanced and felt somewhat guilty about the pace they had set getting to Hugh's. The sheep had been no problem as the three pups had ensured they stayed together, even when unrestrained overnight. The pups had also been outstanding when it came time to round up the pigs and chickens. One by one, they singled out a pig and moved it towards Jack, who grabbed it and then shoved it back into the cage. They did the same with the chickens, but Blue tried to take a nip at one, getting a mouth full of feathers and was chastised by Jack. She slunk back and flattened herself in the smelly mud in the chook pen. All three pups would need to wash before being allowed in the wagon with Bea.

After leaving Hugh's farm, it had taken them three weeks to arrive at Meadow Flat, as Jack called the whole valley.

~

Bea had not had her flow in the three weeks since setting out from Orchard Hills. As it was six weeks since they married, she was sure she was now with child.

As they went through Penrith, Jack had vanished into a store and returned with a large cast-iron hot water fountain and a triangle frame to mount it on if camping. He had seen Bea's delight when she had found one on their first night on the road, and he was determined she would have one for her own.

The hot sweet tea was a lifesaver on the trip through the mountain pass with the freezing nights and cold days. The six travellers enjoyed the hot fluid she doled out along the road. The four drovers had rarely had a contract so effortless. The three pups were more often than not on the road on either side of the sheep, keeping them under control. All the men had to do was follow.

Jack took over the wagon's reins as the drovers could easily care for the small herd. Morning and evening, Jack and Bea shared a blanket, and Blue often shivered under it on Bea's feet. "I'm going to have to make her a coat, Jack. She's so little compared to the other two and gets so cold."

He chuckled. "You're mothering her already. Don't get too close to her, or she'll get jealous of the baby. I've seen it before. Dogs are dogs, and I've known the most placid ones to turn on a newborn child. They are possessive. I certainly would not trust Bounder with a baby; I can tell you that much. Blue has already nipped a chook." Jack thought of the big hunting dog of Hugh's. He continued, "You know he nipped me when I got close to you; he could easily kill a baby, so be careful, Bea, please. These three dogs were born to working parents on a farm; their instincts are strong." Jack was sure that, given a chance, they would turn out like Bounder.

Bea was shocked. "You really think so, Jack? If so, they will never be permitted inside."

Jack looked down at his trusting wife. She was prepared to take his word for everything. He nodded. "I know so, darling girl, but that doesn't mean you can't play with them. I will make them a warm outside kennel. They are affectionate and Blue especially. She already adores you but was bred as a working dog."

Strawberry had slackened her pace dramatically after leaving Emu Plains. The piglet's stench from the cart was nauseating. All of them would be glad to see them released into their yard. It was the one thing Jack had built as he was determined to get some pigs to root out the paddocks and vegetable patch. The chickens were a bonus purchase; they could roost in the lean-to-feed shed with the drovers. He knew they would be free-range and roost where he fed them. He would eventually need to build them a proper coop, even if to keep them safe from the dingos overnight.

Jessie's milk had come in for her calf, and she was full. Jessie was producing so much milk that Bea needed to strip the excess from her each night. Bruce and the new calf, which Bea had named Belle, drank what they could.

Heather had loaded them up with dozens of eggs, and as some had cracked *en route*, Bea made the men a hot custard a few times while on the road. The water fountain was filled and boiled for copious mugs of sweet black tea, and Bea attempted to replicate the omelette and toast. It was good but less tasty than the first one that Reah had made.

The journey of over one hundred miles over hills and down dales in early spring was arduous. Bea was thrilled to hand over the reins to Jack, as she feared this section of the trip. It also meant she could share the blanket with him; even with Blue under the blanket, she was cold. The road, such as it was, was extremely rough in parts, and often there was a narrow drop off one side and a sheer rock wall on the other. The road they had to take was dangerous, to say the least. The carriageway was supposed to be twenty-foot wide all along the route, but in the twenty years since it was completed, sections had worn or washed away, and others had been overgrown and rutted. There had been rockslides, and it was now very rough in areas. Jack did not want Bea in charge of the cumbersome wagon train, as she was an inexperienced driver. Some sections even tested his strength and skill. They traversed the highest passage of the road in a day as Jack didn't wish to stay at the high altitude in early September. They had to break the ice on the pup's water each morning, and the stock had to put up with drinking from the various creeks along the way.

Jessie's warm milk was a delight for them all. Bea and Jack could strip her quickly each evening, and Bea would use the milk to make the most delicious creamy porridge. She would set aside the grains to swell in warmed milk overnight, and they would milk her again in the morning to drink. The creamy porridge was far better than cooked beans, and it was accompanied by fresh cream that Bea skimmed off the porridge milk and lashings of sweet tea and damper that Bea made each night; they ate well. The road in this area was good, so Jack was back on Thunderbolt.

Jack's farm was one of the only cleared ones in the area. However, there were two other currently vacant claims on either side. As he had explained to Bea, he had allowed the tribe to stay in their place, and as they topped the last hill, Jack pointed out the smoke from their fires at the far end of the valley.

Jack came and joined Bea on the wagon as they climbed the hill. He wished to be with her when she saw their home for the first time. He had been so proud of it when he left, but now he realised its vast inadequacies. The building was skew-whiff, and the walls weren't even straight. The roof was only slabs of bark, and the floor was dirt, but he had done it all himself. Jack had been so proud of his efforts, and his heart was in his mouth over her reaction when he saw it.

Bea gasped.

Jack waited to hear the despondency in her words. He braced himself for disappointment.

"Oh, Jack, it's beautiful. I love it. It's just so right for the setting. I can tell you that it will never be a dairy, though; it will be my spinning and craft storage room as I…." She didn't finish that sentence. "I just love it, Jack. I'm going to be so happy here. I imagined a ten-by-four, tiny bark hut from what you described. This house is just wonderful." She was almost bouncing in her seat.

"You like it?" asked Jack with astonishment.

Bea's face was like sunshine. "No, Jack, I love it. This shack, as you call it, will be our first home together. Jack, it's ours, and our child will be born in this house."

He released a long sigh. He didn't realise how tense he had been; she was not rejecting his efforts, but then, she never did.

When they arrived, Jack instructed Tom to ride ahead and open the farm gate. Billy and Netty appeared at their cabin door and welcomed the new arrival home. Jack had heard Bea's gasp when she saw the aboriginal couple. "You trust me, don't you?" he whispered.

She nodded.

He replied softly, "Then believe me when I say you will love these two. It's only their skin that makes them different."

Bea nodded and smiled a welcome and gave a cheery wave. "I shall start as I mean to go on, Jack. A brave face and cheery disposition. It's what Molly told me to do."

Jack had started at that, saying, "Mother used to say that too, Bea, only not so agreeably." As they drove towards the open gate, Jack said, "You always look on the bright side of things, Bea. You could, and really should, have been so bitter about everything, but you aren't. I used to stand outside the dairy and listen to you singing to yourself. You were always happy. At least you seemed so."

Bea rubbed her cheek against his arm. "I was happy there, Jack. The Lacey's were so good to me. To call them friends now is way beyond my dreams." She glanced up at him as he moved the wagon forward. "Jack, life is like sewing, or better still, a tapestry. You make just one stitch at a time, and when carefully placed, it makes a beautiful picture. Life is the same; each day is like a stitch; if done correctly, one's whole life works. Until I met you, my life was like the back of a tapestry. I could not see that there was any pattern to what was happening. I felt it was just all knots and trouble.

My early years were like someone spilled hot fat on me. Even when I arrived at the Lacey's, I felt burned, sticky and unclean. I realise now that it was the healing time I needed to have. Soon after I arrived, I decided that only I could change my attitude. Maddie's talks made me realise I had to make the best of my life. I could not change the past, but I could change my attitude toward the life before me. I had no desire to return to England. Here I could have a life. I rarely have melancholy days like when you arrived, but sometimes life is unfair and gets to me. Now I look back; if all that bad stuff had not happened, I would not have met you. So, even in the bad things, good things have come from it. I'm a survivor, Jack, not a victim. I know it's only a different word, but it is an attitude too. I survived and will continue to do so." As they drew near their future home, she added, "Life is what you make it, Jack, and I'm going to make it the best I can. I want to make you proud of me."

As Jack negotiated the main gateway, he bent and kissed the top of her head. "I already am, sweet Bea. I already am."

~

Within a week, they had everything unpacked and the new foodstuffs stored on the shelving room Jack had built into the small cabin.

Bea had quickly learned to love Netty and Billy. They didn't need to be asked to do anything; they did what needed to be done without fuss.

As soon as the animals were unloaded, the four drovers set their minds to assembling Bea's new bed frame and furniture. A log shed was next for a dairy, and an extension on the chicken coop followed.

Digger and Shep had taken to sleeping at the new barn door and always had half an eye on the flock. Blue now had her little coat made out of a scrap of oilcloth, and she had decided that the chickens needed a companion. She even slept with them; this made everyone happy, as she had already killed one snake as it made its way in to steal an egg.

Netty claimed the dead serpent to eat.

Jack and Billy chose a place for the new house, and they set about clearing it. Billy had asked the tribal leader where Jack was allowed to construct his homestead, and he had taken the drawing of what Jack wanted. Billy returned and pointed to an area that Jack had wanted to build but didn't even think he would be permitted to clear. "Good spot there, Jack." It was perfect. Rather than be under the lee of either side of the valley, it was to be on a knoll overlooking the entire area. From here, they could have a surrounding verandah, as Bea wished, and it would have views in all directions. Their current cottage was on a small hillock at the foot of this area.

A month after their return, Bea woke just after dawn and needed to use the basin she had placed beside her bed. Jack was concerned, but she giggled. "This is just morning sickness, Jack, and confirms that I am expecting. The last time I was in the hulks and had no access to anything. I had to use the slops bucket to retch, which was very smelly. Before we left, Molly gave me a tub of her special powder. It's baking soda and sugar; she said I'm to mix it with a bit of lemon juice or something acidic. But I'm dying for some hot sweet tea. I couldn't get anything hot on board ship."

Jack was up and had the kettle on the hob fire in moments. The big log he had added just before bed had kept the cabin warm, and it was easy to stir the fire back to life. Bea admired his naked muscular body from the warmth of their bed. He made them both tea and then sat watching her.

Bea finished her tea and lay back on the pillows. "Jack, we don't need to get up yet, do we? Come back to bed and get warm. I know just how to do that." The look she gave him had him beside her even before she lay down.

~

Only weeks later, a dust cloud was visible mid-morning, and the three dogs started barking in unison. They flew to the gate and sat waiting for Jack to arrive behind them.

The convict team had come. They not only brought the building equipment but carried a letter from Ned with news that Charles was on the mend. He also said that Maddie sent her love to Bea, and Maddie told him that she would write. Molly sent a lumpy parcel for Bea. She was ecstatic to find that Molly had collected some pine resin from the trees at Government House. Molly had shown Bea how to make beeswax wraps. She had put it on her to-do list but now had the needed resin.

The four drovers, Jack and Billy, had finished cutting the last tree and marked out where the cellar was to be excavated. The drovers had decided to stay for a while longer and go back with the government wagon when it returned, as it meant they would be fed on the way back. The fact that Bea and Netty fed them so well and that they were warm and comfortable in the new stable certainly helped. There would be little work for them in Sydney until late spring, so they were not in a hurry to get back. Jack was paying them far better than they earned droving. A new henhouse and dairy were quickly erected with the logs that had been previously cut.

The building crew consisted of twenty convicts and fifteen soldiers. They had five bullock wagon loads of tools, hewn cedar slabs, and stone blocks. More material would follow, but this would be for the cellar and the house foundations. The logs that Jack had felled would be cut or split and set aside for future use; these were too green to use for the house anyway.

By the time Bea could feel the first flutters of their child moving, the cellar was fully lined with stone, and shelving was wide slabs of cedar timber. The roof of this structure was problematic as they couldn't use rock. Jack suggested they use wide slabs of thick cedar and then daub the underside with thick wet clay mixed with straw. The floor of the house and verandah was of stone, as was the back wall separating off the kitchen and two servants' rooms. The outline of the house slowly rose from the top of the knoll. The inside and front walls would be timber-framed, then panelled and lined with red cedar cladding. Each room had a fireplace; the lounge dining one was double-sided. The kitchen cooking fire was double-width with assorted nooks and shelves for heating and cooking. Jack had even added a built-in bread oven, and when Bea walked through the vast space that would be their kitchen, she chuckled. "Jack, this one room is bigger than our cabin, but I don't wish to move from our special place."

Jack consulted her over every decision of the internal set-up in the house. He had discovered early in the build that, rather than ask her what she wanted, he would usually ask her to choose from two options. She would freeze and then weep, unsure of what to reply. He had learned that an open choice was too big for her.

Bea had realised that a big house meant they could take more girls. However, she didn't realise it was to be so large. She was happy in the shack where she could look after it and Jack by herself. Helping others was the reason that she agreed that Jack should continue with the homestead plans.

Netty often stood watching. "Mister Jack, you build big fella house for plenty them *gurung*." She then giggled and headed back to the fireplace.

Bea asked, "Jack, what's a *gurung*?" The first time Netty mentioned the word, she found out it was what they called their children. Bea had yet to meet Netty's young ones. She had discovered they had four, and they lived with the tribe. She had half expected the couple to be middle-aged, but they were probably in their early thirties, if that. Their abode, as Jack called it, was a domed *gunya*, built of bent sticks and bark. They preferred this to Jack's shed. They slept on a mat on the earthen floor.   Bea knew how sometimes it was easier to be happy with nothing as long as they had each other.

By the time the frame of the house was up, Bea had a small bump on her otherwise flat stomach, and she could feel her baby moving. On the day the roof went on, Jack finally felt his child for the first time. It was a mere flicker, but he could feel it was there.

If Bea had thought her husband was loving and caring before, he positively mollycoddled her for the following months.

Netty would stand watching Bea. She said, "Time you start walking more, Missus Bea. Netty walk too."

Each day after that, Netty took Bea's arm and went for a long walk. They would always be within sight of the buildings but close enough to call for assistance if need be.

Blue was always nearby. She had been taught to "Skitch Jack" when required. The dog quickly picked up the meaning of the word. When Jack threw a stick for her and told her to skitch, she brought it back, and soon Jack was presented with many appropriate sticks. Her fetching skills soon improved, and she could understand various instructions, but "Skitch Jack" meant that she would attach herself to his clothing and tug him to Bea's side. Once when Netty had gone for the day, Bea, large with child, had sat on the floor and couldn't get up. She had said to Blue, "I so wish you understood me; I wish you'd skitch Jack." Blue had beetled out of the cottage and soon arrived with Jack in tow. They had both made such a fuss over her that she realised she would get lots of pats and a bone if she obeyed. From then on, she was often seen near Bea and Netty on their walks. As a practice, they would tell her to skitch Jack for a tea break or some other unimportant reason. Blue would get smothered with congratulations, which she loved.

By Easter time, the new house was nearing completion, and Bea felt like she was waddling. She could do little more than walk, spin and sew. She counted the weeks from their wedding and worked out that she still had eight weeks to go before the child arrived. She was busily making clothing for the baby, but a week-long visit from Heather and Hugh made her realise how unprepared she was. They had no napkins, cradles, or ordinary things babies needed. Bea planned to put the baby in the bottom drawer of their dresser. She didn't know you could buy a baby's bed or even what it was called. She knew nothing; having never had anything to do with children, let alone babies, she was at a loss. Heather had brought a cane baby basket and all the bedding, plus two dozen flannel napkins with her as a gift.

The building crew left after Easter, and peace returned to the valley. Jack and Billy were finishing the last of the work on the house, which included fitting it out with furniture and built-in shelving and then whitewashing everything except the stonework.

Bea would have preferred the timber to be left natural but refrained from stating her wishes. Jack returned from the new house one afternoon near the end of May to find Bea in tears. "I can't do this, Jack; I have no idea what is needed, and I don't have anything ready for the baby."

Bea's hacking sobs tore through him. He was floundering as much as she was, but most of the care would fall in her lap. Jack had no words of comfort. Being the youngest of his parents' two children, he also had no experience with little ones. "Bea, you have learned to have faith, not in me, but in God, and He will be there for us. Like you, I have no idea what to do with a baby." Jack held her close as she wept.

Bea was gathered into his arms and lay against his chest. She said, "I thought I could do this alone, Jack, as I've always been by myself, but I'm so darned scared. This new life is growing in me, and I must protect it. I still feel so guilty that I lost the other one, even though I didn't know who the father was. I had to throw that tiny dead life away like rubbish. It looked like a baby but fitted in my hand." She hiccoughed as she spoke, then buried her head into his shoulder again.

The anguish he felt was nothing to what she was dealing with. "Bea, can we pray about it?"

The two bowed their heads and gave the situation up to the Lord in prayer.

Bea had discovered what a comfort it was to ask for help from an invisible presence. Jack had explained that he was proud to have God as his crutch. It was how he coped with rejection and what his new life threw at him, yet he knew God was always beside him. He understood that he was never alone. It had been Ned who had introduced him to faith and Hugh who had helped it grow. When leaving his comfortable home in England, with servants at his beck and call, he travelled halfway around the world. Having no one to rely on had been hard. He had called on Hugh and Ned, and both had told him to pray. Remembering their short prayers, a simple prayer was what he needed at the moment; it was all he could muster. His thoughts were blank, and the words were gone, so he spoke from his heart, "Dear God, we are so alone and need help. Please send us someone who can assist at this time." They stood silently, wrapped in each other's arms, neither knowing what to say.

Netty had silently entered and watched the couple. She had heard the words and giggled. "You pray plenty good, Mister Jack. I come to tell you *dubas* come to help Missus until she have *gurung*. You fella has been plenty good to us black fella, and we help the Missus. I see she gets weepy and *baragat,* so we come to stay close till *gurung* comes. You not be alone no more, Missus Bea. We all here for you, Missus; no more weepy weepy now, Missus. Us *duba,* we come to help with Billy. Don't be *baragat,* Missus." Netty was now on her knees beside Bea. "Missus Bea, me be plenty *baragat* first time. But the *duba* know what to do. You be all good. Me stay close."

Bea had no idea what her black friend had just said.

Jack translated for Bea. "Sweetie, Netty said the women from the tribe are coming to help with the birth and the child. She won't leave you alone."

Netty nodded and grinned. "You tell her, Mister Jack, no *baragat* too."

Jack did. "Bea, she said not to be frightened either. They will teach us what we need to know." He still saw a frown on Bea's face.

She asked, "What do those words mean, Jack?"

Jack explained. "*Duba* is the local word for a woman; *gurung* is child or baby. *Baragat* is frightened, but I'm not sure about *binya.*" He looked to Netty for an explanation.

Netty giggled. "*Binya* means this." She pointed to Bea's extensive stomach. Then made the shape of an expectant woman and pretended to be with child. Netty was so funny in her mime that Bea giggled at her antics. Just knowing Netty would be close was good.

Netty's big grin lit her face with delight. "That good, Missus Bea; you be all good now." Netty gave her hand a gentle and loving touch, grinned then giggled again. Her beautiful round face broke into another huge smile; two large dimples popped on her cheeks.

"Yes, Netty, I'm good now." Amazingly, Bea realised that she was. Netty would be with her whenever Jack wasn't. She no longer had to have the child alone. Jack was also thankful that he didn't have to deliver their baby. Molly and Sal had given him detailed information about what to expect and do, but he had no wish to have to carry out their instructions. Jack had come home to say that the new house was ready to move into. There were things to finish still, but Jack wanted Bea to be in the new place before the baby came.

Netty grinned. "Then, Mister Jack, we move today as Missus not long to go before she pops." Bea was now up on her feet. Netty felt her stomach. "We move today, Mister Jack *gurung* come, tomorrow or day after meybe." Netty went to the door and called to her tribal friends. She turned and said, "Mister Jack, you walk Missus Bea to house now; we bring things up. Plenty *duba* to carry things; done soon. You go now." Netty shooed them out.

Bea knew the move would be soon, and she had packed most of their belongings. Jack escorted her out of the shack. They both stopped at the door and looked back. The group of ladies were already stowing their possessions into the open cases and boxes that were waiting. Bea gazed at her husband of nine months. "I'll miss this, Jack; this was our first home, somewhere that you built yourself. The new house is nice, but this is my heart home. It is our place, Jack. We will use it for something special. It will not just be a shed." Bea was sad to leave.

Jack was also sad. "I'm pleased you think this, sweet Bea; I was thinking of using it like a chapel or a guest room. Netty and Billy might even want to move in. Whatever its final use, we'll keep it maintained and ready to use at a moment's notice. It's why I bought a new bed for the house. This one will stay here. I have loved being here too, and especially with you." Jack turned and walked his very expectant wife to their new home.

Robert John Barnes arrived three days after they moved into the new house. They chose these names as Jack was John Robert. He was named after both of his grandfathers. Bea said it would be Jessica if it were a girl, not for any reason other than liking the name. Bea had spent the last two days in her nightgown as nothing went around her anymore.

Netty had been correct; Bea had been close to delivery when they moved. Bobby arrived only four hours after Bea's first pains. Jack encouraged her to lie on a bed when the first pains started.

Netty giggled again. "No, no, Mister Jack, we walk. We walk long-time on the verandah, round and round many times. You come, stay with her. When pain comes, she lean on you; give her strength. After longa, long time, and when pain comes plenty quick, then baby comes. Much time yet."

Again, Netty's words proved true. Bea felt she had worn a path around the verandah. They had circled it so often that she was tired. As each pain hit, she leaned into Jack, and at Netty's instruction, she took long deep breaths through each pain. As they got closer together, more women appeared. Netty told Bea to walk near the railing this time. She gave further instructions saying that as soon as Bea vomited, Jack was to get her indoors as quickly as possible after this happened.

Netty took up her position beside an older duba. Jack was placed in a chair and held Bea in a squatting position. He didn't want to be this close, but it was better than at the other end. He could be with her without seeing much.

Bea did as she was told, and Bobby entered the world shortly after. Netty kept telling Bea to breathe deeply and shout if she must.

Bea groaned and pushed, then relaxed against Jack.

The older lady said, "Missus Bea, push again. One big-fella push, Missus."

Bea braced herself against Jack and pushed with all her might.

With a rush, the *duba* caught the baby and held up the limp grey child by his feet; she then gave him a small smack. Bobby took a deep breath and let out a bellow; his colour changed to pink as he cried. Jack and Bea watched in astonishment.

Netty took the child and wiped his face. She had to stay close as the cord was still pumping. She pointed to the cord. "Him go flat soon. You watch."

They did; they couldn't help it.

Soon Bea was holding their son. She wept. "Jack, this small mite fully relies on us. What if I don't know what to do?"

Overhearing her comments, Netty giggled. "We be here, Missus, old fella *duba* she be plenty wisdom." They had seen the *duba* tie the cord and cut it with Bea's dressmaking scissors. She gave them a few minutes, then said, "You give Netty *gurung* as more pain come now."

"More?" Jack asked.

Netty nodded. "Bad pain this one, but not long. Hold tight, Mister Jack. Squat more, Missus Bea." Netty took the child as violent pain hit Bea. Her legs buckled as excruciating agony ripped through her stomach. She let out a bloodcurdling scream.

"Netty, what's happening?" Jack was almost panicking.

"You no worry, Mister Jack; pass soon, Mister Jack. This normal; not long now. One more push Missus Bea, maybe two! Deep breath, in, out; in, out." Netty said with enthusiastic encouragement.

The afterbirth came away, and the *duba* at Bea's feet wrapped it in paperbark and walked out with it. Her job was done, so she vanished.

Netty said to Jack, "All done now, Mister Jack; put her in bed. You feed Bobby baby, Missus, Bea, then sleep."

Jack scooped Bea up and carried her to their bed. He was overwhelmed by what he had just witnessed. While busy with the birth, other women lined the bed with paper bark and placed a towel on top. Then they vanished.

Jack carefully set Bea on their padding, quietly thanking them for their assistance.

Netty shooed Jack onto the other side of the bed. "You watch and learn good, Mister Jack, so you help Missus Bea later. Now you feed Bobby, Missus Bea, and then sleep. You need plenty fella sleep, not much with Bobby here now."

Bea had no idea what she meant. "Feed him, Netty; how?"

Netty pointed to her breasts. "Feed now, Missus. Suck, suck." Netty showed Bea how to let the baby suckle. Bobby knew what to do. He latched on and sucked. His tiny hand sat on his mother's breast, and his blurry blue eyes met hers.

His parents sat in awe at the tiny human they had made. Jack moved and sat beside Bea with his arm protectively around her. "Bea, my heart is pounding; I can't believe we have a son. You were amazing, my sweet Bea. So absolutely amazing!" He kissed the top of her head.

After ten minutes, Netty showed Bea that she had to swap breasts. Again, Bobby opened his tiny rosebud mouth and was soon suckling.

Netty giggled. "Him good boy, Missus Bea, him know what to do." Bobby had fallen asleep, and Netty carefully took him from his mother's arms and showed them how to burp him. "Now you sleep, Missus Bea. Mister Jack, you hold." She shoved the wrapped but sleeping child at him.

He refused to take him. "What? I can't!" Jack said, horrified that the fragile child would break.

Netty chuckled. "You can, Mister Jack, hold him just a liddle-bit. I settle Missus Bea." Without waiting, Netty placed the sleeping baby in Jack's arms. Jack felt like he was holding a bubble. He was scared that he would burst it and make the child cry.

"Him not break, Mister Jack," Netty giggled at his panicked face.

Chapter 12 Coming and Going

$\mathcal{T}$he family settled into their new surroundings. True to her word, Netty

stayed with them in the house for a week. By then, she was sure that Bea was coping, so she returned to Billy. Jack had learned to burp his son. A gassy smile, followed by a big burp, was his reward. Both parents learned to stand to the side when he changed him. The tiny child had already won his parents' hearts. Netty told Jack to put a wet rag on his stomach just before removing the soiled napkin, and the golden showers were caught in the cloth.

The other women of the tribe had vanished as fast as they appeared. Bea had heard them referred to as ghosts of the bush; she now knew why. She had learned to love them, not fear them. In the months before the birth, Netty had often enfolded her dark arms around Bea, bringing love and comfort to the frightened girl as she had never had before. Netty was like the mother Bea had never known. Bea had found love when she wasn't looking for it; she had also found acceptance and security. Jack was again correct; Bea loved Netty; she loved her dearly.

The first of the convict girls arrived on the Bathurst mail coach soon after Bobby's birth. Soon, Rebecca became a friend and companion for Bea.

Winter arrived after a dry autumn. Reverend William Clarke called in and baptised Bobby on his way west. He was on another leg of his seemingly unending Mineral Survey. Each time he would pass, he relished the warm welcome from the Barnes family. More often than not, Reverend William would stay two nights and spend much time conversing with Bea and Jack, explaining the Bible and answering their questions. His delightful visits were always welcome. He would hold a small Communion service for nearby farmers and then bless Jack and his family and their work.

Life on the farm fell back into a routine. While Bobby slept, Bea and Netty often spent the morning making beeswax wraps; this made the house smell like honey or other saleable items. With the roadside stall now a regular stop, the waxed calico cloths could be left for sale on an honesty system. If they were stolen, they had only been made from offcuts, so they would lose little of value.

Bobby grew, and Bea tried to keep busy. Yet each afternoon, she would ensure she stood at the verandah railing waiting for Jack's return from the paddocks. Of late, his work was more often a daily search for feed for their stock. On return, he would put Thunderbolt in the stable, wrap her in his arms, and greet her with a long and loving kiss. She never tired of this closeness, love, and adoration. With Bobby adding to her contentment and a new and growing understanding of Jack's faith, Bea found that she was happy. She had a family, and she was loved; all else was just cream. The stranger she had married had become the anchor that her life revolved around.

It had been a long, hot, dry summer, and bushfires had surrounded their valley. The house and buildings were safe, as Billy had refused to allow Jack to plant any more trees close to the home. She, however, wanted to put a lemon tree nearby, and Billy told her that if she did, it must be near the stone wall side of the kitchen, not the timber walls of the bedrooms. The shack still had a few native trees nearby, but although the bushfires surrounded their valley, nothing on their farm had burned. The tribe had moved into the open empty fields as the flames jumped over their valley.

Jack had ploughed his potato paddock and sent their pigs to root out the remaining weeds. The next crop would be planted and then fenced off from them. The spuds, as Jack called them, stored well, but also, they had enough produce to give the tribal elders. They sold some on their small roadside stall; more were stored in soil-filled wooden boxes in the cool cellar under the house. The roadside stall was an unattended stand, and often stock for sale vanished. Bea didn't like calling it stealing, but that's what it was theft. Other than the wax cloths, the stall only had some fresh fruit and produce, like potatoes and oranges, when in season, but little else. There was also a sign saying more available at the house, but as few could read, they only greeted the occasional visitor. Their cool room had a wide selection of cheeses made by the girls. Jack had been astounded that Bea even knew how to make the rennet. They used some Heather had brought from her farm. During all those years working at Lacey's, Bea had learned a lot, including how to smoke and preserve meat.

Jack's five female piglets had grown, producing two litters each. Each sow had between five and eleven piglets in the first litter, and their second litters were only seven months after the first; they had twelve to fifteen babies each. With nearly one hundred growing hungry piglets and little feed due to the lack of rain, they decided to slaughter or sell the small boars and lay down a good store of preserved meats. Bea made a brine and pickled a barrel full of pork. The underground cool room was slowly filling.

Bea and Rebecca had made all sorts of things and added them to the hooks or shelves in their cellar. They had minced all the offcuts and made sausages which they smoked. With each slaughter, Bea ensured that a selection of pork products was kept in stock. There were smoked sausages, smoked or pickled trotters, hams and slabs of bacon, which were made into pork pies that Jack and Billy loved to take for luncheon. The new smokehouse had been used for not just bacon but strips of dried kangaroo, which Billy provided. From the pig carcasses, they made double-smoked bacon bones. These were wonderful to add to the dried pulse soups in winter. The flavour was delicious. Knowing how easy it was to make these, Bea kept herself busy storing food for consumption and sale. They had a vegetable garden that grew onions, peas, beans, turnips and pumpkins, and of course, the fields of potatoes.

A few months before Bobby's arrival, Ned sent a selection of other goods. There were empty barrels for the pickling, bags of brine salt, four huge sugar cones, a carton of stoneware jam pots and a slab of bee's wax to seal the tops. Ned had also added some dining chairs, a table, three more beds and mattresses, and a large crate of young fruit trees. These thrived in the fertile valley. They included a range of citrus trees, two black figs, assorted apple trees, a plum, two apricot trees, and a peach tree. With nearly a year's growth behind them, the trees had grown and were already producing fruit. Admittedly, there was not a big crop for the first year, but they had great potential. Bea now looked at the small lemon tree near the kitchen. It was laden with juicy fruit. The excess of this was also stored. The peel was candied and stored in jars, and the juice sweetened with both honey and sugar and bottled. Bea also dried thick slices of fruit for use throughout the year. Rebecca also showed Bea how to make marmalade with some of Ned's sugar cones. Bea was intrigued that she added a spoon full of butter to the mix, and it stopped the scum from forming. Rebecca, Bea, and Netty slaved over the food preservation of everything they could. They used the cooled washing water on the fruit trees, particularly her lemon.

Bobby, at five months, was sitting up. He could roll across the floor. His joyous chuckles brought much joy to Bea. Bea and Jack's love for this tiny person vastly differed from how they felt for each other. Neither had known the love from a parent, and they found it hard to credit that their parents did not feel the same affection they had for their son. Jack looked forward to returning home each evening when he would get a hug from them both. He would take over Bobby's care while Bea and Netty prepared the meal. Rebecca would do the milking and set the cream to rise. Billy was occasionally persuaded to come and join the evening meal, but he took his plate outdoors more often than not.

When Bobby was eight months old, Heather and Hugh arrived unexpectedly without their children. They had come to ask Jack and Bea about taking the first proper intake of girls. Rebecca's conviction had expired, and she would return with them. She was now free.

A shipload of women had arrived in the colony, and Hugh had come to ask if Jack and Bea were ready and willing to receive their first needy girls. Most of the ones on the ship, the *Roslin Castle,* were Irish. However, many of the women on board were young, but one was in her seventies. They needed safe placement. All were single, and Hugh assured them that Ned had vetted them well. Little discussion between Jack and Bea was required as they had wondered how they would get Rebecca back to Parramatta for her new paid position that Ned had found for her.

Bea nodded willingly. "Oh, Jack, if we could help other girls as I had been, I will take as many as possible. It's why we built this big place, Jack. It's not for me; it was always for them."

Jack agreed. "Send whom you will, Hugh; we'll make room for them. We have beds for four in the two staff rooms and more in the shack where we can add shelf beds."

Both Hugh and Jack bemoaned the lack of rain. The earth was dry, and the dust intolerable. Hugh would need to find some pasture if the rain did not come soon. Jack's head had jerked up at the passing comment. Long ago, in return for an advance to buy the farm, he had promised to be available to drove for Hugh should the need to go droving arise, but that was when he had been single, and he had nothing. Now he was married with a child. With his life so settled, he had not thought about that promise from so long ago, but he knew he would need to honour it.

The departure of Hugh and Heather made Jack and Bea discuss where their farm was heading. They had not even named it. Bea suggested 'Sunny Haven', but they just kept calling their valley 'the farm'. Jack had previously told Bea of his promise to Hugh and that even though he didn't want to go, he couldn't break his word. Droughts come and go, but this one was bad. Jack didn't want to leave Bea alone on the isolated farm, and the presence of more help on the farm to assist Bea would be good. But his heart rebelled; however, he must honour his promise to Hugh, he knew that which meant he would have to go droving. Hopefully, it wouldn't be for long. His heart hurt; he did not wish to leave Bea; however, he told her when they met that he was a drover, and this was his job. As she now had a child to care for, she couldn't even accompany him. The farm was only ever to be a base when not on the road. Then he had fallen in love. It was now home.

The road west from Penrith was traversed far more frequently these days. More and more people were farming beyond Bathurst; more and more strangers came to the house when Jack was not there. Bea had to cope with an angry customer more than once. The idea for a proper produce shop on the roadside and a stockyard for overnight droving was implemented soon after a particularly obstreperous and obnoxious character tried to grab Bea for a kiss. Blue had barked for some time before she bit the man's heel and alerted Jack to an issue; he had arrived just in time. The man received a neatly placed thump to his jaw, then was grabbed by the collar and marched off the property.

That same day, Billy and Jack set about building the shop and a roadside corral, and he removed the roadside *For Sale* shingle. From now on, only friends would be permitted down to the house. Jack wrote to Ned for the assistance of a convict team. The stockyard came first, as the post and split rail fences were cut and readied as they cleared the land along the road, which was already fenced. The green timber was much easier to cut and shape and could be used for fencing without drying. Other cut slabs and larger logs were left to dry for the new shop. The new building would have a central shop, with two lean-to accommodation cabins on the end.

Ned sent a small team to erect the new holding yard and build the shop. Ned had been the one to suggest a separate store for passing traffic. He knew the types of travellers were heading westward. After coming for a visit, he knew that Jack could be gone from the house all day. Neither man wished Bea to cope with the rowdy and unruly travellers.

Jack read Ned's short note and turned to Bea. "Ned wants to send us an older couple too. Listen to this…."

Dear Jack,

Would you be interested in housing an older couple who need work, convicts, of course, and lifers, so no payment is ever required. Have a think and let me know.

If you are building a shop, they would be suitable storekeepers. They could oversee the accommodation and yards, and if we add an underground cool room, like at the house, you could put your sale stock there. Build a cellar and a room in the shop anyway. You could hire it out for other farmers' stock if you don't want it for the shop managers. The first lot of girls will come on the mail coach in ten days. Thanks for this, Jack. I'm sure they will be of great assistance to you. The two young ones have been trained as nursemaids, the older lady is a needlewoman, and the other two are dairymaids. All have lived on farms in Ireland.

Ned

The westward mail coach had taken a reply from Jack. It was short as it was written as the coach waited for a response.

Thanks, Ned,

Please send them all. Building construction is already in progress, including the cellar.

Jack

Ned sent the convicts with an escort and a wagon load of basic furnishings. There were horsehair mattresses, pots, pans and a vast selection of goods from Government Stores that were typically issued for each convict. The shop was complete when Honor, Eliza, Bridget, Mary and Colleen arrived.

Arriving with them were Harrison and Mildred Titchmarsh. The older couple were in their early sixties and both grey-haired but were still active.

They had been convicted for poaching hares and on-selling them. As they were life convicts, they were delighted with their assignment. They would have a much better life here as convicts than at home. They received life as they had been given numerous warnings before their conviction. The Titchmarsh's settled in the shop accommodation and soon had shelving ready for stock. Jack and Billy moved much of the produce from the house's underground cellar to the shop's new cool room. In less than a week, the mail coach was dropping in regularly for a hot tea and a comfortable stop. The driver and passengers could use the new outhouses at the back of the store for ablutions. The mail coach asked if they could leave a change of horses there and would pay to do so. Even though it did not earn much, it was more income for the farm.

Mildred Titchmarsh regularly made pies and hot pasties, which were hot and ready for sale. From one of the hams, Mildred also started selling ploughman lunches with cheese, ham, hard-boiled eggs, pickled baby onions, and some apples or dried fruit. She also made travelling versions of this food for consumption in the coach. Mildred was also a dab hand at making the most delicious cold pork pies. She also planned to sell hot stuffed large baked potatoes and hot soup in wintertime. She also made small cakes and fresh scones with jam and cream for the travellers. The two mail coaches passed regularly, and the shop soon became a routine stop on the route. Two tea tables were set up in the shop.

The new women who had arrived also soon found their niche. Honor, the eldest one, was a seamstress by trade, but unable to walk much, she would sit and do beautiful sewing for sale in the new store. As Bea had not used all the fabric she and Jack had purchased in Parramatta, Honor started making items to sell. There were drawstring bags, mob caps, aprons, and anything else she could think would be saleable. She made Bea an embroidered reticule.

With the arrival of the new helping hands, Bea entirely relinquished the dairy work to the girls. Biddy was only fourteen and had been a nursemaid, so she split her time between the dairy and Bobby. The others set to work both in the dairy and vegetable garden. With more hands to work the garden, more produce could be grown. Bea concentrated on making hard cheeses. However, only so much could sell in their shop. The mail coach took some to Emu Plains or Bathurst for sale there. The excess milk was either given to Netty for the tribe or poured out for the pigs. As the shop became better known, the farm could sell more foodstuffs; the extra milk was all converted to saleable products. In winter, hot milk chocolate drink was very popular.

Jack and Billy were still battling away, ploughing the virgin ground with a single furrow plough. Much of the new area was rocky, as the flat arable fields had already been ploughed and were under-crop. There was one area Jack dearly wished to prepare; however, he had been told it was a hunting ground, and he was not permitted to till this area. So, he battled away, clearing the permitted area and had two stock horses pull the small plough. It was hard work, but it needed to be done to expand farm production.

Jack had just dug the last of the arable ground and trustingly planted the barley seed when the first of the rains came. The steady drumming of the drops on the shingle roof was a wondrous sound. The morning birds' song sounded happier and louder in the pre-dawn light.

As Jack lay in bed listening to the sweet sounds, Bea turned to him and saw he was awake. "Jack, it's just occurred to me that I've not had my monthly flow since Bobby was born, and I know that even though I'm still giving him an evening feed, it should have come back. But my breasts are sore, and yesterday afternoon I threw up for no reason. I have a feeling I might be expecting again already."

Jack was delighted. "Sweetie, this is wonderful news! With the rain arriving, you have made a good day even better." He drew her into his arms for a morning kiss. "Darling Bea, with the rain overnight, I won't need to leave you and drove Hugh's sheep for him. I told you when I met you that I was a drover. When he last came, he asked me if the promise still held good. I owe him a lot, Bea, for we are here because of Hugh. When I wrote to him about what was happening at home, he told me to come and settle here."

He leaned over and kissed her. "As you know, I promised him that I would drove for him whenever he needed me. He put up the money for my farm until my inheritance came through from home. He never even asked for interest. Of course, I paid him, but he didn't expect it." Jack held her close, "Bea if they don't get rain, we can now have his stock here. I won't leave you unless I must. Be assured of that." Jack had told her of the debt to Hugh, and she realised there was more than just friendship between the two men. Jack would not skimp on a debt. However, the arrival of the rains meant he could put it off for some time. He pulled her into his arms and showed her how happy he was at both bits of good news.

~

The following months saw Bea concentrate on her reading skills. She and Jack would spend at least an hour pouring over the old black leather-covered Bible each day. It was the only book they had. Jack would make her read aloud to him, and he gently encouraged her to keep trying when she stumbled. He explained his persistence one day. "Bea, if ever I do have to go away if you can read and write, you can reply to my letters."

With this as her motivation, her efforts and concentration became a daily priority. Time that had previously hung on her hands was now spent studying. This was an excellent occupation as her growing condition increasingly incapacitated her. Jack would also answer her questions about his faith. He had started her reading the second half of the Bible, which he called the New Testament. He explained that this was about the life of Jesus. The Old Testament was about all the times before Jesus was born. She hadn't been reading for long before they reached words familiar to her. "Jack, this is the Lord's Prayer that we say together. I had no idea the words were actually a direction from Jesus and came straight from the Bible."

Jack looked over her shoulder and said, "Let's read Matthew chapter 6, verses 9 to 13 together, sweetie. They read, '*After this manner, therefore, pray ye: Our Father which art in heaven, Hallowed be thy name. Thy kingdom come, Thy will be done in earth, as it is in heaven. Give us this day our daily bread. And forgive us our debts as we forgive our debtors. And lead us not into temptation but deliver us from evil: For thine is the kingdom, and the power, and the glory, forever. Amen'.*"

Jack saw Bea's excitement as she had not made a single mistake. "Do you know what the words mean, though? The first bit is worshipping God, as we should always do. Every day we should acknowledge that He is in charge of all Creation. They say God's love is like a father's love, but Bea, neither of us has had that. We only know what my love for Bobby is like, and we have to go from there. Then the next bit asks for what we need, like food and rain. God is Lord of all His created order, and for some reason, He is withholding the rain on the land for now, but He will send it in His good time. We just have to trust Him. But, sweet Bea, it's the last bit that is the hardest. We have to forgive those who have hurt us. Those who owe us something, be it money or an apology for hurting us and will never repay us or say 'sorry' as we wish to hear. For us, it is those people who have hurt us so much. For you, my darling, it was all those who have abused you. For me, it was my parents' disregard and neglect."

Bea's eyes welled as she thought about his parents' neglect of the two small boys. "I can never understand that, Jack; how can a parent not care for their child? I love Bobby so much; I could no more hurt him than hurt you."

Jack had often wondered the same thing. "My parents didn't have a happy marriage, Bea. I don't think that either of them knew how to love. We do have to try to forgive, not to love or even like them or what they did to us, but don't hold it in, or it eats you up from the inside out. Trust me, I know!"

Bea nodded. "I learned that long ago, but I didn't know what it was called. What happened I can't change; I can only change my own actions, and the actions I choose are now doing everything I can for my family, and that's you and Bobby. I love you both so much."

"That's great, Bea! I love you too." Jack bent and kissed the top of her head. If he kissed her on the lips, he would get too distracted. He took a deep breath and said, "The last bit is asking for God's protection over our lives and decisions. Then the last word, Amen, is a Hebrew word that means 'so be it', which means that you agree with all the words."

Bea rested against Jack and thought over his words. He had never explained them like this before, but it made sense now. He lived his life like this prayer; this was why he was different. Ned and Hugh did the same as Jack's other friends in Parramatta. They stood out from the rabble in town. Molly had already told her about having to forgive her abusers, or it would eat her up inside. She knew that and had tried hard to take her advice. The change in attitude came when she realised that she wouldn't have Jack if it had not occurred.

Bea's second confinement was beginning to tire her out. Jack sent a letter to Ned for a full-time cook as Bea and Netty could no longer keep up with the food production. Netty still was in the kitchen, but she was often busy on the farm with Billy. Bea had stopped feeding Bobby soon after she realised her growing condition. Soon afterwards, she felt the first flutter of their second child and knew her suppositions were correct.

Jessica Mary Barnes arrived in October at the end of a brilliant harvest. The farm was growing faster than they could imagine. The four convict girls were followed by two more, and two new, very young male farmhands came to join Jack. The new men moved into the shack on new shelf bunks, and Honor slept inside the house in a small back visitors' room. Other bunks were added to the girls' room, and everyone settled in quickly.

The work digging the enlarged vegetable garden on top of the stock and crop work was beyond Jack and Billy. These two new Irish teenage lads knew how to garden. Neither had been on horses, so they took over the hoeing vegetable garden and potato crops. Both were Irish political prisoners, as were all the girls, and both men claimed they were innocent of any crime except being Roman Catholic. As this was common for many Irish convicts, they got along well. Eon and Miles were young and fit; they were not afraid of hard work. Soon the race to see who could till out a row of weeds was watched by the giggling girls. Their sweaty muscles rippled in the sunlight as the perspiration dripped off their muscular bodies as they tilled the soil. The girls had taken to having their tea and damper sitting on the fence watching the boy's work. Honor watched the six young people and kept the two groups well apart. The new cook was a middle-aged woman used to feeding many people and coped well with producing food for the entire household. The Titchmarsh's cooked for themselves and rarely left the shop.

Jack had realised that they could also sell other foodstuffs from the store and added dried foods like grain, rolled oats, sugar, flour, etc. Each bulk bag of grain stood in a row of large frames. Each had a scoop and was sold in pre-packed brown paper bags. Fresh produce from other farmers, like eggs, butter, cheeses, and honey, was added to the stock. Hetty Walker had sent some products from Loganberry Farm along the Hawkesbury River area. She had the most magnificent honey and a range of baskets. These all sold well. There also sold dried fruits like apples, apricots, prunes, bottled peaches, and pears; the cold storeroom had meats and cheeses on shelves. The Titchmarsh's were told they could use any food they wished, as long as it came from the home farm or the bulk bags.

~

Happy years followed, and Jack and Bea had their third child, Edward Hugh, in March 1839. The drought had hit hard on the range; even Jack's potato crop had failed due to lack of water. Jack didn't bother to plant much grain in the new field. Although he had dry-sown some barley in one older rock-free paddock, they had little hope of germination. He was right; not one grain germinated. The dairy cows were slowly munching away at the silage that Jack had laid down two years before when they had a bumper year. Jack's father had made him learn about farming, and how to lay a silage pit was one of the lessons he remembered. However, he never thought he would need one; a few years earlier, they had spare fodder and some barrels of molasses, so they laid a pit down. Jack said, "It's just in case of drought."

More young convicts had come and gone over the years. The Titchmarsh's had the shop humming. Mildred, baked goods sold well. The takeaway food was enough reason for people to stop and come inside. She made various sorts of small pies, pasties, and apple turnovers. All of which could be eaten on the coach.

Ed was only a few months old when Honor died. She had been sewing when she slipped away peacefully. Bea had found her sitting, staring sightlessly over the back paddock. Bea turned to Blue and quietly said to her faithful shadow, "Skitch Jack." Honor would be the first burial on the property. The dog flew off the verandah and soon returned with Jack in tow. Bea had not moved. She had stood watching over the dear old lady who had become her confidant.

Billy followed Jack, wondering what the emergency was. When he saw Jack close the old lady's eyes, without a word, he went to find Netty. He and Jack must dig a grave for the dear old lady. Netty would need to help Bea. Honor's failing health had been a recent topic of conversation, so her passing was not unexpected. Jack had even told Billy where she would be laid for eternity. He had even made a cross for her grave. Billy collected a spade and a pick and walked away silently. They had no coffin, so Honor was wrapped in a blanket and buried near the shack. It was a spot that Jack had chosen for this purpose but had hoped not to use for many years. Years before, Jack and Bea had decided to be buried in the picturesque venue, as it was close to their first home. Hopefully, that would not be for a long, long time. After the small service, Jack and Bea slipped away from the others. They stood at the sliprails and prayed for more rain. Bea stepped close to Jack and was enfolded in his loving arms. Each drawing comfort from the love and acceptance of the other. Jack knew he had to write to Ned and inform him of Honor's passing. The letter would catch the next eastbound mail coach, but for now, Bea was his priority, and she always would be.

Chapter 13 The Long Paddock

$\mathcal{B}$y March 1840, the drought had hit everywhere hard. There had been little to no decent rain for over six months. Hugh's place was even worse. At least in their valley, they had had a shower or two, which filled the tank at the house. Thankfully, their well water was holding up. Whatever grass that was left now crackled underfoot. The crops failed again.

Over the summer, it had been so hot that fruit bats were found dead under some roost trees. The birds were silent, and the crickets didn't chirp. Snakes were on the move, searching for water. The roos and wallabies had gone bush hunting for hidden sources of water. The heat was oppressive, and their small valley was frequently enshrouded in smoke from bushfires. Bea knew that Jack expected a letter from Hugh any day. He didn't want to leave his family, yet he knew he would have to. He had killed three big brown snakes that week, and Billy had taken them to the tribe for food. Thunderbolt had been seen acting strangely one afternoon, and Jack found he had stomped on another one.

Billy had taken to collecting the wood for the kitchen fires as Netty had seen the tail of a snake invading the pile. Shep made short work of that one. Again, Billy took it to eat. Jack didn't mind killing them for food, but he let them live if he saw them in the bush. They were God's creatures, even if he didn't like them. However, he would not endanger his family. Standing at the verandah railing, Jack and Bea looked out over the dusty and dry valley. The farm stock was now suffering. Jack had sold as much as they could. "I'll have to go soon, Bea; there's nothing left for them to eat. As you know, the autumn rains have failed again."

The dust was now suffocating; she had given up dusting as the wind swept the fine brown dirt into the air, and it settled on everything. Twisting willy-willy winds were seen scouring off the topsoil as they spun across the parched paddocks. Bea's nose even bled with the dryness of the air.

Everyone's tempers were fraying, and the children were miserable. The flies were driving everyone crazy. They were seeking moisture wherever they could. The last thing Jack wished to do was leave his family, but now his stock was suffering, and these beasts were their livelihood. His allowance from England had long ceased, and he heard from Hugh that his brother had spent the family's fortune.

Another month passed with no rain, and Jack received a letter from Hugh saying he had sold many of his sheep but wished to keep his breeding stock. There was some grass along the Hawkesbury River, but too many other farmers were grazing there. He was going droving and wrote to ask Jack to join him. Jack was shattered; he knew he would have to head west. Bea couldn't even come as Ed, the baby, at fourteen-month-old, was too small to travel on the wagon, and the other children were too old to sit still for so long.

For weeks Jack had debated over what to do. He knew he had to take them to the long paddock, or they would all die. The death of one of his prize ewes one morning decided for him.

Bea wondered what "the long paddock" was until Jack explained that it was the grassy verges along the roads. The fodder on the roadsides was all that now remained. It was how many drovers fed their stock in drought times. All he could take needed to be carried in his saddlebags. He would live in the saddle and sleep under the stars.

Two days after Jack decided to leave, Hugh sent a note with the mail carrier that he would be coming through with his mob and was happy for Jack to add his sheep to the flock. That gave Jack a week to prepare.

The two men would head west to keep their stock alive. Jack was thrilled that he would not be alone on the road. He and Hugh must leave their hearth and home, for their family's future.

Bea was resigned to his departure, but she didn't want him to go. Yet, she knew they would lose their stock and possibly the farm if he didn't leave. Jack's inheritance money was all but gone. They still had some money saved from stock sales, but he had purchased hay for the horses a few times, and their savings had dwindled. He had panned a bit of gold, and it was all that kept them afloat. Bea knew she had married a drover who had done no droving. Their last night together was tearful for them both.

As they lay entwined, she had felt Jack's tears as they freely flowed. "I don't want to go, Bea. I don't want to leave you and our munchkins."

He was still amazed that he had married for convenience to a girl he liked, but they had fallen in love. He gently moved a strand of hair from her forehead and touched her lips with his.

Bea wrapped her arms around her beloved and drew him to her. They lay holding each other tightly, knowing it would be their last time together for a long while. They did not hurry their lovemaking, but once done, they fell asleep, still entwined.

The morning departure was not rushed. It was hard enough to leave as it was. The mob was in poor condition and could only move slowly. Thunderbolt stood waiting at the slip rails. Digger, Shep and their latest four grown pups slowly rounded up the stock.

Jack and Billy opened the side gate and sent the dogs to move the mob onto the road. The dogs were the only animals with any stamina and soon had the sixty sheep headed towards the open roadside main gate. As the last animal dawdled through, Billy was about to shut the internal stock gate to the fields. "Don't bother Billy; leave them all open except the main road one next to the grid. There are only your two horses and the dairy cows left. The pigs won't last long anyway. Let all the stock wander where they wish. They can't get over the log grid at the front gate, and they may be able to find something to eat."

"Right, oh, boss, will do. You take care, boss man; you come back real soon." Billy rarely spoke, and it was only a word or two when he did. For him to string together, so many words made Jack smile.

Jack replied, "I'll take care, Billy, but you must look after my family for me. I would not leave her and the little ones if I didn't trust you." He didn't dare look at Bea yet. He knew she would wait on the verandah until he was out of sight. They had said their farewells.

"We take plenty good care, Mister Jack. You see." Billy waved a hand in farewell as he walked away. He did not even look back.

As Jack rode out of the gate with the mob, Hugh was waiting on the road. He only had thirty of his stud flock with him. The two men shook hands; only then did Jack turn in the saddle and raise his hand in farewell.

The dogs moved the sheep westward, with the two men bringing up the rear. Jack stayed twisted in the saddle, watching until he could see Bea no more.

Bea had not stopped waving and blowing kisses. She fell to her knees when he was out of sight and wept. He was gone.

Netty stood shaking her head and watching Bea. She muttered to herself, "She gonna need watchin' that one, she will. Billy 'n' me, we move close." By the end of the day, Netty and Billy had moved from their *gunya* in the back of the home paddock to Jack's old original cottage they all affectionately called 'Jack's shack,' so they were much closer to Bea. With winter ahead, Netty knew the lined shack was more comfortable. It had beds, not that they used them, and an indoor hob stove which she loved.

The two young convict stockmen who had occupied it for years had moved on months ago when their time expired. Jack had not replaced them as the vegetable plants had died in the drought. The three remaining dairy cows subsisted on household scraps and whatever grasses they could find. Bea used every skerrick of household wastewater to dampen dust around the house, allowing some areas for the grass to grow. Bea only took the milk they needed for the house, and the rest was left for the growing calves. The three cows, two with calves, and the two horses were all the animals left on the farm. The bull, Bruce, was somewhere in the scrub as he had pushed down a back fence and gone last year when the drought hit. He had obviously returned at some stage, as two of the cows recently had calves. Jack had sold all the sows but one long ago; she had piglets that were to be collected and sent to Bathurst. Bea would slaughter her soon as they had room for the meat.

Bea was pleased that Blue and two of her grown pups were to stay close. The six other sheepdogs, including Digger and Shep, travelled with Jack and Hugh. They were working dogs and could do the work of six men. Jack had trained the two older dogs when they first came to the farm; they taught their pups by example. All responded to his various whistles. Each different tone was an additional instruction. They would drop on command and wheel the flock left or right; even a beast that had broken away could be rounded up with a single whistle. All the dogs obeyed instantly. And better still, they never tired and were aware of dangers that even Billy missed. More than once, they had alerted Jack or herself to the dangers of snakes, especially the insidious tiger snakes or big brown ones that were lightning fast. Digger had even killed one that had come too close to the house.

As Jack and Hugh had less than a hundred sheep between them, they hoped to mix with another small farmer or two to help with the drove. Hopefully, the men could keep alive the nucleus of their breeding stock.

Bea realised she was now like every other drover's wife; she was alone, as was Heather Lacey. Although Heather and Hugh's son Hugo, was now old enough to help on her farm, Bea knew she would have to pick up the reins and run the farm alone. Harrison Titchmarsh and Billy would be on hand if needed, but both had their own work. Netty was wonderful as moral support and would often have them howling with laughter when she mimicked the various animals or held them spellbound when she told her Dreamtime stories. The children were four, three, and eighteen months old. Ed had weaned himself a month ago from his comfort feeds, and Bea missed the closeness of his suckling. Bea only had two convict girls in the house with her. Hannah cooked, and Alice helped with the children, milking, and whatever else needed doing. As the younger and more agile of the two, she would be the one to collect the mail and was also often outdoors playing with the children. With the bleating of the sheep now absent, an eerie silence settled in the valley. Bea looked down the road in the direction Jack had gone. How long would he be away? How long must her arms stay empty? At least Jack promised to write, and she could now read well and even write a reply. Jack had promised he would send mail when he could and send directions of where to address letters for him.

He had only been gone a week when the first letter arrived. Poor

Harrison had walked down to the homestead with the screed. "Mornin' Missus, mail's come, and Mister Jack has sent you a letter." He handed over the dirty missive. Knowing that the arrival of Harrison meant news, everyone had left their various chores and was awaiting information.

Bea thanked Harrison. She chuckled as she flipped it over to open the seal. Jack had drawn lips on it as though kissing the letter. She said to everyone, "I'll read it first, then read out any bits suitable." She walked onto the verandah, sat in her rocking chair, and opened the tightly written double-sided letter. Everyone else sat chatting on the steps while she read her screed.

My Darling Sweet Bea,

We arrived at Bathurst safely. I thought it was dry at home, but here it's a dust bowl with no blade of grass in sight, so we have decided to head south. Few others are on the road with their stock, so we are lucky in that respect. Many have just walked off their land, abandoning the remainder of their beasts. We are collecting some of their starving stock as we travel. Not intentionally, as they join the mob as we pass. We have met one poor farmer trying to keep his horses and rams alive. He only has twenty ewes left of his original thousand-strong mob, so we have joined up with him. He is a young squatter named Graham Barry. He is tall to the point of gangly, but he's a nice bloke. Here, trying to farm against the odds is hard. He would like to go further west but will wait until they get rain. He said he'd then take up a selection and farm grain.

We are both well, as are the dogs.

No exciting adventures have happened yet; therefore, I will tell you about a funny incident from Bathurst. I needed a shave and took the opportunity to head to the barber. I was seated under full lather when a stinking old bushman came in. The barber had been joking about the state that some fellows arrive in and expecting the barber to work miracles. I noted a sly look between the two barbers, and the elder one seated the scruffy swagman and proceeded to do his darnedest to fulfil the man's wishes.

I figured he was going to trim his hair and shave his beard. The younger lad working on me whispered for me to watch. He turned my chair a little so I could see the other customer. What beheld my eyes still makes me laugh. Darling Bea, from where I sat, I could see the cut-throat razor sitting in a tub of boiling water on the hob at the back of the shop. The man's hair was now neatly cut, and the beard trimmed to make lathering and removal easy. If left like that, he would have still looked good. The barber had shaved under his chin, and being freshly shaven, it was tender. Anyway, to continue, the older barber met my gaze and winked. He pulled out the scalding razor and wiped the flat side across the bushy's newly shaved throat. The searing hot metal left a red line but caused no damage. The poor customer thought his throat had been cut and cast aside the covering and, with hands clutching his throat, fled the store yelling blue murder and numerous other cusses. Before he left, the bushy swung at the older barber laying him out flat. I could only sit and watch. I do not think he will repeat his so-called game.

I shall write again when I find a place to post a letter. Be assured of my love, my darling sweet Bea.

Yours always

... a very lonely Jack.

The household staff anxiously anticipated news, so Bea read the story to those gathered nearby. They all chuckled, and then all but Harrison went about their duties. She had kept him back intentionally. Bea hoped this would be the first of many letters. But the delivery had made her think. "Harrison, we'll have to work out a flag system so you don't have to walk from the shop yourself. We can see the back of the building from the kitchen, and if a letter comes that needs collection, you can put up a flag, and one of the girls can collect it."

By late that afternoon, Billy had cut down a tall thin sapling and rigged up a flagpole. It was now bolted to the back wall of the shop. With the pull of a rope, Harrison could hoist up a flag. Red for urgent and white for mail or some other collection.

At least once a fortnight, there was a letter from Jack. He would add to the back of his letters where they would be heading next. Hannah and Alice would alternate collecting the mail or whatever had been delivered.

Bea wrote happy newsy letters in reply to Jack about the doings of the farm. She tried not to include any bad news. She told him she had killed the last pig. She set the various cuts of meat to smoke or pickle for their use over winter. She had learned to slaughter beasts on Lacey's farm, never realising she would one day need this skill to survive. Few chickens were left, but somehow, they managed to scratch out a free-range living on the farm. Bea fed them some of the grain from the store each night and locked them away safely lest dingos got them. She filled her pages with the children's antics.

It was not until Jack had been gone for eight weeks that she realised she was with child again. She waited until she was ill before she told him the good news. Hopefully, Jack would be home for the birth. When she counted back, she realised she had conceived about a week before he left. Hopefully, by November, there will be rain. Hopefully, he would be home by then.

Her prayers continued. Bea left her letter for collection.

The wait between Jack's letters was longer and longer as there were fewer places to post them. Each one was longer and more loving, and many included funny stories.

My Darling Sweet Bea,

I am writing to let you know of our new direction.

My love, sadly, we have had to head a long way south to find fodder for the stock. The feed around Bathurst is gone. There the rains are but a dream for yesteryear. I dream of you at night like a ghost haunting me. I wish to wrap you in my arms and declare my love and adoration for your adorable body. We have just left Coura Rocks, locally known as Cowra, and will head south-southwest.

We are planning to go through Lambing Flat; however, I hear they have no post office there, so I do not know if I can post a letter. From there, we will head to the ford on the Murrumbidgee River. I hear there is lots of good grazing land down that way as there is permanent water. Again, I do not know if they have any post office there, but if you address your letters to the inn, I shall check at each town we pass through. If I do not get your letters on the way south, I will collect them on the way north. We will go no further south than the river area. We have heard that Wagga Wagga has a settlement of sorts, and I'm sure there must be a produce delivery there who will bring the mail. I live for your news, my love. Please continue to write.

The nights are colder than I've had before. We sleep with our feet to the fire, but love, it's cold enough to freeze the balls off a brass monkey. I must explain that comment, my sweet. We met an English sailor turned farmer, and he told me of the cold nights on board the warships when fighting the French, although he called them froggies. That is something to do with them eating frogs' legs, eww, I hear you say, and I agree wholeheartedly. Anyway, he said that the cannonballs were stored, piled in pyramids, and the dimpled brass plate they sit on is, for some unknown reason, called a brass monkey. It contracts in the freezing weather, and the cannon balls roll off it. I thought this term was amusing.

My love, this vast country is desolate. We see many dead kangaroos around the dried-up puddles. As we move further south, finding water for our stock to drink is a challenge. The waterholes are mostly dry, and at some, we must shovel out the mud to reach fresh water. Before we finish, the local birds are swarming about the tiny puddle and quenching their thirst. We let them drink as they also need to live. We have rescued many animals stuck in the mud of such holes and then have dug safe areas for them to drink from.

Bea, my darling Bea, I do so hate death. To see the condition of the wildlife here is gut-wrenching. We rarely need to hunt, as finding an animal near death from thirst or starvation is not difficult. They all have not a scrap of fat left on them. The roos are so weak that you only must slice their throats to dispatch them, for they are too weak to hop away. As much as I dislike killing them, this ends their suffering quickly and supplies us with food. The dogs get the carcass, and we eat the tail. Many drying waterholes have fish floundering in the remains of the mud. We learned very quickly to chop the heads off before cooking the catfish. They have sharp spikes that are nasty. I didn't know that and was spiked. The pain kept me awake for two nights. Putting my hand in hot, almost boiling water relieved the agony. I feel your birthing pain was like this, my darling one; I've not felt such pain before.

Take care, my darling Bea; I will return when the rains come. Know that I love you and our sweet children.

Give Bobby, Jess, and Ed lots of kisses and cuddles from their Papa. My paper is now full, but my heart is empty and lonely.

I will love you forever, my darling.

your Jack

Bea quickly replied to his letter telling him again of her discovery about her growing condition in case he missed her last letter. Their fourth child would be here before Christmas; however, she was unsure if Jack would be. She prayed for the autumn rains to come. She had nearly finished writing when Hannah came in covered in flour. "Ma'am, the red flag has gone up at the shop. Can Alice go down, please? I must do the bread."

Bea smiled; she needed some activity. "No, Hannah, she has the children; I will go myself. If you see my blue handkerchief go up the pole, send Billy with the cart. I think I might permanently add a third blue flag to the rope, as we've had to bring things back a few times." Bea quickly set off to the shop to attend to whatever Harrison needed. It wasn't far, and she felt like stretching her legs. Within ten minutes, she was drawing close to the back of the small building and could hear an angry, discordant voice through the walls.

The furious female said, "You said someone would come. How long do I have to wait in this God-forsaken place? Everything is filthy, and look at the dirt…" The harsh voice went on and on. The woman sounded far more than merely angry; she was positively vitriolic.

Bea could not yet see what she looked like. But she noticed that the mail coach had already departed, which was unusual. Before entering, she tied her blue handkerchief to the rope and tugged it up the pole. Whoever it was had nowhere else to go but the homestead, and from the sound of her, she would not want to stay in the shop bunks. Why she had alighted here, Bea had no idea. Mayhap, she had been offloaded. She took a deep breath and went to face the fire-breathing dragon. She forced herself to smile before she entered the small shop.

An over-dressed older lady was seated on a barrel of pickled pork. She had an embittered look on her face, and her arms were folded in a stance of absolute annoyance. She would not have been out of place at St George's Church in London. However, she was in a roadside shop in the middle of nowhere on the other side of the world.

Rather than greet her, Bea was lost for words at her volatile temper.

The angry shrew demanded, "Well, who are you, girl? I suppose a convict wench, eh? How am I supposed to get to the house, and who will take my luggage?"

It was only when the lady said that Bea saw the mountain of luggage sitting at the side of the shop. Why would this woman need nine metal travelling trunks? Who was she? "Welcome, ma'am; I am Bea Barnes. How may I assist you?"

The woman gasped, looked her up and down, and then repeated the investigation, motioning for Bea to turn around for further examination. Bea remained silent but passively obeyed the rude woman's order. She knew just what this sort of woman was like. Miles's mother, her first employer, was similar. She knew it was best not to argue.

The woman harrumphed. "Well, in that case, Beatrice, I am your mother-in-law. So, you're the convict that married my son. Where is he?"

Bea was horrified to find out that Jack's mother had arrived unannounced. What she had heard of this female was not encouraging. Regaining her equilibrium, she gently said, "He's not here, ma'am. He and Hugh Lacey are off droving. They won't be back for months. It's the drought, ma'am." Bea presumed her words would explain everything.

However, the woman nearly exploded. "Ahhh, sheesh! Oh, damn, damn, damn and botheration." She paused for a breath, then asked, "And what the blooming heck do you mean he's not here? And why is he droving his own animals? Are you serious?" Edith Barnes was outraged.

Harrison and Mildred Titchmarsh shrank back into the shadows. They felt for their mistress but could do little to assist her. Both had been horrified to hear this gorgon was their wonderful Mister Jack's mother. They had already received a long tongue-lashing from this harpy.

There were words for this female that flashed through the minds of all three people. She was a harridan and a shrew.

The volley of questions that spewed from the fire-breathing dragon did not require answers.

Bea had taken a step backwards in shock at the vitriol almost spat at her. She felt belittled and unsure of herself for the first time in a long time. What was she going to do with this woman? When she married Jack, they assumed she would never meet her; now, the she-devil hellcat was to stay with her. She now fully understood why Jack had left. Bea was wondering what to say and do when Billy arrived with the wagon and not the cart. Bea smiled; of course, Billy would know about the luggage; somehow, he always knew what or who was coming. Considering how quickly he had arrived, he probably started harnessing Cassie when the mail coach took off early.

As the verbal diarrhoea continued to assault Bea's ears, Harrison and Billy managed to get the heavy metal cases out of the shop and load them onto the wagon. All the while, Edith Barnes was verbally shredding Bea. She had hardly taken a breath.

Mildred wondered how to rescue Bea when the resident carpet snake lowered its head from the rafters. Bea stood passively and took the verbal diatribe without flinching; this only riled Edith more.

Mid-sentence, Edith screamed at the attacking serpent and fled outdoors. As soon as the door banged shut, Mildred took a now-shaking Bea in her arms. "Oh, Missus Bea, I'm so sorry. She's been here screaming at us since the carriage arrived. I so felt for the other passengers. Most feigned sleep on arrival, but I heard them cheering as they drove off. I passed in a free basket of fresh goodies I had for sale. They deserved it. Ma'am, we're all in for a bit of a tough time, but please know we're here for you. Come here for respite when you wish."

Bea had not heard Mildred say so much the entire time they had lived with them. "Thank you, dear friend; I may occasionally need to escape and be rescued." Bea gave the kind lady another hug and a kiss, then she took a deep breath, "Keep up the prayers, Milly; we're all going to need them."

Mildred nodded, "I will, Ma'am."

As Bea walked to the door to leave, she looked up and thanked the python, "Mister snake, you have the most perfect timing, although a little earlier would have been nice." The serpent was still hanging from the rafters. Its tongue flicked as Bea swung the door closed behind her. The tinkling bell rang a chime of doom. She didn't mind the serpent as it kept the rats away.

The sight of her mother-in-law standing with her mouth open nearly made Bea chuckle. Billy was naked to the waist and had one of her cases on his shoulder. Jack and Billy's physiques were similar; only the colour of their skin differed. The muscly inky black-skinned aborigine lifted them like they were weightless. He was used to doing heavy work on the farm with Jack.

Harrison helped arrange the nine travelling cases so they would all stay on the wagon without falling off. He knew he would have to come and help get them off as they would be too heavy for the girls, and he knew Bea was with-child, so she was not to lift anything.

Billy offered to help the stranger, but she refused and stayed as far from him as possible without falling off the seat.

Harrison stepped up and helped both ladies onto the seat. Edith made Bea crawl over her so she didn't have to sit beside the half-naked black man. After telling Mildred he would go to help, Harrison hopped on the back.

The trip was silent; there was little to say. The farm looked dead; it was. There were no stock and virtually no grass. The paddock gates were left open for horses, cows and wildlife to try to eat what they could. Thankfully, the well still had water, keeping the remaining animals from perishing. The patch around the lemon tree was the only green in sight.

The chickens were culled, and they kept only the ten best-laying ones. They feasted on roast chicken twice a week until the henhouse was down to a more manageable number. The chickens could breed up again when the rains came. Hannah had made chicken stock with the last of the wilted vegetables and bottled it for later use.

Staff were now kept at a minimum, and Netty and Billy's tribe had gone walkabout back to the Nepean River. Jack said that some of the tribe lived on their friend Hetty Walker's farm. They could manage with the clean water from the well and the food they had on hand. With Jack's mother's arrival, she was one more mouth to feed, one more unwanted problem. Edith Barnes had come to disturb the peace, and Bea would not allow that.

It had taken Bea some time to discover why the tribe had settled on Jack's land. It was the far western boundary of their territory. The *Dharug* people were the Freshwater people of the Hawkesbury-Nepean River system. Over the years, Bea had learned their names and could speak quite well to many of them. For each of Bea's babies, the tribal ladies would appear, do what was needed, and then vanish as quietly as they came, often before they had been thanked. An ample supply of food was left for them or given to Billy to take to the camp.

With the drought holding tightly, the tribe had gone. Netty said, "Them go walkabout, Missus, them come back, bye'm'bye when the rains come. You see."

Bea desperately hoped the tribe would be back before the baby came. She figured Edith wouldn't be much help.

As the wagon pulled up to the front verandah of the house, Edith waited to be handed down from the vehicle; however, both men had seen Bea shake her head and motion not to assist her visitor. The men smiled and nodded.

Bea slid off the seat behind Billy. She turned to look at Edith. "Mrs Barnes, I would say welcome to our home, but your timing is poor. We are in the middle of a severe drought and have minimal help and less food." She drew a deep breath and continued, "Jack told me one of your favourite sayings was 'start as you mean to go on,' well, I will take you up on this. We do not have maids to assist you or footmen to help you down. Here, if you do not get things for yourself, you will go without them. It's all hands on deck, and we eke out a living as best we can." With that, she walked up the steps onto the verandah and went to warn Hannah and Alice what they were to expect. A she-devil had come to stay.

Still sitting in state, Edith realised no one would assist her, and she quickly climbed down from the wagon. She was about to give instructions for her cases and opened her mouth to say something when Billy appeared in front of her with his hands-on-hips. She snapped her mouth shut, and with skirts hitched up, she stormed onto the verandah. She would sort the luggage out later.

The homestead had a series of double French doors along the entire front. Bea had gone through one, but Edith had not noticed which. She stood and called, "Beatrice, come here at once."

The call remained unanswered.

Bea was attending to the needs of her children. They had to be warned to behave and stay as silent as possible.

Bobby said, "Mama, she sounds really angry."

Eventually, Bea followed the sound of the berating voice, still audible from inside the children's room. She arrived at the front of the building to see the woman still there. In a calm voice, Bea said, "Ma'am, these are your grandchildren, Robert, called Bobby; Jessica, known as Jess; and this little one is Edward, known as Ed. I will add that they have never heard a raised voice, and I hope that will continue. This house is our home and is a place of peace. It is also a haven for the hurt. You may stay if you wish, but I will not have the children or my staff upset. If you do not wish to conform, the mail coach will return tomorrow, and you may await Jack in Bathurst or Penrith. The choice is yours."

Edith was about to explode and complain about her insolence when Jess asked, "Why are you angry at my Mama?" The child had her hands on her hips and was frowning.

The small child's question had no answer.

Edith saw another small urchin holding onto Bea's skirt fearfully.

The little girl teared up and wiped her eyes. Jess whispered, "You is mean!"

Bobby asked bravely, "Is that why Papa left your home, 'cause you're always angry?"

Edith didn't know what to say. Bea had no time to word them up, yet they knew they spoke the truth. Edith was angry; she was always angry. She was angry that her husband had died, angry that Jack had left, angry that she had no home to go to now except here, and angry that her other son, Paul, had shot himself. Edith watched the peaceful decorum of her daughter-in-law, then the fear etched on the faces of the children. Eventually, Edith knew the child needed to be answered. "I think it was Bobby. I..." She stopped. "I..." she tried again, but her words wouldn't come.

Bea saw her struggle and stepped in. "I think we will find you a room, and you can work out what you want to do later." Without waiting for an answer, she turned and led them in through a double door.

The guest room was light and airy; there was a large bed with solid-looking red-coloured timber furniture. The room was lovely.

Edith swallowed her pride. "Thank you, Beatrice, this will do beautifully." She put her reticule on the bed and turned around to say more when she realised she was already alone.

Bea had quietly shut the door behind their exit.

Chapter 14 A Dog's Day

$\mathcal{E}$dith was left alone much of the time.

Alice would serve breakfast in the dining room and then set about her chores. If Edith weren't up and ready to eat, the porridge would be left on the table, covered but unheated.

Hannah was in the kitchen with Netty, and Bea and the children were milking the cow and collecting the eggs.

At four, Bobby could do various jobs around the house. Jess, at three, was his shadow. They knew where they could go and what they were allowed to do. The vegetable garden was the limit of the area they could wander, and they knew that any further and Blue would round them up and nip at their heels until they returned home. One of the other dogs would then get Bea, who would gently scold the two wanderers.

Edith had taken up residence in Bea's rocking chair and sat biding her time uselessly. They rarely spoke to her, and she made no effort to assist with anything.

Bea had made it abundantly clear she was not wanted nor welcome. Edith had arrived with her mind made up to dislike the girl her son had chosen. However, the more she watched her, the more she admired how Bea got on with the work required.

No softly-spoken English aristocratic girl could cope with what Jack asked of her. Bea never complained once. She hummed or sang most of the time, and the children and staff obviously adored her.

Bea frequently tied Ed onto her back as she worked. The four headed off for a walk with the dogs bounding around them. They would return with a large bag full of kindling for the fires. Ed would be between his siblings, toddling bravely, and a large bundle would be on Bea's back.

Edith would not even know how to set a fire, let alone the sort of wood to collect. Even Jess knew how to make a good fire. Edith had found that her three-year-old granddaughter's job was to clean the cold fireplaces each morning and reset them for use that night. Bobby and Billy would bring in logs, and Jess would tell them where she wanted them placed. The baby, Ed, rarely cried. Edith didn't remember her sons at that age. She had seldom seen them. She couldn't even remember if they looked like Jack. Guilt embedded itself as she watched.

Bea had finished the letter she was writing when her mother-in-law arrived. She added only one line, informing Jack that his mother had descended upon them without notice. She knew it could be months before he received the information. She was sure he did not know his mother's intentions. She had not had a whole conversation with Edith yet, so she had no idea why she had come. So much for pulling her weight! Edith had not attempted to assist with any of the household chores.

~

For three weeks, the frosty stand-off continued between Edith and Bea.

Netty had stayed out of sight as much as possible; however, she missed their daily morning cuppa on the verandah. Then one morning, in her normal singsong voice, Netty had said quite loudly, "Quick, Missus Bea, your chair is empty; come have a nice cuppa with Netty." Alice and Hannah had just appeared with the tea tray with only four cups. They sat on the verandah next to Netty.

Bea smirked at the very unsubtle method Netty used. She was aware that her mother-in-law was close by.

Edith stood just inside the door and heard every word. Rather than object; she took the not-so-subtle hint. Edith went to the dining room, collected a cup and carried a chair out to the verandah for herself. It was the first thing she had done for herself besides making a cup of tea. Edith sat listening to the chatter of the four ladies. None spoke to her, and she didn't understand what they discussed.

Netty said, "Missus, with new *gurung* coming, you be careful. The *duba* still on walkabout, and it will be just us unless Mister Jack come back. You bin *bunya* four times now and not *baragat* no more."

Bea smiled at her comment. "No, Netty, I'm not frightened anymore. This baby will be my fourth confinement, and I hope your tribal ladies return before it comes."

Now seated near Bea, Edith was stunned. She bit back the nasty words that initially sprung to her mind; instead, she said, "You're with child? And you're still working?"

Bea looked up at her mother-in-law. She showed no hint of bitterness. Bea said, "The work doesn't stop, Edith, and while I can work, as everyone else has enough to do, I will continue to do so. We are short-staffed; the cows still need to have their milk stripped, the fires still need setting, and the food needs to be made. We have no shops to buy things from, and no one delivers our food. If I don't work, we don't eat. Your arrival has added to the workload as you are an extra mouth to feed."

Edith could only reply with, "Oh." She realised she should have written; she should have stayed in Sydney until she heard from Jack, but she had no money to pay for the hotel. She caught the mail coach in Sydney on the spur of the moment. However, Bea knew none of this. Edith's pride would not allow her to admit the dire situation she had found herself in. No matter where she went, she was now just an inconvenience, unloved and unwanted. Edith teared up; she looked away from Bea and Netty.

Alice and Hannah saw the watery eyes of their visitor.

Hannah bent and whispered to Jess, who was sitting on her lap.

Bea watched Jess shake her head violently.

Then saw Hannah nod and whisper, "Yes, go on."

Jess shrugged; she toddled over to the watery-eyed lady. "You've never given me a hug, Nana." The three-year-old held out her arms and obviously would not take 'no' for an answer.

Nana! She was this child's Nana. She had not thought about that. Edith didn't remember when she had hugged a child last, but it certainly had not been a granddaughter, for she only had this one. Edith reached out for the small child and soon received a two-armed hug and a sloppy kiss from her granddaughter. She felt the first chink in her self-imposed armour falling away.

The hug and Bea's silence had broken through where animosity and society had failed. "Bea, I need to tell you why I'm here. I need to tell you all. You see, I have nowhere else to go. Eustace, Jack's father, is dead. He died some years ago. Paul then inherited; he was living the high life in town. For the last two years, he's been living well beyond his means, and things came to a crunch. He was about to be arrested and taken to Fleet Street prison when…" Edith paused; she could hardly admit to herself what had occurred, "…Beatrice, Paul shot himself. Jack is all I have left. I was ostracised and homeless, and I had nowhere else to go. Paul sold the house but didn't tell me. When he died, the bailiffs came and cast me out. With the money I had left, I came here. Hugh and Heather Lacey had written to tell me where you were living, and they have fed me scraps of information over the years. I knew you had one child, but not three. I could not believe that you were all they said and that you were good and honest. You were a convict, and I thought they were lying. I was wrong."

Bea sat listening, inwardly smiling to herself that, finally, the woman was getting her comeuppance. When Bea had first met Jack, she couldn't believe a family could be as horrible to a child as his parents apparently had been. Her words belied her feelings. "Edith, you are welcome to stay, but if you do, you will need to do something. You must find your own niche. When I was growing up, I was envious of people who had parents. You see,

I don't know who mine are. Then I met Jack. He said he wished he didn't have any. He fled your country to find peace. He left you and found it here with me, an ex-convict, and we are happy, Edith. Oh, and we are all on first-name terms here, and you will be no different. I will not allow anything to destroy that hard-won peace of my family or home. However, if you wish to change, we will welcome you as part of the household for the moment. As to being part of the family, that is up to Jack." Bea saw her nod. "You will need to find a place for yourself; however, if you do this, you are welcome to make your home here."

Edith's tears returned. Nodding, she replied, "If you can still work while with child, with another one tied to your back and one in each hand, then I'm sure Bobby and Jess can teach me to at least collect sticks and set a fire."

~

Within weeks Edith had thrown herself into doing small things around the house that she saw had been overlooked. The dusting was certainly not up to scratch, but she realised that jobs needed to be prioritised. However, Edith quickly discovered that dusting during a drought was an unprofitable use of her time and soon abandoned it. No sooner had she finished a room than a breeze blew in and replaced what she had just removed. Edith didn't know how to milk or cook. She couldn't dig what remained of the vegetable patch, but she could water it. Alice had just finished the washing and needed to hang it out. Edith soon learned that dresses were hung by pegging under the armpits. She volunteered to water the garden after helping hang the washing, but Alice warned her not to put the hot water on the plants.

Another loathsome job that Edith learned to do was ironing. Alice taught her to fill the iron with hot coals and iron the clothing. Edith had no idea calico was so hard to smooth. She had growled at her staff so often as their starched aprons were often creased. Since she learned to iron with Bea's coal-filled implement, she learned how truly nasty she had been. Hannah had advised her to iron the calico slightly damp, wet, and straight from the copper. This produced a much better result.

A month after Edith's unexpected arrival, another letter arrived from Jack.

Harrison hoisted the white flag at the shop.

Edith volunteered to wander down and collect the mail. She had previously apologised for her behaviour to the Titchmarsh's, and she and Mildred even shared a cup of tea. They all came from Kent and were much the same age but from vastly different walks of life. They reminisced about home and found they came from much the same area. Harrison even knew about her husband's folly of planting an acre of walnut trees. As her husband had left it to Jack, it was the only land left. Edith admitted that it was now the only property that Jack owned. Paul had sold or gambled away everything else, but the walnut farm was not his. Being still immature trees, no one wanted the walnut farm. It could not even be gambled away as Jack needed to sign the papers.

After tea with Milly, Edith took her son's letter to his wife. She wondered if he had received the news that she had arrived. When she arrived, Bea was asleep in the rocking chair and had a book on her lap. Edith was astounded to see it was Jack's old Bible. She had learned that Bea was as nice as Hugh Lacey assured her. She had not been malicious when she laid down the rules. This house was her home, and these were her children. Once Edith had sorted herself out, her welcome had been warmer. She knew she had yet to apologise to her son. She didn't want to do that in a letter but knew it was better than not doing it at all. While Bea slept, she set about writing a long overdue missive to her son.

Bea woke after her nap and saw a letter tucked into the top of her Bible. She slipped it open and read the contents.

My darling sweet Bea,

We have arrived at the Murrumbidgee River. There is plenty of feed here, and we shall stay here until we hear the rains have come. The place is called Wagga Wagga, a funny name but lush with feed. If you write to me here, I will get your letters because they have a post office. There is not much else other than a blacksmith and a public bar. Mail comes overland, so continue to send via the Bathurst mail coach. A regular bullock train passes through, bringing and taking produce north and south.

My darling sweet, I find the months away from you are getting harder. I do so hope the rains come soon, yet I know that even then, it will take some warmth for the grasses to grow. Pray hard, my sweet, for I wish to wrap you in my arms again. I will finish this tomorrow.

J

My darling girl,

Hugh has just collected your latest letter. You did not tell me before of any suspicions that you were with child again. To say that I am excited is such an understatement. If you are due, as you say, in late spring, we will endeavour to return by then. My darling, the weather is even colder by the river than in the desert, so I will be more than content to snuggle up in bed with you and warm my toes with yours.

Now my sweet, I always endeavour to tell you a story.

This one involved the demise of a rogue dog, but the story behind it is all too true to life down here. Along the river, the farmers need to remove many large tree stumps so they can plant crops. The trees themselves are easy to fell compared to removing the stumps; they often blow them up with a stick of explosive. One day two farmers had made some of these waxed bombs, ready to remove the stumps, but a new friend decided to see if they could catch some fish with one stick of explosive first. They thought they would finish off their mugs of tea before taking the selected explosive to the river. This stick had an exceptionally long wick. One fellow had laid it on the box and set to boil their billy. How he planned to get it in the water, I don't know. However, the story goes that while they drank their tea, a friendly lanky pup came for a game of chase-the-stick. With a perfectly good stick of explosive on the box, the dog grabbed it and sat ready for a game. However, the wick brushed against the fire, and it soon caught alight. With the wick fizzing loudly, the men set off in different directions and hid as best they could. The lanky pup found the men's hiding spot and chased them for a game. One man upped and ran off at full speed and, now running for his life, headed for the town.

At this point, the lanky pup with a new toy came to the notice of the town's guard dog. This gigantic beast, a mangy mongrel much like Bounder, was the town's terror. He fought often and had beaten most other dogs in town and the local dingo pack. When the mongrel saw that the lanky pup had something fun, the mangy dog wanted it. By this time, they had come close to town. The man, seeking a haven, ran into the taproom and slammed the door behind him. Unbeknownst to him, the lanky pup found a back way. There followed a mass exodus of running feet followed by the two dogs. Once out in the courtyard, the mangy mongrel caught the tail of the lanky pup and made him drop his new toy. All the inn's patrons were hiding behind anything they could. The wick, by now, was very short, and as the mangy mongrel sniffed to take up the toy, the wick burned to the end. The patrons held their ears as they all saw the end was nigh.

Unbeknownst to the farmers, the powder inside the new explosive was a new brand that had twice the power of the old variety. The remains of the old mangy mongrel landed on the inn's roof; at least most of him did. Other bits were scattered over the courtyard. One by one, the farmers stood from behind their shields and shook the dirt from their shirts. The dog's owner started apologising for the mangy mongrel's demise and the trouble his pup had caused, and he was surprised that all congratulated him. The mangy mongrel was a sheep killer, and none could shoot the beast.

Oh, my Bea, I must confess this was us. We were in no real danger, but the town congratulated us on the mangy mongrel's demise. Shep naturally was severely chastised by me, but as he was unharmed, it all turned out well. However, I shall never touch explosives again. Not that it was me who made the darned thing. I will confess that we thought of the idea of using the bomb to catch fish.

My darling love, I twaddle on because I want my time with you to last forever. However, I have again filled my sheet of paper and must send this to you. Know that you are loved, and I miss you so much. I will endeavour to be home as soon as I can. I will be there for the child's arrival, even if I must return afterwards. I do love you so much, sweet Bea. Keep up your prayers for me, my darling girl. I need them to sustain me until I am home again.

Your very loving
Jack.
PS Keep praying for rain.

Bea sat on the rocking chair, chuckling to herself. She had seen Shep often help himself to a stick or anything to play a game of fetch. To think how close he had come to being hurt made her heart go to her mouth. From the story's beginning, she realised that it was the sort of naughty thing their dog would do. She lay back in the chair and realised she could feel the child within her flutter. She laid a hand gently on her stomach, relieved that Jack would be here for the birth. She sighed in delight. If Edith remained as helpful as she had been recently, things might improve dramatically.

Bea heard movement behind her. Edith appeared and sat in the cane chair beside her daughter-in-law. An uneasy accord had settled between them. Bea was still uncertain about Edith's demeanour; the letter should resolve any doubt of Jack's affection for his wife. It was something that Edith had never had. According to Jack, there was outright animosity between his parents. Bea passed her the letter.

Edith sat reading the love letter from her son. No one had ever poured out their feelings to her like this. It hurt to know what she had missed.

Bea saw her put the letter down, draw her handkerchief from her sleeve, wipe her eyes, and then read again. She then refolded it and handed it back to Bea. They sat in silence for some time until Edith said, "I'm jealous of all you have, Bea. It's part of the reason for my attitude to you. You have everything I have not had. My parents forced me into the marriage, and the children came through being forced to conceive them. He forced himself on me but made sure his bruises were not visible. He was a bully and a horrible person. He took the babies from me in case I became too close to them. So, I threw myself into the social whirl of London society. I hated the shallowness of it, but it was all I had. I realised I had lost my boys already, and my life was empty. He only came near me to slake his lusts. I was totally and absolutely empty. I clung to what society valued, position, wealth, and beauty. All failed me. Then my husband died, and Paul treated me as I treated him; he shunned me. I deserved everything I got, Bea. I won't ask for forgiveness because I'm not worth it." Edith sat with her hands folded in her lap. Her tears fell silently.

Bea sat gazing out over the parched land. "Edith, we are like the land. What do you see out there?"

Edith lifted her watery eyes to the dust caught in a willy-willy blowing across the back paddock. "It's so dry, Bea. Is that someone coming?"

Bea smiled when she saw the twirling wind, "No, that's the wind. And it's like our life. When I first met Jack, I was milking a cow and thinking back over my life. Yes, I was just twenty-three, but much had occurred in the years before. I, too, had been taken against my will by my master's son, his friends, and some staff, and all within a few hours. I was also beaten up so severely that other staff did not recognise me. I was arrested for housebreaking and streetwalking, which I wasn't, as I was employed there. That was my crime, being abused where I worked. The reason for my conviction was non-existent, but they needed to get rid of me. Did Jack tell you that?"

Edith shook her head. "He has not spoken to me for nearly ten years,

Bea. It was Hugh who told me you were here."

Bea nodded and continued. "Well, Jack arrived weeks before my time expired. He had seen me before, but I didn't know that. Mister Hugh had many visitors, and I was only a dairymaid and, as such, never even entered the house when visitors stayed, so I never conversed with them. Even before Jack arrived, he had decided to woo me. I thought he was a swagman passing through. He told me Mister Hugh had employed him as a drover, which he had, but that's all I knew. He told me that day he wished to marry; he didn't say he had chosen me already but did ask if I was interested in a marriage of convenience. He courted me, and I knew I'd marry him within a week. I thought my option was to go on the streets as a prostitute, and I would rather die than do that."

Edith sat silently. She was so sure it had been Bea that entrapped her son.

Bea saw the change in her mother-in-law's face. "Edith, Jack proposed again after I was free, and I said yes. I thought I would be a drover's wife and live with him on the road. Yes, he said he had a shack that he had built himself. It's the cottage where Netty and Billy are living now. Edith, I've never been so happy as when we lived in that wonky shack with only Jack, Billy and Netty. Bobby was born the week we moved in here; it's a beautiful house, but it's just a house. My home is wherever Jack is. Every now and then, we pack the wagon and go camping down the back of the farm. Just us and the children, the river is our happy time. Edith, I don't love Jack for what he has. I just love Jack because he loves me. He knows I have no idea who my parents are, and he doesn't care; neither do Hugh and Heather. They all know me just for who I am. I could barely write my name when we married, but I studied hard and learned everything possible. Netty and the local *duba's* deliver our children. Netty will deliver this one too." She rubbed her stomach. The bump was hardly noticeable on her slim form. "Edith, if you are serious about wanting to stay, you have to make it right with Jack, not me. But let me make one thing clear that you are very wrong about; we are all worth loving. God made each one of us special. I knew nothing about God when I met Jack, and after we married, he taught me about Him."

Bea heard Edith gasp, and then she said, "I saw a Bible on your lap; you honestly believe all that?"

Bea chuckled. "I more than believe it, Edith; I try to live it. The words at the end of Jack's letter are not just words. He really wants me to pray for him and his return, and yes, I will 'up' my prayers for rain. I want my husband back, but you must make amends with him before he returns."

Edith smiled at Bea, then dug into her pocket and waved it. "I've already made a start, Bea. I won't let you read it, as it contains specific things you don't need to know. But I need to ask for Jack's forgiveness for some graphic things. But be assured I've been very apologetic. I do hope he can forgive me. I need him to do so." She fell silent for a few minutes. "Bea, will you teach me?"

Bea looked confused. "Teach you what, Edith?"

Edith blushed. "Teach me about this Bible thing and how to be a person, not a mannequin, in society."

Bea was ashamed of her previous thoughts. "Yes, Edith, but you only have to learn about the 'Bible thing', as you put it, and then the rest should fall into place."

Edith smiled. "I shall take my letter to Mildred once it's addressed; then we'll start."

Bea chuckled. "You already have Edith. Think back to what you were like when you arrived. You're not that same person, are you?"

Edith replied with her own chuckle, "No, but three weeks of absolute silence makes one rethink oneself, doesn't it?" After reading Jack's letter, Edith addressed it and walked to the shop to leave it for collection.

As she walked away, Bea was thankful for the postscript she'd added to the letter she had sent Jack on the day Edith arrived. She had added in the tiny space at the bottom of the letter. '*PS Your Mama has just arrived*'. Jack would be receiving that letter soon. He would be stunned. Her following letter explained more, but at least if Edith's letter arrived first, it wouldn't be entirely so unexpected.

Edith's change of attitude saw her throw herself into everything she could. Within weeks, she even had Bea teach her to milk a cow.

Strawberry didn't like the new cold hands. She bucked and tried to push her away.

Bea took hold of Edith's hands and noticed they were cold. Bea giggled. "You need warm hands, Edith. Think of cold hands on your chest. You have to treat her like a friend. Rub them together and try again."

Edith did. Soon, Strawberry relaxed and let her milk down, and there was a steady stream of steaming milk into the bucket. "Oh, Bea, this is so rewarding." The sound of milk hitting the pail was soon rhythmic.

Bea explained. "We only need to take what we need. She has a calf, and he will drink the rest. We only need a bucketful from all the cows, so don't take all of hers. Once she is done, move the bucket, and she'll go out by herself. Josie comes next, then Trixie; we sold the rest as three were all we needed. Bruce, our bull, went bush and only returns when the cows are in season. He is usually as gentle as a lamb, but he's now a scrub bull, so don't trust him too much. If he does turn up, he likes dried apples."

Edith stopped milking and moved the bucket back.

Strawberry reversed and then gave Edith a slobbery lick and sauntered off. Josie took her place at the feed trough, and Edith stretched and, remembering to rub her hands to warm them, then went to work. Josie turned and looked at the new milker before giving a soft low, then put her head back to the trough.

Edith wasn't used to bending over for so long, so Bobby did the last cow. She said, "Bea, doing this work makes me appreciate the food we eat. Before living here, I had never thought about where our food comes from." This milk was for the household and some for Harrison and Mildred. At the time, Edith also started reading the Bible for the first time.

Chapter 15 Jack's Shack

*E*very day Edith would read another chapter of the New Testament and then ask Bea about it.

Bea usually had her afternoon nap in her chair on the verandah, but for once, she went to her room to lie down. A breeze wafted through the open doors and caught the muslin curtain, floating it softly in the draught. Edith was sitting at the table in the dim dining room and, by the light of a candle, wrote Jack another long letter, then she read a chapter in the book of Matthew. Now tired after helping with the dawn milking, she rested her head on her arms and dozed off.

Edith awoke to the sounds of something crackling and a bright light. The cotton muslin curtain had caught alight. Edith had time to grab the things on the table, including Jack's Bible and call out, "FIRE, FIRE." Rather than run outside herself, she ran for the children and Bea. Everyone was having an afternoon rest.

Edith shook Bea awake and shoved Ed into her arms. She assisted her up and pushed her outside. Edith then raced back in and grabbed the two older children.

Pandemonium broke out, and Hannah and Alice soon joined Bea and the children in the yard, ensuring they were well away from the fire. Alice took a coughing Ed from Bea and moved the children further away.

Bea watched as piles of clothing and other items were thrown over the verandah railings. The smoke billowed around the front rooms, but the bedrooms remained clear. Only the front room was currently alight. Bea saw the Bible sitting on the dirt and picked it up. Where was Edith? Everyone else was safe. Bea started screaming at the top of her voice, "Edith, what are you doing? Get out of there; it's only a house. Leave it and get safe."

Although engulfed by the smoke, Edith ignored Bea and continued to grab armloads of whatever she could and threw it out on the parched grass. Clothes, bedding, mattresses, bolts of fabric, and even Bea's sewing box were thrown clear. Edith saved everything she could. She cleared out everything in the linen cupboard and the wardrobes. Even the cutlery canteen that Jack had purchased in Parramatta was saved.

Bea was hoarse from screaming at Edith. "They are only things, Edith; get out of there."

Soon Nettie and Billy joined Edith. They realised Edith had shut the inside doors, and it had slowed the burn. The living room side of the house was well alight, but the bedrooms were still safe enough for their activities.

Alice handed Ed to Bea and went to join them. Bea could do nothing to stop them all.

Mildred and Harrison soon appeared from the shop. They could do little, so they held the older children.

Bea realised that in her condition, she would be risking too much to assist, so she stayed with the children and the dogs.

Although it was just a house, it was sad to see it like this. Bea sat and watched their home burn. They were all safe, and that's all that mattered. The shack that Jack built remained. That was her heart home.

One hour passed, then another. The fire licked its way through every room. It was pointless trying to quench the flames. Their water was just too precious, and their lives even more so.

After three hours, it had all but burned itself out.

The house was gone. All that remained was the stone base, verandah floor, kitchen walls and the stone wall of the staff rooms. The double-sided stone chimney also still stood.

Thankfully the fire had occurred during the day, and no one received any burns. Edith had covered her face with a woollen scarf but still breathed in some smoke. She sat on the hillside and coughed.

Thanks to Edith, many of their possessions were saved. However, Bea noticed that Edith had not tried to save any of her own clothing. The girl's staff rooms on the far side of the kitchen were virtually untouched, having just lost most of their roof. Those walls were stone and attached to the kitchen wall. The kitchen itself was almost still usable. The chimney and hob were covered in burnt timbers but should still work. Even the kitchen table was unburnt. Bea worried about the cool room downstairs, but it was still too hot to enter to check it out.

As they sat on the dry and dusty hillside, watching the smoke rise from the ashes, a very sooty Edith came to Bea's side and almost collapsed onto the dirt. There was no sign of the London socialite in the filthy woman beside Bea. She was sooty from head to foot, and her greying fair hair was covered in cinders.

She coughed for a few minutes before saying, "Bea, it was my fault. I started it. I was reading with a candle, and the curtain blew in and caught alight." She expected a blast from Bea. "You told me not to, and I didn't listen. I'm so sorry."

Bea drew her into her arms, and with a chuckle, she said, "Now we can all start with nothing, Edith. And to top it off, you will have to wear my clothes until you can make more with the fabric you saved. You will be a real colonial lady, Edith. I believe I saw you throw out bolts of calico and drill. Thankfully you also saved my sewing box. So at least we can sew."

Edith was so close to tears that she leaned into her daughter-in-law's shoulder. "Bea, I'm going to say something I've never said to anyone on the face of this planet. I love you, sweet girl. I love you so very much, and I can see why Jack adores you too."

The two women sat hugging, with a child under each arm. Ed had snuggled to Bea's neck and gone to sleep. He had received a lung full of smoke and coughed for a while before falling asleep. At nearly nineteen months old, he was usually running everywhere.

Bobby and Jess had never experienced a large fire before, let alone see the only home they had ever known go up in smoke. They did not realise the impact this would have on their lives. Gone was the luxurious, warm, and comfortable home they had been born in. Gone was their security; they now only had each other. Jack's shack would now be their home.

Netty saw the family sitting together and said, "Big fire makes best friend you two. You all sleep in Mister Jack's special house now. We go back to *gunya* Missus Bea, all good; big fire tells tribe big trouble. They come back plenty quick time now, Missus. You watch, me bring my family too. You get to meet my *gurung* now. It's time you meet my *gurungs*. I bin hiding them, Missus Bea. You see why soon."

By the time the initial shock of the fire had worn off, Billy had harnessed the wagon, and with Harrison's assistance, the men were loading the vehicle with everything Edith had saved. They would take the family clothing down the hill to Jack's shack.

Bea shook her head, still unbelieving this had happened. She looked at Edith's face and saw fear and sadness; then she looked at the children's sooty faces. It snapped her back to reality. She shot directions and soon mobilised everyone to get themselves sorted out. "Come on, everyone, we're moving home. Edith, you've done enough, stay there and hold Ed. He needs you. Bobby and Jess, come and help me and help gather the things in the yard. Hannah and Alice head down to the shack with Netty, prepare the place for us, then get your own things and move to the shop bunks. Billy and Harrison can help you take your things to the shop rooms. You two will have to stay with Mildred and Harrison in the guest quarters. Sorry, but the shack will be crowded with us there."

Within minutes, only Edith was still sitting, and Ed was asleep in her arms. She was overwhelmed by Bea's reaction and her forgiveness. The unadulterated love of a child was something she had never experie-

before. Ed had come to her willingly; she knew that he loved her.

Billy was heading down the hill with the loaded wagon when the group roused themselves. Netty had quickly gone down to the cabin to pack their things.

Bea had no idea how these two dear people lived and thought it would be a mess. She entered and saw that the cabin was pristine. The bed was unused; a bark sleeping mat was on the floor before the fire with a possum skin blanket. The room was pristine. Alice and Hannah had nothing to do but help bring things inside. They started filling the bed with the rescued items.

Netty saw Bea enter and look around. "Your bed too soft for black fella, Missus Bea, so we sleep floor. Fire nice, though; we sleep there." She pointed to a mat. She added a folded pile of their scant possessions and rolled them in the rug. There was little else visible.

Edith had never been into the shack her son had built, as Netty and Billy had moved in before she had arrived. From the outside, the log cabin looked dark and uninviting; through the open door, the room looked welcoming. Years before, Jack had built sleeping shelves for the young convict men along the side walls of the cabin. After the boys had left, the family had camped here, and the children adored their home away from home. Edith realised the mattress Billy saved from the burned house would have to be for her. She either used that, or she slept on the earthen floor. Edith entered the single-roomed building. She saw that the family had not been joking when they said it was small. She also saw one bed and the mattress Billy had just thrown on the floor. She took stock of everything and realised that would be her bed. She said, "Well, I won't have far to fall out of bed." She gave a nervous giggle. The luxurious bedroom she had in England was bigger than this entire cabin, but here, in this tiny hand-built room, she could feel the warmth and love of the place. What was more, her son had built it himself.

Jess shared the bottom bunk with Ed and very generously offered to swap with her grandmother. "Nana, you could have my bunk if you like. Ed kicks, though, just so you know."

Edith said, "Thank you, darling girl, I'll be happy on the floor, but you can come and sometimes snuggle, just in case you are lonely or get cold."

"I might, Nana, I just might." Jess jumped up and ran to her mother to help with the mountain of clothes being dumped on the bed. Jess helped sort out her own clothing. Bobby helped carry the items in, then assisted in sorting and folding the various piles, and each took an armload to their b   d placed them in neat piles.

watched, astounded, as they did things without being asked. She
ng the towels, flannel napkins for Ed, and other household
had flung from the linen cupboard. "Bea, you didn't even ask

them to do that."

Bea didn't pause in putting away Ed's flannel napkins, "Do you remember I said that we all have our chores? The children have to sort the laundry with Alice. As she is busy elsewhere, they get on to it unasked." Bea opened the top dresser drawer and slipped in the Bible. Jack often came down here for prayer times and to do the farm books. The ledger still was in the drawer. She felt like it was home too. The farm ledger had sat virtually untouched since he had left. There had been few farm sales, except the piglets the week he went.

Bea realised she had been short with Edith. She was tired, her house was gone, and she wanted Jack to enfold her in his strong arms and ease her worries. "Edith, I'm sorry, I'm short-tempered, but believe it or not, I'm not worried about the house. If it had been this shack that had burnt, I would have been far more upset. Jack built this himself. We lived here so happily until the big house was finished, so this is my heart home. The only reason I let Jack and Ned build the homestead was so we could help other girls. With the drought, I can't do that anyway." She sniffed and rubbed her eyes. They had welled with unshed tears. The tiredness she now felt was overwhelming. "I'm tired and grumpy, and I want Jack back, that's all." With that comment, she burst into tears. "I miss him so much, Edith, and I wish it would rain and rain so that he could come home. I want him with me."

Edith's following words stunned them both. "Then we'd better pray for rain, Bea. We all want him home." Edith enfolded Bea in her arms and let her weep.

Bea's melancholy mood didn't last long.

Edith drew Bea to a chair by the fire. "Let's pray right now. Children, come and join us."

The small group sat in a huddle and begged for rain.

Jess had heard them talking about her papa, and she also wanted him home. "God, please let it rain so Daddy can come home. Please, please, God, just do it. Lots of rain, too, everywhere, so he'll know when to come."

Bobby, Bea, and Edith added their pleas. Having taken a momentary breather, they left the worry in God's competent hands.

They soon returned to work and prepared for their new life in the cottage. As they sorted the clothing, the women chatted. "Edith, tomorrow we'll be able to get back into the house and see what we can salvage. The wood will be too hot today to go near, but as the roof has already fallen in, it should be safe enough as the foundations are all stone. I particularly need to see that the contents of the cellar have survived. Much of our shop produce is down there, not to mention our food store. Hopefully, the stone lining and thick earthen roof will have protected it. Jack built it as a bunker."

Billy knocked on their door. "Tucker ready, Missus Bea. Har- you come to shop and eat. Cart ready, and me and Netty com-

has no time to cook tucker for us today." The group filed out of the door, and Edith hoisted herself up onto the high seat of the cart and took Ed on her lap. Billy flicked the reins, and Cassie whinnied and then trotted down the track to the shop.

Hannah, Alice, and Mildred had cooked up a feast. Most of the food was perfect, if a bit smoky; the cart had made three trips bringing up equipment and the girls' smoky possessions. Unbeknownst to the cabin occupants, Billy and the girls had been busy emptying the kitchen contents and taking them down to the shop.

After dinner, as they stood at the cart waiting to return to the shack, Billy looked down and watched tiny ants on the ground. He said, "Missus Bea, we gotta get moving clearin' burnt house plenty quick. Rains are coming soon; look, see, ants are building plenty high." There was a trail of ants surrounding a tube of soil. "There, see that sign of rain. Next, you hear them black *garmit's* squark. They tell rains are real close. We sort house tomorrow, no more time." He made the action of a bird flying and pointed.

Bea smiled; she had heard some black cockatoo's screeching earlier that week. "Billy, that's wonderful news, as this means Mister Jack will return soon."

Billy's white teeth shone in the lamplight. "Not just Mister Jack, Missus. Walkabout over, they come soon too, and you meet our *gurungs*."

Bea didn't ask how he knew, but he'd not been wrong yet. "That is so good to know. I like having the tribe close by, Billy." As they spoke, everyone climbed back on the cart. "I feel safe when they are near."

Netty explained the mystery to Edith. "Nana Ediff, here on farm, Missus Bea, Mister Jack, keep us all safe. But we are Freshwater people from down river long way, that way." She pointed towards Sydney. "We should be on the river, this edge of our land. But we can stay here with this white fella; here we safe. You need us, and we need you. Work both ways. We happy help you, white fella. Tomorrow we clean up the firehouse and make it ready to build again. You see, friends come help." Netty folded her arms and giggled.

Bea saw Billy give Netty a nod of permission. Netty smiled broadly at him, then said, "Missus Bea, you not met my *gurung* yet as you get shocked. Two *gurung's* white man's doing when Netty plenty young. They beat me plenty bad, too, so Billy and Netty not go back to the river with the tribe. No more walkabout for us. *Gurungs* go with tribe, though. They go see tribe at Hetty Will... She good woman that one."

... t and took her hand. "Oh, Netty, I'm so sorry."

... ore alike than they had realised. All three women had ... ntly abused. Bea and Edith certainly had been. She ... ks were similar.

... onger afraid of these two people. They looked so ... ed their similarity when Netty saw Edith sewing after dinner; then she pricked her finger, and a dot of red blood appeared.

Her joyous giggle of the woman rang out. Netty said, "See, Nana Ediff, we all bleed red. All-a same under black skin. Happy, sad, laugh, cry, all-a same."

Edith did see. She saw beyond the prejudice to what both Jack and Bea saw in these beautiful people.

Netty patted Edith's hand. "All us girls get done-over by bad men, Nana Ediff. All-a same, we survive and grow strong. We *dubas* stick together."

The chill had descended when Billy dropped them at the shack. Bea was so tired but still had to milk the cows and settle the children. She sighed deeply, knowing it would be hours before she got to bed. The cows were already lowing in their stall, and she just wanted to sleep.

Edith and Netty saw her yawn with fatigue.

Edith had learned Netty's fear of the big-horned cows, so she wasn't surprised when Netty said, "Missus Bea, I put *gurungs* to bed; you do cows, you take Nana Ediff too, get done real quick."

Edith nodded. "Come on, Bea, at least I can help with this, dear girl."

Half an hour later, the cows were back out in the paddock, and the two weary women covered the pail of milk with muslin, leaving it in the cool dairy, and they walked to the cabin. It had been a big day.

Netty had the fire going, and she had washed the three children, who were already asleep. The small room was tidy, and all the clothing and linen had been put away.

Netty was about to go out into the cold of the evening when Edith realised she had no jacket. Although she had none of her own clothing but what she wore, she still had blankets and shawls. Edith shrugged off her thick overcoat and said, "Netty, you need this more than I; it should keep you warm. Keep it, please."

With a big grin, Netty enfolded Edith in a warm embrace and said, "Nana Ediff, it good thick coat and will keep Netty warm. Thanks, Missus Nana." Netty was enveloped by the darkness within moments.

Edith shut the cabin door and went to settle for the night.

Bea was already washing and soon climbed into the big feather bed.

Edith stoked the fire and turned the lamp off. Bea was asleep before Edith had finished her ablutions. Edith looked at the mattress on the floor. It looked warm and inviting. Soon only the owls outside were awake. No one heard the crickets start to chirp.

Dawn came all too soon. A dawn chorus of kookaburras laughing and magpies carolling stirred the shack's occupants.

Edith had slept better than she had for months.

Bea woke with a groan; she knew that today would be exha
Soon Jess and Ed were being helped up on the big double bed by B
breath clouding as he worked. All snuggled under the blankets

room while Edith stoked the fire and warmed the cabin. The hob stove was soon hot, and a camp oven full of water was quickly boiling.

Edith had seen Hannah make the porridge and was planning to try her hand at feeding the family. Her family! It had hit her in the middle of the night that the room was full of her people. And not just that, but she loved them all. She could reach out and touch them, hug them, and she was not afraid to show them affection. No one would take that from her this time. It was as though the final shred of her defences had fallen away. Edith was determined to learn everything she could, as Bea had done. Bea was born with nothing. The little she had worked for as a girl had been stripped from her. Convicted in nothing more than a nightgown and robe, she was still happy. Now living in a tiny cabin that her son had built, Edith realised that what had made her happy was love. She adored the small arms of Jess creeping around her neck or slobbery kisses from Ed. Bobby had yet to learn to trust her. Hopefully, that would come. She had missed these things from her boys and had never even realised that before. She had never nurtured a babe at her breast or known that bond and adoration of an innocent child. But she hoped it wasn't too late to change that.

Chapter 16 Solace at the Sliprails

*N*etty didn't knock. The door swung open and, in a sing-song voice, said, "Morning everyone, Netty's here, cook tucker. Look!" She held up a large chunk of smoked bacon. "Me find him in the smokehouse, Missus Bea. We sleep there last night; too far walk *gunya*. Forgot this fella one, Missus Bea." In her other hand was a long hollowed-out *coolamon* that contained some eggs. "I cook 'em up tucker for all-a you fella. Big day of work, need good tucker." She placed the bounteous food onto the table and pulled a heavy bark flap in the wall open.

Edith had not realised there was a door in the cabin leading to another room. She followed Netty inside and discovered a plethora of items. The small room was a treasure trove of goods. All sorts of kitchenware, piles of blankets, some men's clothing Edith presumed were Jack's or possibly the stockman's, and goodness knows what else.

The children were already up, and they dressed themselves, with the room now warm from the fire. Edith told Bea to stay in bed and have her sweet tea.

For once, Bea didn't argue. From her warm bed, she didn't miss any of the activities. She knew the day ahead would be trying. Soon, the group sat at the rough-hewn table, eating fried bacon and eggs, followed by porridge. Bea ate hers in bed.

Billy had joined them for the meal but, as usual, took his food outside to consume.

By the time the sun fully hit the remains of the homestead, all were up and about their chores. Strawberry was already calling for attention.

As soon as Bea was dressed, she wrote a letter to Ned Grace, addressing it to him at the Military Barracks in Parramatta. She told him about the fire and that she needed help. She included the last twenty-pound note that Jack had left for her use. It was the very last of the money they had. Bea would join Netty and Billy at the house as soon as she sent off this letter and did the milking.

Alice would collect the children and take them to Mildred at the shop. Bea's letter would catch today's mail coach eastward.

The children were not to be permitted near the remains of the smouldering ruins, and Mildred loved having them. Everyone else had left to start sorting the debris.

Bea's letter was short and to the point.

Dear Major Ned,

First, I need to say that we are all safe and totally unharmed. I am writing to tell you that the house is gone; it burned down yesterday. Jack's mother, Edith, is here and helped save much of our clothing. However, we now only have the furniture in Jack's Shack, which is safe.

Ned, I need a team to rebuild at some stage, and I know that you arranged the last one, so I hope you will understand what I need. The stonework all survived. I found this drawing of Jack's dream home in the shack. I will enclose that for you. Jack's still droving with Hugh Lacey, and I don't wish to trouble him. Before you arrange anything, please let me know the costs, as I will need to sell a cow to pay for the materials. I enclose what money I have on hand.

Jack said he would try to be home before the baby comes in late spring. Last we heard, he was at a place named Wagga Wagga.

Thank you, Ned; I hope this is not too much trouble.

Bea Barnes

Bea realised that with the forthcoming activity at the homestead, she would no longer find peace standing at the remains of the verandah railing and praying for Jack; not that much of the railing had survived anyway. It had been her favourite place of solace. Now it was gone. After finishing the milking, she usually relished the morning silence with a mug of tea at that railing. The paddocks were quiet and refreshing in the cool of the day, even in the drought. This morning, she realised the air was moist, not the dry and dusty feeling of the previous months. She could already hear noises from her burnt home, and she didn't want to face it. She and Blue moved to the slip rails of the holding yard, and she leaned against the split log fence. It wobbled as she rested her weary arms on the top rail. Stabilising this post was another job she needed to fix. There was so much to do. She didn't want to face the chores today, she wished to go back to bed and sleep, yet Bea realised she must be strong for everyone else. She always had to be resilient; everyone relied on her. The work would not do itself. Bea felt the child within her kicking. She was getting too large to milk and knew the others would soon need to take over. Bobby was now old enough to have this added to his regular chore list; soon, he would have to do it with Edith.

Bea put her head on her arms and leaned against the split slabs of timber. She prayed aloud, "God, give me strength. I can't do this alone anymore." Bea softly said the words, and she didn't expect an answer; however, she received one.

Netty and Edith had seen her stance and knew things were getting her down. Both knew the tiredness of carrying a child; both understood that discomfort. Bea felt arms of comfort and support go around her from both sides. They had come to be a support for her.

"You are not alone, Bea, and neither am I." It was Edith who spoke, but Netty's huge grin met hers. Edith continued, "And Netty is here for us both, dear."

Netty grinned. "You be good now, Missus Bea; we got many helpers, look." Bea turned and became aware of the sound of singing and laughter floating across the still valley. "I come to tell you my *gurungs* come to meet Missus Bea, come."

Even after years on the farm, Bea was yet to meet Netty's children, and Edith had yet to meet the tribal people. Edith saw about thirty very dark half-naked people emerging from the bush and walking towards the house. She nervously stood close to Bea.

Bea saw her fear. "Edith, they are as lovely as Netty. Smile and talk normally. Most can understand us, but they speak a sort of baby talk like Netty does to reply. You'll get used to it."

Edith clung tighter. "I already am, Bea; I love Netty. I just don't like strangers, any strangers. I never have." She took a deep breath and straightened up.

Bea chuckled. "Then put on your best London smile."

When the tribe arrived, Bea introduced Edith to the group, and soon they were all set to work. A white man obviously fathered Netty's two oldest children. Their skin was pale, but they had Netty's beautiful round face and deep dimples. They looked like teenagers, meaning Netty would have been only a young girl when they were born. Bea's heart went out to her. Some men were hateful beasts who just wanted to gratify their lusts.

The men of the tribe set to work moving the burned roof and beams and making the access safe.

Bea had explained what she wanted to be removed first. She had to know about the produce below ground. They soon cleared a pathway into the trapdoor to the cellar. Finally, it was uncovered. Although scorched, the fire had not touched the thick slabs of timber and thick mud-daubed covering that Jack had used to seal the room. When Billy lifted the door for Bea, one glance showed her that the contents were smoky but unscathed. The cool air from the room also showed that the cheeses had not even melted. She heaved a sigh of relief. A year's work of cheese, hams, and bacon was stored in that room, along with preserves, ginger beer, and numerous other goods. Bea shut the trapdoor and thought about where to start with the rest of the house. She need not have worried.

Billy had tribal men sorting through everything. He piled the partially burnt wood for later use in the house fires. Usable clothing was sorted and placed out for washing. Soon the remains covered the verandah and courtyard in assorted piles. Billy had moved the wagon to the verandah's edge; they piled on everything beyond use or repair. They would have a big bonfire when it was safe.

The broom cupboard was intact, as it was built into the back of the stone kitchen wall. Edith's metal cases had also escaped undamaged. She had only opened one of her large metal travelling cases, which had fallen closed. Discovering these bags brought a smile to her lips. She had already decided on making over many of her gowns for the children and Bea. Netty's acceptance of the coat yesterday made her think she would make clothes for the rest of the tribe. She knew there were furs and velvet cloaks in her bags. She would keep one serviceable thick woollen coat for herself, but she would give the rest away. She would not need them here and had no intention of ever returning to England. The wardrobe in her room was in cinders, as was her bed. But she had slept well on the floor, and being close to her family gave her a contentment she had never experienced before. Edith paused in what she was doing; she realised she was happy. Happier than she had ever been before, and she had virtually nothing. She smiled, and she started humming an old hymn she had learned as a child. She thought of the words as she hummed them. "Amazing Grace, how sweet the sound that saved a wretch like me." How apt those words were.

~

For three days, they cleaned the shell of the house. The original stone walls were still sound, and as Billy had said, the kitchen was almost intact; it just required the roof to be replaced. Soon, only the floor needed sweeping. Bea's rocking chair had been scorched but was still solid. Billy had rescued that too.

Over the next few days, after the morning and evening milking, Bea took a few minutes to stand at Thunderbolt's sliprails and pray. It was the only time she managed to get away on her own.

Six days after the fire, Edith saw the red flag hoisted up the flag pole. Before she had time to tell anyone, she saw a bullock wagon approaching. "Bea, come quickly; you have a visitor." Bea stood beside Edith and watched the procession of the wagon. Another and then a third followed it.

The team of builders had arrived.

Bea turned and took Edith's hands. "Edith, it's Ned; Jack knows him from home, as do you." It occurred to Bea that Edith would also know him; with panic in her voice, she said, "Edith, here, this man is Major Ned Grace. If you know him by another name in London, please say nothing. Please!" Edith saw the pleading look on her daughter-in-law's face. She had no time to reply but nodded.

A tall blonde soldier was walking toward them.

Edith saw who it was and gasped.

She felt Bea grab her arm. "Please, Edith, stay silent; and for goodness sake, do not curtsy to him." She squeezed her arm.

Edith turned and gazed at her. Was Bea on first-name terms with this man? Edith knew of his parents, but the Duke and Duchess of Gracemere had never even given her the time of day.

Bea introduced them officially. "Major Ned Grace, this is my mother-in-law, Edith Barnes. Edith, Ned is Jack's good friend."

Ned smiled. "Yours too, I hope, Bea." Knowing his men were watching, he turned to Edith and politely said, "A pleasure, ma'am."

He walked up onto the unroofed, singed verandah and approached the two ladies. He held his arms towards Bea, and she almost fell into them. "I thought you would need some moral support." Over the past five years, Ned had come for a week-long visit a few times. He had become a good friend to both Bea and Jack. Ned flicked her cheek affectionately. "It's good to see you again, Bea. It's been too long. I want to have a long chat with you later."

Bea gave him a welcome kiss on the cheek. "Nice to see you too, Ned; thanks for coming yourself. And yes, I would love that chat."

Edith stood watching the friendly welcome. Ned Grace was, in reality, Lord Edward Lockley, the second son of the Duke of Gracemere, and he was cuddling her ex-convict daughter-in-law. Edith had met him only twice at home. He was only a lad back then. However, he was unmistakably the same man. He was here as a soldier and looking after convicts. Edith stood and watched the view of Bea in Ned's arms. Bea was now in tears and slowly pouring out the story of the fire and her loneliness with Jack away. Both were oblivious to Edith. Bea was an illegitimate orphan ex-convict, and Ned was from almost the highest level of the aristocracy.

Ned stood hugging Bea, listening and giving her the strength of his support. Eventually, they drew apart.

Edith forgot and was about to curtsy to him when she heard Bea whisper, "Edith, no, he's just Ned here. A simple soldier and a good friend. Please be careful."

Ned heard what Bea said; his eyes grew wide in surprise at her tone. No one spoke to Lady Edith Barnes like that. He waited for an explosion, but it didn't come. With a curt nod to her, he took his leave.

By lunchtime, a tent city was set up in the old vegetable patch. The bullocks were set free in the front paddock and fed with fodder carried on one of the wagons. Ned had even brought feed for the beasts. He supervised the tent encampment and did not have much time to chat.

The team set about unloading what they had brought. At Billy's suggestion, they placed much of the building timber on the verandah.

After dinner that evening, Ned knocked on the shack door. He had some private news for Bea. She welcomed him inside the small cabin. After greeting Edith and the children, he said, "Bea, this is my last job before I retire. I know I didn't say anything on my previous visit, but there are reasons. Would you walk with me for a moment?" The look he gave Bea puzzled her. He obviously had something he wanted to tell her privately.

She walked him to the door, then wandered a few steps from the shack's verandah. He said, "Bea, I've met someone and want to be close to her. I had no idea what Jack felt for you until I met her. The sad thing is, I can't marry her. I have no prospects, and although I've purchased a tiny cottage near her, I can't ask her to share such a life."

Bea took his arm and moved further away from the shack's door. She wondered if Edith would try listening. "Why Ned? If you love her, she won't care; look at Jack and I. Don't hold back. Be happy; make her happy too. We all need someone to love. Don't miss out because of a tiny house or a lack of money. I have been happier in Jack's tiny homemade wonky shack than in the beautiful homestead you had built for us." She was looking up at him with compassion etched on her face. She knew the need for love and acceptance for just being herself. Jack knew it too. "Ned, love is not reliant on wealth or money. It's way beyond that. You know that I married Jack thinking he was a drover. I had no idea he had more than what a drover made."

Ned looked down at the confident young woman beside him. She had nothing; she had just lost her house, battling alone in the middle of a drought, with small children and a shrew for a mother-in-law, and yet she was concerned for his happiness. "I'm nearly forty, and I'm still scared, Bea. You know about my last engagement. It's taken me over twenty years to allow any woman under my armour." He looked a little embarrassed. "A few of you girls have each chipped away at my protective shell. However, I was more than content to see each of you happily settle with your chosen men."

Bea gave a huff of frustration. "Ned, don't do this to her or yourself. Please don't make her suffer any more than she has. She will be lonely too, and I'm sure she needs you as much as you want her."

Ned was amazed that this compassionate young lady made more sense than any argument he could give himself. "Bea, I will say this, if the opportunity arises, I will declare my feelings. In the meantime, I will stay close to her. Somehow Christina Meadows has managed to breach my defences without trying. Her need is desperate, but I cannot assist her much due to society's rules."

Bea chuckled. "Blow the rules, Ned. There are ways around those if you are serious. Again I say, look at Jack and me."

Ned gave a nod of acknowledgment. "Bea, I'm also committed to helping out Charles and Sal. His broken leg has healed, leaving him with a bad limp. How he even walks amazes me. Having said that, I sneak Christina food each week, but I can do little else. She lives alone, and so do I. However, I came to tell you myself, as it's not the sort of thing you can put in a letter."

Bea argued her point. "If she's that poor, then sharing one house will save money." Bea understood. "Ned, I didn't expect you to come at all. I asked for a quote."

Ned chuckled. "No one is paying for this rebuild, Bea. The material is left over from a government project, and I was told to put the remainder to good use. You are 'good use,' Bea. I told Governor Gipps that your house had just burnt down, and he told me to fix it, so I am. It's all above board, and all this is free, as is the labour, of course. I put your money to use purchasing some of the bits, like glass for the windows. They are a good team who cause little trouble. We will get the roof done before attempting the walls and the outside. I had Old Tom in Parramatta tell me the rains are coming soon and that they will be heavy."

Bea nodded. "Billy said the same thing. He said the ants are building tall towers and added that when the black cockatoos start squawking, the rains will start soon afterwards." Bea placed a loving hand on his arm. "Ned, think about what I have said. You will be able to help her more married than not. And Ned, you will have companionship too."

"I will, Bea, thanks for listening." Ned gave a slight bow.

They said good night, and Ned slowly walked back to join the other soldiers in the tent city. He had much to contemplate. Mayhap Bea was correct. Maybe he could court her in private.

For the next week, the homestead was a frantic construction site. The verandah was widened to fit Jack's new design. Then the frame went up in no time at all; the roof quickly took shape. When the rains started, the building team had just finished adding the last of the shingles to the new roof. The team worked well into the twilight; they nailed on the last shingle as the first dew for months settled on the completed roof.

For the previous two days, the team had worked from sun up to sundown; now, they had finished it. All other work had ceased so they could complete the waterproofing of the roof.

As Ned stood under the verandah roof, he could hear the black cockatoos screeching their warnings for the first time in many months. Tonight, many birds were giving their warning cry at dusk; then, an eerie silence settled on the valley. A cricket sang here and there but soon fell silent.

The following dawn, everyone was woken by a raucous flock of screeching black cockatoos. Clouds were gathering overhead, but the parched land was still dry and dusty.

Billy greeted Bea with, "Morning, Missus Bea, the big rains come today. You ready?" Billy walked with her to the milking shed. "Big, big, rains, Missus, see them ants, they build high towers, really high. Them soldiers get washed away in veggie patch. Move up here in house, Missus."

Bea told Ned, and with waterproof protection overhead, the team and soldiers collapsed their canvas town and moved into the warmer, dry shell of the new house. The team brought all possible building materials and workbenches onto the covered verandah.

The children did their chores in record time and stocked up piles of kindling. The washing was taken from the line and brought inside. Edith had unpegged the last of the sheets when the first drops fell. She would stay in the shack looking after the children. Ed had never seen rain like this and didn't like being cooped up. He had only ever known drought and dust.

Edith smiled at the antics of the small toddler; soon, mud pies would be his new toy. She pulled an empty half keg under the corner of the roof. Bea had pointed out that Jack had built the roof so it drained to one side. Only a few months ago, she would not have even realised water needed to be drawn from a well, let alone know where to find an empty half keg and then move it to where it was required.

The odd drips turned into drizzle.

Work continued on the verandah.

Bea wrote to Jack saying that the rains had arrived. The mail coach came through and collected the letter, taking it westward and carrying the good news on its journey to Jack. Bea had kissed the message before sending it on its way.

The initial fine drizzle of rain turned into sheets of water channelling through the dust in the paddocks; it brought snakes out of hiding, one of which had taken up residence in the shack.

Bea entered to see a giant brown snake sliding under Edith's mattress. She had walked in as the last of the tail vanished. Too scared to move in case it changed position, Bea stayed rooted to the spot. Blue was told to "Skitch Ned."

Ned arrived minutes later and saw her frozen like a statue. Knowing how the nasty brutes could strike in a moment, he said, "Bea, you need to get out, but slowly, very, very slowly, move backwards."

Bea's voice shook as she spoke. "It's under Edith's mattress, Ned, and it's a big brown; please, be careful."

He hated snakes with a loathing. They were a symbol of all that was evil. Yet he knew they were just another of God's creatures; however, he had dispatched many in his time here. This one was endangering his friends. He was on duty, so he had his loaded musket with him. It was soon primed and ready to fire.

One of the other soldiers had seen Ned's unusual departure, with a dog hanging off his coattails, and had followed to assist. The dog had grabbed Ned's coat and almost dragged him from the verandah. Something was up.

Ned sighed with relief when his Captain arrived. "Phil, grab that clothesline pole. A damned snake is under the mattress."

"What sort, Ned?" Phil asked as he grabbed the pole.

Phil heard a shake in Ned's voice. "A brown and Bea says it's a big one. So it will be quick. I will shoot it once you lift or move the mattress."

Phil flicked over the mattress, and the snake reared and was ready to strike in only milliseconds. Ned fired. The explosion brought everyone running, but the remains of an eight-foot brown snake were quickly removed from the shack. Ned was thankful he had not missed it.

Billy claimed it and said, "Him good tucker, Mister Ned. Netty cook him up good, and him taste like chicken." Billy left, grinning, carrying his prize aloft.

And still, it rained. The water turned from trickles into torrents.

The dust quickly turned to mud, which stuck to whoever ventured outside. Overnight the chill air froze the slush and made conditions more than treacherous. The stack of burnt timbers from the old house was now piled on the new verandah. It was sawn up and now supplied warmth, not to mention dry fuel for the stoves. The double-sided stone fireplace, where the lounge room had once stood, gave a coziness and comfort to the room and to the soldiers and convict builders alike. All praised Billy's forethought for keeping the partially burned timbers dry. This convict team was not chained at night, as Ned knew these men, and to add to the overnight guard duty, Blue's two pups were set to watch both doors. Both would bark at anyone stepping outside the newly erected external walls of the house. Not that there was anywhere to go, as they were two day's walk to anywhere.

Blue slept outside the shack and stayed on guard over her family. Bea was only permitted onto the building site when accompanied by Ned, and even then, only if he needed to consult with her over the positioning of a wall or discuss some element of the rebuild. Bea noticed the new house was from the design she had sent of Jack's dream house, but with no second story.

One by one, the rooms took shape. All the time, the rains fell. The dry dirt was now a memory, and the glut of water turned to brown rivers of sludge, then later a flowing creek. The big dam was full again, and the creek flowed once more, but the rains didn't stop.

The torrent continued for one week, then two, until the yards and paddocks were mud pools as far as the eye could see. Bea smiled at the welcome sight. Dips in the fields were filled with brown muddy lakes of water. The paddocks themselves were sodden.

Billy had tried to move the bullock teams into the holding yard at the house, but there was no feed there for them. Bea watched him slide on the custard-like gloop. As Jack had said as he was leaving, Bea repeated, "Let them wander, Billy; they can't cross the grid."

He did. He dropped the sliprails in each paddock and let them roam.

Her horse Cassie, and Strawberry, with her latest calf, took refuge from the deluge on the verandah of their shack. When the rains started, Josie and Trixie headed to the back paddocks with their calves.

Billy and Netty decamped from their *gunya* onto the verandah.

Netty and Hannah were cooking for everyone. Alice was occupying the frustrated children as best she could. Edith even sat and told them some stories of Jack and Paul when they were young. Edith realised how few memories she had of her boys. She had never once visited them in the nursery. She had never been permitted to. However, she was sure Bea would have found a way. Netty was delighted at being back in the big kitchen. It was warm and dry.

After sixteen straight days of rain, they awoke to the sunshine. The ground was frozen solid, but the sky was clear.

Bea laughed as Strawberry decided she didn't mind being milked on the shack verandah. The path to the dairy was all but impassable; Bea didn't mind at all as she was very ungainly. Strawberry and her calf would present themselves for the morning ritual at her door.

Bobby had become a dab hand at the job of milking, and even little Jess helped. Strawberry had turned and licked the little girl when she started learning. Jess had given the gentle cow a big hug. The hug had become a regular occurrence before milking each morning. Jess took her three-legged orange stool, climbed up on it, and hugged the great horned beast before setting to work on the milking. Working on either side of the red cow, Bobby and Jess soon had enough milk stripped from their favourite farm animal. The other two cows had still not made a reappearance. With so many extra mouths to feed, all milk was consumed rather than made into cheese.

Edith watched on in awe as the children worked without instruction. Even Ed would sit beside Bobby and open his mouth. Bobby aimed the teat and squirted the warm milk directly into his little brother's mouth. More often than not, he missed; but it was a cause of great merriment for the children. Bea rarely needed to correct their behaviour or stop their harmless antics. During the enforced confinement, the children had not fought once. Instead of fighting, the family drew close. Bea taught them to play knuckle-bones and made them simple spinning toys with lengths of yarn and a button.

Most mornings, after the chores were done, Edith read Bible stories to the children while Bea carded a fleece and spun.

Every afternoon, Alice would come and give both ladies a break from the children. Bea would rest, and Edith would sew. She had cut up the most elaborate ball gown and made a new dress for her granddaughter. Jess had chosen this fancy peacock-coloured dress as she adored the colouring. It had once been Edith's favourite dress, yet she had willingly sacrificed it for her granddaughter, and the story times had made Edith realise that the children could not read. So, as she read to them with the three children sitting on her lap, their education began.

Chapter 17 A Fresh Start

*T*he day after the rains had stopped, Ned visited the shack.

Edith had been sitting reading to the children. Jess was getting changed after helping Bea milk Strawberry.

As Ned arrived, he heard Bobby say, "I love you now, Nana." The young boy had just thrown his arms around her neck and told her for the first time.

"I love you too, Bobby." Edith's eyes were glassy as she looked up and saw Ned.

With a smile, he asked, "Is Bea around, Edith? I have some news for her."

Edith returned his smile with a nod of acknowledgement. "She has gone to return the milking bucket to the dairy, Ned." Edith watched the handsome young man leave. If she had had a conversation like that in England, she would have given a deep curtsy and kept her head bowed while addressing him as sir. Here, she was on first-name terms with him and had not even stood when he entered.

Ned found his quarry standing in the yard with the bucket held firmly in her hands, and Blue, as usual, was at her side.

Bea was gazing at the sliprails and looking out over the muddy paddocks. She had her milking mob cap covering her hair and her special calico milking apron. Bea looked for all the world like any English milkmaid from home rather than co-owner of the beautiful valley she gazed so lovingly over. She was the picture of contentment, but Ned saw a wave of sadness cross her face. She looked almost forlorn.

Ned flicked his eyes to where she was looking. He noticed there was now a soft green blush on the paddock in the distance. He spoke softly, without wishing to startle her, "It's amazing how fast the grass can grow, isn't it? However, considering how cold it has been, I thought it would take longer than that to sprout."

Bea gave him a beatific smile. "Those are the potatoes, Ned. Jack didn't even get to harvest last year's crop. It just withered and died. I had no idea any had survived. The paddock beyond that is barley, and look, it's also growing. Jack dry-sowed a single paddock on the off-chance there would be rain. I thought the birds would have eaten all the seeds. But, Ned, it's sprouted. See the mantle of green on the hillside over there? And that one we call the cow paddock, but it's where the sheep have been last as it is fenced. They ate off the few bits that had grown; the heat got everything else. It's the only paddock that's secure enough for sheep."

Ned stood beside her and leaned on the railing. He noticed its wobble as they looked out over the greening valley. He watched the wave of emotions sweep across her face; a tear of sadness moved to a flicker of a frown. He knew she wished Jack was home to see their beautiful valley return to life. He said, "Bea, I've come to ask if you could tell us where you want the wardrobes."

Bea didn't reply. She met Ned's gaze with a steady look. She was sad, and she was lonely. She knew the crew had been busy but had no idea they were already at that stage. She silently returned the bucket to the dairy, and they left the dairy yard.

As they walked, Ned said, "I've been thinking about what you said about my lady love, Bea. I think I will ask to court her. Christina's year of mourning is up, and if I am careful, we might be able to see each other on the sly. You know what some catty people in town are like; they can't stop their tongues running away with them." Ned saw Bea's head lift, and she gave him a questioning look. Still, she remained silent.

He smiled. "Did I not say she was a gentleman's widow? Sorry!" He looked around to make sure no ears were listening, "She is, Bea, and a very beautiful one. If push comes to shove, she will also make a wonderful Duchess, but that's jumping ahead of myself somewhat. However, it is also something I must consider. If I marry, you know the role I could have if, God forbid, one day I inherit. Any whispers I have heard from home have not mentioned David's children. However, he's only a year older than me. He'll be around for many a year yet."

Bea nodded as she walked. "I do know, Ned. He certainly had none when I left, and Edith has not mentioned any. I presume Christina is not a convict?" Bea asked. She had stopped walking.

Keeping his voice low as they were closer to the house, he said, "No, they arrived free years ago, but her husband died. She's had a rough time, as I think he drank, and Elizabeth Macarthur said she had seen her with bruises on her. She was the person who drew my attention to her. I dare not tell Christina I know what she has endured, but she had no food and little money. After her husband died, just enough was left for her to buy the tiny cottage. I have recommended her as a piano teacher, and she also takes in sewing." As they were still standing in the yard, Ned said, "Bea, I have other brothers."

Bea nodded. "Yes, I know, but do they have the training for the role as you do? Ned, you know what may happen; therefore, you must have children to inherit after you."

Ned frowned. "Ahh! I see what you mean. But am I not too old for fatherhood?"

Bea gurgled a chuckle and answered simply with, "No!"

Ned continued to chat about other things as they approached the building. They walked up onto the verandah of the newly constructed homestead. Bea saw that the immense pile of assorted timber planks they had brought had dwindled to only a small stack. One team of carpenters was knocking up freestanding shelves from the remaining cedar slabs; another group was making wardrobes; a third group were working on a solid-looking dining table with elegantly shaped curved squared legs. The last group were making large bench seats that looked like church pews. There were two long ones and two shorter ones. Bea remained silent but took in the efforts of the team. She heard more hammering from inside. Various red-coated soldiers were either lolling against the new railings or holding timber planks for the workers. All were laughing or chatting freely with the prisoners. Ned had chosen this team well, as Bea knew other soldiers rarely offered to lift a finger to assist a convict.

Ned escorted Bea through the new extra-wide, double French doors into the main sitting-cum-lounge room. These doors had slats in them instead of glass panels. "Bea, you can replace these later, but this was the best the men could do without door glass. I did bring some completed windows, but not glass doors. Sorry, but that's all you'll have to purchase. The rest of the house is finished from your plan. The furniture they are making will see you through, but it will be usable and serviceable until you replace them." Ned explained guiltily. "Before we leave, I'll get them to bring up your old bed, plus bedding and all your possessions from the shack. We should be done and tidied up in a few days, Bea. You can then return home."

Bea touched his arm. "I am home, Ned. The shack is more a home to me than the old fancy house ever was. It is what I said to you before. Jack knew that, so he has not high-tailed it home to me. Not that he has had much time. He may not have even received my letter to say the house burnt down. This house is just as nice as the other one, but our shack is special. Jack and Billy built it themselves, with Majors Tim and Humphrey helping cut the wood. So the shack is where I feel closest to him. Bobby was nearly born there, and I thought this one might be." She rubbed her hand gently over her distended stomach. It was just over eight weeks until she would hold the new child in her arms.

Ned smiled; he was a little jealous that Jack would soon have his fourth child. Even Tim and Maddie had two now. This new house was fifty per cent larger than the old one. They were standing in a room with a twelve-foot ceiling. The new taller ceiling was lined with cedar panelling. The doors had opening vents above them, so the rooms could be closed off to keep the warmth in, but the vents also let out the summer heat.

Bea liked what she saw. It was similar to the old house but had improvements she had not even considered. Not only the vents, higher ceilings, two extra bedrooms and a summer sleep-out. "Ned, it's lovely. I love the smell of the timber too. It's clean and fresh and not whitewashed." She gazed around the room; the baby kicked as she turned. "I hope Jack makes it home in time for the arrival of this one," she murmured almost to herself. She gazed around the vast living room that shared the fire with the dining room. "It's wonderful, truly lovely. It's so much larger than before. We shall sit in here in comfort and pray for you. I love the opening vents. You've been here in summer and know how hot it gets. Ned, it's wonderful," she said as she walked through the rooms. "This is Jack's dream home, even to the summer sleep-out on the verandah."

They had just walked into the kitchen when they saw the red flag hoisted up the pole at the shop. "Look, I wonder what they want. That means urgent. Can you send someone up to ask?"

Ned had seen the white flag come down and the red one going up. "Great system, Bea!" He went to call for a soldier and then returned to her side.

They saw the mail carriage leave and head east along the road to Parramatta. Hopefully, it had brought news of Jack. Bea stood watching and waiting. Impatiently she moved outside on the new back verandah and stood waiting for the message to arrive.

Ned watched her face. It softened, and then a frown crossed her brow. It vanished as a smile hovered on her lips, and then her eyes filled with tears. The range of emotions she experienced in such a short time intrigued him, just as they had done earlier at the sliprails. He had never noticed a woman's face before Christina had come into his life. He felt slightly guilty as he had not even let Charles and Sal know about her. Unable to stay silent, he said comfortingly, "He'll be fine, Bea; I bet he's on his way. I presume you wrote and told him Edith had arrived?"

Bea nodded. "Yes, Ned, but I gave no information. My first note to him was an addition to a completed letter with just one line to say she was here. She then wrote, but it was as though a different person was here by then. Ned, she's changed so much. I'm worried about their reunion, for they must sort things out. She has nowhere else to go."

Ned gave a soft chortle, "She's certainly different from the few times I met her in England. I would never have expected her to be content in a log shack. She has finally won Bobby over, you know. I caught him throwing himself into her arms and telling her he loved her."

Bea smiled and gave a nod. She watched the long strides of the returning soldier. Ned could see her change feet in anticipation of the impending news. Her mind was still on Edith. "I've learned to love her too, Ned. I didn't think I would, but I do. I don't think she's ever been loved before. I'm not telling tales out of place when I say you know of my convictions and the following abuse on board?"

Ned nodded.

Bea continued, "Ned, it could well have been her; only her husband had the rights of matrimony to abuse her. It sort of makes sense of her treatment and neglect of the children. I know what she felt. They were both forced on her with much violence. They are a permanent physical reminder of the vile abuse she had suffered. She told me she had poured it out to Jack in her letter as she knew he needed to know before coming home. Ned, I don't know how he'll cope with the news that both Paul and he were unwanted by her. I at least know my mother cared enough for me that she left me safe and warm at a church; otherwise, I would have been thrown in the river, like so many other babies. I can never thank her enough for that, for it showed that she cared. It was more care than Jack's parents gave him."

Ned was reeling at her words. Coming from a loving family, he found it hard to understand. He was stunned that Edith had been raped too.

The soldier arrived puffing and handed her a letter with familiar writing. She nodded thanks to the man, then turned her back to them to read her letter. Her hands were shaking as she flicked open the seal. She saw that Jack had filled every skerrick of paper available.

My darling wife, the delight of my eyes and desire of my heart,

I am writing to tell you that we are on the way home. Mother's letter reached us the day after yours. I prayed hard when I read your single line. I could not even admit to Hugh that she had come. I can imagine your shock. My sweet love, I hope her attitude has changed as her letter seems to show. Somehow, I doubt it, but I shall hold my judgement until we meet. I won't write more of this now.

My darling girl, I will never do this again. The stock is not worth the time apart from you and the children. I have had much time to think and pray while dawdling behind the mob. The light is fading, so I will write more tomorrow.

He had written more the following day.

My darling heart,

I have just received your letter about the fire. Sweetheart, are you sure you are safe and well? The mail also included another letter from Mother, admitting it was all her fault. To say I am angry is a vast understatement. How dare she ignore your instructions about leaving candles unattended? I hope you have written to Ned and let him know about your predicament.

Sweet Bea, we have had to while away time while finding feed for the mob. We have wandered over hill and dale in the area and went slightly east of Wagga Wagga to a gully called Sandy Creek. I saw a familiar twinkling in the sunlight that caught my attention; you know of my activities in our creek at home. With just my frying pan, Hugh and I decided to test the gravel in the stream. Guess what, my beloved? Our saddle bags are now well-balanced and weighed down. I shall bank my share so we have some security behind us. As there are only the two of us now (the other fellow has returned home), we have gone halves in what we have found. This discovery must also be kept quiet, and once smelted, no one will know its origin. This bounty will allow us both to restock fully.

Bea gasped. Ned looked at her, concerned but saw a huge grin on her face. "Bea, is everything all right?"

She looked up at him, her eyes misty with happiness. "Yes, Ned, everything is fine." She looked around to make sure they were not overheard. "They found more gold, Ned, lots of it. It's not just here in our creek but in other areas." Bea knew that Ned knew about the mineral finds in their own creek. He had even done a bit of panning with Jack on one visit. Those finds had kept the farm going for the first year when the drought hit. Ned had slowly been cashing in the tiny ingots that Jack had made; however, they were now gone. The twenty pounds had been the last of their money.

Jack could only pan their creek while the tribe was on a walkabout, as it was in the same area as their camp. Billy knew of its presence and sometimes came and helped, but he could not see the use of the golden dust. To him, it was just heavy yellow dirt.

Bea's eyes returned to the letter. She saw that the following paragraph was written a few days later.

Sweet Bea, we have left the South and are en route home. By the time you receive this, I will post this in either Young or Cowra or possibly even near Bathurst. From there, we should be only a week away as we find that the rains went through here some weeks ago, and there is plenty of grass along the roadway. I wish I had Strawberry with us to lead the way home at a quicker pace.

My darling girl, I can't wait to hold you in my arms and declare my unending love. I must say that if my Mother is causing you any problems, I shall send her away. Your last letter told of her invaluable assistance at this time, but leopards rarely change their spots. Only with God's help would that happen. I do wish I could hurry time. Be assured that I love you and look forward to our reunion very soon.

Your loving and lonely husband
Jack.

Bea lifted her head smiling. She was so pleased that Jack had continued her reading lessons. "He should be here soon, Ned. He's coming home." She released a long sigh of contentment.

"Wonderful news, Bea, as I don't like leaving you here alone. I thought I still may stay until he returns." He knew that some of the men working on the property were soon to be released, and they knew she was here all but alone. With Edith in residence, they would be adequately chaperoned. He was worried as she was vulnerable. Harrison and Billy would be no match for a violent, virile ex-convict. "Bea, if Jack ever does have to leave again, consider going with him or employ a young man or two to guard you."

"He said he won't go droving again, Ned. Ever!" Her eyes were dancing with delight.

Throughout the rest of the day, the hammering and sawing continued. The pile of timber planks had dwindled to almost nothing.

Bea knew that Ned would soon leave, but having him close had been lovely. He, too, enjoyed talking to her about things he could discuss with no other. He couldn't even speak to Charles and Sal about Christina, his family, and their societal position. Only Bea would understand his reasons for confiding in her. She knew he was a titled lord, and she realised he could never marry a convict, or a woman with a tainted past, as she would never be accepted if he became the Duke.

With a light and happy heart, Ned realised he wished to see Christina and progress their friendship to the next stage. He could then retire with a clear conscience and court her as he desired.

By the time the sun was overhead, the mud had solidified. After being stuck inside for nearly two weeks, the children were allowed out to run and play.

The farm was slowly coming back to life. That morning a chicken in a hidden clutch of eggs hatched. Bea had not even missed the broody red hen.

That morning the green valley also saw the return of Bruce, leading the two runaway cows and the half-grown calves. The warmer weather after the rains had made the green tinge turn to a thick velvet mantle.

Once again, the crickets and frogs were heard every night. The birds called their dawn chorus in the mornings again. Life had returned to their home, but Jack was still missing.

The children loved helping their mother. Bobby and Jess stripped the milk from Strawberry very quickly. With the two cows returning, the children milked the three cows each morning. They handled the extra work with joy and song as they worked, just as their mother did. Once the children had finished the milking, they left the clean-up to Bea and returned to rescue their Nana from Ed. The three children adored her now.

Bea sent the two older children to the shack and once more took her place at the sliprails as she went to return the empty bucket. She bent her head and prayed for Jack. As she prayed, her eyes rested on the verdant hills. The valley beyond looked like it was shrouded in a green gossamer veil. Bea was amazed at the growth in just one day; she stood gazing at the beautiful sight. She had once seen a shawl that was the glorious colour of the fields, and it was made from cashmere and had been so soft to her touch. With a sigh, Bea turned to walk to the shack. She had noticed that Ned had sent someone to fix the wobbling post. She smiled at his thoughtfulness.

That day, Ned gave the order for the clean-up to start. The pack-up would take at least a day, possibly two. The team still had the furniture to complete, which would hopefully be done by tomorrow.

Those men who were not building were set to work moving stores. Ned arranged that all the food taken to the shop after the fire be returned to the main kitchen. Once done, they set about scrubbing the scorched implements. The furniture and personal possessions in the shack and Edith's heavy scorched cases had to be moved back into the house. Ned planned their departure for the following day.

The team then moved the family's remaining possessions to the new house. Netty and Billy didn't take long before moving some of their things from the verandah back into the shack, but not their sleeping mat. They would stay close until the builders left.

Netty told Ned, "We not tell Missus Bea, but gunya fall down in the rain. We sleep in the smokehouse before we move to verandah. We stay close tonight, then move back to Mister Jack's shack." She put her finger to her lips. "Shh, no tell. She got nuff worry, Mister Neddy. All good as Mister Jack, he come real soon; one day, maybe, two!"

Ned smiled knowingly. He had never known their knowledge to be wrong. He had one of the bullock wagons pushed to the side of the verandah. Throughout the day, the men loaded the wagons with the tools no longer needed. The long-horned bullocks wouldn't be brought from the front yard until the team was ready to leave.

Bea knew that Ned was wonderfully thoughtful, even thinking of bringing feed for the big beasts. The giant animals were gentle, and the wagon drivers even allowed the children to pat them as they fed the hungry beasts hay.

With the work all but done, Ned seconded the assistance of two burly convicts, and Bea pointed out a large keg of home-brew ginger beer. It had fermented a little too long and was a potent brew. She knew the men would like it as it had fully fermented. She had completely forgotten about it until now, but the treat was well received.

At dusk, the workmen and soldiers huddled around a big bonfire. Billy had not burned it before as he had used whatever he could. During the clean-up, they threw all the offcuts from the new works and things destroyed in the fire on a massive pile in the middle of the back roadway.

On the final night, they planned to light the bonfire.

Ned had the men sleep on the verandah for the last night rather than put the tents back up.

Netty fed them kangaroo tail stew and damper, followed by treacle dumplings with fresh clotted cream. She and Hannah had been busy cooking up a feast. Some of the food had a slightly smoky flavour but was still edible. The underground cellar still had potatoes in storage; even a few turnips were left and added to the stew. After the big meal, they all settled for the night.

The new doors had internal bolts on them, Ned didn't tell Bea, but he had purchased those from Thomas Tindale and Eddie himself, so he could be sure she could be kept safe. Ned insisted that Bea and Edith lock themselves inside the new homestead for the night while the convicts were still around, especially after imbibing the somewhat potent ginger brew. The doors would have been closed anyway, as it was cold, but with convict men and soldiers so close, he did not wish to put his friend's family at risk. Once again, the three dogs were on guard. The house fell quiet as, one by one, they slept.

Bea lay on the feather mattress in their huge new bedroom, thinking about the last few months. The smell of the new cedar timber reminded her of the day she had Bobby. The first homestead had been new back then, and now just over five years later, she lay alone waiting for the birth of their fourth child. Eventually, she slept.

The sounds of snoring soldiers and convicts broke the stillness, but everyone slept on peacefully; all enjoyed the dreamless sleep of exhaustion. Blue had taken up her guard spot outside Bea's French window, and not even the children would gain access without her four-legged angel stirring and rousing the entire household.

Again, the pre-dawn chorus of birds woke the household and stirred the morning into action. Netty and Billy were up first, and soon the chimneys were puffing belches of smoke. Netty put the massive vat of barley porridge on to cook. Billy tidied up the last of their things on the verandah and took them to the shack. Bea was up, and by the time she had her morning mug of tea, Bobby and Jess were at her side and ready to help with the milking. The morning ritual got underway.

Bea heard the activity outside of the house but stayed well clear. The last two weeks had been wonderful, as Ned's presence had given her a sense of security. Bea hadn't even realised how being here alone had weighed so heavily on her.

Bobby and Jess had only taken thirty minutes to relieve the cows from their milk, and this morning Netty wished for some of it to be taken to the kitchen. Billy waited and returned with the children, carrying the full pail of frothy white milk.

Relieved of any duty, Bea took time to be alone to take her place at the sliprail and pray. Today she had a smile hovering on her lips. Her prayers had been answered; the rains had come, and Jack was coming home. For some reason, this morning, she decided to drop the last sliprail on Thunderbolt's yard. This rail had been lifted when Ned had the post repaired. As the holding yard was next to the dairy, she subconsciously prepared for Jack's homecoming. She even put some fodder in the trough. Her heart was racing; she found it hard to catch her breath. The baby moved, and she placed her hands on her stomach.

In the distance, she could hear a horse coming down the road at pace. Not an unusual sound in itself, but Billy was in the kitchen, so she knew it wasn't him, and none of the soldiers had horses.

She listened with only half an ear as it neared. She turned to watch, but the sound died. The house had muffled the hoofbeats. A frown crossed Bea's brow; who would be riding like that? Was there an emergency? She thought the lathered horse looked like Thunderbolt, but the filthy bearded man on him couldn't be Jack. He wasn't due home for a week.

Then welcome surprise finally sank in; it *was* Jack. He looked like a dirty version of the first time she had seen him. His beard was scruffy, and his hair matted, but he was home.

He threw himself off the horse and gathered her into his arms for a long whiskery kiss.

He was home, and he was safe.

Bea was weeping and laughing all at once. Finally, she managed to say, "Oh, Jack, I missed you so much."

He held her at arm's length, then cupped her beautiful face before gathering her to him and kissing her as he had never done before. "I missed you so much too. I couldn't wait for Hugh; he'll be along later with our flock. My darling, wonderful wife, I love you so very much. You, my darling wife, are the delight of my eyes and my heart's desire. I wrote that in my letter, but I mean every word. And Bea, I will never leave you again. My droving days are over. Unless you are on the saddle in front of me, as you were on that very first trip, I'll not go away again."

There was no more talking for some time as they relished the welcome.

Chapter 18 Home Sweet Home

*T*hey were unaware that they were being observed by not just Edith and their children but Netty, Ned, and most of the workmen were watching too.

Netty's giggle finally broke them apart. She had appeared at the homestead railing next to Ned. "See, Mister Neddy, I say Mister Jack come real soon."

Jack turned to see who was there. With Bea tucked under his arm, Jack patted Thunderbolt and released him into the yard. He noticed that there was both food and water for his steed.

He was about to lift the railing when Billy appeared from nowhere and said, "You leave him with me, Mister Jack; I fix him real good." Jack shook his hand and led Bea to the house.

Jack smiled. "Not too good, Billy; leave him saddled, as I have to return and help Hugh bring in the mob."

Jack noted the bonfire embers as he left the holding yard. "Looks like you had a bit of fun recently."

Bea was almost bouncing with excitement. "Yes, Ned and Billy arranged a clean-up of all the scraps and fire leftovers. We had a big bonfire last night." He had not even looked at the house as he passed. He had seen wagons, but all else vanished when he saw Bea's mob cap at the sliprails. He now stood looking at the rebuilt house of his dreams; only then did he notice the people on the verandah. He lifted his hand in a wave, unable to put off the forthcoming meeting any longer; they walked arm in arm to join them.

The three children raced into his arms as he reached the steps. One by one, he kissed them. Jess was garbed in her new peacock-coloured teal-green dress.

Jack recognised the material and gasped; it was made from his mother's favourite ball gown. His eyes flew to the woman on the verandah.

She was wearing one of Bea's drill work dresses. She had pulled her long fair hair back into a serviceable bun and was grinning at him.

He reluctantly mounted the stone steps to meet his mother.

Bea saw his face. "Jack, come and let me introduce you to someone. You have never met this woman, but she wants to make your acquaintance. By the way, she left her evil twin in England, either that or threw her overboard halfway." She giggled while pulling Jack's hand towards the verandah.

Ned stood back to let them pass. Jack stopped and took his hand, squeezed it warmly but passed without comment. His smile said more than was required. He needed to do this and move on.

As he reached his mother, he felt Bea tug his arm. "She's changed, Jack, really changed. Trust me."

Jack stood before his mother and didn't know what to say or do. He looked at Bea, then at his mother. Should he shake hands? Hug her? Bea motioned for him to do the latter. He gave a subtle nod and coldly embraced his mother for the first hug he had ever received from her.

Edith broke. Her tears flowed as she hugged Jack back. She muttered, "I'm sorry, Jacky, I'm so sorry," into his shoulder over and over and over.

Jack met Bea's eyes over his mother's head. The pleading look on his face was one of utter confusion.

Bea touched Edith's wet cheek with a hooked finger. "Edith, let's go inside in private." Bea motioned to Ned to follow.

Edith pulled herself from her son's arms.

Jack flinched; Bea called his mother by her Christian name. No one did that, ever. Maybe things had changed, and hopefully, for the better. Jack escorted his wife and mother away from the prying eyes of the building team. Ned followed with the children.

Netty was awaiting them with the tea tray. In her sing-song voice, she said, "Mister Neddy, I told you, Mister Jack come home real soon." She threw her head back and laughed.

Bea's family was back together again; she had not been this happy since the birth of their third child.

Netty took Ed from Bea and motioned for the children to follow her to the kitchen. As the door closed behind them, Edith sat and patted the seat beside her. Jack reluctantly came at her bidding. This new mother of his would take much getting used to. They had never had a relationship of any sort. He had always been an encumbrance and an unwanted one at that. Her first words floored him.

"Jack, I love you. I always have but didn't know how to, nor was I permitted to show it." While sitting on the edge of her seat, Edith continued, "Son, I arrived unannounced on Bea's doorstep to find you gone. For the first three weeks, she did not speak to me. No one did, and I was hurt. I shouldn't have been, as it was virtually the same treatment I gave you boys. In my short time here, Bea's silence broke through the tough protective shell I had carefully built around myself. No words could penetrate my shield. I discovered that you couldn't fight a war when the enemy didn't attack. Jack, a battle raged within me. I discovered that the war I was in was facing the wrath of God. I let both of you boys down badly. Initially, I had no choice, but as you grew and when your father was away, I could have tried, but I didn't. I told you in my letter what had happened, and with Paul's death, I fled. I had nowhere else to go. I don't know what I expected, but a conversation of some sort would have been nice. Bea withheld even that, and I'm glad she did. It didn't take long living here with her to see her love for God and her family, and Ned, that includes you too. The welcome you received on arrival was as part of her extended family. I was still well on the outer."

Bea looked guilty. "I never had a mother, Edith, and I had dreamed of finding mine and knowing she loved me. I didn't understand your reasons. I'm so sorry."

Edith smiled at her beloved daughter-in-law. "Don't be, sweet girl. Your very few words made me rethink everything. Then one day, I found you asleep with a Bible on your lap. I recognised it as the one I'd given Jack at his Confirmation." Edith met Jack's gaze.

His face was like a blank canvas. Even Bea could not read what he was feeling. She motioned for Edith to continue.

Edith gave a nod of acknowledgement to Bea and continued her explanation. "Bea told me of your words, 'The wrath of God is God's love meeting sin.' Jack, I only knew of God's wrath; and little else but that. I didn't know of His love or His forgiveness. Then I burnt the house down. Bea wasn't angry at me. I saved what I could, but she didn't want possessions; it was just you, Jack. I could have dealt with anger. I deserved it; I could have dealt with hate; I knew that well too. But forgiveness was foreign to me. Then, I found myself sleeping on a mattress on the floor; I thought all my worldly possessions were gone. Jack, I realised I was happy for the very first time in my life. Little Ed's love was unconditional. But Jess was quite happy to tear into me if I did something wrong, but Bobby just saw I made his mother unhappy, and he stayed distant. I knew I must change. So, I did. I cast off the old me and wrote to you. Only yesterday did I get my first hug from Bobby."

Bea moved to the bench seat beside Jack and took his other hand. "She really has changed, Jack. I didn't intend to be so mean, but I wasn't coping with everything. She arrived when I was at my lowest. One more mouth to feed, one more day without you, and one more day without rain. And I was so tired with this child." She rubbed her swollen stomach. "But I could not rest. I could not understand her rejection of you and Paul. I adore our children, so I could not understand her rejection of her family. So, I didn't even speak to her."

Again, Bea met Edith's glance and saw her nod to continue.

Bea knew that Ned knew of her abuse as a convict. Long ago, she had also told him that she had lost a child as a result. Bea now realised that Edith would have had the same feelings for the children she carried against her will. When she realised she was with child that first time, she had a sense of both anger and detachment from something that had been forced upon her. "Jack, eventually, we talked and shared. The scales fell from both our eyes. I have seen a new Edith growing in the weeks since Ned and his team arrived. It started with your ball gown, Edith. I cried to myself when I found you had cut that up. I have dreamed of owning a gown like that so I could wear it just for Jack. But you cut it up like you were shredding your old life."

Edith smiled. "That, my dear, is exactly what I was doing, and it felt so good. Jack, you would know that particular gown. It's why I brought it with me. I wore it often, as it was the only one I was allowed to choose for myself. My husband gave me little free will throughout our marriage. Strangely enough, it was why that dress was given away first. Because with the new me, this was to be my choice. Eustace had forced everything on me, so that dress, my favourite gown, my only free selection, had to go." Edith looked at the three pairs of eyes fixed on her. "I hope you will let me stay, Jack, and be part of the family, for I've never had that before, and I find I quite like it. However, I also want to hear more about how God can continue to change me, for I know I need that even more."

Bea squeezed Jack's hand and said, "I'd like her to stay, Jack."

Jack's heart was hurting. He wished to lash out at his mother for the hurt she had inflicted on him for so long, yet he knew he both shouldn't and couldn't. He swallowed his pride, turned back to his mother, and said, "If Bea is happy, then I am happy. Mother, she and our children are my priority. I just want you to know that."

Edith nodded; she was content with that. Only time would prove she really had changed. All heard her sigh with relief.

With the heavy explanations done, Jack turned to Ned. "I hopefully will get a chance to talk to you, Ned. I saw you packing up, but can you stay? You have no idea how comforting it was to know that Bea could, and did, turn to you for help."

Ned met his query with a smile. "We were leaving today, but I think I will still send them off without me. I might stay on if I may. Hugh must still bring his flock home; I will help him from here. It's a long time since I spent days in the saddle. I will ache, but I will love it." Ned grinned, "You see, as of today. I'm officially retired."

Jack flinched in surprise.

Ned grinned. "Bea will fill you in if I don't get the chance, but there's a good reason, Jack, a very good one. And Bea, thanks to you, I will take your advice as soon as I return." Ned's dimples appeared as he met Bea's eyes; they danced happily as he grinned.

Jack rose, not letting go of Bea's hand. "Come on, show me through our new house. It looks like we are all in for a fresh start." Jack drew Bea to him and, regardless of the two watching them, proceeded to kiss his wife again. "I missed you so much," he said eventually.

The emotions that surged through the two people watching them were vastly different.

Edith watched with relief. Although she was somewhat jealous that she had never had love such as theirs.

Ned watched with compassion mixed with anticipation. Yes, he would return and ask to court Christina, even if it needed to be in secret. The excitement of this event was mounting within him. One day soon, he wished to draw Christina into his arms and kiss her like this. Ned knew he must protect her reputation. Hopefully, he could pull off what amounted to an almost illicit relationship. He was sure Charles would notice a change in his attitude. It was so lovely that Jack and Bea were in on his secret. He would have told Marcus and Jess if they had still been here, but they were now back in England. As he stood, he said, "Leave off, Jack; I will get jealous." He said it with a laugh. "Come and look through your new house. Bea sent me a plan from your farm journal."

Jack admired the new house's solid construction and was impressed by the vents above the doors. He was thrilled that the double fireplace he had designed for the first house had survived the fire. "Darling Bea, I agree with you, my sweet; this is a house. It's a wonderful house, Ned, but Bea and I were so happy in my shack. However, here we can help people." Jack spoke as they opened one of the visitor's rooms. He saw the mattress on the floor and his mother's familiar, slightly singed, travelling cases. One chest was open, and he realised it was a travelling chest with drawers and even a large hook off the side to hang her clothing from. Jack turned and looked at his mother. He raised his eyebrows questioningly.

Edith met his look with a chuckle and said, "Jacky, it's easier for the children to get into, but I believe Ned has a team making a bed frame with the last of the timber they brought. I said it was only to be done if there was enough left after everything else was completed."

Jack didn't know what to say, so he remained silent. He could not believe that his mother had put herself last. That was so unlike the woman he knew in England.

Ned silently slipped away as they were talking.

After seeing every room, Jack said, "I must go and help Hugh with the mob. Sweet Bea, your runt dogs have been amazing. They do the work of six men each and cause much less trouble. Plus, they also keep us warm at night."

"I'll walk you to the sliprails." Bea knew Jack had to go, but he would return in a few hours. She could cope with that.

As soon as they were out of earshot of the house, Jack asked, "What's with Ned? Why has he retired?"

Bea was almost bouncing with happiness. "He's found someone named Christina, and he's going home to court her. Jack, I'm so delighted. I think that it's why he has sold out. When he arrived, he couldn't wait to tell me about her, but he had decided not to do more than stay friends with her. I think I have persuaded him to take it to the next step. He said he didn't have the money and tried to say he was too old, but I pointed out that I was happier in the shack even before the house burnt down. And two can live as cheaply as one in a single house; it would halve the costs. We all want and need to be loved; I think God built that into us all. I think of it as a God-size hole in each of us. I also pointed out to him that he could care for her much more easily if they were married. She is all but next door to his new cottage."

Jack had time enough only to say, "Wow!" before they arrived at the holding yard. He was surprised to find Ned was up on Cassie and Billy on the nameless old nag. Both were waiting and ready to help the drove.

Ned was holding Thunderbolt's reins.

Jack quickly kissed Bea. "Until later, my sweet. I'll want a long bath and a shave as I refused to go to that barber in Bathurst." He chuckled as he mounted.

The three rode off and out of the side front gate. Billy had swung the main gate over the grid so the side access into the farm was now awaiting the animals to come home.

Ned had left them earlier to tell Captain Phil Bryant he was now in charge and to take the team back to Parramatta. He would stay to assist with the mob. Even before leaving Parramatta, Phil suspected Ned would likely remain with the family. Phil knew Ned had sold out but not the reason why. He wondered if Bea was the reason, especially as she was alone, but Bea's passionate welcome of Jack blew away that idea.

Phil harnessed up the bullocks; Edith's bed frame only needed a few finishing touches. By the time the carpenters had the bed completed, the wagons would be ready to roll.

Netty loaded them up with fresh bread and food for the trip. The team headed out the main side gate mid-morning. The bullock wagons would travel even slower than the mob of sheep; Ned and Hugh may even catch them before they got to Penrith.

Ned smiled at what he called his dereliction of duty. The weight of leadership was now lifted from his shoulders, and he was once more with friends. He relaxed.

Billy rode on ahead to go to Hugh's aid. He sat upright and was rock solid in the saddle, even at full gallop.

As they rode, Ned said to Jack, "I should feel guilty to have sold out early, Jack, but I don't; I feel free. I'll be on hand to help Charles at the inn if required. His leg healed, but he now has a pronounced limp." He glanced at his friend before saying, "Bea had made me see that I must commit to the next stage in my life. Hopefully, she has told you that I have met someone and, on my return, will ask to court Christina." The delight at the smile he saw on his friend's face brought him comfort. "So, you don't think I'm too old? I turn forty in October this year."

Jack threw back his head and laughed. "Not likely, Ned! This is wonderful news. I gather she's not a convict. Knowing what is possibly ahead of you."

Ned shook his head. "No, she's a gentleman's widow. She came free with her husband, who was landed gentry. She doesn't talk about him. I haven't told Christina what I've heard, but I understand she's been through a terrible time. Elizabeth Macarthur filled me in some years ago. That was before I had even met Christina. Her husband was a drunkard, and, from what I have heard, he was an unpleasant fellow with a tendency to violence once he had consumed a few or more drinks. Elizabeth had business dealings with William Meadows and had warned me about his temper. I had heard of him but had no idea it had also led to violence against his wife. Christina will not say a thing against him, although she rarely speaks of those years. While John Macarthur was away in England, Elizabeth went on a visit to their farm; it was there that she saw Christina after William had taken to her with his fists one day. I, therefore, watched over Christina when she arrived in town because of what Elizabeth told me. At first, we would only meet at church, but it didn't take long before I realised I wanted to be close to her. Knowing she was short of cash, I recommended her to friends for some work like teaching piano, sewing and the like, but I've been unable to do much more. I still only get to walk her home from church, as any more will bring gossip for us both."

Jack was thrilled for his friend. He knew about some females Ned had befriended, but all had been convicted women. None had dented Ned's defensive armour. "Ned, I want you to be as happy as I am. Bea is serious when she says she is happier in the shack than in the house. I'm sure Christina will be much the same, especially if she has had it tough. Don't hold back, Ned."

Ned said, "I won't, Jack, but I won't rush things either. When I realised how deeply I felt for her. I purchased the cottage all but next door to her so I could be close at hand; I told you about that, but not why. Charles thought it was because it was near to them. It took time to process my retirement. I was going to stay on here with Bea for a while to deal with Edith, but she has that under control." The two fell into a companionable silence as they rode, both deep in thought about the women in their lives. After some time, Ned said, "Jack, I wonder if your mother had a similar experience to Christina. If so, then the woman you knew is dead. Edith has changed, trust me. I met your mother in London, and that facade is well buried."

Jack doubted if the woman he called Mother could change. He wondered if too much water had gone under that bridge. "We'll see," was his non-committal answer. They rode on silently.

By mid-afternoon, they had met Hugh, and after their arrival, they picked up the pace of the mob. The grass beside the road was long and had not been grazed since they left. Jack realised that until the paddocks grew, he would have to let the mob feed along the verges for a few weeks. He could be home each night and in his warm bed with his wife beside him. The desire inside him grew. He was keen to return home, but work needed to come first.

About fifteen minutes from home, Ned came close and quietly spoke to Jack about his mother. "Jack, if Edith has been through what Christina has, she may not wish to speak about it, but it would explain much. Bea also had a bad time that way, but she's strong. But I emphasise that I have noticed a dramatic change in her."

Jack was torn; his anger at his parents boiled over. He almost spat his following words. "Ned, you don't know what living in a war zone was like. I know they hated each other, but we had no idea we were, in reality, the product of Father's violent temper; you met him; you know what he was like. How do I reconcile the new person at home with the one I hated for years? How do I treat her as though nothing has happened? She had many opportunities to explain, and she never did. And yet, how do I cope with being the product of what is, in effect, legal rape?" The growl of pain he released came from deep within. "Paul obviously couldn't; did you know he shot himself?" Jack was gutted, and he felt ill when he thought about it. He had not even told Hugh what was going on at home.

Ned was worried for his friend. He hoped that Hugh would stay a night or two so he could talk to him longer. It would be good if he could talk and pray with his friend. "Jack, there is only one way through this, and that's with prayer and then forgiveness."

At that moment, a few sheep broke away, and they had to stop them from doubling back on the mob. The dogs set off after them and soon had them rejoin the flock. Ned had caught a fleeting glance from Jack before he kicked Thunderbolt to chase the rogue sheep. Ned thought that if looks could kill, he would be dead. There was almost venom dripping from Jack's eyes. Ned was stunned. He was now determined that he must stay to sort this out. This was not like Jack. He ached for him and what he was dealing with. Jack didn't join Ned again, but Ned wasn't surprised. He knew that Jack's faith would be challenged. He must face the raw truth and forgive his mother, and he would not like to do it either. Edith needed to make her home with him, and Jack had to work through it.

Ned slowly made his way towards Hugh; he would ensure they stayed a couple of days and see if they could sort it out. Ned tried to sound breezy, but he didn't feel it. "Hello, Hugh, I haven't had a chance to chat much, but I'm coming back to Orchard Hills with you if that's all right. I'll ride one of your horses if that's okay?"

Hugh was delighted to see his friend. "I'd love that, Ned, and yes, I have three nags that should carry your weight. You should have seen them when we found them. I think the stallion has some Arab in him. I intend to breed him. All the horses but my own steed were from an abandoned farm, along with a paddock full of sheep and a few skinny cows. As we passed by, they broke the fence down and followed. We were going to take them anyway, as the farmer next door was going to shoot them to save them from suffering." Hugh pointed out which beasts they had adopted. "You should have seen them, Neddy, all skin and bone and barely able to walk." They chatted about the trip then Hugh asked, "What's eating you, Ned?"

Ned gave a sideways glance to his friend. Jack was well out of earshot with Billy. "Did Jack tell you his mother is here?"

Hugh almost fell from his horse. "Cor! Lady Edith is here? No, seriously? Not a word, Ned!"

Ned nodded, "Yes, she arrived unannounced and was still the abrasive, rude woman we knew in London."

"Blimey," said Hugh, then added, "Oh, poor Bea!"

Ned realised that Jack was now the Baron and, therefore, Lord John. But he owned nothing but a walnut farm that would not produce for at least ten years. Knowing Hugh would understand the ramifications, he continued, "Lord Eustace is dead, and so is Paul. He was rolled up and shot himself, well, that and other reasons." It was not his place to tell Hugh what Jack had just said. "It was that or the Fleet Prison. According to Bea, Edith has undergone a change since her arrival. I've been with a convict team there for over two weeks, staying with Bea and rebuilding the house Edith accidentally burnt down. I have certainly seen a difference in even those two weeks." He fell silent.

Hugh again looked over at Ned. "And...?"

Ned smiled; Hugh had fallen into the local habit of saying little but asking much. "And... Jack just looked at me with daggers when I said he had to forgive her."

"Ahh," said Hugh. "So, we hang around for a couple of days and see if we can sort them out?"

Ned nodded, "Could you? Would you mind?"

Hugh chuckled. "I wouldn't miss this showdown for the world, Neddy. I'm game for it."

"Hugh, you really will not recognise her. We must make Jack realise that God has touched her heart." Hugh's grin of delight made Ned release his held breath.

"She's that different? Seriously? How?" Hugh asked. "I was the one who wrote to her about Bea, so I sort of feel responsible."

Ned dipped his head in acknowledgement that he knew that; Bea had told him. He replied, "Bea did it in her own beautiful way!" He chuckled, "She didn't talk to Edith for over three weeks after she arrived. I don't think any conversation would have made the same change. The silence broke down Edith's defences quicker than anything else could have done. Bea was soldiering on, coping with a farm in drought, three children, and another growing child within her, and then Edith's violent, tumultuous arrival happened. Then she burnt the house down. Did Bea complain or abuse her? No, she hugged the woman. She put Jack's teaching into action, and Edith changed. Truly, you wait. You won't recognise her, even to Edith Barnes wearing drill and calico." He paused before adding, "Bea's not going to like that she now had a title, you know."

Hugh nearly choked, laughing. "I know, but I don't think Jack will tell her. He won't go back, so what's the point of her knowing?" They came to the top of the rise and saw the luxurious green valley before them. The grass was now ankle-deep in the few days that had passed since the rain stopped. Hugh gasped. "No wonder Jack wanted this place; it looks like Eden now, but Ned, you should have seen it when he first showed me the place about seven years ago. He had to clear all the rubbish and dead trees before making it look like this." He glanced at Ned. "Sounds like Edith's life, doesn't it? Now all the dead stuff is gone; she's changed too."

"Exactly, Hugh! If only we can make Jack see it." Ned kicked his horse to drive the mob inside the open gate at the farm.

With the arrival of the eclectic herd, the house and all those in it were soon a hive of activity. The animals were left to wander where they wished. The sheep took off into the barley crop, and Billy closed the gate. Jack noticed but let them go. He had more significant problems to deal with. Knowing Bea awaited him, he turned and went inside. Jack managed to avoid his mother as he walked toward his room. He had just reached their bedroom door when words from his past assailed his ears. However, they were not said in the same tone, nor were they spat at him as they used to be.

"John Robert Barnes, please come here." Edith stood at the door of her room across the corridor.

Jack slowly turned and faced his maternal nemesis. His heart was pounding, and his mouth was dry. The emotions of yesteryear came rolling over him like a tidal wave. He stood before his mother like a chastised, overgrown little boy. He obeyed her as he always did. "Yes, Mother," was all he said.

Edith recognised the stance of her now-grown son. "Jacky, it's over twenty years since I last spoke those words, but I must sort this out before Ned and Hugh leave. Because I will leave with them rather than hurt the family you have built." She saw a look of stunned amazement on his face.

"What?" The single-word question was forced from him in a strangled voice.

Edith smiled shyly. "I mean it, Jacky, I'll ride one of Hugh's horned cows if I need to, and I will go to their place, then I will find a job somewhere as a governess. I'll leave if I have to either walk all the way and sleep on the roadside as they do, or as I said, I'll ride one of those horned beasts and do it astride in a calico gown if I need to, but I'll go without a fuss. Jack, Bea is everything I could want in a wife for you. I love her so much." Edith saw Bea standing at their bedroom door and beckoned her over.

Jack watched as his wife walked to his side. She slid her arms around his waist. Bea looked up at his worried face. "Jack, listen to her."

Jack's astonished gaze turned back to his mother.

Edith saw Bea nod for her to continue. "Son, Bea taught me about forgiveness and being washed clean. She can also tell you that I was the same shrew I was in London and at home. Yes, when I arrived, I was still the same horrible person that you knew. But I really have changed, Jack. I ask that you give me a chance, son. Give me a week or a month; then, if you want me to leave, I will go. And I'll go without argument. But I don't want to leave, Jacky; I want to be part of your wonderful family. I want to be loved and cherished, but above all, I want and need to be forgiven. I realise I'm a work in progress, but I acknowledge that I need to start afresh and become a new person. I didn't like who I was, Jacky, but I find I quite like the new me." She looked up at him somewhat nervously. "All I can say is that I beg your forgiveness; if not, then I plead for your mercy."

Jack looked at Bea, then said to his mother, "I will not have Bea or the children hurt or upset in any way. If Bea wishes for you to stay, then you may; but know this, Mother, she is the most important person in my life. Bea married me thinking I was a mere drover; she had no idea of my status or that I was The Honourable John Barnes. She loves me because I'm me, just Jack. I would do anything to make her happy." He drew Bea closer to him.

Edith gave a long sigh of relief. "So would I, and I know that, Jack. I promise that, and I will ask again in a month and get your final answer."

Jack felt Bea's hand pushing him to hug his mother. He didn't, but he did gather them into a group hug. "A month, Mother, but I doubt I'll need that long, as there is no way the mother I knew would ever have given that speech. If you have changed, as I do hope you have, then we would love to have you as part of the family for all time." He swallowed nervously, wondering if he had said the right thing.

Ned and Hugh were about to enter when they heard the conversation. They met each other's looks with a smile. Without intentionally eavesdropping, they had overheard the words and knew their planned conversation with their friend would be unnecessary.

When his friends walked inside to wash up for dinner, Jack greeted them with an abashed look. Jack now had a lady under each arm. "Ned,

Hugh, sorry I've been like a bear with a sore head. As you know, it's not like me, but there's been a lot going on."

Hugh jabbed him. "You could have let on your mother had arrived, Jack."

Jack looked sheepish and glanced at his mother, then said, "Well, the one I knew in England isn't here. She seems to have managed to get lost sometime after arrival. Hopefully, it's now all sorted. Mother will be staying here, so you do not need to saddle a horned cow for her." Jack grinned, trying to imagine his previously elegant mother sitting astride on a great-horned cow like Strawberry in a peacock-coloured ball gown or a calico dress for that matter. He knew Bea would do it, and somehow, he had a feeling that his new mother would try. With that thought floating through his head, he said, "Let's eat. I'm famished. I'll wash up and join you in a moment." He released his mother but not Bea.

After dumping their bags in their rooms, Ned and Hugh escorted Edith to the waiting children at the dining room table.

Jack took Bea into their bedroom and, while washing his face and hands, said, "Bea, I mean what I said to Mother. If she upsets the family, she's the one who will leave."

Bea chuckled. This emotion was not the reaction he expected. She said, "Jack, you are the one who will get the shock. She really has changed, and I bet by the time this child is born that you will have fallen in love with your mother, too, for I certainly have. Jack, she will be the mother we both want and need."

Dinner that evening was a delight; the long refectory-like table fitted everyone. Edith both served and was served.

Bea was not permitted to do anything.

Even the Titchmarsh's had come from the shop, and for once, Netty and Billy joined the extended family with the convict girls plus Ned and Hugh.

Netty had cooked a butter-basted, roast pickled pork with lashings of dried apple sauce, roast potatoes, baked pumpkin, and boiled mint-flavoured dried peas; this sumptuous repast was followed by a substantial hot apple cobbler with dollops of clotted cream. Somehow Netty had managed to remove the rind of the pork, and the crackling was salted and so crisp that it crunched.

Bea relished the tender meal and mentioned that this was the last of the sows. "Jack, this was Pinky, the last sow that was here when you left. When we butchered her, we decided to pickle her for our own use. She's delicious!"

Edith looked down at the deliciously tender meat and salted crispy crackling on her plate. Before moving to the farm, she had never thought about where her food came from. Her cutlery was held aloft; she found it somewhat off-putting that she was about to cut into a meal with a name.

Jess noticed that her grandmother wasn't eating. "Nana, don't you like roast pickled pork?" she asked innocently.

Edith gave a minute shake of her head. "Jess darling, I love pork; I've just never eaten an animal with a name before."

Jess frowned. "Yes, you have; we ate Snowflake, the chookie, last Sunday, and we have had some of Pinky before, too, as sausages."

Edith swallowed. "We did? I didn't know, Jess. It's sort of like eating a friend."

Jess was not deterred. "But Nana, they are friends; it's why they taste nice. Mummy gives them hugs and cuddles and fills them with love. They live a good life. With the love they are given, they taste good; otherwise, they would be all bitter inside."

"Like me," she muttered softly, but Jack heard her words. Edith frowned, and then she gingerly took a bite of the meat.

All eyes at the table were now focused on her.

Jack wondered what she would do. He watched as she took a deep breath; she had a look of determination on her face as she cut into the soft meat.

After taking another deep breath, the fork made it to her mouth. Edith chewed and swallowed. "Jess dear, you are so right. I can feel the love infusing into me, right down to my toes. I feel I am a new person." She met her granddaughter's anxious gaze. "I think you will need to get some more pigs, Jacky. Bea, you must teach me how to fill them with love."

A wave of laughter rippled along both sides of the table.

Jack was astounded that this woman who braved eating a pet pig was his mother. His big smile went all the way to his eyes this time. He settled down to eat the delectable dish in front of him. He bit into the crackling with a joyful crunch. Pinky really was delicious.

Bea saw the twinkle return to her husband's eyes. Her smile lit her face too. She was sure everything would be all right.

Ned and Hugh decided to leave the following day, both giving promises to return soon.

The following morning, both men reluctantly bade farewell and headed eastwards to their respective homes. Jack had given Hugh one of the dogs as a thank-you gift. Hugh said that Jack needed the roadside fodder for his beasts, and the larger mob would quickly eat through the new growth.

Hugh returned to Heather and his family with a message of love and some of Edith's first batch of preserves in his saddle bag.

Ned returned to Christina to ask if she would consent to court him. He also carried two small bags of gold dust from Jack to pay for a list of purchases plus more stock and the other to bank. Ned was to buy some furniture and glassed French doors for the house and send them up on a wagon. He had also arranged for more piglets and chickens to be sent. He would add a few things for the family, including Edith. He had access to bolts of water-damaged fabric and would send a bolt so that Bea could have her special gown to wear for Jack. He would also choose some fabric for curtains and upholstery and send more muslin and cheesecloth to keep the flies out. He had a list in his pocket, and now he had the time to do this as he did not need to return to work. He would ask Christina for advice in choosing some fabrics and sneak some in for her, too, even if it was some fine lawn for unmentionables. All ladies needed underclothing; while he could not buy those for her, he could purchase fabric, and it was up to her what she would make with it. He would make sure they all had everything they needed and more.

~

Within days, Jack saw how vastly changed his mother was. He welcomed the new Edith to the family. The hurt was still there, but with a new understanding from an adult perspective, he began to understand much about his childhood. He had previously talked with Bea about how she felt about her first child. She confessed that she had not cared when she lost it but was sad that she needed to throw it away as though it was unwanted. She had, however, done nothing to intentionally lose the child. He began to understand the violation his mother had felt. He found the circumstances of his conception still hard to swallow, but with Bea's help, he realised that they needed to put the past behind them to grow together.

With England now part of their history, the growing family bonded. It was not often that so many had the chance to start over and change their future, but that was before the three of them now.

The children were delighted to know that Nana would be living with them from now on. Jess and Bobby were overjoyed that they could teach her all manner of things about life on the farm, including how to hug piglets. They had taken to their daily reading lessons with her.

Ned had sent a selection of books for their new shelves, and he had included an extensive collection of children's story books plus some slates and chalk for their education. He had added some poetry books for Edith and a prayerbook for her personal use.

As Bea's condition grew, Edith and the children milked the cows without her assistance.

Jack had returned with a few more cows; some had calves at foot. Thankfully they were beef cows and didn't need milking. The volume of milk from their three dairy cows was huge, and Bea had taught Edith how to make soft cheese. This was a delicacy that Edith loved eating, and she had previously never thought about how it was made. She absorbed the lessons on setting, skimming the cream from the milk, and then churning it to make butter. Before this, butter appeared on her table in curls or perfect cubes. She had complained if it didn't curl correctly or if there was not enough for everyone. Now, she took great pleasure in making her butter pats look neat and ready for sale. Each one was wrapped in waxed calico and stored in the cool room. The cheese, however, was a more labour-intensive task.

First, the milk had to be raised to the correct temperature; then, the milk was curdled, and the rennet was added. Once put through these various processes, the curd needed to be diced, strained, and put into cheesecloth-lined moulds. The full moulds were left to drain or hung until they stopped dripping. Each full cheese mould needed to be pressed to turn it into cheese wheels. Edith learned that a cheese needed to be pressed for twenty minutes, and the excess whey drained from it.

Once sufficiently set, the new cheese would be turned out and put in the cool room alongside the butter pats and other produce. The now-trimmed cheesecloth formed part of the cheese skin. Edith loved making these tasty products and had a great sense of accomplishment when each cheese was turned out. One job Edith delighted in was to rub the maturing cheeses. She had once seen Bea doing this. It looked like she was caressing each wheel of cheese, but she found Bea was actually covering each cheese with soft white lard. This substance formed a thick skin on the outside, and the flavour penetrated the cheesecloth; it flavoured the cheeses beautifully.

Edith also learnt the knack for making the waxed calico cloths they used to wrap saleable produce. Melting the resin into the beeswax was the most challenging part of this process. Once she had learnt not to be hasty and remove it from the stove too quickly, the waxed calico cloths were just the right stickiness for use. She had seen them used before but now discovered the pleasure of making them herself. These activities were far more rewarding than painting a watercolour or sewing a tapestry unless it was to repair a chair. She thought back to how pointless her life in England had been. For the first time in her life, she felt useful and was achieving something.

Bea and Jack had discussed their belief in the Bible teachings. She thought she was beyond redemption and said as much, but when Jack realised she was serious about changing her life, he shared more of his faith. It was his conversation about God's judgement that hit home. Jack had been surprised when she said he would get straight into Heaven. "Mother, what makes you think Bea and I are beyond judgement? We all will stand before God and be judged by Him. From Queen Victoria to young Ed, every one of us will be judged fairly by God. If we have begged forgiveness and made an effort to change, then we are, in essence, given a free pass. I'm sure it's not quite that simple, but you get the gist of my meaning. Mother, I can see a change in you already; I have already forgiven you. However, I'm not the one whom you need to submit to and ask for forgiveness. The church calls it penitence, as does Jesus."

Edith absorbed his words, and she realised how right he was. She now understood Bea's words about being washed clean. No amount of rain could wash away her past, but she had made peace with it, and therefore she could put her old self away and move forward. Once alone in her room, her tears of sorrow and repentance flowed.

~

As the spring progressed, the warmer weather encouraged more growth, so the stock had plenty of feed.

The hidden dormant potatoes had germinated by themselves, and the crop would be astounding.

Even the sheep grazing the new barley turned out to be a blessing as the single stalks of grain had each turned into multi-stemmed plants. The barley should also be a bountiful harvest. Jack estimated that the yield from this one paddock would be more than the entire farm in the last three years combined. He realised that sheep grazing on the new growth fertilised the crop and multiplied the return. He would do this in future years.

In the weeks leading up to the birth of their fourth child, Jack learned to love his mother. They took time to sit and talk often; Bea was usually beside them. She had never known her mother, and she relished the new relationship that had developed between the three of them.

Both mollycoddled Bea as the time for the birth drew closer. Bea grew unsteady and could no longer go to the dairy with the cobbled floor or help outside. However, she could follow the new level path to Thunderbolt's holding yard. There, she would stand at the repaired post and wait at the sliprail for Jack's return from his day's work on the farm. She was there, waiting at the railing when the first of the birth pains hit. Knowing that Jack wished to be at the birth, she turned to her small dark shadow and said, "Skitch Jack, Blue, and fast."

Blue had appeared at Jack's side as he and Billy were finishing the cover of the new silage pit. Hopefully, the farm would not need to use it again for years, but the security it gave the farmstead boded well for the future. The grain harvest had been a bumper one, and the straw stalks had been laid down as silage to further drought-proof the farm during the next dry spell. Jack had promised Bea that next drought, he would sell the stock and leave the farm fallow. Next time, Billy and he would pan their gold when the tribe went walkabout again. He would never leave his family again.

They stood looking at the finished job, and Jack realised that Blue had come for him. Blue was insistent, so he returned to support Bea through the birth of their fourth child.

Their second daughter was born on November 6, 1840. Netty, Edith, and the *dubas'* were at Bea's side, as was Jack. He was again supporting her and giving her encouragement. He gave her his strength and prayed constantly as she travailed through the birth. Eden Grace Barnes was born with a minimum of fuss; Bea had worded Netty up that Edith was to have first hold of her grandchild.

Edith had never been permitted to hold her newborn baby. Both Paul and Jack had been whisked away from her within moments of their delivery.

This child would be shared by them all.

Eden's name meant *Place of Pleasure*, and Grace is what Edith felt her new family had given her. Bea and Jack had not even discussed a boy's name. All had felt the child would be a girl.

With Eden's arrival, the farm seemed now complete. The joyous sounds of laughter frequently echoed through rooms, and they often all sat or worked on the wide verandah.

~

Ned's bounteous load of furniture had arrived only a week after Eden's birth. A smaller wagon followed with two new pens of animals. There were seven piglets, twelve hens, and a big black rooster. Edith was given the job of naming them all, knowing they were destined for her plate.

The furniture Ned had purchased included new mattresses for the extra guest rooms, feather-filled pillows, glassed French doors with hinges, dining chairs and all manner of other things, replacing those consumed by the fire, also a replacement bed for the shack.

There were new bolts of fabric; some were the same blue Bea had originally chosen so many years before, and there was more lawn, muslin and cheesecloth.

Ned had also purchased three new rocking chairs. He had labelled them. A sturdy one had Jack's name on it, and a massive box of vegetable seeds was tied onto the seat. A delicately carved and padded velvet upholstery chair was for Edith, with a paper-wrapped parcel on the seat with her name inscribed in Ned's calligraphy. This gift was the new gilt-edged leather-bound Bible. The third chair had a padded tapestry upholstered seat and was for Bea. Her chair also had a long parcel tied to it, but it had a note attached. Jack had declared her fire-singed chair unsafe and returned to the shack.

The note was in Ned's elegant script.

Bea,

You were correct; she said yes. I can't believe that I am again contemplating marriage after twenty years. As a thanks from me, this is for you to make your special gown to wear for Jack.

Ned

Although nothing material mattered to Bea, the flat bolt of gold damask silk fabric sent her heart beating wildly. From this, she and Edith would make her dream dress that she would wear just for Jack. Clutching the golden fabric to her, she lifted her eyes to her husband. Her family was happy; that was all she wanted. Jack had been correct; they had learnt what a family was and grown closer through the years.

After nearly seven years on the farm, it now had a name, *Eden Vale*. That had grown out of a stray comment from Hugh rather than their daughter's name. Eden Vale's Cheeses were now transported from Bathurst to Sydney. They were not as good as Kit Kellow's cheeses in Parramatta, but they were delicious.

Life on the farm was good. Girls came and went, and Bea would watch the sunset from the sliprails where she waited for Jack at the end of each day. Netty had claimed Bea's old chair, which was again returned to its original place. She often joined them with a mug of sweet black tea.

~

Edith celebrated her first year on the farm and now stood on the verandah in a serge gown, watching her daughter-in-law. She found happiness in her new and fulfilling life. Jess and seven-month-old Eden were usually close to their grandmother. Titles meant nothing to any of them. Jack had not even told Bea she was now Lady Beatrice, and he doubted that he ever would.

Jack finished repairing the fence around the new barley field, and he turned to head home. That word, home, now brought a feeling of contentment and deep happiness. He smiled and turned Thunderbolt's head towards his beloved.

Bea was by the sliprails at Thunderbolt's yard once more. She could see him approaching. The magnificent steed brought her beloved Jack back to her loving arms.

He waved when he saw her.

She responded with a two-arm wave.

Today she had more news for him. She was waiting at the sliprails to tell him their fifth child would be born at the end of the summer. If it was a girl, she would name her Christina after Ned's new wife.

Thank you for reading my story. I hope you enjoyed it, and the following pages are more from the same era.
Sara

If you loved this book, these are similar.

Unlikely Convict Ladies - Trilogy

Dancing to her Own Tune

Co-authored by Sheila Hunter and Sara Powter

Sydney 1790s to England 1830s

Annie White is released after serving seven years as a convict in Sydney. She gets a visitor who, with his help, she can start a baking business. She is then asked to assist another sick man, **Sam** Corbett. Annie nurses him back to health, and a relationship develops. They settle into a life together, barely making ends meet; she realises she's expecting a child. Sam has his past laid bare and must adjust to the revelations. They both must face their accusers and find that the answers to their questions are not what they thought. Their life experiences seem to cling to them, and unable to shake it they finally, they end up back in England, facing their ghosts and discovering they are not who they think they are. How can they turn their anger and spite into love and forgiveness? The Dance of Life goes on.

ISBN 9780645110715 ISBN9780645110722

Long-listed in the Historical Fiction Company Competition 2022

October2021

https://amazon.com/dp/064511071X https://amazon.com/dp/B09JC378YV

Amelia's Tears

Parramatta 1828 – England 1840s

In the Parramatta Female Prison, **Amelia** awaits her assignment. Forced to leave the relative safety of gaol, she is assigned and now faces her worst nightmare. A foul man claims her and makes her life a living hell. Then her world goes black. A glimmer of hope arises when she hears from her brother, Jim, who has enlisted a friend to help her. She writes to Jim, pouring out her heart and telling him of the horrors of her new life. He encourages her to stay firm in her faith. All she can do is pray. When Major **Ned** Grace, her brother's friend, enters her life in Parramatta, he starts to ease her path. Things have changed, as now she has a child in tow. How can Amelia forge a new life for herself? What man could want her with her background and a child at her side? Who is the gentleman who turns her tears of sadness into tears of great joy?

ISBN: 9780645110739 eISBN: 978-0-6451107-4-6 Hard Cover ISBN 979-842061-7953

April 2022

https://amazon.com/dp/0645110736 https://amazon.com/dp/B09SS855BR

A Lady in Irons

England 1800s - Parramatta 1808+

Katy is mourning the death of her husband after he dies in a shooting accident. Barely coping, she awaits the birth of their child. If it's a girl, she must hand the family home to her husband's brother. The day after giving birth to a daughter, she and her daughter are left on the side of a road. She collapses and is found by someone she thought had died in a fire ten years before. **Perry**, badly scarred himself, nurses her back to health. They marry and move in with her widowed friend, Mary.

After some years, she discovers her husband and friend in each other's arms. Now living in a love triangle, she flees. Grasping the only straw available, she intentionally gets arrested and is sent to a colony far away. By doing this, her marriage can be annulled.

What happens in the Colony is different from what she expects. Governor Macquarie comes to her rescue.

But what of Perry and her children?

ISBN: 9780645110784 eISBN:9780645441505

November 2022

https://amazon.com/dp/0645110787 https://amazon.com/dp/B0BCWSXB9Z

NO MORE, MY *Love*
Hunter Valley, NSW 1820s

Jess Elkin is distraught when tragedy ravages her family. She becomes the victim of a carriage accident and is nursed back to health by the driver, **Marcus Ryan**. Marcus was not expecting to fall in love. Yet, when Jess's fortunes suddenly turn for the worse, Marcus must decide how far he will go to pursue her. As time passes in Newcastle, Australia, Marcus must take a business trip and is taken by pirates. Jess is left wondering if her will keep his promise to return to her... Will she ever see him alive again?

ISBN: 9780645441536 eISBN 9780645441581
April 2023
https://amazon.com/dp/0645441538 https://amazon.com/dp/B0BSBH143Q

The Vine Weaver
Hawkesbury River area 1820s+
New Beginnings and Old Threats

In the 1820s, Australia, **Joel and Hetty Walker** live on a secluded farm on the Hawkesbury River which becomes a healing haven for the protection of young convict women.

A series of events brings **Fran Rea** to the attention of Hetty, and she is taken to the farm. Fran and Hetty develop a cottage industry under the compassionate eye of farmhand **Hector Macdougal;** Hector's loving words change lives. It is to him that Fran turns when threatened.

The vines now must draw them close to survive the future revelations, and of those, there are many.

ISBN: 9780645441512 eISBN: 9780645441529
June 2023
https://amazon.com/dp/0645441511 https://amazon.com/dp/B0C6Z552Y2
The story continues in Scotch at The Rocks...

Waiting at the Sliprails
The Bathurst Road 1830s
A Convict's Tale

Bea Dawes's term of conviction nears an end, and she has few options other than marriage to a stranger or going on the street.

Jack Barnes, the hired drover, wants a wife. Bea accepts his offer; then she discovers that he could be gone for months, leaving her alone with **Billy and Netty,** part of the tribe of aborigines who live on his secluded farm. Bea learns to love her husband and also this wonderful aboriginal couple.

Drought ravages the farm, and Jack must hit the long paddock with the flock. In his absence, a visitor arrives, destroying everything she has worked so hard for.

Can Bea cope? Will the drought ever end? And when will Jack return?

ISBN: 9780645441543 eISBN: 9781923097032
Coming August 2023

SCOTCH AT THE ROCKS
Glasgow, Scotland, early 1800s to The Rocks, Sydney 1830s

Orphaned children Brodie Stewart and Heather Anderson live on Glasgow's streets. Although hungry, somehow they survive and keep out of trouble. Heather finds a job and looks to be settled; things go pear-shaped for them both. Eventually, they marry by declaration, yet even that gets messed up, and they are both arrested soon after they make their vow. In 1838, they got transported to Sydney as convicts. Heather arrives within weeks of Brodie, and they are assigned close to each other. They are now living on the docklands in Sydney, called The Rocks. They now have to forge a new life halfway across the world from their homeland.

Adventures abound, and Brodie gets press-ganged. While he's away, Heather's life changes and soon, she's officially selling Scotch Whisky at a shop in The Rocks.

You can take a Scot out of Scotland, but where did the Scotch come from?

ISBN 9780645441550 ISBN ebook 9781923097001

November 2023

Convict Shadows of the Past
Two Jennifers, two hundred years apart

When aged eight, **Jenny** Kellow learns of her convict family history and discovers that she was named after a convict from nearly two hundred years ago. Her grandfather's stories inspire her to dig deeper into her ancestors' convict past. From her grandfather, she hears stories of bushrangers, convicts, and life in the infant colony of Parramatta. She sets about retracing the footsteps of her convict great-great-great-grandmother to honour her. Jenny's search starts with microfiche back in the 60s, and she learns about the small tin mining town in Cornwall and the production of a cheese that sets London afire. Then she discovers her ancestor has brought these cheese-making skills to Parramatta, where she taught others her craft. Echoes of the past can still be heard if you know where to listen. But who was the first **Jennifer**? Why is she so elusive?

ISBN: 9780645783315 ISBN ebook 9780645783322

A NaNoWriMo 2022 book winner

January 2024

In Defence of Her Honour
London 1800s to Parramatta 1819

Bill Miller had been raised and educated with the sons of the family. The youngest, Bert, had been his best friend. However, jealousy intervenes when Bill's excellent schoolwork curtails their friendship. He wins a scholarship and enters Oxford University. When Bill's father, the old butler, dies unexpectedly, Bert insists that Bill take over the position, but it's more to oppress him. Bert's jealousy grows and festers. Now looking for a way to rid themselves of their new butler, a ruckus ensues, and Bill is arrested for assaulting Bert. The housekeeper and her daughter **Molly** vouch for him, but it's too late; Bill has been arrested and sentenced to be transported. With Bill gone, Molly now needs to defend herself from Bert. After hitting him with a pan, she is arrested and sent to Sydney. Bill and Molly arrive with letters of introduction and compensation from Bert's father. Soon they are running the best Inn in Parramatta with an endorsement from the Governor.

ISBN 9780645441567 ISBN ebook 9781923097049

April 2024

Gentle Annie Soames

A 1788 First Fleet Convict Story

Her dreams lead to unexpected outcomes. An Australian First Fleet story.

Annie Soames is shattered by the cancellation of her debut into society, so when she hears of a position as a carer for the nearby Marchioness, she grabs it.

Oliver Quilpie, the recently married Marquess, discovers his arranged union is not to his taste; he is drawn to his wife's companion. Unfortunately, he is unable to keep his hands off her. For revenge, Annie mimics his every move while riding but is dressed as a highwayman. However, she had now fallen in love with him. This action finally leads to her arrest and transportation to a faraway land.

After some years, Oliver's wife dies, and his thoughts turn to Annie. He seeks to find her, but she has vanished. He is horrified to discover she was transported to New South Wales as a convict on the Lady Penrhyn. He follows with a shipload of supplies.

Will Annie want to see him?

ISBN 9780645441574 ISBN ebook 9781923097063

July 2024

ℐ can't stop Tomorrow

Irish Famine 1840s to Avoca Beach, Australia

Escaping bigotry and prejudice in Ireland, the **O'Shane** family live on a secluded farm on the west coast. The potato blight soon decimates their farm. It's always darkest before dawn, and they cling to the hope of a new life. With the kindness of strangers, the oldest girls, **Clare** and **Kerry,** head to their cousin, Sal Lockley, in Parramatta, Australia. A new wonderful life awaits them both.

Shéamus Connor is the annoying teenage boy who reluctantly draws Clare's affection. However, living in a convict town means ruffians abound.

John Moore is an angry and troubled Irishman, content to live alone on another secluded farm until he discovers Clare and two other lads need rescuing.

Can John protect her from the pain inflicted by an evil world?

Can Shéamus find his lost love?

ISBN: 9780645441598 ISBN ebook 9781923097056

October 2024

Madeline's Boy

England 1830s to New South Wales 1840

All is not straightforward when money and a title are involved.

Madeline is asked to care for her best friend's son when his life is in danger.

Christopher is the pawn between a greedy, unscrupulous uncle and his inheritance. Maddie must do everything she can to keep him safe, including moving halfway around the globe to take Chip to his guardian, Major Humphrey Downes, in the Australian Corps in Sydney. Humphrey's best friend, another soldier, Major Tim Hinds, meets Maddie, and with the support of these two men, a chase around the colony ensues.

Will Maddie and Tim be able to find happiness together?

Can the three adults keep Chip safe until he's old enough to claim his inheritance?

ISBN: 9780645783308 ISBN ebook 9781923097094

January 202

Tuppence to Pass

London 1800s to Parramatta 1820s - Governor Lachlan Macquarie

Josh Callan is a London lad who makes the best of the life that has been dealt to him. Stealing from the man who killed his father gives the family a change of direction. Josh is arrested, but the judge belittles him and says he's not worth tuppence. He is sent to the penal colony of Sydney as Governor Macquarie's term starts. He proves his worth and falls on his feet, becoming the Governor's groom. Life in the Colonial town opens opportunities they never could have dreamed about in England, but can Josh find his niche in life?

Where will this new life take Josh and his family?

ISBN : 9781923097070 eISBN: 9781923097087

Coming 2025

WHEN UPON LIFE'S BILLOWS

Sydney 1795-1800 - Governor John Hunter

Captain John Hunter is born to a life at sea. The wind blows where no man knows, and John is caught up in the gale. From the wrecking of his ship, the HMS Sirius, in 1790 to becoming the second Governor of the colony of NSW, John seems to always be in the wrong place at the wrong time.

Helena Rosedale is not a typical female convict. She fights tooth and nail to stop the men from abusing her. She gains the name of Helena Hellcat.

Crispin Milroy is one of the Governor's security detail. Can he win the fair lady's heart? Life in 1795 in Sydney Cover. I it raw at best. Food is scarce, and disease often ravages the settlement. Life throws them everything possible except death. Somehow they survive. What trials will the young couple face to make a new life in this raw town? How can John ease their path?

Coming 2025

A 100-year, six-part Australian Colonial series
Lockleys of Parramatta
Hands upon the Anvil
A blacksmith's life and love are more than work
Parramatta 1830s

Eddie Lockley's parents were transported for their crimes. Can a steadfast lad rise above his origins and guide others to succeed in a land of opportunity?

Ten-year-old Eddie longs to help his mum and dad. Living in a convict town with his family, the keen youngster has been working with the local blacksmith since his sixth birthday. But when a lieutenant doesn't stop abusing his older brother, the young boy yearns for the day when he can stand up and end the torment. Though he's thrilled when his mentor offers to send him off to learn his letters, Eddie fears he won't be around to watch his sibling's back. But as he takes on the biggest adventure of his life, the brave believer soon discovers God is looking out for everyone he loves. Does this young man in the making have what it takes to change everything for the better?

ISBN 9780994578235 Ebook ISBN 978-0-9945782-5-9 Hardcover 9798496177368
Released 2021
https://amazon.com/dp/0994578237 https://amazon.com/dp/B08TB51L19

Out Where The Brolgas Dance
Gold is found, and so is love
Parramatta 1840s
How can a question change so many people?

It's the 1840s, and discoveries across the Blue Mountains continue. Major Mitchell's new road is complete, and towns are planned and being built. Abundant land is available for those who want it.

William **"Wills"** Lockley, 18, has laid a solid foundation for a respectable career as a blacksmith, but the Lockley lust for adventure flows deeply within his veins. He dreads the monotony of work at the blacksmith's forge and yearns for adventure in a new frontier. Wills meets six Englishmen who have the means to make his dreams come true. What they discover changes the Colony and their lives forever. Gold fever ensues. Now on the road West, Wills has to deal with an uncertain romance. Does she even want him?

ISBN 9780994578242 Ebook ISBN 978-0-9945782-6-6 Hardcover ISBN 9798755445504
Released 2021
https://amazon.com/dp/0994578245 https://amazon.com/dp/B08T6NS3XX

Diamonds in the Dirt
Diamonds, love and money… but there is much more to life.
Parramatta 1850s

Luke, the youngest Lockley son, has completed University, and his life has no direction. No job, no money, and no love. Desperately alone, he prays for guidance. How can Luke trust that God has a plan for him if he can't even find a job? He does the only thing he can … he prays. Within a week, life has changed … oh, how it has changed as his brother Wills turns up with a suggestion. Would Luke be interested in joining the expedition with John Evans? Reverend William Clarke needs assistance on a Government Mineral Survey. The challenge, adventure and finds are life-changing for many. However, it gives Luke meaning, purpose and direction. The condition of his heart problems also takes a turn. Can he walk away?

ISBN:9780994578273 Ebook ISBN: 978-0-9945782-8-0 Hard cover ISBN 979-8788011141
Released 2022
https://amazon.com/dp/099457827X https://amazon.com/dp/B09NH1MLXZ

The Earl's Shadow

Who or what is the 'shadow'? How does it affect so many?

Parramatta 1860s

Charles is the Earl of Coxheath and spends his youth as a convict in Parramatta; he had no idea he was an Earl. He had minimal education and few social skills. His eldest son **Charlie** is no different.

Now faced with his own mortality, Charles has to work out how to live the remainder of his life after a near-death experience. He is called to step way out of his comfort zone in London. His action will change the world for many. The echoes from the past still haunt Charlie. London is calling the family, and they can't postpone the trip. How does **Jim**, the Cobb and Co coach driver, fit in? And precisely what is *'The Earl's Shadow'* that he speaks about? What happens if the 'Shadow' is gone?

ISBN: 9780645110708 Ebook ISBN 978-0-9945782-9-7
Released June 2022
https://amazon.com/dp/0645110701 https://amazon.com/dp/B0B158SKSK

Once a Jolly Swagman

An old black Billy Can contain the secrets of an incredible life

An Australian Historical Novel

Set in 1870s Parramatta and Kent UK

Rick Lockley, battling his family's expectations, runs away to become a swagman. Jack, a jolly swagman takes him under his care. Even after years together, Rick knows little about the old man.

On his death, Jack leaves Rick his precious Billy Can; the contents reveal Jack's identity. Stunned, Rick must travel to England to finalise Jack's wishes. There he uncovers Jack's life of love, betrayal and a link to his own family. Rick discovers there is much more to learn about this enigmatic man.

ISBN 9780645110753 Ebook ISBN 978-0-6451107-6-0
Released Sept 2022
https://amazon.com/dp/0645110752 https://amazon.com/dp/B0B5JN1WCV

Jonty's Journey

Gems, Love, Artists and a Golden Lion

Australia and South Africa 1880-1902

Sydney Jeweller, **Jonty** Evans' passion for gems takes him to Africa at a volatile time. He finds the diamonds he wants and gets given a lion cub. Jonty gets all but kidnapped. His experiences in the Transvaal plunge him into questioning everything he knows of life. Soon nightmares haunt him.

On return home, he nearly messes up his love life with **Lottie** before it even starts, and he struggles to settle. Lottie's father, **Luke** Lockley from Parramatta, takes him in hand and points him to someone who can help.

Jonty is then recalled to Africa as a liaison and reconnects with his lion, Chimbu, when he saves the life of his security detail. His life journey introduces him to the most amazing Heidelberg artists, politicians, poets, rebels, and the scapegoat soldier Harry Breaker Morant. Can Jonty bury the past and regain the peace he's lost?

ISBN 9780645110777 Ebook ISBN: 978-0-6451107-9-1
Released Feb 2023
https://amazon.com/dp/0645110779 https://amazon.com/dp/B0BLJ7ND1Q

Australian Colonial Trilogy
By Sheila Hunter
Co-Winner of 1999 NSW Senior Citizen of the Year, In the Year of the Senior Citizen

Mattie
Coming of Age in Convict Australia
Woodslane/Hand in Hand Publications ISBN 9780994578204

Twelve-year-old London street urchin **Mattie Paul** is convicted of petty theft and sentenced to seven years of transportation to the penal colony of Port Jackson, NSW. Peg, another female convict, takes Mattie under her wing and gives her a chance to make something of her life by teaching her to read. Mattie seizes every opportunity that comes her way. Though life is not particularly kind to her, she battles through earning her freedom, marrying and becoming a mother in her homeland. On this journey, she encounters bushrangers, is widowed, and becomes an entrepreneur in the Bathurst goldfields. She mixes with escaped convicts, but her spirit is indomitable, and she becomes a pillar and much-loved treasure of her adopted community. Mattie may be a fictional character, but her experiences are only too real and invest us in immersing ourselves in the lives of those remarkable women who helped to make Australia what it is today.

ISBN 9781503252370 & ebook AISN BOOTTEDBTO
(The Story continues in The Earl's Shadow)
Released 2015
https://amazon.com/dp/150325237X https://amazon.com/dp/B00TTEDBT0

Ricky
A boy in Colonial Australia

Ricky English and his mother immigrate from England to join his father in the new Colony of Sydney. On arrival, there is no sign of his father. Ricky's mum uses the tiny amount of money they brought to get lodgings in a run-down building. Things go from bad to worse when his mother dies, he is thrown out of the rooms, and the caretakers confiscate all their possessions.
Ricky lives on the streets of Sydney Town as a street waif. Ricky finds safe places to sleep and befriends freed convicts who can help him survive. One day he encounters a lost child and helps reunite her with her family. These people try to help him, but because of his stubbornness, he insists on doing things his way, but he has found a mentor and confidante. The story follows him through his life. He survives and turns his life around, helping others along the way.

Paperback ISBN 9780994578211 Kindle ASIN: B00MLYN6IG
(The Story continues in Jonty's Journey)
Released 2014
https://amazon.com/dp/1500770574 https://amazon.com/dp/B00MLYN6IG

The Heather to The Hawkesbury
Four Scottish families brave a new life in a strange land.

Mary Macdonald and husband **Murd** and family; her brother **Fergus** MacKenzie; sister-in-law **Caro** MacLeod; cousin **Alex** Fraser and all their families who have had to emigrate from the Isle of Skye during the "Clearances."
The story follows the four families from Scotland on the ship out to the NSW colony in the 1850s. Mary does not cope with the changes and losses that occur in the first months in the colony. The other women in the family rely on her, and she nearly crumbles. The families struggle together through accidents, losses, trials, floods, and hard work and forge a strong bond with their new country. Trials, tribulations and triumphs see the four families make a firm mark in their new homeland. The immigrants from Scotland helped make Australia what it is today.

ISBN 978994578228 ebook AISN B01A21JYWQ Large Print ISBN1533473641
Available on Amazon/Kindle & Large Print
Released 2016
https://amazon.com/dp/1503251438 https://amazon.com/dp/B01A21JYWQ

Author Bio

Sheila Hunter and Sara Powter were a passionate mother-and-daughter team of amateur genealogists. While working together on their family tree, Sheila and Sara made many captivating discoveries. The greatest of these was finding four convicts, and these four had very different perspectives. They were sent to Australia from 1792 to 1814 during the height of Convict transportation. Before her passing in 2002, Sheila adapted some of these histories into enchanting stories, her Australian Colonial Trilogy. Sara later had these published. A fourth she left unfinished, and this inspired her to finish it. However, before she did, **The Lockleys of Parramatta** were created. The first two in the series were completed before she completed 'Dancing to Her Own Tune' for her mother.

Vividly living through the Colonial Era, these books delve further into the theme of overcoming adversity in Colonial Australia and how it developed, the demise of the Convict system and the discovery of mineral wealth.

Sara intricately weaves accurate, archival data and a charming narrative to create a series of tales of faith, love, loss, and redemption.

And so, two hundred years after her family arrived in Australia, Sara continues the Australian Colonial stories started in *Lockleys of Parramatta,* followed by the **Unlikely Convict Ladies** Trilogy. **No More, My Love, The Vine Weaver** and **Waiting at the Sliprails** are stand-alone novels.

More Historical Fiction books are to follow… as six more are already in the editors' queue.

Amazon Aus QR

See her web page to keep up to date with more stories.
With an online store available for a signed copy of Sara's books.
www.sarapowter.com.au
(Australian Postage only)

Feel free to email me at
saragpowter@gmail.com

BOOK BUB
https://partners.bookbub.com/authors/6273615/edit

FACEBOOK
https://www.facebook.com/profile.php?id=100063887262514

FREE Newsletter signup
https://preview.mailerlite.io/preview/41388/sites/
77987646202184961/wCAAcK

Bibliography

Chapter Drawings
by Henry & CW Lawson and Frank Malone
https://www.sl.nsw.gov.au/stories/unique-editions-henry-lawsons-early-poems
Henry Lawson - pictures and most drawings.
https://gutenberg.net.au/ebooks20/2001121h.html
Photos converted to sketch chaps 7, 9 & 18

Darug Language
https://dharug.dalang.com.au/language/dictionary

Glossary

Tucker = food - Australian slang

Aboriginal words - Dharug/Dharawal dialect
Dharug Tribe - the Aboriginal people from Western Sydney to the central Blue Mountains area. Known as Freshwater People. (Eora Tribe are the Saltwater people)
https://dharug.dalang.com.au/language/dictionary

Gurung = child/baby
Duba/s = Aboriginal woman/women
Binya = pregnant
Baragat = frightened
Fella = pidgin English for person
Chook = a chicken
Gunny = aboriginal tent
Garmit = black cockatoo (large black parrot)
Garraway = white cockatoo (large white parrot with yellow crest)
didgeridoos = hollow branches used for instrument
gunya/humpy = Aboriginal dwelling

Characters

Beatrice Dawes b 1803 raped and convicted in late Sept 1828. Dec court case.
Hulks 6 months then *Lucy Davidson* convict transport 20/7/- 29/11/1829
m August 1835 John Edward (**Jack**) **Barnes** from Kent
    (parents **Edith** and Eustace Barns) older son, **Paul**, died 1839
Children 4
#1 Robert John (**Bobby**) b June 3 1836
#2 Jessica Mary (**Jess**) b Oct 1837
#3 Edward (**Ed**) Hugh March 1839
#4 **Eden** Grace Nov 1840
#5 ? Jan 1842

Hugh and Heather Lacey,
(Hugh knows Jack & soldiers Ned, Tim & Humphrey from England)
5 children
Hugo & 4 girls (Hugh at School with Jack & Ned)

Major Ned Grace -from Kent, 2nd son of Duke of Gracemere
Once engaged to Elouise Wickham, who marries Ned's, Bro David
In love with Christina Meadows, a widow.

Charles & Sal Lockley, *Jolly Sailor Inn, Parramatta*
6 children,
Charlie, Eddie, Liza, Anna, Wills and Luke

Bill (Bill) Miller '*Rear Admiral Duncan*'
m 1821 **Molly Miller** (Par and Ma)
Timmy   b 1822
Gracie   b 1824
Samuel   b 1828
Ellen   b 1830

Harriet and Dorothea (**Harry & Reah**) convict girls assigned to Hugh
Joe, Tom, Iain and Fred. **Drovers**. Tom spokesman
Madeline (Maddie) & Christopher (Chip) - see '*Madeline's Boy.*'
Eliza, Bridget, Mary and Colleen 4 maids - gone by 1840
Harrison and Mildred Titchmarsh - shopkeepers
Hannah and Alice - new maids - Hannah is the cook

Trigger - Hugh Lacey's horse
2 convict girls (sisters) for Heather & Hugh's place
Jack's animals
4 dairy cows, **Strawberry** (calf Bess) & **Josie**(calf Belle), Daisy, **Trixie**
    & **Bruce** - a six-month-old bull calf
4 horses on the wagon, plus two other horses - Bea's horse **Cassie**,
Jack's horse, **Thunderbolt**

Printed in the USA
CPSIA information can be obtained
at www.ICGtesting.com
LVHW051538060923
757370LV00002B/163